ROYAL LOVERS, RUTHLESS INTRIGUES

LEAH

Her radiance, her beauty, her cascading golden hair had tempted many a heart . . . but at fifteen she had yet to taste of life and of love. Only marriage to the lusty Lord of Radnor awakened her tender passion, to transform her from reluctant bride to willing lover.

CAIN, LORD OF RADNOR

A giant of a man whose iron will had toppled enemy forces and women's eager hearts, the rugged Lord of Radnor was bonded by destiny to a shy young flower.

THE EARL OF PEMBROKE

Leah's unscrupulous father, the Earl of Pembroke cared less for his daughter's happiness than for Radnor's estate. Blinded by ambition, he would readily kill the Lord of Radnor to win his greedy ends—though to do so would snuff forever the mounting flames of his daughter's love.

D0712006

ROBERTA GELLIS
BOND OF BLOOD

AVON
PUBLISHERS OF BARD, CAMELOT, DISCUS, EQUINOX AND FLARE BOOKS

To my beloved husband Charles
without whom
I could never have written anything

AVON BOOKS
A division of
The Hearst Corporation
959 Eighth Avenue
New York, New York 10019

Copyright © 1965 by Roberta Gellis.
Published by arrangement with Doubleday and Co., Inc.
Library of Congress Catalog Card Number: 65-10601

ISBN: 0-380-00714-2

First Avon Printing, May, 1976.

AVON TRADEMARK REG. U.S. PAT. OFF. AND
FOREIGN COUNTRIES, REGISTERED TRADEMARK—
MARCA REGISTRADA, HECHO EN CHICAGO, U.S.A.

Printed in the U.S.A.

AUTHOR'S FOREWORD

THE MAJOR POLITICAL EVENTS of this novel actually did take place in 1146–47 in England, and the book is based upon the chronicle of these events in the *Gesta Stephani*[1] (*Deeds of Stephen*), the most reliable source for the period of Stephen's reign. Only the central characters and their retainers, their influence on affairs, and their relationship to the other characters are fiction. The entire reign of Stephen was one of hopeless confusion and continual warfare on both a national and a private scale,[2] and frequently national and private quarrels blended so that it is difficult even for historians to sort out events into a clear pattern. No chronicle could even attempt to record all the petty enmities or all the minor engagements which took place, and therefore the *Gesta* gives only a record of the major events concerned with the struggle for the throne. Under the circumstances, the author felt free to involve the hero in any personal conflict necessary to the plot, provided that the involvement did not alter the truly historical events with which the book is concerned.

On the physical conditions of life—clothing, housing, and food—the author has attempted to be accurate within a period of about one hundred years, except in one matter. Mentions of money used for purchasing items like cloth or needles or spices are an anachronism. In the twelfth century, nearly all commerce was carried out by the barter system; however, a literal description of this method of exchange would have been so complicated as to impede the progress of the story with very little gain.

One more explanation about social and political concepts must be offered to those readers not familiar

---

[1] *Gesta Stephani*, K. R. Potter, ed. and trans., Thos. Nelson & Sons, Ltd., London, 1955.
[2] *The Peterborough Chronicle*, under the years 1137 and 1140. A review is given under these dates of the situation of England during the reign of Stephen.

with medieval civilization. In the twelfth century, most men had no idea of a country as a national unity nor of our concepts of individual freedom, equality, and patriotism. Their lives were regulated largely by personal attachment which was achieved in several ways. First and foremost was the bond of blood, or blood relationship. This included families related by matrimony and the tie of godparent to godchild. This bond, even when not enforced by affection, had deep religious significance based on the precepts of the Bible and the dogma of the Church. Next in importance was the bond of fealty which a man contracted with his overlord when he did homage to him. The act of homage was also invested with religious as well as personal significance, since fealty was sworn on holy relics. Thus a man who violated his homage had sinned against God as well as smirched his personal honor. Related to the bond of blood, but apart from it, was the tie of fostering. Most male children of the nobility were sent away from their own homes between the ages of seven and ten to be educated by other noblemen, and these children were often very loyal to their foster parents and foster brothers and sisters. Below this level were further bonds which determined the lives and actions of medieval people: the bonds of friendship; those of responsibility to the lower-class people (all too often neglected) who labored on their lands; and those of hospitality and charity.

It will be noted that every important bond of moral obligation mentioned had religious aspects, and the Church encouraged this in every possible way, attempting to make every living action come under its influence in one way or another. In whatever light we regard this at the present time, it was by no means all bad in the medieval period. The Church was the chief influence for good, mitigating to some small degree the brutality of life in this period, in spite of the abuses to which religion was put. One of the abuses, the superstitious belief that the devil walked the earth in human form marked off from his fellow man only by some deformity such as a tail, horns, or a horn hoof, is one of the themes of this novel. The reader should not allow a twentieth century freedom from superstition to prevent him from recognizing the real terror and horror with which medieval people, even those who were themselves so afflicted, regarded congenital deformity. The question of whether all deformity was a bond with the devil because God created only perfect things was a real one at this time.

The frequent mention of peace in this novel must also be clarified. No medieval person dreamt of either peace or war as we know them today. War was never total, although it meant that large armies devastated large tracts of territory for political reasons. Frequently the devastated areas belonged to men who were not technically involved in the conflict. As frequently the possessions of one or more of the active belligerents were totally untouched. On the other hand, peace never meant a cessation of fighting. It merely referred to a condition in which minor bands of armed men attacked clearly defined objectives for personal and private reasons rather than for reasons of state. When, therefore, the hero of this book strives so desperately for peace, he does not mean that he wishes to give up all fighting, which every medieval knight enjoyed. He means that he wishes to avoid large-scale devastation for causes which usually meant nothing to the people who were hurt.

IRISH SEA

IRELAND

WALES

ST. GEORGE'S CHANNEL

SEVERN

Chester

Painscastle

Hereford

Cheltenham
Gloucester

Dursley
Bristol

BRISTOL CHANNEL

Bath

Devizes

Bruton

Ilminster

Bridport

Seaton

N
W   E
S

Miles
0   50

map by palacios

Stockbridge
Tuxford
Lincoln
Nottingham
Corby
Norwich
Oundle
E N G L A N D
AVON
Burford
Bampton
Oxford
Faringdon
Shrivenham
Henley
LONDON
Wallingford
Hungerford
THAMES
Downton
Arundel
ENGLISH CHANNEL
FRANCE
NORMANDY

CHAPTER 1

EDWINA, LADY PEMBROKE, looked with pleasure on her daughter who was teaching a maidservant to spin. It was the twenty-fifth day of April in the year 1147, and Leah was just fifteen years old that day. Her figure was entering its first blossom, and even the ill-cut homespun gown revealed high young breasts, a narrow waist, and rounded hips. She was not a great beauty, but to her mother's intense pleasure she had kept the fair hair and white skin of her childhood, and her large eyes had long silky lashes which she used unconsciously with great effect. The girl's gentle manner and soft sweet voice also had great charm, but Edwina felt that these would be wasted on a hard man so much older than her daughter.

"Do you know that you are fifteen today, Leah?"

"Of course I know it, mother."

"Well, I have come to tell you something of great importance. In a few weeks you will be married."

The spindle dropped from the girl's fingers. "To whom, mama?"

"To Cain, Lord Radnor, son to the Duke of Gaunt. Do not ask questions now, child. Dress yourself in the blue sarcenet bliaut and the tan tunic and come to the hall. His lordship wishes to see you."

Leah stood up obediently, but she was powerless to follow her mother's commands. She had dreamt, like all girls, of marriage; dreamt of a home much as her mother had described, where there was peace and happiness, where she would be her husband's "lady" and life would be one long alternation of fairs and tourneys. But Leah was fifteen now and knew that those were dreams, not life. No knight had come to court her, to ask for her sleeve to carry as a favor. Dream knights, knights one heard the minstrels sing of, or knights that one read about in a rare romance borrowed from the convent or monastery, did such things. Real marriage was a hard fact; her life itself might de-

1

pend upon her husband's whim, and there would be no mother to hide her and protect her.

"Leah!" Edwina's voice was sharp. "Dress quickly and bite your lips before you come down. They are white and you look sickly. This is no time to be a silly chit."

She saw, however, that the timid girl was shocked, and called the maids to help her. Leah was the one great passion in Edwina's life, the one person she really loved, and she longed to tell her not to be frightened. No matter what kind of monster Cain of Radnor was, Leah would not need to endure him long. Doubtless if Pembroke's plans succeeded, Leah would be a widow very soon after she became a wife. Edwina did not offer the assurance; Leah was too young. She would not be able to behave naturally with the man if she knew she was to be the bait that would draw him to his death.

Leah's homespun gown was cast aside and in its place a soft wool tunic of tan, high-necked and long-sleeved, was pulled over her head. This was followed by a blue bliaut which the girls laced as tight as possible at the sides to pull in the narrow waist still further. The underclothes and shoes they left alone for it was unlikely, though not impossible, that Leah would be asked to undress. Finally they pushed her, trembling, down the stairs, coming to the foot themselves to peer curiously into the hall. On the last step Leah remembered her mother's order and bit her soft lips until the blood came back to them. She came into the hall slowly, with downcast eyes as she had been trained to do, although she was quivering with curiosity as she walked to the fireplace.

"Drink up, drink up," the Earl of Pembroke was saying, and then as he saw her, "Ah, here she is. Look up, girl."

Leah obeyed with the promptness of habit, and her eyes fell on the scarred and grizzled warrior standing beside her father. Only years of submission and terror held her still as the old man reached out and grasped her arm to pull her closer.

"She favors you," he said, whistling through broken and missing teeth. "She will be well enough when a couple of children have put flesh on her bones. Well, well, she is as you said, and for my part, I am satisfied. She understands, of course, and is willing?"

"She will do as she is told," Pembroke replied. "I have bred no crotchets in her. She is handy and biddable and her mother says she is well instructed in housewifery."

2

"What is your name, child?"

Leah started. She had not known that anyone else was present, but the voice came from a seat thrown into shadow by the glare of the fire. It was a low husky voice—a priest, Leah thought, and swallowed convulsively.

"Leah, her mother called her—that she might be fruitful." Pembroke answered.

"So she told me," the voice spoke again. Leah strained her eyes to see into the dimness. "But I would hear the girl speak. She is not simple, is she?"

"No, no! Curse you, Leah, open your foul mouth. You chatter enough when I would you were silent, but when you are asked to speak you are mute."

"Yes, father," the girl whispered. "I am only surprised. I did not know."

Slowly a huge form rose from the seat and limped painfully forward into the light. Leah had the impression of enormous power, of bitter dark eyes, and of shabby clothing. "Let her go, father," the younger man said. "Come here, Leah, for I would look at you." His husky voice was very gentle and gave her a little confidence so that, when the old man dropped her arm, Leah followed willingly enough to the window embrasure.

"How old are you?"

"Fifteen today, my lord."

"And already a famous housewife." There was a faint note of mocking laughter in the voice, but when Leah, stung, looked up, the face was grave enough. "Come, I will not hurt you, and, although I am no beauty, you must learn to accept my face," he continued as Leah hastily dropped her eyes again.

"My lord," she murmured, "I am unaccustomed to much company. Usually when knights come to visit my father I must stay in the women's quarters."

She did look at him then, however, and saw that a once handsome countenance was marred by one scar which drew up his mouth in a perpetual bitter smile and another which crossed his forehead and divided one brow in half. When she could detach her attention from those startling marks, she noted that he had a dark, weather-beaten complexion and a full head of rather lank black hair, that the lips, had they not been set so firmly, would have been full and well contoured, and that the large dark eyes were not only beautiful but held, in that unguarded moment, a rather soft expression of sadness.

3

"You need not always call me 'my lord,'" he was saying, "indeed, I have a wish to hear you say my name."

"But I do not know it."

There was a moment's silence, and Leah could see the eyes and the mouth harden. "I am Cain, Lord Radnor."

"You! Oh, then it is you—" Leah sat down suddenly on the window seat. She did not see the angry shade that passed over her future husband's face, and it was just as well for that would have frightened her badly. As it was, her relief brought her smile and, in a moment, her laugh trilled out. Her laugh was one of her greatest assets; it was like the song of a blackbird, a tinkling, musical cascade heard far too seldom. Unselfconscious in her relief, she put out her hand to touch his sleeve. "How glad I am. I thought—" She left that unfinished, merely repeating with a sigh, "How glad I am."

This man was certainly no beauty, but he was younger than the other and spoke gently. Leah looked at Cain squarely again, color flooding back into her face and making her glow into something approaching real beauty. For a moment she was surprised by his puzzled expression, and then realized that her remarks must have seemed incomprehensible to him. She laughed again, explaining.

"When I came in, I saw only your father. I thought he was the man I was to marry. I—it is not my place to object, of course, but I was afraid—I thought he was a little—a little elderly."

It was Lord Radnor's turn to laugh then, and he too sat down, grimacing as he took his weight off his feet. "And if it had been he that was to be your husband?"

"I would be obedient to my father in whatever he bid me, but I am—I hope—I do not know, but I think, perhaps it is easier to please a younger man. My lord—I mean Cain—what an odd name. I would think—" Her voice drifted away because of the scowl that spread over Lord Radnor's face.

"An ill-favored name, but my own." The husky voice was still low, but there was a snarl in it now.

"Nay, my lord," Leah touched his sleeve again, but timidly this time, her color fading slowly, "it cannot be ill-favored to me." She could say no more. An angry man was terrifying.

"So pretty a compliment must needs make me reconciled." His tone was clear then, and sharp with sarcasm, and Leah felt crushed and helpless. Her eyes filled with

4

easy tears and she looked away. For a moment the silence hung between them, and Leah was startled when Cain spoke again in his normal voice, a little uncertainty in the words.

"I am sorry. That was unkind. Nay, I pray you, do not weep. I was only—I pray you, do not weep." Cain moved closer on the window seat. They had, in that place, all the privacy that the great hall afforded, because the window opening in the walls, five feet thick at that level of the keep, formed almost a private room around them. "Come, you shall have your revenge for my unkindness. Set me a task, or ask me for—for—oh, Lord, what do women like—a jewel, and you shall have it."

Leah looked at him. To her surprise, for she had expected only a frown or the sly expression her father wore when he set a trap for her, Lord Radnor's face was perfectly serious, even concerned. The thought that her lord and master should offer her "revenge" for a harsh word was so ludicrous to her that she was surprised into laughter again. The sunlight filtered in a haze through skins scraped thin and oiled that covered the window to keep out the April chill; it made an aureole of light of the fine ends of fair hair that escaped from Leah's plaits and warmed her enough to set free a delicate odor of lavender that seemed to float about her like the shimmering light. Leah could not know her own charm with the teardrops sparkling on her long lashes, and she did not understand the curious expression that crossed Lord Radnor's face, but she took courage for it was certainly not anger. In reply to his repeated request she smiled shyly and shook her head.

"Will you cherish your hurt, then?"

"But I have taken no hurt. I was only frightened when you frowned, for I am sure that if I make you angry my father will—will kill me." Leah was telling the literal truth when she said that if the plans fell through because of something she did her father would kill her.

Lord Radnor's mouth hardened again. He intensely disliked Gilbert Fitz Gilbert, the Earl of Pembroke, and the daughter's fear did not improve matters. "No one will do you any hurt. As we are betrothed, your care is in my hands. Do you but please me and all will go well. And be not so timid for a frown. You will find that I frown often enough about matters indifferent to you."

Oh, God, Leah thought, no matter is indifferent to a

5

wife. Does not my father beat my mother when the crops are poor? Is not the will of God a matter indifferent to my mother? And yet, do not the blows sting just as shrewdly when the matter is indifferent? But she had training enough in concealing such thoughts, and she continued to smile. There was a pause. Cain studied the slightly downcast face of his future bride. He had not wanted this marriage, but he was a good deal better pleased than he had expected to be by the girl, her gentleness and soft beauty striking a chord to which he could not help responding. Leah racked her brains for further ground for conversation, inquiring politely at last how long her lord would stay.

"This night and perhaps another. I would not have come at all except that it was agreed that the betrothal should take place on the morrow." Lord Radnor stopped suddenly and became conscious that he had been extremely rude and tactless. "I should not have said that, I suppose, but I do not mean that I did not wish to meet you, of course. These are dangerous times in Wales, and if a full scale rebellion is to be averted I must keep close watch on my men and lands. I can ill spare even these few days—although—I am glad now—"

"I hear very little of these matters, my lord."

"And you are little enough interested, I warrant." Radnor smiled, wondering briefly what most women thought about, if they thought at all.

"No, no, I am interested. If you would but have the patience to pardon my ignorance and explain simply. I do, indeed, wish to know what is happening in the world, but my father never speaks of aught but hunting and gaming and my mother is so glad to be at peace that she will say no word of war. I remember when I was a little girl that there was much fighting and the house was full of strange knights always and my mother wept all the time. Why are these dangerous times?"

Lord Radnor passed a hand across his face, gently touching the scar near his mouth, seeking for simple terms to explain a complicated situation to this child who was watching him with an expression of eager interest. There was no need for him to tell her anything, of course, and he had not the smallest expectation that she would understand him since women, with the exception of she-devils like Joan of Shrewsbury, never did understand anything. He was amused, however, by her eagerness, like a child begging for a story, and it could do no harm to tell her.

6

To Leah, hearing of what was happening in the country around her was almost as great a marvel as reading a new romance, for news traveled very slowly and, since Pembroke stayed very seldom at the keep to which he had banished his wife, often missed them completely. Leah's life was filled solely with the household chores of the castle, and perhaps that should have been sufficient for her, but Lord Radnor like everyone else underestimated how much her wits had been sharpened by living with the father she had. She was very capable of understanding, and she longed for the stimulation of information beyond her household chores.

"When old King Henry died—no, I must go back before that, I guess, if you are to understand. King Henry had but one son born in wedlock. That prince, unfortunately, was drowned in a crossing from France. When the prince was drowned, King Henry, wishing to keep the throne for his own blood and having no other legitimate son, bade the barons do homage to his daughter, the Empress Matilda."

"Do you mean, my lord, that a woman could rule this land?"

Well, she had picked that up keenly enough. "Wait, let me go my own way or we will become enmeshed in explanations that take us nowhere. Many barons were willing to take her as queen, many were not, but after the pledge was made, even those that were willing regretted what was done."

"Why? Because she was a woman?"

"Not that so much. It is more that she is proud and overbearing. In a man a high stomach may be borne, but in a woman it is insufferable. When Henry died, therefore, some sent messages secretly to Stephen of Blois, the king's nephew. He was pleasant, well liked, and a strong fighter—also weak-minded, which was discovered later, but that is treason to say, so do not repeat it."

"I will repeat nothing you tell me, unless you bid me especially to do so."

Lord Radnor was startled, but he realized almost immediately that she responded to an order like a good, obedient child and continued his tale. "At first all went well except for a few disaffected—Robert of Gloucester, the king's natural son, held by his sister's right to the throne—and, although my father hesitated long, he finally was brought to do homage to Stephen by the representations of many of

7

our friends. But Stephen did not hold his promises; ever he listened to the last man to have his ear and, by turning first this way and then that, accomplished nothing and allowed every abuse. The result of this was that no man fears him, and the whole country has gone mad."

"Was that why there was so much fighting when I was a child?"

"Ay, but you are little more than that now, and there is more to the story which you will not hear if you continue to interrupt."

It was very kindly said, and Leah could not forbear a mischievous smile. He was a delightful man, even if he was not handsome, and, when one came to think of it, the marks were not so dreadful. They gave manliness to a countenance that might, from the looks of the eyes and mouth, have been too soft.

"Now the Empress Matilda—you remember, the king's daughter—had been waiting for just such a situation and she came posthaste from Anjou where she had been living. Once she arrived, serious rebellion broke out. Some were dissatisfied with Stephen; some had troubled consciences and feared the wrath of God because they were forsworn; but most seized gladly on the opportunity to attack and rob under the pretense of supporting one side or the other."

Leah had her hands gripped tightly together in her effort at concentration on this history. "Then the Empress Matilda is at war with King Stephen, I see, but—"

Glancing at the tightly intertwined fingers, Lord Radnor had to smile. He had a swift memory of himself concentrating on his tutor's lessons with just such hands. "Wait, wait, you leap ahead. It is not so simple in truth because the Empress Matilda now has a son who is very nearly a man. It is rumored that he is to return again to press his claim—he was here with his mother once before, but he was only a child of ten then."

"I see that this does not please you. Is he also unworthy to be king? Do you think that King Stephen can be brought to better ways?"

"The priests tell us that there are miracles," Cain replied dryly. "Perhaps God will think that England has suffered enough and perform one. Short of that, I do not believe that the king will—or I should say can, because Stephen is a well-intentioned man—change his ways. You are right though in saying that Henry's coming does not please me— and very clever, too, to have read that in my face—but it

8

is not because he would not make a better king. Almost anyone would, although Henry is too young, about sixteen, but I am sworn to be Stephen's man, no matter how little my heart lies there and I must hold to my oath. Of more immediate importance though is that Wales is like a pot just on the boil. One little thing more will make it run over."

Leah heard little but the last statement because she had been thinking that she could read far more in any man's face than whether or not he liked or disliked a king. When the price for every misreading of a flicker of expression that shows a mood is a blow and a bruise, the eye grows quick and the mind grows keen.

"But why should England's troubles affect Wales?"

"God in His omniscience, He knows why He made the Welsh as He did. I give them credit for their courage, but they are lunatic. They know not when they are beaten. They will not lie down and die when they are wounded unto death. They will not acknowledge us their masters although we have proven our claim again and again by force of arms. Each time the crown changes hands in England, the Welsh think that we Normans will be so concerned that we will pay no mind to what goes on in our own lands. Therefore the Welsh rise in rebellion, seeking to be free of the yoke we have placed upon them. Each time an overlord, like your father's brother, is slain or is deposed by the king, they rise to fight, flooding down from the hills and out of the forests."

Radnor had not turned his face from Leah, but his eyes stared unseeingly past her. He had forgotten she was there and was merely speaking aloud of something which puzzled and hurt him. "God knows that I would more gladly give my protection to them than slay them; their blood runs in my veins, and I have offered peace again and again. I would even, perhaps, give them what they say they desire—freedom. Little enough can be wrung from unwilling people in labor or gold, and the cost of fighting them to make them pay is more than my gain. But they will not live in peace among themselves nor let me live in peace. They kill my serfs; they burn my land. I cannot bear to see the earth a black ruin. I cannot bear it when the serfs bring their starving children to me and cry, Master, help us. Can I bring crops from scorched soil? It must be stopped before it begins. At all costs there must be no war in England and no change of overlordships in Wales."

"There will be no change in overlordships," Leah

soothed, frightened by Cain's intensity. "Why should there be?"

Cain started and flushed slightly as he realized he had exposed rather more of his personal feelings than he had intended. "I hope not," he said more calmly. "Our marriage will assure peace between Pembroke and Gaunt. If only Fitz Richard can be extricated from Stephen's grasp and Chester will keep the promises he has made to me, all will be well."

"Do you mean my cousin Fitz Richard? My lord, why does the king hold my cousin Fitz Richard?"

"You have a special affection for him?" Radnor asked sharply.

The jealous note was lost upon Leah in her concern for a childhood playmate. "Oh, yes. When I was a little girl, he told me stories and taught me chess arnd other games. Please—is he in danger?"

"Not in any personal danger, I believe." Cain was ashamed of himself. It was perfectly reasonable that a girl should be fond of her cousin. "You see, the Earl of Chester has rebelled often against the king. I love Chester well; he is my godfather and has been very kind to me, but he is a man of strong passions and when he believes the king to be wrong he tries to mend matters by war. War cannot mend matters now, so my father and I and your father made peace between Stephen and Chester."

"But my cousin Fitz Richard, what has he to do with this?"

"Chester is Fitz Richard's uncle on the mother's side, as your father is Fitz Richard's uncle on the father's. Also, Chester loves Fitz Richard well. Therefore Fitz Richard thought that if he offered himself and his lands as hostage for his uncle's good behavior, Chester would be more likely to keep the peace. This is all very well for England and for Chester, but it leaves your cousin Fitz Richard's lands without an overlord. This in itself is bad, because, as I told you, the Welsh are always restless."

"Then why does not the king send Fitz Richard home to govern his people?"

Cain sighed. "I have said I love Chester, and it is true, but Chester is not, alas, always to be trusted. The king keeps Fitz Richard because"—he knew he should not be saying these things to this girl, but he was carried along on a wave of bitterness—"because the moment Chester is bound by nothing but his word, he will break his word.

Stephen hopes that Chester will be quiet out of fear for Fitz Richard. Oh, God, I should have stopped it before it went so far, but I was so tired of this war and Stephen would have only Fitz Richard as hostage—and the fool of a boy was willing. Every man makes mistakes. If the peace had not been made, the Welsh would have rebelled. To quiet them we all agreed Fitz Richard should go. Now they threaten to rise for lack of an overlord and we must get Fitz Richard back—and I am so weary."

"But if you cannot get Fitz Richard away safe, and the Welsh do rise—Wales is large and well-peopled. How can you withstand them?"

What a fool I am, Cain thought. I have frightened the poor child. He ran a hand through his hair, and then smiled. "Some of the Welsh are satisfied to till the soil in peace and are content with their Norman masters. We take a tax from them, of course, but we protect them also so that they are not exposed to the wild tribes of the hills. Even so we would be in an ill case except that the Welsh are different somehow. Usually when there is a great cause for a people, that people unite to fight for it. Men will set aside petty quarrels to go on crusade, for example—and fools they are to do it too. It is most fortunate for us that the Welsh can never be brought to do this. They love to fight, but it is all alike to them whether they kill Normans or English or other Welsh. They are ever forsworn—I am not sure they believe in the True God, so they swear easily by Him without fear—so they do not trust one another, and this makes our task far easier. By my faith, they are brave fighters. It is just as well that they do not readily agree. I would not wish to meet the Welsh nation united on the field."

"You have been in many battles, have you not, my lord?"

"Many and many." Lord Radnor put up a hand to touch his scarred face and smiled more grimly. "Do you think I had cut myself while shaving?"

Leah's eyes glistened. "It must be very exciting to see a battle. I have rea—" Her voice hesitated and she dropped her eyes. To Leah's father it was a sin for a woman to be able to read. Her mother had taught her, but she knew she must keep her knowledge secret. "I mean I have heard many tales, and—"

Cain threw back his head to laugh, exposing white teeth and a powerful, corded neck. "Very exciting, provided you

11

are on the winning side. You are bloodthirsty for a maid, are you not?" he asked, teasing her.

Leah missed that. She was trained to take remarks literally. "I do not think so. I do not like to see the serfs hanged or maimed. Only it is so very quiet here, I think I should like to see brave men fight. The serfs scream and grovel so, I can hardly bear it."

Cain's laughter faded. "Not all men are brave in battle. It is sometimes hard to die." He shook his head sharply as if to rid it of a thought or picture and then smiled again. "In heaven's name, what a subject for a maiden. You will have excitement enough of a better sort for women, and soon enough too. Sometime this summer I must ride to court. Stephen has once more summoned the barons together. My father prudently remains behind so that one of us at least will have freedom of action no matter what befalls. Will you like to ride to court?"

"I am to go?"

"As you desire."

"Do you mean that I may really choose whether to go or to stay?"

There was a silence, and then Lord Radnor said rather dryly, "You would rather stay at home than ride to London with me?"

"Oh no," Leah gasped, "no, but it was lovely to think that I could choose to stay behind if I wished. No one has ever offered me a choice before," she added naïvely.

Edwina now reappeared in the hall and went toward Pembroke and His Grace of Gaunt. As she passed Leah and Lord Radnor, she directed at her daughter a definitely monitory glance. Leah cast wildly around in her mind for what she had done or left undone, and turned anxiously to the man beside her.

"Please forgive me. You must be tired for you have ridden far and over a hard road. I see you are all muddied, and here I have kept you talking. I pray you come to the east tower chamber and I will disarm you and prepare your bath."

"Gladly. It will be well come. We have ridden three days from the west and I am galled by the steel against my body."

Leah was instantly all concern. She led the way to the stairs and then, becoming conscious of Lord Radnor's halting step, offered her arm. "My lord, you are hurt. There was fighting in the west then?"

"Some fighting, but I am not hurt." Cain stopped and perforce Leah did too, turning to look questioningly at him. What she saw in his eyes turned her cold. She had read in the book of saints' tales of agonies of the spirit, but until that moment she had never believed that they could be more violent than those of the body which she had witnessed. Without consciousness of what she was doing, only feeling a rush of desire to offer comfort, she put out her hands and took Cain's. "I am a cripple," he continued, so harshly that, but for her hold on his hands, she would have physically recoiled.

"Alas, I am sorry."

"If I can bear it, you needs must. You will hear tales enough about me, and I tell you that I have a crippled foot. I am a crippled man, nothing more."

Leah's lashes hid her eyes. A fierce surge of protectiveness almost maternal, a desire to salve the apparent raw hurt, made her stammer a little. "No, no." She pressed the hand she still held tightly, and Cain became aware of her grip. "It is of no consequence to me; if I am sorry it is only because you looked so—." She could not go on, for what she had seen was indescribable. "Come, I pray you, you are tired, and if you will we may talk later. It is ill done of me to delay when you have told me of your weariness."

For Lord Radnor there was nothing more to say. Certainly he would not discuss with this raw girl the nameless superstitious fears which he denied he felt. She would run screaming from him in horror when she heard the tales of the demon son of Gaunt—and how was he to keep her from hearing? Mutely he permitted her to draw him out of the hall and up the stairs. In one of the towers of the keep, the area had been cleared of war gear and made fit for habitation. There were no true windows here, only arrow slits to let in light, and the circular room was dim, but the rushes underfoot were clean and intermingled with herbs so that the room was freshly scented. A fire burned brightly on the hearth, illuminating the grotesque carvings in the dark wood of a low-backed chair set before it. Into this chair Leah pressed her betrothed, and he sank into the cushioned seat with a sense of relief which was sharply broken when the girl released his hand and moved away.

"Stay, my lord, I must go to my mother and—"

With one bound he was upon her, grasping her forearm in his right hand. "Do you go to your mother? Will you ask

13

her to plead for your freedom? Do not be foolish. Crippled or whole, man or demon—oh, yes, I know what they say of me—I am a great matrimonial prize. Your lands march with mine. It is in every way suitable."

Shocked by his attack, Leah instinctively tried to pull away, and Cain tightened his grip until she went down on her knees. "No, no. Oh, my lord, please. I am in every way willing. Indeed, indeed, I was only going to ask my mother for herbs for your bath. Have mercy," she cried, her tears spilling over, "do not hurt me so."

"Oh, God." Radnor released her arm as if it had burnt him. "I am sorry. I did not realize—" He walked away to the fire while Leah leaned against the chair rubbing her arm and trying not to sob. Cain muttered something under his breath and then, more clearly, "If you wish to be free, tell me, and I—I will contrive so that you will bear no blame. I have used you shamefully, poor child."

"I swear I am content. I pray you to say nothing to my father. He will kill me. Dear lord, what have I done? What have I said? Do not be angry." He walked back toward her and she cringed. "I will go nowhere. Do not beat me, my lord."

"Beat you! For what? For my own shame and bad temper?" Cain touched the bright hair gently. "You will not think it after this, but I wish to use you kindly. I do not desire that you should fear me out of reason." He closed his eyes and laughed harshly. "I have begun well, have I not? Bruising your arm and frightening you out of your wits." Bending, he lifted her to her feet. "You must not let me frighten you, Leah. Your fear makes me cruel." The remark was ridiculous and Cain laughed. "There, I know you are young—I have led too hard a life—but I will try to remember. Are you truly content? Can you forget that I have been harsh to you?"

With a surge of thankfulness that the storm seemed to be over so quickly and with so little damage done, Leah summoned up a smile, tremblingly. "Oh yes, I am content, and you are not cruel. My father often uses me much more hardly and never has said he was sorry for it."

"Does he treat you ill?"

"No indeed," Leah said, afraid that Lord Radnor would think she had the temerity to criticize her father, "but I am very foolish and do many things amiss. It would be wrong in him to overlook my errors, for how should I ever learn if he did?"

14

She looked up at Lord Radnor to see the effect of this statement and noticed that he looked positively ravaged. This too was a revelation to Leah, for Pembroke always seemed to be refreshed by raging. All men were like that, Leah had assumed, having no other but her father for comparison, yet here was Lord Radnor, exhausted and ashamed. Leah could recognize the emotions because, sorely tried, she too could blaze into a rage. Her reaction, however, paralleled Lord Radnor's, and shame and fatigue followed temper.

Although Leah's reading of her betrothed's emotion was correct the reasons she assigned for it were wrong. It was not Radnor's burst of temper that exhausted him but his struggle with his private fear that he was something unclean. The fear went so deep and the struggle was waged so constantly that Cain suspected every emotion he felt and often considered the natural cruelty that exists in every human being as a sure sign of his damnation.

"I pray you, sit down again."

Leah pressed Cain gently toward the chair. Insensibly he was soothed and obeyed the urging, turning his face to look at the fire, and Leah, taking advantage of his apparent inattentiveness, rearranged the cushions on the chair more comfortably. Since this service caused no adverse reaction, Radnor continuing to stare at the flames and rub one hand with the other, Leah knelt and fumbled at his sword belt. She was pleased by the richness of the gold wire filigree snakes and birds which were riveted to the soft, strong leather, because her father was a veritable miser and locked away all the pretty things in strongboxes. Lord Radnor leaned back and sighed as the buckle gave and Leah lifted the weight of sword and belt from his hips. She folded the surcoat back away from his hauberk, and slipped the worn, rust-stained velvet over his shoulders. It was a source of great wonder to her that he would wear so rare and precious a fabric for such a purpose, for velvet was still imported into England in very limited quantities and brought fantastic prices, but it was not her place to ask questions. He leaned forward to permit her to remove the surcoat completely and docilely raised first his hips and then his arms so that she could pull the mail shirt off over his head. The weight of the mail made her gasp with effort. Technically a squire should do the heavy disarming, but neither Lord Radnor nor his father had a squire.

In spite of their prowess as warriors and their great position, not too many men wished to trust their sons to Gaunt's training. He had peculiar ideas about serfs and had infected his son with them. Furthermore they frequented the court only when summoned; they were not in particular favor with Stephen, although he listened with respect to anything they had to propose, because they had supported Robert of Gloucester in the late civil wars to the limit of their ability without actually fighting for him. Those barons whose political opinions concurred with Gaunt's had other reasons for withholding their sons. For one thing Gaunt never offered a place to a young nobleman, preferring to fill his ranks with well-paid mercenaries; for another, a boy entrusted to them could not come by the training in arts such as conversation, dressing, carving and so on, which were considered necessary for a noble.

The woolen tunic and linen shirt beneath the mail were stained with rust and blood, and Leah shook her head over the marks. "My lord." She touched Cain's arm and he started and looked at her with blank eyes. "You must have a fresh shirt, and a robe, and—"

"Yes, well?"

"Have I your leave to fetch these things?"

"Yes, certainly."

"But my mother has the keys to the storeroom. I must go to her to get the keys. You bade me—"

"Do not be so silly. Could you think I meant you to avoid your mother forever?"

"It is not my business to think what you mean," Leah answered simply, "only to obey you."

"Yes, very proper, but you must have a little sense too. If you do not leave the room and it should happen that no one came in, we might starve to death finally, and I should never get the bath I am very desirous of having."

It took a moment or two for the puzzled girl to realize that he was laughing at her, so grave was his expression, but she did understand finally and smiled. "You are teasing me," she said.

Her betrothed started to answer, but shivered suddenly, hunching his massive shoulders, for the room was dank and chill in spite of the fire. Leah ran at once for a woolen bed covering from a chest near the wall and draped it over his back. As she knelt before him to fold it around his body, she stroked his passive hand, hard as steel and scarred across the knuckles. She was remembering how kindly he had answered her questions and how tired he looked. Lord Radnor held his breath, hardly daring to move his eyes to look at her. She reminded him just then of nothing so much as the wild birds that perched near him as he lay in the woods of his home and, as he had held his breath then not to alarm them, so he held it now for this shy bird. How long they would have remained thus lulled by the hiss of the flames and their own quiescence was doubtful, but the idyl was broken when a log snapped in the fire, causing Leah to jump out of the way of the sparks. Lord Radnor did not move; his hand, like a lure to a bird, lay quiet on his knee and the quiet was indeed a lure to Leah. Daring greatly because he had been kind, because her comfort and possibly her life depended upon her pleasing him, Leah dropped a kiss on that quiet, scarred hand and ran lightly away on her errands.

CHAPTER 2

LEAH RAN HASTILY down the dark turret stairs. At the foot she met a maidservant whom she ordered to bring a bath to the east tower room and to ask her mother for the keys of the storeroom. "I will be here on the battlements," she said breathlessly. "Give me your cloak."

Away from Lord Radnor's presence, her excitement threatened again to overwhelm her and she felt that she had to breathe. She needed, too, peace to consider her fate, and the noisy, bustling hall where she might come upon her father or mother and be told to do something was not the place for thinking. Actually she knew more about her future husband than her mother suspected. As closely as she was watched, because highborn girls were guarded well to ensure their marriage value and Pembroke's household was rough and ill-regulated outside of the women's quarters, she listened often to the maidservants' talk. Many of these girls had lovers among the men-at-arms, for Pembroke laughed at such matters and in the face of his indulgence Edwina's prohibitions had little force. They told tales of the warriors who held back the Welsh, who fought in civil war, and who were embroiled in the current upheavals. The Duke of Gaunt and his son were high on the list of heroes.

Tales of their prowess were many and varied and, even the simple Leah suspected, sometimes exaggerated, but one thing was sure. Father and son were a strange pair and were held together by a strange and reputedly unholy bond. The father was well known to hate the son who obeyed him much as a dancing bear obeys his keeper; sometimes docile, sometimes snarling on the border of rebellion, Lord Radnor, like a bear, was always dangerous. Still, Gaunt was said to repose absolute confidence in his son and sent him alone to the councils of state, and the confidence, so stated rumor, had never been misplaced. Some said too that Lord Radnor—reported invincible in war—was not Gaunt's son but the child of the devil whom Gaunt had received because he could father no heir. Certainly twenty years of marriage to a second wife had produced no other child. Leah shuddered briefly because she knew that such things were possible. He said he was crippled, but was he? Or was the foot he limped on the horn hoof which marked Satan in his human form? Leah pulled the borrowed cloak closer about her, chilled by fear more than by the April wind.

It was useless to dwell upon such fears. This man, whatever he was, would be her husband. Her father had so commanded, and so it must be. Only what would she do if—. No, whatever else was uncertain, there could be no doubt that Lord Radnor was a great knight, and that she would be a great lady, the equal of any in the land save the queen alone. He would not have wanted to marry her if he planned to do her harm. If she were very obedient, Leah thought, she might be able to please him. With her father obedience did not always serve, but Lord Radnor was much younger than her father. Perhaps he would be kind to her—he had said he wished to use her kindly—or at least not unkind. If that were true, how proud she would be in the ranks of ladies with such a lord.

After Leah had left, Lord Radnor drew a shaken breath and swallowed hard several times. "Madness," he said to the fire. "It comes from reading those accursed romantic tales."

Then the sound of his own voice embarrassed him, and he scowled at the blameless flames. For twelve years Lord Radnor had spent few days without a sword in his hand and few nights in a safe bed. He had fought up and down the borders of his father's huge holdings keeping out robber barons and forcing the Welsh, who always desired to throw off the yoke of the Norman conquerors, to continue to serve them and pay taxes. Before that time, however, he had been taught by the priests his father supported, for Gaunt had not only peculiar ideas about serfs but equally peculiar ones about the value of education. The duke felt that if a man could read and write he could never be at the mercy of the clerical scribes; if he could speak and understand all the languages used by the people around him, including Welsh and Latin, he could understand things it might be dangerous to miss and would never need a translator.

In the mass of tutors needed for such an education, one man—Father Thomas—had recognized the qualities of the irritable, high-strung lad who was such a good student and such a difficult pupil. Father Thomas was not, perhaps, a very good priest, but he was a perceptive, gentle man. For a little while he had tried to foster the streak of gentleness he recognized in Cain with talk of the love of God and the beauty of faith. To this there had been no response; the fear that he was born damned as well as crippled was already too strongly implanted in the child. Father Thomas promptly abandoned all attempts to save his pupil's soul and saved his reason instead. He had introduced Lord Radnor to the Latin classics available, particularly Virgil's *Aeneid*, and to the "romance." In these popular tales, knights lived by their honor; they were gentle to all women and loved only one thoughout life; they fought for the oppressed and for the right without thought of self. Lord Radnor knew this was not life as it was, but it was a dream to cling to and an escape for his tormented mind. Through all the years of war and brutality and blood and death, he had clung to his dream, yearning for something beyond sordid reality and for a proof, in his endeavor to imitate the heroes of those tales, that he was a good man.

The Duke of Gaunt, a hard and brutal person, but shrewd and long-sighted beyond most men of his times, had added reality, all unwitting, to his son's dream. He had seen that serfs who had sufficient to eat and who were not totally prostrated with fear of their masters somehow produced better crops. Still harder work and better results could be obtained, Gaunt found, by allowing these virtual slaves to keep a slightly larger proportion of the crop than strictly belonged to them when the yield was particularly good. Confidence that they would be protected from the wars which ravaged and ruined the crops they labored so hard to produce and from rapacious minor barons also improved the willingness of the serf to labor for his master. All these things, then, the duke had provided, and the fact that he had become richer and richer and that his lands lay quiet when others endured rebellion proved the maxim that he had drilled into his son—that the way to a fat land was through fat serfs. Fat serfs came through peace which permitted them to till the soil. Lord Radnor's duty, then, was to keep the peace for his serfs by making war on those who threatened them, and the righteousness of the accomplishment of that duty, the protection of the weak, lent a glow of reality to his dream.

Not that Lord Radnor hated war. His nature was dual; it contained much cruelty as well as softer dreams. He loved his own prowess with sword and lance and his power on his own land and in the councils of the nobles of the realm. It was only that under that satisfaction was a desire for—for what? Cain had not formulated his thoughts, although he was a man given to introspection, and he was not sure what it was he lacked. He did know that the romances of Chrétien and Béroul satisfied and stimulated that longing. If life could be like that! He stirred in his chair and passed his hand across his face feeling the puckered skin of his scars. He fed his desire with reading and reading, buying and borrowing manuscripts wherever he could lay hands upon them, and the more he read the hungrier he was. For the courtesy, he had brutality; for the shining armor, he had rusty mail, hacked to pieces and mended to be hacked to pieces again; for the lovely ladies, he hardly saw a woman except the ragged, dirty women of the fields and the sluts of the court.

Lord Radnor rubbed his forehead impatiently—love, he shied away from the word, but that was the be-all and end-all of the romances. All the battles, all the trials and tribulations of the shining heroes were motivated by the love of fair ladies. He grunted and turned more toward

20

the fire as the maidservants brought in the bath and the leathers of hot water. Clumsy lumps with thick red hands. He stirred again, restlessly, and made an indistinct sound of discomfort as his shirt tore loose the scab of a half-healed cut on his shoulder. The girl—Leah, that was her name—her hands were smooth and thin and white. Love! Suddenly he had a clear picture of himself; his torn face, his skin nearly black and leather-textured with exposure. Oriented by his reading about blond and handsome heroes, Radnor did not understand the male attractiveness of his dark, harsh-featured face with its redeeming softness of beautiful eyes and sensitive mouth. He could only think of the horror at the end of his left leg with which he had been born instead of a foot. He did not see the grace of movement in spite of the limp or the appeal in the promised virility of his great body. All he knew was that he was no golden-haired, perfect knight of the romances, and no woman had ever loved him.

There were women, of course, the women of the fields that he used like an animal in heat, and the women of the court where he attended Stephen every so often. Some of these had offered love, and, years earlier, filled with the tales he had read, he had disregarded the fact that they were betraying husbands to "love" him. Was not Tristan's love illicit but true and faithful? Lancelot's? But he had learned that, outside of the leather-bound parchments of the romances, a woman who betrays her husband betrays her lover too—or charges a high price for her favors. Lord Radnor's mouth grew bitter with memory. The women who had betrayed him and laughed, who had sold him their bodies to steal secrets or gain political ends, had scarred his emotions badly. He had accepted the bond of matrimony as necessary to the continuation of his line, but he had accepted it reluctantly. What was more, he had objected particularly to marrying Pembroke's daughter because Pembroke hated and feared the Gaunts. His father, however, had been adamant, insisting that the dower lands Pembroke offered were not only great but particularly well placed with respect to Radnor's own property and that a blood bond between Gaunt and Pembroke was the best assurance possible of peace among the Norman barons of Wales. Finally Radnor had accepted marriage even with Pembroke's daughter, driven by the fierce desire to have a son to succeed him.

Leah had been a shock to Lord Radnor. He had not expected so pretty, but above all, so gentle and timid a girl. His experience of women had not included pure, highbred young girls. He felt, therefore, that Leah was different, something exceptional. He was worried now that this delicate bird would die of his rough handling as a lark caught in his youth had died of fright when he tried to caress it. Cain shivered again just as Leah came back into the room.

"My lord, you are chilled. It is all my fault. What a poor thing I am compared with my mother." She needed some excuse for she had wasted much time standing on the battlements and thinking. "Your father is already bathed and dressed. I pray you pardon me, but I will be quick now." She gave orders to the maids and soon the scent of the herbs she had thrown into the water filled Cain's nostrils. "Will you have me bathe you?" As she spoke, Leah blushed. She had never bathed a man before, although her mother had taught her how it was done and although many girls like herself did perform that task. Edwina took the burden of that duty on herself for all visitors of sufficiently high rank, but Lord Radnor was Leah's betrothed and she assumed that he was hers to care for. She put her hands on his shoulders to pull off the cover, since she had received no reply, and Cain made a strangled sound that caused her to step back. "At least let me help you undress."

Her lord cleared his throat and finally turned away from the fire to look at her. Her hands, exactly as he remembered them, graceful, pearly white, were held a little toward him. He stared at them and at her delicate, fine-boned face for so long and so intently that Leah blushed again.

"No, I thank you. I will bathe myself. I always do so. It is too old a habit to be broken."

His voice was so soft that Leah started forward. "You are well, my lord?"

"Yes. Perfectly well."

"I will leave you then, before the water cools. I pray you call me before you dress. There was blood on your shirt and I will anoint your wounds so that you may be comfortable."

"Very well."

Cain undressed slowly, the physical action masking his thoughts, and stepped into the tub. He grimaced as the hot water stung a dozen sores, but he was so inured to physical discomfort that the movement was wholly unconscious.

He washed, lifting the water in cupped hands to rub over his face, shoulders, and upper arms, before he noticed a small irregular cake of yellow soap. For a moment he stared at it, unrecognizing, for he had not used soap more than four or five times in his life. After he had taken it up, however, he bathed more briskly, lathering himself luxuriously, even washing his thick black hair. Finally he stepped out of the bath, standing on his right foot alone and holding the other up off the floor. He stood steadily, through long practice, to dry himself roughly, reached for the shirt, remembered that Leah wanted someone to attend to his wounds, and instead took up his chausses, a garment that combined stockings and underpants. When these and the special boot that masked and supported his crippled foot had been drawn on, he raised his head and bellowed for attention.

Leah herself came in bearing pots of ointment, responding so quickly to his call that she must have been waiting outside the door. Lord Radnor looked faintly surprised—he thought she would send a servant to attend him—but when she asked if she might dress his wounds he agreed willingly enough. He returned to his chair by the fire and returned, too, to his contemplation of the flames.

"Oh," Leah commented after anointing various hurts with a salve from one of the pots, "there is proud flesh here."

"Yes, an old wound that does not heal. It is of no consequence."

"But it is, indeed. It must be attended to. Let me get a knife and I will make all clean. I assure you that it will heal properly if cared for."

Lord Radnor made an impatient gesture. "I must be away two days hence. Who will care for it? Let be, I say. I have borne it so long, a little longer, or forever, can make no difference."

Leah had never in her life questioned or contradicted a statement made by a man, and she did not think of doing so now. For a while longer she worked over the rest of his body. She rolled down the loose top of the chausses and knelt to salve an angry-looking weal very near his groin. Suddenly, she felt Cain's body stiffen.

"I will not hurt you, my lord."

"Hurt me?"

"I know that I am young, but I have been well taught. If you do not trust me, let me call my mother. She—"

"How could you hurt me?"

He did not even know what he said. Innocent as she was, Leah could not know the rage of desire that had suddenly flooded him. He had been hurried in the last few weeks and there had been no woman immediately to hand that he had wanted to take to his bed. Being alone in the dim room with Leah had made Cain achingly conscious that she was to be his bride and that she was very desirable. Worst of all, the sustained caress of her hands as she dressed his wounds had aroused him, and the thought of her hand between his thighs nearly made him lose his control.

"Nay," he said at last, seeing the trouble in her face, "if you are in such earnest, fetch your knife and do as you will. I only did not think it worth your trouble."

If she would go and not touch him for a while, he could master his desire, but it was no easy thing to do. She is no lady greensleeves, he told himself, nor yet a serf on my lands. When I have her, it must be with honor. With honor, he repeated, as Leah returned. He winced slightly as she cut his flesh, and she put a cool hand on the back of his neck to steady him. Unfortunately, the coolness did not communicate itself to him. Where she touched him, he burned, hotter than the blood which he could feel running down his back.

"This will sting a little, my lord." Leah spread an unguent on the raw flesh and Cain drew breath and released it in a long sigh. Leah misunderstood the trouble he was having with his breathing. "I am sorry," she murmured. "It is finished now. Only the one bruise below and I will let you be."

Lord Radnor braced himself to quietness and knew even as he did so that he could not bear it. "Give it here, I will spread it myself." She handed him the pot, but her lips trembled. "Fool. It is not because you hurt me or because I mistrust your skill. It is——." What was he going to say? Cain burst into laughter. "Oh, Lord, girl, I cannot explain to you."

"You are trembling. You are cold. Here, put on your shirt."

Cain laughed even louder. "No indeed, I am not cold. By God's eyes, I am far, far too hot. Perhaps, though, the shirt will do as well to cool this heat as it would to warm the cold you fear."

He pulled the garment over his head and added tunic

24

and gown quickly, feeling vaguely that the more clothing there was between them the safer Leah would be. When she came up close to offer a soft leather belt to close the gown, however, Radnor's mixture of desire and curiosity conquered him. It could do no harm, after all, to take one kiss from her lips. He caught her wrist and pulled her still closer. The hand that held the belt dropped when he pushed her face up to his, but she made no effort to withdraw. Slowly, watching for a sign of fear or revulsion, he put his mouth to hers. His lips were hard and rough and forced her soft mouth open; Leah's breath would not come evenly. For an instant her hand moved aimlessly, then pressed him away, and then, as she felt his lips begin to withdraw, went around his neck to pull his face closer.

"A pox take me!" Radnor exclaimed and roughly pushed Leah away. "That was ill done, my lady. A little more and you are a maid no longer. Think you I am made of the snows of the mountain?"

She could not speak. Scarlet to the roots of her hair, she stood with head dropped before him. So this was the sin of lust. How quickly it had overtaken her. She could not rid her mouth of the feel of his lips. Worse yet, she did not wish to do so.

"D-do n-not th-think ill of me, my lord. I could n-not help—"

"The fault is mine. I am sorry now, though, that I did not agree to be married today as your father and mine wished. I felt that you would like to have time to prepare yourself. Your obedience is such, however, that I see this to have been unnecessary. Are you sure, Lady Leah, that you do not know overmuch of kissing?"

Now Leah's tears flowed in earnest. How quick was retribution on the head of evil doers. "Oh, no," she sobbed, "you may ask my mother. None but she has ever kissed me before, and she not often. My lord, my lord, if I have done ill, it is only in listening to the tales of the maids and the singing of the jongleurs."

He knew it had to be so. She was watched too close, no doubt, to come to harm in her own castle, and she had never been away from it. His fierce jealousy leapt to life in fear of no particular man, but if she kissed him with such warmth—ugly and deformed as he was—what would happen when the bright young men of the court were made available to her?

"Stop that crying! Do you want to have the whole castlefolk in here? Dry your eyes." He bent and picked up the discarded belt, fastened the gown together, and came toward her. "The fault was mine." Lord Radnor spoke more gently. "There is no wrong in a willingness to kiss your betrothed. I should be glad you do not shrink from me as I half expected. Alas, for someone who wishes to please you, I have made you greatly unhappy this day."

Leah shook her head. Cain watched her. If her response had been planned, it would not occur again; if it was involuntary—

"Come here," he said austerely, "and kiss me once more, quite properly."

She came to him obediently and raised her face, still wet with tears. This time, it was true, she made no effort to embrace him, but, when he kissed her, she trembled and leaned against his body. Lord Radnor checked himself with an effort, calling himself ten times a fool, as the taste of desire rose again in his throat.

"Go now. Go before I shame myself and do you some hurt."

Through the meal which was served in the evening because Cain and his father had missed their dinner, Leah sat mute as a stone. She was so exhausted by the emotional upheaval she had suffered that day that she could make no further effort, although she knew that she should make some conversation with the Duke of Gaunt who sat beside her. The old man did not trouble her with a word, but his keen glance moved from the drooping girl to his son's slightly pale face. The great ox has frightened her, he thought, and the chit is Pembroke's daughter. She will have to be watched close.

As soon as she dared, Leah crept away to seek solace in quiet. She shut the door of the tiny wall chamber which was called hers, struck flint into tinder to light the stub of a candle which she was allowed, and began to ply her needle. The familiar activity did little to calm her, but one clear idea took possession of her. Her betrothed's clothing must be put into fit condition for him to wear. The garments had been left in Edwina's chamber, and Leah easily picked out Lord Radnor's clothes. The stillroom supplied remedies for rust and blood stains, and Leah set to work. While the shirt soaked, she damped and brushed the brown velvet surcoat lovingly. She would not soak that precious fabric, but blotted and brushed patiently at the

26

stains. When she was through, the surcoat was in far better condition than it had been before, but it was clear that the garment was too worn and badly neglected to be reclaimed. She noted too that though the cloth was of the finest, better than any she had seen in her entire life, the making-up was coarse and ill done. As she stared at it, the idea came to her of making Lord Radnor a lavish robe for a wedding gift. She did not know whether it would be possible, for her father would have to supply the cloth and jewels and might not be willing, but there was a chance since he would be eager to please his powerful son-in-law.

After cutting rag strips to indicate length and width and carefully putting these away in the chest with her own clothing, Leah took the shirt out of the soaking tub. The stains were nearly gone, but the shirt was badly torn in several places, as were the chausses. These too were of good material but poor make. Leah set the shirt to dry before the fire in her mother's room—there was none in hers—while she mended the dark blue chausses, frowning over the awful combination of colors. She knelt close to the flames for light, scorching her face but taking tiny, careful stitches. She would not light candles without her mother's permission; candles were expensive and Pembroke was not generous.

Edwina found her thus employed. "What are you doing, Leah?"

The girl, immersed in her own thoughts, started and blushed. "Mending his clothes," she replied, as if there was only one man in the world. "They are in sad condition. Oh, mother, I have some linen laid by for a shift. May I use it to make a new shirt for him? I think there is enough cloth, and if I sew tonight I can have it ready in time. I can be quick."

Edwina regarded her daughter for a long puzzled moment. "Certainly, if you wish to give up your new shift." Edwina would have given up anything for her daughter, she thought, or for her own parents while they were alive, but to make a sacrifice, even so small, for a strange man who would use you as he pleased was beyond her understanding.

"Oh yes. I have two which are still good." Leah's face was pink in the ruddy firelight, and her mother could not tell whether she was blushing or merely overheated.

"Light some working candles, child, you will burn your hair." Leah obeyed at once, and Edwina watched her as

27

she brought the candles to a table near the hearth. She caught her daughter's arm, as Leah was about to touch Lord Radnor's shirt to see if it was dry. "Are you content, Leah?" Now it was plain that the girl was blushing rosily, and Edwina was surprised.

"Yes."

"Of course, you could not be otherwise when your father has so decided. But—you had much talk with Lord Radnor. Is he content, think you?"

Leah stood submissively before her mother, but she did not raise her eyes. "I do not know. He was—very kind." She spoke with an effort which her mother interpreted wrongly in the light of her own feelings.

"Leah, you must be happy with what God sends. He has offered you much to be happy with. If Lord Radnor is not so young or so handsome as you may have desired—if he is not just like the knights in the tales which you hear—he has many things to offer you. Lord Radnor is rich beyond avarice, the lord of many manors; he is a great warrior; he will be one of the greatest and most powerful men in the kingdom when his father dies. You must be grateful that he has chosen you."

"I am grateful, mother. I am content."

Edwina was baffled by Leah's reticence. Her confiding child had withdrawn into her own thoughts. She released Leah's arm. "There, the shirt is dry now. Mend it, and I will help you cut the linen for another."

CHAPTER 3

THE HIGH TABLE the next morning was lacking in conversation since all of its occupants were heavy-eyed. Pembroke and Gaunt had drunk far into the night. Edwina had lain awake tortured by fears for her daughter's future and disturbed by Leah's emotional withdrawal. Leah herself had sewed almost all through the night, and Lord Radnor had tossed and turned and then walked the floor until he was exhausted. When he finally slept, he was disturbed by dreams which brought him awake, sweating, to walk the floor again until the pain in his bad foot was unbearable. He had spent the rest of the night dozing uneasily in the chair by the fire. One thing he had to be grateful for—he thought his father had been too drunk to notice his behavior.

Leah rose first from the table, not usually set up for breakfast except on the infrequent occasions when there were guests. Cold meat, pastry, and eggs were added to the usual bread and wine, but of these she had not partaken. Murmuring excuses, she retreated to the women's chambers. She found that her calm was not proof against her betrothed's presence. She could barely choke down her bread and wine, and the few glances she had dared steal at him showed a sullen, angry expression intensified by heavy-lidded, red-rimmed eyes.

The Earl of Pembroke and Gaunt went off to hunt for a few hours, issuing an invitation to Cain which he refused rather rudely, shrugging aside his father's even ruder remarks on his manners. Alone, he wandered out into the battlements and then down through one of the towers and across the moat into the field adjoining the castle. Edwina, passing from one tower to another on her household business, saw him there and, after considering, sent Leah to him. She was reluctant to do so, but felt that they would both suffer if Pembroke heard that Lord Radnor had spent the day alone. He was sitting beside a tree with his eyes closed when Leah came up to him, but the sixth sense of all successful fighting men warned him of her presence.

"Good day, my lord."

"What brings you here?" Cain spat.

Leah recoiled. "My mother did not wish you to be alone. She sent me to you, but I will return at once."

"No!" Radnor was ashamed of himself. He should have known that this child was too well brought up to force herself upon him of her own volition. She was no court lady, puffed up with her own importance. "I do not even know what made me say that. I was half asleep. Stay, now that you are here. Would it be too cold for you to sit still? Would you prefer to walk?"

"It is a fair day." Leah was about to suggest a walk in the water meadows to see if the wild crocuses were still in bloom, but she remembered his limp in time. "Let us sit here quietly, if that would please you. It is not cold.

Indeed, it will be pleasant to sit and do nothing for I was awake most of the night."

Lord Radnor was startled and a trifle displeased. "You too?"

"Alas, did not you sleep well, my lord?"

"Well, did you?" It was not, perhaps, proper for a girl to confess to so much passion, but it was certainly innocence which permitted her to do so. Lord Radnor could not help smiling as he asked his question.

"Oh yes, when I went to my bed at last."

Now that was a wholly puzzling remark. "What kept you from it then?"

"Why, my lord," she replied laughing, "I mended your clothes, and cleaned them too."

He burst out laughing. That would teach him to overrate his attractions. "But why did you mend my clothes?"

"Surely you do not think it is our custom to allow our guests to go forth all mud-splattered from our house." She frowned. "I fear I could do little enough with them. They are sadly neglected. Do you not carry a change of clothing with you?"

"No. I used to do so, but if the things were not lost in fording some stream or left behind by carelessness, I found I never had time to change anyway and finally gave up trying. I have clothing in all of my own keeps, of course, and I change when I can."

"If you were not in such haste, I would have—but at least I made you a new shirt. You are so very big, my lord, that it was not possible to give you my father's clothing, which my mother would have been glad to do. Indeed," Leah said both shyly and slyly, taking a chance because of the pleasure mirrored in Lord Radnor's face, "I am very glad there is no one of import to see us here. For although you are a very great lord and I of little account, I could never hold up my head again if I were to be seen with a man so clad."

Radnor was startled into sitting upright and looking at himself. In truth, he was a sight to behold. His cross-gartered legs protruded from the bottom of a gown at least eight inches too short for him and hastily patched to accommodate his tremendous breadth of shoulder and chest. He grinned, exposing handsome teeth.

"You have touched me, my lady. Although it must be plain to all that I care little for such matters, I must say that to be seen in this guise causes even my spirit to quail.

Your mother has certainly made you a good housewife. She bade you, I suppose, show me all your virtues. She seems troubled that I am not satisfied with my bargain."

"She did not need to tell me aught. I hope I know what is every guest's due—and how much more is yours, who are my own good lord." Her gentle dignity drew Radnor's eyes again to Leah's face. Embarrassed by the forthright stare, Leah sought hastily for something to say. "If it is not improper for me to know, where exactly is it that you go in such haste? You look tired to death; it is shameful that you may not rest here longer."

A swift memory of the night he had spent almost made Lord Radnor laugh at that comment. He had a good idea that he would get little enough rest in Leah's company until he could satisfy himself with her, but he repressed his laughter, and answered her direct question.

"Two of the petty barons who hold land of my father have found a cause to quarrel. From insults I fear they will leap to assault, and this is no time for a private war on my land." Lord Radnor squinted in the strengthening sunlight of April, and Leah, alive to his smallest gesture with a sensitivity new to her because it was not born only of fear, put her hand on his shoulder and pulled gently.

"Rest your head on my lap while you tell me. I will shield your eyes from the sun."

Cain yielded to her with a sigh and closed his tired eyes against the glare. "There is little enough to tell except that a rumor grows that Henry of Anjou will come again to claim the throne. If so, Chester may break his truce with the king, your cousin Fitz Richard's lands will fall forfeit, and the Welsh will doubtless rise. I will need every vassal I have to subdue them. I dare not allow my own men to become embroiled with each other. When the Welsh run wild—"

"But were not the Welsh subdued in King Henry's time?"

"I told you yesterday, they have never really been subdued. The Welsh—" Lord Radnor made a helpless gesture with one hand. "They are all mad together and say that we oppress them. A man may not leave Welsh lands unguarded to indulge in private war. The Welsh will strike—they say for freedom, I say because the devil is in them—the moment their lord's back is turned."

Leah could feel the muscles tense in Cain's shoulder under her hand. "Rest. There is no need to tell me more if it disturbs you. Let us talk of something else. Here, at least, is peace. There is nothing to guard yourself against on this land and in this keep."

"It does not disturb me to tell you how matters lie if it interests you, but it has come to my mind that the Welsh Marches are no place, in time of rebellion, for a woman not of their blood."

"I do not think I should be afraid. If they wished to kill me, that would not matter. If I thought they should do worse, I hope I could have the courage to end my own life." That made Cain laugh gently, for it sounded to him as if a dove had offered to take the place of his gerfalcon. Leah was a little hurt. "You need not laugh at me, my lord. Even a woman can find courage when she must defend her husband's honor."

That remark made Radnor open his eyes in surprise. The women he had known had given him little reason to think that they concerned themselves much with their husbands' honor except to stain it.

"Now who has given you ideas like that?"

"My mother and the chaplain have taught me my duty, I hope."

'You never learned talk of self-slaughter from your chaplain—or your mother, I'll be bound."

"No, but I have—have heard many tales of brave ladies. Now you are laughing at me again." Radnor assured her he had merely been smiling because of the pleasure her pretty face gave him, and begged her to continue. Watching him suspiciously for further signs of mirth, Leah added, "I know that the priests say that to take your own life is a mortal sin, but do you not think that God, who is so kind, would understand that although you might be willing to suffer yourself you could not permit another, especially your husband, to suffer because of you?"

Radnor did not answer for a moment. Her theology was certainly original. He should have been horrified, for he knew better, but instead he was charmed and amused. Just now he would do nothing to hurt her feelings at any cost, certainly not argue a theological point. He quelled the impulse to laugh at her earnestness, but even so he sounded a little choked.

"I am sure that the Lord would understand, being omniscient. Whether He would approve or not, of course, I could not take it upon myself to say. Tell me, Leah, do

32

you spend your time listening to tales and thinking these thoughts?"

The girl laughed at an experienced man's naïveté in household matters. "No indeed. You must not think me so idle. Women must learn many things too, even if they are not such interesting or exciting things a men learn. I can cook, and spin, and sew, and even weave, although that I do not do too well, for it takes long experience to make a good weaver. I have learned to nurture herbs and to use them. Now if you will permit, I will show you something else I have learned. I have urged you to rest, but you lie on my lap as if you were ready to spring to your feet at each moment. Turn a little on your side, my lord, and I will teach you how I have learned to make a man rest."

Cain was surprised again. Always tense, he had not noticed his own rigidity. He did as he was told, however, and Leah began to rub the back of his neck and shoulders gently. She continued to speak in a low voice of the daily life of the castlefolk, and her voice grew fainter, her words slower, until finally she drifted from words into humming a simple tune. Radnor's eyes grew heavier, his muscles flaccid; at last he slept soundly, his battle-scarred hands relaxed open on the ground and his face pressed against her dress.

When he woke, the sun was beginning its afternoon decline, and Leah was smiling down at him. "Are you rested now?" she asked.

"Wonderfully. You must have bewitched me. It seems to me that I have not slept so well since I was a child."

"You were very tired. How difficult must be your life, my lord, to tighten your thews so hard that you cannot release them. It is grievous to me that you cannot stay longer."

"Truly?" Leah did not answer but smiled and pressed his hand slightly, for they were walking now in the formal manner with her hand resting on his. "Where do you lead me now?" he continued. "I am so bemused that you might lead me off the edge of a cliff and I would not notice."

"What a gallant speech," she laughed, "and how evil you think me. Even if I had such dreadful intentions, you must see it to be impossible—we have here no cliffs. I mean kindly to you, however, I assure you. I do but return to your sleeping chamber. I would look again, if you permit, at your wounds, and I hope to induce you to change your attire. Perhaps when your limbs do not hang out of your

33

garments, I may think of you as a swan instead of a duckling."

That remark was puzzling, but Radnor connected it vaguely with their previous talk about clothes and did not pursue it, surrendering with a voluptuous sense of luxury to Leah's ministrations as she unfastened his belt and drew off his gown. "I tell you," he replied, "it is no light thing to be so much larger than other men. It is always my head that sticks out on the field of battle." His voice was dreamy and a little muffled as Leah pulled off his shirt. "It is no doubt by God's special grace that I have kept as much of it as I have. One day the good Lord will grow tired of over-seeing His long mistake, and I will—"

"Oh, no!"

"Why, Leah what is it?"

"I did not think when I laughed because you are so big that it was not matter for jest at all and that it might be a danger to you."

"No, no. It is indeed a matter for jest." Seeing the tears in her eyes, he tried earnestly to reassure her. "Leah, I did but jape with you. Do not weep. I am in no way endangered. Truly, on a horse all men are the same size."

But Leah was badly shaken. She had suddenly realized that true fighting did not take place in the romantic way in which it was described in the minstrel's tales where the hero always won and was never hurt. The marks on Cain's body showed clearly that he was not invulnerable. Adjusted as Leah was to absolute obedience to her father, she would have tried to love any man he chose for her, no matter how old, ugly, or brutal. With Lord Radnor she had not even had to try; he was not old nor, in spite of his scars, ugly, and he certainly was not brutal to her. She was desperately anxious that nothing should happen to interfere with their marriage, for she knew that her satisfaction was a matter of total indifference to her father and that it was unlikely that she would be equally lucky in Pembroke's second choice. Her hands clung to Radnor's mighty upper arms and she bowed her head on his breast.

"Leah, I am long tried in war. For God's sake, if not for mine, do not weep—I cannot bear it." Whatever women had offered him in the past, not one had ever cried with fear because he might be hurt. "Good God," he said, at last, more moved by her tears than she was herself, "you will unman me."

At that Leah raised her head. "My lord, I do not weep."

34

Tears trembled on her lashes. With an effort she steadied her voice. "Men must fight and women must wait. It is the will of God. But may I be dead, as I most certainly will be damned, if I should make you less than yourself." The words were bravely said, unconsciously copied from the romances, but her hands clutched so tightly at Cain's arms that her nails bit into his flesh.

"You will have more wounds to dress if you do not let me go," he said gently, and then with an attempt at lightness, "and I shall take cold and die of that if you keep me standing in this cold room much longer with nothing but my hose on."

Leah smiled uncertainly, bade Cain sit again, and went to fetch her ointments. She smoothed the salve into the raw spots, exclaiming that the infected cut was now healing well. "I wish you did not go so soon."

"I will make haste—the best haste I may—to return. Will you be as tender of me then? Will you salve my new cuts and bruises?"

"You said"—her hands tensed and Cain winced as she pressed too hard on an open sore—"that there might be no fighting."

There was always fighting, one way or another, he thought. "A man may always tumble off his horse, or fall down a flight of steps when drunk," he replied lightly.

"I am sure that you are in the habit of falling off your horses," Leah laughed, and then bit her lip to force back a new rush of tears. "And now, my lord, you may anoint the bruise above your thigh. I must go and change my gown for dinner because it makes my father furious if I am late. Your clothing is here on the chest."

She left quickly and ran to her room, not to dress but to throw herself on her bed in a passion of tears. She knew he would never return. She was too happy; she could not be permitted to have such joy unpunished. She cried hysterically, and Edwina, coming in to dress, heard her.

"Leah! What is it? What has happened now? Heaven and earth, what has befallen you?"

"Oh, mother, something dreadful will happen. I know it. I know it. Nothing good can come of this."

Edwina's face went white as wax. Could Leah have discovered that Pembroke planned Radnor's death? If Radnor was warned and did not go through with the marriage, the whole plan to make an independent kingdom of Wales with Pembroke as its king and herself as its queen would

35

collapse. If Radnor had been warned through Leah's foolishness, Pembroke might really kill his daughter. But how could Leah have heard? What, and how much, had she heard?

"What are you talking about? What happened? Where is Lord Radnor?" But Edwina could get nothing from Leah except an incoherent repetition that something dreadful was about to occur.

Leah could know nothing definite, that was sure. By the time Lord Radnor had entered Pembroke's plans, Leah had been carefully excluded from all the conversations as had everyone not perfectly trustworthy. At first Pembroke had spoken only of obtaining control of Fitz Richard's lands, since the young man was kept a virtual prisoner in London. Slowly the notion of obtaining the lands permanently through forfeiture had developed in Pembroke's mind. It would be so easy to make Chester violate his truce; it would need no more than a hint that the king did not trust Chester and did not treat him with enough courtesy. That was where Radnor had come into the picture. Pembroke knew that the Gaunts would oppose any change of overlordship in Wales, partly because they feared it would wake the wild tribes to rebellion and partly because they did not want Pembroke's power to be increased.

Edwina herself had suggested the marriage. She knew that Leah had to marry, although she hated the idea, and Radnor was out fighting so much that he was the least of the evils in that Leah would be little troubled by his presence. Pembroke had hesitated because he hated the Gaunt family, root and stock, until Edwina pointed out that the blood bond would be a particularly strong one since Radnor had no other close relatives. Surely, she had urged, he would not oppose his own father-in-law's aggrandizement. Edwina remembered very vividly how Pembroke had stared at her, how long he had remained silent with his cold, round eyes getting blanker and blanker. Then he had begun to laugh, and he had actually leant over to kiss her. Even in retrospect, Edwina drew herself together in fear and distaste. Gilbert was so cruel, so wily, and in spite of her efforts he could read her very soul like an open book. He had laughed and laughed.

"How would you like to keep your daughter?" he had asked. "A rich widow with a father to care for her property does not need to marry again. How would you like to be the first lady of Wales?"

36

There had been no need to wait for an answer. He had touched the only two sensitive spots in Edwina's heart, her love for Leah and her pride. Pembroke had repeated over and over, af if he were savoring the flavor of the words, that Radnor was the only child of an only child. He had neither kith nor kin who could inherit his property or his father's property. When he married, every rod of land and every copper mil would belong to his wife if he died childless.

"You are right indeed, my clever wife. Why should Radnor not marry our Leah? Why should he not die? Even if there was a child, would not that child be best guarded by his wife's father, since Gaunt is so old?" Pembroke had stopped laughing and was picking nervously at his clothes. "It would not be easy. That devil will not be easy to kill so that no man knows I have done it—but it might be done."

Little by little the plan had grown. With Radnor and Gaunt dead—and Gaunt would die by nature very soon for he was nearly three-score years old—there would be no real power in Wales except Pembroke himself. He would be like a king. Like a king? He would be king!

The easiest and least suspicious way for Radnor to die was in battle, but Radnor was cautious and not greedy. He would fight only to defend himself and on his own land. While Pembroke began negotiations for the marriage of Leah to Cain, offering as bait a magnificent dowry, he also began testing this man and that for weakness. Most of Radnor's vassals were steadfastly loyal, for the Gaunts were good overlords, but finally a man with a grievance had been found. He was Sir Robert, the castellan of Radnor Keep. Pembroke had nearly wept with joy, for Radnor Keep was not far from the border of Fitz Richard's territory. If the Welsh in Fitz Richard's territory could be incited to attack any keep near Radnor Castle, Cain would be caught between the Welsh army and the disloyal Norman garrison. It was a good plan, but not good enough. The Welsh were undependable; Sir Robert might have a change of heart; or Radnor's own great skill as a fighter and leader might save him. Having received some indication that the marriage proposal was being favorably considered, Pembroke began to seek auxiliary methods of insuring his future son-in-law's demise.

Pembroke made a quiet trip to London in the winter when few men traveled. Stephen could not make nor keep secret a plot, but in Queen Maud's luxurious solar a man could speak of devious plans and be understood. Even to Maud one could not simply confess a desire to murder one's daughter's husband nor, of course, could one admit aspirations to royalty, but clever as she was she was only a woman. Pembroke found her ears very open to a plan to attack Gloucester from the rear and end the civil war once and for all. If Chester and Hereford could be attained when they were at court and could be taken prisoner easily, their estates would not make a solid bar against a royal invasion of Wales. Then only Radnor was left to resist the King's march through that country. Radnor was too cautious politically to fall into the trap as his godfather Chester would, but when Stephen called a council of his barons a tourney would be given. Men died in tourneys too; not as often as they died in war, but matters might be expedited without too great difficulty. Pembroke did not speak his mind fully to Maud. When he needed to express himself, there was always Edwina, who feared him more than she feared the devil because she was more surely in his power. To her he added the fact that Radnor might not fight in the tourney—that would be the last, most certain, device. There were knives that slipped between ribs in dark passageways; there were arrows that sank deep after singing through quiet courtyards.

Edwina did not know, and did not wish to know, the details. She knew enough to horrify and revolt her, but Radnor was nothing to her and the prize to be won by conniving at his death was invaluable. Desperately she slapped Leah until the girl's cheeks were flaming red and her sobs quieter. "Whatever you have heard, or guessed, or dreamt, hold your tongue. If this marriage does not come to pass because of a slip of your tongue, your father will rip it out with hot pincers. Now, wash your face. Dress in your best gown, but do not dare show yourself in the hall until I send for you. Whatever you have marred, I will do my best to amend it. God help us both if I may not make matters smooth."

Edwina threw on her own clothes and rushed into the great hall. Here the sight that met her eyes filled her with relief but also confused her. Lord Radnor, Pembroke, and the Duke of Gaunt were laughing pleasantly enough together over ceremonial goblets of wine. What was plainly the document of marriage settlement lay on the table bearing all three signatures. The clerics who had written out the settlements and witnessed them were making copies to be deposited in the church in case of future argument. Nothing could have exceeded the surface good will of the scene. If Leah guessed something, she had not spoken and now would not. It was more likely, considering Pembroke's care for secrecy, that the child was merely unwilling. That would be excellent as long as her distaste did not communicate itself to Lord Radnor—no, even that did not matter for the betrothal was complete and he could not now withdraw.

What was going forward at the moment Edwina arrived was a discussion of who must be asked to the wedding. Actually this was a serious problem, because Gaunt and his son stood midway between the sides in the civil war. Their sympathies were with Henry of Anjou; their fealty had been given to Stephen. Unlike many others, they were faithful to their sworn word and, although some hated them on both sides, by most their behavior was grudgingly accepted and even respected.

Matilda, the empress, was no problem; she was just about to return to France and would not be likely to delay her departure. Henry likewise was no problem because he had not yet arrived and might not come after all. The most serious question was what to do about King Stephen and Robert, Duke of Gloucester. Both were far too important to ignore, and to have both come to the wedding would be a catastrophe. Finally Gaunt said that he would write personally to Queen Maud and tell her that she must dissuade Stephen from coming because of the danger to him which would arise from being so deep in enemy territory. To give the king credit, no such argument would have weight with him both because he was a brave man and because he would love to annoy Gloucester. Lord Radnor engaged to contact Philip of Gloucester, Robert's second son and his own close friend, and ask him to keep his father away on the chance that Queen Maud could not control her husband. Most of the other great magnates who would be invited either were neutrals or had changed sides in the conflict so often that they could mix with each other in relative safety. There was some doubt whether men like the Earl of Chester would be able to remember which side they were on at the moment.

The duke's attention, once the major question was settled, wandered, and he engaged Edwina in conversation. "I am well pleased in this matter." He smiled grimly. "It is

39

good for a young man to have a wife to his liking. I told him two years since to throw off the slut he was playing with and make a marriage, but then he was so hot after her that he would not listen. It is no light thing to ride and fight all day and wander about half the night. Things will be better thus." Gaunt laughed coarsely. "Your daughter had well caught his fancy—so well that he could not lie quiet last night. He thought I slept, but I heard him walking. He will return in great haste. I hope he may keep his mind enough upon the business in hand that we do not lose the northern provinces. I have half a mind to go with him. I had forgot how it was." A bitter expression crossed the old man's face. "But it was so with myself for his mother. I was so fine-drawn by the time we came to bed that I had a fever and lost two stone."

He paused a moment while his mouth grew harder yet, and Edwina felt sick as she thought of what Leah would have to bear. Gaunt had continued speaking, however, and she wrenched her thoughts from her own bitter memories to what he was saying.

"He murdered her—killed her in the bearing, her and the twin who was born with him. I can never forget that, for the other boy was whole and the woman was dear to me. If there had been another to take the lands and the name, I would have strangled him then with my own hands, but I had no other son and as time passed—. God Himself has punished him sufficiently; he fears damnation without hope of redemption, and he thinks he bears the mark of Satan on that lame leg." He snorted contemptuously. "With such things may a man torture himself if he chooses to meddle with his own soul. I will say for him though that he bears the pain that keeps the memory green bravely, and he is not free of it day or night. That I taught him; I have that satisfaction. And in other ways too he is a good son, but I cannot forget the bitterness he brought with him. I have helped him remember also; I named him Cain for the fratricide he is."

"Your Grace." Edwina was shocked at the words although there was a puzzling note in the voice that she did not take time to try to understand. Enmity between father and son was common enough in these terrible times, but not for this reason. "I speak as a woman who has borne, and I say that it is no fault of the child if the mother—ah, well," she said as the duke turned away angrily, "you

40

know your own affairs best. My concern is with my daughter only. Will he be kind to her?"

"When he is so hot for her that he cannot sleep? Oh yes, he will be kind—at least while the heat lasts." Edwina grew pale, but Gaunt did not notice, absorbed by his own thoughts. "No," he said with a frown, "I do him an injustice. He holds hard by his word and is in no way changeable in his affections. Doubtless as he begins he will continue. If your daughter is not as a queen in her own keep and as happy as mortal lot can be, the fault will be in her—not him. Look at him, he is besotted."

Edwina could not help but feel that this was true, although it did little to comfort her. Lord Radnor was talking soberly enough with her husband, but something about his manner, his expectant glances at the door, an eagerness in his expression, all betrayed that his interest was centered elsewhere. Edwina motioned to a page idling about and told him to fetch Leah. When the girl entered the room, Cain saw at once that she had been crying in spite of the bright red bliaut she had donned to help conceal her blotched complexion. He limped across to her to hand her through the room.

"You are not still concerned for that silly jest of mine?"

"No."

"Then why are your eyes so heavy? There are tears in them still."

"Oh—oh, it is a woman's foolishness to cry for joy."

Thus far in his life, Radnor had not found that to be true, but then, he had not found a girl like this before either. "I know little enough of the ways of such women as you. If you say this, I will believe you, but I urge you to speak the truth to me. As things are with me now, I will forgive you anything—if you tell me plainly—almost anything. If you lie to me, I warn you, you will be sorry for it."

In her naïveté Leah did not realize that what Lord Radnor said did not apply to the type of lie she had told. She took his words quite literally, as she had learned to take her father's statements. Her hand trembled slightly on his, yet her reply took a liberty she would never have dared taken with her father.

"Later, I will tell you later. Please, not here, not now."

Their low voices had not carried in the noise the servants made setting up the tables for dinner. Only Edwina was watching, and she could make nothing of what she saw. If Leah was unwilling to take Lord Radnor as her husband, the girl was displaying a duplicity Edwina had never believed to be part of her character. Yet it was apparent that her crying had not been caused by any quarrel with Lord Radnor, for there she was speaking with him in the low, intense tones of intimacy. Of course they had been together all day. It was barely possible, in the light of what Gaunt had said, that Leah had yielded willingly or been forced to yield to him and was suffering the revulsion which Edwina was sure came with that. Even this notion did not seem to be correct, because when Lord Radnor was separated from Leah by the seating arrangements of the table, he watched her with a look of avidity that did not, to Edwina's limited knowledge, augur satisfaction.

"Lord Radnor," Pembroke called across Edwina to him, "you go to the summoning of the barons this summertide. What do you think Stephen wants?"

"What does he always want but money and men? What he hopes to achieve when he knows that he has let all power slip from him is more my question. He has probably heard the rumor of Henry's coming and, I can but believe, seeks to gauge the support he will have or seeks by bribes and intimidation to gather more."

"So I think too. But why, when you believe this and you know he cannot compel you, do you go? I do not."

"He goes," growled Gaunt, "because I say so."

"Yes, I suppose he would not if you bid him nay, but why do you say so?"

"Because I have done homage to Stephen. I am his man, damn his eyes, and I will not be forsworn. We are sworn to provide him with men and arms for the holding of our lands and each time we must prove anew to the council that those forces are honestly expended in defense of the realm against the Welsh. It is a waste of time for Cain to go so far, and it puts me to great labor for which I am growing too old in taking his place on the field, but I would not have it said of us that we did not obey our overlord's summons honestly."

"My father speaks the truth, but there is more in it than that alone. God only knows what imprudences the king may be beguiled into committing—or paid to commit. It is most needful to be there to oversee what occurs and, if necessary, to counter against what is intended. I should think the head sitting a little loose on my shoulders if I were not there when the wolves gathered."

"Your head may sit a little loose on your shoulders through being there."

"Mayhap. But I may be able to ward the blow that will overset it completely if I can see it coming."

"Ah, well, you know best the state of these matters. I would not run when Stephen called unless it suited my purpose." Pembroke's eyes held an odd, calculating expression. "But in these times, would it not be better to leave your wife behind?"

"Oh no!" The protest was startled out of Leah who had been listening intently. She covered her lips with her hand immediately and drew back, but not quickly enough to escape the backhand blow her father dealt her.

Almost before the smack had landed, Radnor was on his feet, his hand fumbling for the sword that was unaccustomedly missing from his side.

"How dare you!" His voice was choked with rage. "My wife! How dare you strike my wife!" Radnor would have launched himself bodily at his father-in-law, but Edwina stood before him, clinging to his arms, and Gaunt had interposed his own body in front of Pembroke.

Leah cried out in agony, "Oh, my lord, I pray you—" and the men at the long tables in the hall began to growl and rise.

Pembroke, yellow-pale, forced himself to laugh heartily. "Such a to-do over a slap to a girl." And then as Cain snarled like an animal and threatened to break from Edwina's grasp, "Nay, nay—I beg your pardon, Lord Radnor, but think you, she has been my daughter longer than she has been betrothed to you, and it is not my custom to be said nay in my own household."

Slowly the alarming red of Lord Radnor's scars faded to their normal white. "No doubt that is true, and I beg pardon in my turn for offering you violence in your own home. But her behavior is my problem now. While I am here, I pray you, let me attend to it." They all resumed their seats; Leah could eat no more, however, and although Cain went on with his meal he had little enough appetite and his lips were set in grim lines.

Pembroke shook his head, wondering what had caused Lord Radnor's excitement. He could only decide that his son-in-law had a tremendous sense of possession. What he failed to see, never having experienced anything similar himself, was the passionate attachment that Radnor was developing for his daughter. "I have heard also," he con-

43

tinued as if no interruption had taken place, "that Stephen gives a great tourney. Are you entered in the lists, Radnor?"

The Duke of Gaunt's head lifted sharply and Cain stared fixedly at Pembroke. "You above all should not ask," he replied. "You, *I* hear, suggested my name as king's champion for that tourney."

Pembroke shrugged. "He put it upon me because he desires to make bad blood between us. You may believe I suggested no such task for my son-in-law. You should have had sufficient sense to refuse to go to London at all. What if Stephen should hope to take this simple way to be rid of you?"

Leah gave a small gasp which Pembroke ignored, but Cain's eyes flew to her. "Much hope he has of that," he replied with assurance. "I have spent fifteen years under arms. Am I likely to be overset by a dulled jousting lance? There will be little enough to fear on Stephen's score. I take a full complement of well-tried fighting men with me, and I am no babe in arms. Also, my father remains behind as a free agent. While he holds Painscastle and our lands, it would be madness for the king to attack me."

"Openly! Which is why I beg you to beware the tourney."

"Nonsense. If I have not been killed in war, no man will kill me in a game of of war."

Gaunt lowered his head over his food and did not lift it again, but his eyes were at once wary and blind-looking.

Cain continued speaking. "I am truly concerned about matters other than Stephen's like or dislike. This business of Henry's coming, if it be true, is like to throw all into disorder again. The new Earl of Hereford is solidly behind him and is a hotheaded youth. Gloucester is always willing to spite Stephen, and might contrive, although I know him to be drained dry by these years of war, to send the boy some help. If Chester should again change sides, the whole bloody war will be in full force and with as little hope of success this time as last."

"True enough, but I cannot see what good can come of meddling. Sit firm on your own lands. As you yourself said, you have enough to do there."

"Ay, if I could, mayhap I would, but with each change of fortune in England, the Welsh seek to be free of us. If I could but see some hope of success for Henry, I might close my eyes and let happen what will, but Stephen is still

44

too strong. Many feel still as you said you felt last night—that Stephen's yoke is lighter than Henry's may be. If Henry comes, the land will be bled white again; crops will rot in the fields because there will be none to harvest them and famine will stalk us all. And all for nothing!"

"But you cannot prevent him from coming."

"Alas, I cannot, but mayhap I can convince him to go home again—I and others—until the time is more ripe. If Stephen can be made to renew his promise to make Henry his heir and speak the boy fair, I think it can be done. His disposition, as I remember it, did not seem unyielding like his mother's. He seemed a reasonable lad."

"But in this melee of policy, is it well to bring an untried girl?"

Radnor's face darkened alarmingly, but his voice did not change. "I hope she may listen and hold her tongue. To be silent at her time of life is meet and fitting, and by listening with closed mouth one may hear much. It would be well for me to know what is said in the women's quarters."

"Radnor," Pembroke said scornfully, "a girl of fifteen?"

"I think, Pembroke, it would be better not to discuss this matter further. I count on your training to enforce silence on her and your assurance that she is not simple to enable her to repeat what she hears."

"Who can trust a woman among women?"

Radnor's eyes kindled, showing red lights in the brown, but Gaunt veiled his and began to laugh. He swallowed a huge chunk of venison from the blade of his knife and raised his harsh voice into the tense silence. "You will never convince him, Gilbert. Can you not see that he cares nothing for her head if her body is with him. Look you, he is so hot after her that he shows blue beneath the eyes already. How he will last out these two moons, I cannot tell." A slow dark flush dyed Cain's face, causing his scars to stand out whiter still. Gaunt laughed again. "Well, Gilbert, look. Have I not touched him on the raw?"

The victim of the gibe stood up, rocking the table, said that he had eaten his fill, and that Leah should accompany him for he had something to say to her. This caused a new burst of merriment from the older men. Cain turned his head from one to the other like a dog-baited bear and then left the hall precipitately. Leah rose immediately. For the first time in her life she looked neither at her mother nor her father for permission but followed her new master out on to the battlements.

In the hall, Pembroke had continued the argument with Gaunt. He pointed out a variety of disagreeable results that could come about from taking a young girl to Stephen's loose-lived court. Gaunt only laughed.

"You Norman-Saxons do not undertand the hot blood of the Welsh that runs in our veins. Cain has double portion—both mother and grandmother came from the mad tribes of the mountains—princesses in their own land and heavily dowered when their menfolk—er—died." There was meaning in Gaunt's eyes, and he paused infinitesimally before continuing. "Besides, it would serve him right enough if she wrung his withers by casting her eyes about."

"So his blood runs hot," Pembroke expostulated. "Are there not women enough in the fields and the town to cool it on? A man's heir should be his own. Thus it is that women are kept in their own castles."

"Well, he was never one for either serfs or greensleeves. Not but what he is a man, after all, and driven to it often enough." Gaunt shook his head. "He will keep her too busy to look elsewhere, if I know him, but mainly, I think, it is the nonsense that comes from the south that he is forever reading. The true lord and his true lady—love—faugh! Women bring nothing but grief. They either die or are dishonest. If a man must love, there is God or the Virgin."

"But that is stuff for women to mawdle their brains with."

"Ay, ay, but there are men enough caught by it. Just because you and I are sensible men, Gilbert, do not think that others are also. You know the tourney prizes are all women's gauds now. It is the latest fashion. Once a man could win a prize that was worth risking his head for, good arms or good horses. They give the jewels to the women too. There would be some sense in it if the men kept them. Of course, there is still the horse and armor ransom to be gained. Cain and I have both made good golden coins enough by that road, and he will surely reap a rich harvest at the royal tourney. Times are changed, sadly changed. I tell you that if your girl gives my son a man-child, I will be glad enough to finish here. Of course, if she does not breed, the lands will not go through her."

Pembroke grunted and drank. Whom did Gaunt think he could fool? There was no one else, for Gaunt had been an only son and Cain was an only son. When Radnor was dead everything would go to his girl whether or not she bred. Would he have planned this marriage so carefully if there had been a chance that the lands of Gaunt could go elsewhere than to Leah?

CHAPTER 4

MORNINGS IN APRIL were still rather cold and damp. It was also dark when Lord Radnor swung his legs out of bed, pushed back his hair with his fingers, and began to put on his hose and shoes. Edwina was waiting for him in the hall and provided viands so that he could break his fast. She helped him into his hauberk and set his helm beside him on the table. Both were cleaned until they shone. His fur-lined cloak, discarded on the day he arrived and forgotten, was also cleaned and laid ready for him.

"It will be cold," Edwina said softly, "until the sun rises."

Cain, longing to ask for Leah and wondering where she was, nodded his thanks and continued to consume food. He would not eat, at least not food like this, for a long while. He was disappointed that the girl had not risen to take leave of him but was grateful at the same time. He was finding it unexpectedly hard to leave this place and did not doubt that seeing Leah again would make it harder still. Draining the wine in his goblet, he rose to go.

"I thank you for your kind care of me. Tell my father, please, that I will write as soon as I know what to say and bid your daughter—nay, only give her my farewell. There is no need or you to come with me. I will find the court-yard easily."

"God speed you, my lord, both your going and your coming again."

Lord Radnor went out into the passage, looked briefly up in the direction of the women's quarters, and turned resolutely away.

"My lord."

47

He started and half drew the sword he was carrying, then replaced it in the scabbard with a sheepish expression. "What are you doing here in the dark?"

"I thought my mother might say it was not fitting for me to come down, but I could not bear—I could not let you go—"

"I must go. Nonetheless, I am glad to see you. I forgot something very important the other day. Here is your betrothal gift." He held out a small package wrapped in soft cloth. While Leah unwrapped it, he continued, "I was going to give it to your father to give you, but I thought you might like to have it from me. I would have kept it until my return, but since I see you now—I will bring you something prettier when I come back, if you will think of me kindly when I am absent."

The girl gasped at the magnificent ruby which glowed even in the dim light of the passage. "What is it?"

"Your betrothal ring. If the size is wrong, the castle goldsmith will mend it for you."

"Am I to wear it?"

Lord Radnor found his amusement at her question strangely painful. "Of course, what else would you do with it? On the setting are carved the arms of Gaunt." He tried for a lighter tone. "It puts my mark on you, makes you mine. You must never take it off."

"Am I truly yours, my lord?"

"Yes, truly."

"And does—does that make you—mine?"

"Yes."

"Truly?"

"As true as my life or my honor."

"You—." Her voice failed and she tried again. "You do not love any other lady?"

"No." His face was hard with memory.

"Do not be angry." Leah put our placating hands. "I came to say farewell, but also to give you this to remember me by." A slender ribbon embroidered with pearls and gold thread worked in a design of fantastic beasts was pressed into his hand. It was obviously meant for a woman's hair. "It is mine. Indeed, it is the only thing I own besides your ring. My mother gave me the pearls and I worked the design."

Cain stared at it. "I cannot take your only ornament," he said finally, although he wanted very much to have it.

"Have I been too bold?" she whispered. "I know that in

48

the tales I read a knight must sue to his lady for a favor, but—"

"You can read?" he exclaimed with a tremendous sense of relief. Two months was a long time for a child to remember someone without a spur to memory. Now at least all contact between them need not be broken. Leah did not reply because she was frightened. Cain took her silence for assent, fortunately. "If I write to you, then, you will be able to read my letters?"

"Yes, my lord, oh yes." So he did not mind that either. Surely this was a man far different from her father. How hard it was to let him go!

As if he read her mind, Cain said, "I must go. My men wait."

Leah nodded, and he limped down the passage and disappeared in the stairwell. She ran after him, her voice catching him just as he reached the courtyard.

"Lord Radnor, wait one moment." He stopped unwillingly, his lips white and his eyes shadowed. If he did not soon tear himself away, he felt as if he would not be able to go at all. Leah was fumbling at her neck. "I pray you, bend to me." He obeyed mutely so taken up with maintaining his composure that he hardly noticed as she fastened her crucifix around his neck. "Let me buckle on your sword. There." Leah smiled into the rigid face. "Now you have my favor and I have buckled your sword—you are truly my knight. God speed you. God keep you safe. God bring you back to me."

He had been watching her lips, soft and full, quivering a little, and was drawn to do what he had promised himself he would not. He kissed her, and even as he was thinking, "Let Wales be damned!" he tore himself away to limp to his horse. Not until he was safe in the saddle did he dare turn to look at her and wave goodbye. He gestured the troop ahead and Leah watched them ride, hooves clattering, over the drawbridge. She ran then to the battlement and watched as the long double column of men wound away into the distance. Her mother found her there later, leaning against the stonework, dry-eyed in spite of her fears. Leah had learned her first real lesson as a wife—that tears in parting avail nothing.

Lord Radnor did not look back after his farewell wave. He made his way automatically to the head of his men and rode along the track that led away from Pembroke's keep with a mind turned completely inward. It was hard for him to understand how he could have fallen so entirely under the spell of a chit of a girl whom he had not cared at all about forty-eight hours earlier. She had certainly used no arts that he recognized to charm him. She wore no magnificent jewelry, and even her best clothes were obviously made over from her larger mother's and were not particularly becoming. There were dozens of women at court who were more beautiful—a few of them he had had. Why also was this burden of fear on him? He knew death too well to fear for himself; that was simply not to be and to face God thereafter, and whatever his doubts he could cling to the knowledge of the infinite mercy of Christ. Life was the fearsome thirng. What would become of Leah if he should die? It was the first time he had faced this personal type of responsibility, for his father could care for himself and his care for his dependents was unmixed with emotion. Cain's eyes, fixed between the ears of his horse, saw nothing, but Odo, one of the newest of his recruits, gazed around with the beginnings of a great awareness in his glance.

Odo was with the troop solely because he was rather more intelligent and enterprising than most of the villein stock. Giles, Lord Radnor's master-of-arms, had heard Odo loudly protesting at the village alehouse that all masters were alike bad and that any man could fight for himself given the proper weapons. Giles, not wishing to hurt the promising young man, had proposed a bout with the quarterstaff and made his point—that all men were not created equal—by breaking Odo's head. Giles had detected, however, a real spirit and willingness to fight, and had called this to his master's attention. Odo had forthwith been removed from the farm upon which he had been born, and upon which he had expected to end his life, to the garrison of Painscastle. There he had received some basic instruction in the use of arms and was now on his way to try out the effectiveness of that instruction.

Thus far Odo had enjoyed his new position without thinking too much about it. His self-made principles had forbidden him to be grateful to Lord Radnor, and he had continued to assert that all masters were the same and all bad. Now as he looked about him, his opinions were shaken for the first time. He could still believe that all masters were bad, but obviously there were varying degrees of badness. Here, although the countryside was fruitful, the cringing peasants they passed wore the gray and hollow look of continued hunger. No man came out to greet the passing riders as was common in his own home; instead the few people out in the open ran for shelter in the miserable huts, which were surely more miserable than those to which Odo was accustomed, or dropped to the ground where they pressed themselves against the earth in the hope of being overlooked. It was clear that to these people the lord of the land meant oppression and horror.

The visits of the Duke of Gaunt or his son were not usually eagerly awaited events at home, but this was because they meant that tax-collecting time had come again. Nonetheless, no one particularly feared their coming. Those who had handsome wives and daughters hid them if they wished to avoid their lords' attention; sometimes they did not hide them, even sending them with poultry or produce to the castle, since it was rumored that even a left-handed son would be welcome to Gaunt and because both father and son were reasonably openhanded to the women they took to their beds. There were times too that Odo remembered when the coming of the duke or Lord Radnor had been anxiously looked for. When there were knightly robbers in the neighborhood, when there were rumors of the mountain Welsh coming, when there was murder or a legal dispute to be settled, then lookouts were posted and the sight of the gold and black Gaunt blazon coming from the hills or through the fields brought sighs of relief and shouts of pleasure.

Odo had been hearing things in his two-day stay at Eardisley which, when he could separate his mind from his saddlesoreness, were a revelation to him. Disputes brought before Pembroke were settled by which disputant brought the larger bribe. This was unheard of at home. Both lords were strictly just, Odo knew; they were very different in their ways, Gaunt being more severe but more consistent and Lord Radnor being often more lenient but always unpredictable. Justice, however, was always done, and Odo himself remembered a time when his village had united to complain of a bailiff who was gouging them by collecting more than was due the manor. Lord Radnor, trying that case, had listened to the complaints and the defense with a perfectly indifferent expression and had dismissed the complaint. He had descended unexpectedly upon the bailiff's home, however, a week later and had found there the evidence that had been wanting to prove that the complaints were justified. The bailiff had been publicly whipped, then drawn and quartered alive; his remains had hung in the village square until the flesh rotted from the bones as a warning that it was not healthy to tamper with the workings of the Gaunt estates.

The troop came to a division of the road and Cain turned left, the men following. Old Giles, who had been bringing up the rear, passed Odo at the gallop. He pulled up beside his master and hailed him respectfully. Radnor started.

"Do we return to Painscastle, my lord?"

"No," Radnor replied testily. "Why do you trouble me with stupidities? I told you that we go direct to Fitz Herbert's keep."

"As you say, my lord, so you told me. But nonetheless we are on the road to Painscastle."

Giles' face was totally wooden, but there was a gleam in the old eyes that brought a dark flush to Lord Radnor's complexion. He gesticulated angrily, and Giles shouted the orders that turned the men on their tracks. At the crossroads they now turned right, and, after traveling some miles further, turned more sharply right and cut across the fields.

Edwina had come upon Leah on the battlements staring blindly in the direction that Lord Radnor had gone. "Come down to the women's chambers, Leah. You waste time and gain nothing here. I thought you were still abed."

"I rose to bid my lord farewell. And I watched him go forth without weeping. And I do not weep now, mother, but—"

The girl was mad. She knew the man but two days and she looked after him as if she had lost a precious thing. "What is between you and Lord Radnor?"

Leah looked surprised, having finally brought her eyes from the distance to her mother's face. "Why, we are betrothed," she said idiotically. "Nay, mother, do not be angry. I do not know what you mean."

"Then you are either stupider than I think, or lying. Do you believe I cannot read you? It was I who taught you to mask your thoughts, but you cannot hide them from me. Why should you hang, blushing, over the man's clothes. For what were you weeping like a madwoman yesterday?"

Lifting her hand to shield her expression, Leah temporized. "There is nothing between us not proper to a betrothed pair."

"Where did you get that ring?"

"He gave it to me. It is my betrothal gift."

"Good God! If that is not a man—to give such a ring to a chit of a girl to lose. Take it off at once and I will put it in the strongbox."

"No!" Leah pulled back her hand and clenched her fist.

Edwina was shocked. Leah was always so docile. "Leah! Such vanity! How sinful to be disobedient and say me nay."

"It is not vanity and I am obedient. Indeed, mother, he told me I must wear it and never take it off." A frightened but resolute expression came into the girl's face. "I am not vain and disobedient, mother, but I will not take off the ring unless he bids me remove it."

"He! He!" Edwina cried furiously, agonized by a sharp pang of fear. "Is there but one man in the world that you say 'he' and everyone must know of whom you speak?" Leah remained silent, puzzled and a little hurt by her mother's vehemence, but she made no move to take off the ring and a mulish expression marred the normally sweet curve of her lips. "Well," Edwina gasped, "if you will not answer me, you may set about your work with no more ado. Did you think that just because you were betrothed to a great man you would have no more duties."

"No, mother. I am ready to do anything you bid me."

"Wait. Where is your crucifix?"

"I gave it to him—I mean to Lord Radnor. He wore none. His need was greater than mine."

Where was her docile, confiding daughter, Edwina wondered. In two days she was left with a heavy-eyed stranger. "Are you sure, Leah? The hurt of the body is not so dangerous as that of the soul."

It was as if her mother could read her mind. Leah blushed until tears filled her eyes. "He has done nothing, said nothing, that was not honorable," she whispered.

"But I desire to know what you have done, not what Lord Radnor has done or said."

"I—I have done nothing." There was a slight emphasis on the word done, however, and the sentence had an unfinished sound.

Plainly, scolding would get her nowhere in this instance. Edwina led Leah to her own room and sat on the bed, pulling her daughter with her. "Leah, I love you. You are my child. I can still remember the pain of the bearing and the pleasure of the suckling. Could I desire your hurt? I have had sorrow enough to have gained some wisdom. I only desire to smooth your path, to make you ready for the sorrow to come so that you may endure it more easily."

The dark blush that had dyed Leah's skin receded as she listened, leaving her face very pale. "You are not used to speak to me this way, mother."

"But now I fear to lose you. What matter to tear the heart a little sooner, when it will soon be torn from my breast altogether."

Leah could not understand, but her mother's softness drew her to speak of what, presently, troubled her most deeply. "How quickly," she said in a vague, abstracted voice, "how quickly sin steals upon us."

Edwina's lips twisted but Leah was not watching her and she did not see the grimace of pain. "There is one way, my child, in which God and mothers are alike. No matter what their sins, both continue to love their children."

"I hope it is so, most truly I hope so, for I have committed the sin of lust."

"What?" Edwina shrieked, her face becoming as pale as Leah's. "When? With whom? When? I have watched you so close!"

"When he kissed me." Leah began to sob, frightened by her mother's violence. "Before I could think, before I could guard myself. So suddenly it was upon me, I could not hide it."

Edwina gripped Leah's arm and raised her face. "No wonder you have been so strange. You must tell me all now. First, who was the man? One of your father's men? A serf from the fields? Who?"

"It was my lord, Lord Radnor himself."

"Lord Radnor! Nay, then, the matter is not so very bad. Stop trembling child. It is not well, but with the contract made—. He may think ill of you for so yielding yourself, but he should not have—." Then a puzzled look crossed her face. "But when could this have happened?"

"When I took him upstairs that he might bathe."

"That first day? He took you that first day and you said nothing until now? Yet he made contract the next day— well, it was ill done, but no doubt he is a man of honor. So be it he does not think to void the contract by saying that you are no maid when you are bedded after the marriage—"

"But I am a maid, mother." Leah blushed painfully

54

again when she realized what her mother thought. "Oh, he did not—he—mother, I would not lie to you. I told you he did nothing dishonorable. He only kissed me. It was I who—who lusted after him. Oh, mother," Leah's voice dropped and became tremulous, "I do so desire him. I tremble still. I feel his lips still upon my mouth. I have sinned in my desire and I am punished, but I cannot confess for there is no repentance for the sin in me."

Edwina watched Leah during her simple confession, a mixed look of tenderness and horror on her face. So soft-hearted a child. If she gave the man her love, how bitterly she would be hurt. No, soon enough the poor child's lust would be changed to disgust when she was given what she thought she wanted.

"It is a small sin to desire your own husband. My child, sweet child, what can I do for you? Men are not like women. They desire something and then, when they have it, often and often, they desire it no longer. Leah, it is well to love nothing but God overmuch. All human love brings pain. Parents die, children die or go away, husbands take other women to their beds—." She sat silent, absently stroking Leah's cheek. "Child, listen. It is not well to fling yourself upon a man. Often a man thinks that if a woman's blood is warm for him, it is so for all men. If it is true for you, you must guard yourself very carefully. Once your honor is lost, no man will have you—if your husband does not kill you outright. Do not believe men's blandishments; avoid their pleas. A woman who gives herself, even to her husband, without modesty, with too much willingness, is suspect. Tend him, clothe him, feed him. In these ways you may show your love with honor. But do not hang upon him, for you are more like to bring disgust by such behavior than love."

Knowing her mother spoke the truth, for she could remember Cain's reaction when she responded to his kiss, Leah could only sigh. "I will try," she whispered unhappily.

Lord Radnor's first messenger arrived two weeks later, mud-splattered and fatigued. He gave to Leah a small roll of parchment covered with writing. Radnor's hand was like himself, firm, plain, and strong. His message was simple. He was well; his business moved on apace; he still hoped to be able to keep his promised day of return. The letter contained no word of affection, but some lines at the end had been scraped out. Over them was written a brief thanks for her crucifix. Leah read the terse lines twice, then folded the slip and hid it in the bottom of her chest for further perusal later. Although her heart leapt at the thought that he had remembered her, something equally exciting was happening that day. The spring fair was in the town of Eardisley, and Leah was going with her mother to buy stuff for gowns for herself and at least one for Lord Radnor.

Completely happy, Leah ran down into the court where Edwina waited and was flung up into her saddle by a young groom. They had not far to ride before the tents and awnings of the fair appeared. Leah caught her breath. Even at this distance she thought she could smell the odor of spices that came from lands beyond those where the crusaders fought. She would have to watch closely what her mother did; it might well be that next year at this time she would be buying salt and spices for her own huge family of servants and retainers.

Edwina hid a smile tinged with bitterness, for Leah's thoughts could be read easily in her transparent face. Possibly she would be mistress in her own castle. More likely by this time next year, even if Radnor was still alive, he would have tired of her and some other woman would have the thrill of shopping at the fair. Nonetheless Edwina explained carefully to her daughter. Salt was the first, great need of every keep, and salt was purchased in huge quantities. Edwina showed Leah how the quality of the salt might be tested. First, it must be white; grayish or brownish salt was contaminated with the earth of the pits in which it was made and the sand would grit in the teeth. Only a hundred pounds or so of this white salt would be purchased, however, for the salting of the food for the high table and the salting of venison for use at the high table. The poorer quality of salt was purchased, at a much lower price and in much greater quantity, for the servants' food and for giving to the serfs. Also, Edwina pointed out, some salt should be taken from each sack, not always from the top of the sack either, and put into a little water. Of the white salt, not a speck should remain and the water should be as clear as it was before the salt was added. Of the brown, the dark matter should sink instantly to the bottom, leaving the water clear in a moment or two. Clouded water meant that the merchant had mixed chalk or some other matter with the salt to make it whiter or to make extra weight.

Pepper was the next need, and Edwina moved to other booths after making arrangements to have the chosen salt delivered. She reminded the merchant before she left that the salt would be tested again at the castle and if the quality was found to be changed, woe betide him. Pepper too might be tested for quality. The little peppercorns should not break between the fingers; when they were broken by a hammer blow, they should crumble to tiny pieces; they should not fold together or stick or form lumps. The black peppercorns should burn the tongue greatly when applied; the gray should be sharply pungent but burn a little less. Leah should be sure, Edwina said, glancing up at her daughter's absorbed face, to make the merchant spread out his wares on a light cloth so that she could see the little black bugs that sometimes infested the pepper. Leah was never to buy what was not perfect for food. If she was sorry for the merchant, she could throw a few coins, but she must not buy bad spices.

Finally they came to the tents of the cloth sellers. The other matters had interested Leah as something for which she would be responsible, but the booths of the cloth sellers she approached with bated breath. All her life she had been dressed in homespuns for every day and Edwina's made-over dresses for special occasions. Now she was to choose all new cloth for gowns for herself, cloth of the very best materials, and no limit she had been set on the amount or the price. She turned from side to side, blushing with pleasure as more and more rolls of material were laid out before her.

"Leah," Edwina said finally, "you jump from one thing to another and accomplish nothing. Come, let us do this right. Look first at the fine linen for your undergarments. When you have chosen that, we may look at what will be needed for your tunics and then the bliauts."

Leah sighed and turned away from a roll of lavender silk so thin that it would float. She chose finally a bolt of linen fine enough to see through and a bolt of wool the same, both in white. Two more bolts of heavier wool and linen for winter undergarments were also selected. Cloth for tunics, the long-sleeved, high-necked garment worn under the bliaut in such a way that it showed at the neck, sleeves, and sides, was chosen in pieces just large enough to make one tunic each of different colors. Edwina shook her head over this piece of extravagance for she wondered what Leah would do when they started to wear. You could not patch different colored garments from each other. It was true that Lord Radnor promised generously, but Leah should know that men were not so generous after another woman had taken their fancy. Well, Leah had to learn some things the hard way, and after offering her advice, she allowed the girl to make her own choice.

For the bliauts, the sleeveless, wide-skirted, low-necked dress that laced up the side to fit the figure, Leah chose a deep mossy green wool, heavy and warm but soft as a kitten's fur, and similar pieces of cloth in a rich, warm brown, dark mustard, and tawny orange. She looked longingly at a deep red and deep blue, but her mother held them up against her and said that those colors made her look faded. For summer wear, lighter-colored linens and wools were selected.

While Leah was engaged in this business, her mother had been in conference with the merchant. "Come here, child," she called when Leah, selection completed, stood sighing with repletion. "Do you like this cloth?"

Leah gaped. Never in her whole life had she seen anything so gorgeous. It was a pale silvery green brocaded silk, embroidered throughout with silver thread. "Oh!" Leah gasped, perfectly speechless, "oh!"

"For your wedding gown, Leah, and you may use it for great occasions at court also."

Leah touched the cloth with reverent fingers. Such things had only been known in England for a few years. The men who had gone on the First Crusade, a hundred years before, had brought some back and now such cloth together with silks of lesser value and the precious and rare velvet cloth came regularly into the lands to the south—lands whose romantic names were the only things about them that Leah knew—Italy, Sicily, and Spain. From there the cloth traveled slowly north through Europe until, finally, it reached England. Ordinarily a piece of such value would not be displayed at a country fair; it was meant for the great markets of London, but Edwina had asked for something very special and the merchant felt it worthwhile to take the chance of displaying his better wares.

"Then we will take it at the price of twelve marks." Edwina spoke in a firm voice, for she had bargained for a long time before she had a price she considered reasonable. The merchant had whined and expostulated at great length, actually he was well pleased. In London he would have had to sell to another cloth seller who would have paid far less than Edwina.

"Let us go now, Leah. We were to meet your father at noon and it is nearly that time now."

"Mother, I have not chosen the cloth of Lord Radnor's gown."

"Well, be quick." Edwina had grown colder and colder as the weeks passed to any mention of her future son-in-law, for his name brought a glow to Leah's whole countenance that not even discreetly lowered eyes could hide.

"There is a nice piece of dark blue wool of good quality. Take that. It will make up well and wear well." It was hard to hide the impatience in her voice, and Edwina felt a faint pang of conscience as Leah looked at her, puzzled and hurt.

"No," Leah said slowly, unused to acting against her mother's advice but determined to have what was best for her lord. "I do not think that color would become him." She wandered around the booth with the merchant in anxious attendance. "Ah," she cried finally, "there, that is what I want."

The merchant drew in his breath softly and lifted down a bolt of the heaviest and finest velvet made. If he sold this too, he could leave his apprentice to dispose of the rest of the lot and return to Italy for more stock. Never had Eardisley been so profitable—this was going to be a great wedding. The cloth spread on the trestle used for a counter glowed with the same color and life as Leah's great ruby. She lifted a fold and put it against her cheek.

"Leah," Edwina said sharply, "do you know the cost of such a piece of cloth for a man of Lord Radnor's size?"

"No," Leah replied with a little tremble in her voice, "I had not thought, but it must be very costly." She turned away to look at some fine wools.

"Madam," the merchant interposed, "I have only this one piece of value left. I will make a special price on it. You will benefit in the amount it would cost me to travel to London, for that much will I save. Look again. How perfect the weave. How light as a feather, not to be oppressive in summer. How warm for winter, still without weight. At what I will charge, it will be like paying nothing, for the cloth is so good it will last many, many years."

"How much?" Leah breathed.

"A pittance for such a piece of cloth—nothing for the value received."

"How much?"

"Ten marks."

Tears rose to Leah's eyes. She had never seen that much money, let alone spent it in opposition to her mother's will. "No. It is far, far too much."

"Well, what will madam pay?"

Leah looked at her mother. She knew that Edwina had many coins, gold and silver, in her saddlebags and that she had paid for the salt and spices from this hoard. What was left Leah did not know, nor if she had known would that knowledge have been of much value, since she did not really understand money. But Edwina would offer no help, and Leah turned again to look at the woolens. She touched a wine-red serge, and suddenly the mulish look that Edwina had seen several times in the past few weeks took hold of her face.

"What was the cost of the brocade?"

"Twelve marks, madam."

"Very well," Leah said, swallowing her disappointment. "Then I will have the red velvet and a plain silk of the same green color."

"Leah!"

"Madam!"

"I will have that," Leah said, setting her jaw, "or nothing at all."

"Ten marks is too much," Edwina said slowly. What the devil had taken hold of her daughter, she wondered. Could the stories about Lord Radnor be true? Could he have bewitched the girl? Most women would sell their eyes, not to mention their souls and their honor, for a dress like that. "I will give you half."

"No, madam, I beg you. You will beggar me. I have a wife and children—"

"My daughter says she will have nothing if she may not have the velvet, and I will not pay that price."

"Nine marks then."

"Five and a half."

"Eight and a half. Madam, I paid more for the cloth than that. I can go no lower."

"I will pay seven and not a mil more." Edwina flushed with rage. She was not angry with the merchant, of course, but with Leah. Yet she could not criticize her daughter for an act of self-sacrifice. Also it was growing late and Gilbert would be in a foul temper if they delayed him. It was she who would suffer too; Gilbert had grown very cautious about chastising Leah since his scene with Lord Radnor.

"Madam, I beg you—"

"Seven, I said. Quick, decide. My husband is waiting for us."

The merchant was beaten and nodded his acquiescence. He had not done as well on the velvet as on the brocade, but he had a fair profit and was well satisfied.

Leah caught the bolt of cloth to her with a cry of joy, but Edwina, completely out of patience, pulled her away roughly. "If we are late, your father will be furious." Leah came at once, a little pale at the thought of Pembroke's wrath. Edwina was a little pale too as she tried to think of explanations for the huge sums spent. Gilbert had told her clearly that he did not care what the cost was, but it seemed unlikely that he should have changed so radically overnight no matter what he said. She spurred her horse forward when he came into sight. Leah hung back at first when she saw her mother and father in earnest conversation, but she moved toward them again when she heard her father laugh.

"What do I care," he was saying. "It is a fine joke, for Radnor himself left the gold to pay for the chit's clothes. So he has paid for his own too." His face darkened momentarily. "He said he would ask for an accounting, so it might as well be spent as given back. Are you finished here?"

"As you will, my lord," Edwina replied submissively. "There are still ribbons and laces and such matters, but—"

"Well, go and finish your spending. I will return to the castle. But see that you are not late and that you are finished today. I will not have you running about at your own will every day only because a fair is in town."

CHAPTER 5

EDWINA had no mind to linger at the fair. The huge task of preparations for the wedding had fallen largely on her, and two months was a very short time to prepare for the reception of about a hundred important guests, each of whom would bring his own retinue. All of these people had to be properly housed, fed, and provided with drink. Pembroke would see to the arrangements of the tourney and the hunts to amuse the male guests, but Edwina had to arrange to entertain the women. Every serf in the area was impressed for extra service at the castle, and every animal which Pembroke could lay his hands on, legally or otherwise, was rounded up to be fattened and slaughtered when the time came. Leah too had been pressed into service, and she was responsible for every task that could possibly be delegated by her mother. It was just as well; had she been idle she would have worried herself sick over Cain's welfare. As it was, she was so busy that she scarcely had time to think. By the end of each day, Leah was so tired that she shook, but she forced herself to remain awake and she sewed, night after night, with tiny, careful stitches at the magnificent robe of red velvet, now fur-trimmed and jewel bedecked—her wedding gift to her lord.

For Lord Radnor, things were not going quite as smoothly as his letter indicated. The vassals were not easy to pacify, and their preparations for war had aroused the nearest Welsh tribes. Cain found it necessary to pursue groups of the rebels through the mountains. It was hard, dangerous going and even harder and more dangerous as they moved further and further into purely Welsh territory. He had not been wounded seriously and he fought as well as ever, but the joy of it was gone; his mind and heart were elsewhere. Radnor had personal problems. He was so tormented by his passions that he had turned aside in the middle of a day's march to ease himself with the first woman he could find. To his horror, he could not take his pleasure of her. At a town still further off his road, he had sought out a prostitute, but this served his purpose no better. Nothing the woman could do would arouse his body, yet every night he tossed and groaned, awake or asleep, tortured by the lewdest visions. He was obsessed and terrified by the idea that he had become impotent, that this, just before his marriage, was his punishment for matricide and fratricide. His father had called it murder, although Cain tried to believe that accidents of birth could not be held against the newborn infant. If Gaunt was right, however, he was damned, and his line was meant to end with him.

Lord Radnor's second messenger arrived at the end of May. Leah came out into the courtyard with her arms and dress white with flour. She grabbed at the scroll held out, regardless of her mother's presence, for she had been seeing her lover with wide dead eyes for two weeks past.

"Stay," she bade the tired rider, and she read. "He says he is well." She turned to the man who stood leaning on his sweating horse. "Was he well when you left him?"

Cedric cleared his throat nervously; he was not accustomed to speaking much to highborn ladies. "If my lord says he is well—then—he is, I suppose."

"You suppose? Has he been wounded? Has there been fighting?"

"Fighting in plenty, my lady, but his lordship hasn't caught it. Only, he looks—. His temper is mortal bad, my lady. No one don't dare say him a word but old Giles."

There was a little pause as Leah made, for her, a momentous decision. Then she drew a trembling breath. "Do you return to Lord Radnor?"

"Yes, my lady, as quick as I can."

"Before you leave, come to me and I will give you a message for him."

Cedric strode off to be refreshed in the servants' quarters and Edwina came up to Leah who was rereading Cain's brief note anxiously. "He writes you his welfare?"

Leah started. "Yes. He offered to do so."

"You did not tell me. Do you reply to him?"

63

"I have not dared, but—but his man says that he does not look well. O God, I knew this would happen. I knew. O God, do not punish my sin by hurting him."

Edwina slapped her daughter's face. "Pray for him if you like, but do not question the ways of the Lord. Whatever Christ sends us is ultimately for our own good."

"Yes, mother. Oh, mother, I did not mean to—but I love him so."

"To love a man of flesh and blood can only bring you bitter sorrow."

"I know. But if the Merciful Lord will leave me my love, I will bear whatever other sorrow he sends with patience, I swear it."

Edwina shook her head furiously. Nothing she said seemed to penetrate her daughter's mind, and she had come to wish that Lord Radnor would hurry his return. Edwina had little enough faith in the ways of men and believed that Radnor himself would speedily cure Leah's doting.

To write, Leah found after she had obtained pens and ink from the chaplain, was not so easy. It was easy enough to pour out her hopes, her fears, and her prayers, but this she did not dare to do. She feared that her boldness in writing at all when she had not been bidden to do so would be offensive. Radnor's own terse lines also militated against freedom in her, and her short epistle, when finished, was a model of decorum. She prayed her lord excuse her boldness. She thanked her lord of his great courtesy for forgiving her weak fears. Only in the last lines did her terror peep through. A woman cares for foolish things, she wrote. Did he eat enough? Did he keep dry and warm? Did he have his wounds dressed? Humbly excusing herself for her presumption, she signed herself all obedience to him and affixed her name, for she had no seal.

The sun, that late June, was so hot that the dank rooms of the keep were a pleasure. Leah, however, was unconscious alike of heat or cold. Tomorrow was her wedding day, and neither message nor Lord Radnor himself had arrived. The Duke of Gaunt had come, laden with baggage, the day before. He had laughed at her anxiety and assured Edwina that he had heard on business matters from his son who was quite well.

"A little fined down, according to his man, but still worth marrying."

Leah could do nothing, and fortunately nothing much remained to be done. She paced the battlements, straining her eyes into the distance without avail until her mother, free for a moment from greeting guests, caught her and furiously confined her to the women's quarters. Even when news that Lord Radnor's cavalcade was in sight came, Edwina did not relent.

"Sit still," she hissed at her daughter. "Where do you go, you wanton. Will you show the whole world what you feel? Tomorrow you marry. You will see Lord Radnor enough after that, no doubt. Until then keep close. It is not fitting. Will you shame your father and myself and Lord Radnor too?"

Submitting, because she could do nothing else, Leah clung to her mother's hand. "See if he is well. His man said—. You will bring me news of him?"

"You need have no fear," Edwina replied coldly. "I will take every care of my son-in-law."

Lord Radnor was just entering the courtyard when Edwina arrived there, and already a press of the younger male guests was waiting for him. As his troop pulled their horses to a halt and the clatter of hooves died down, a clear young voice rose from the waiting crowd of men.

"Lo! The bridegroom cometh!"

Radnor, who was in the painful act of dismounting, swung around with a black scowl on his face, but when his eyes fell upon the slight, fair youth who had spoken, his expression cleared and he held out his hand.

"Hereford, by all that's holy."

The Earl of Hereford pushed his way through the laughing group and held Radnor off with one extended finger. "No," he said positively, "I will not clasp your hand nor give you the kiss of peace. The last time I took your hand, mine was numb for a week, and the last time I gave you the kiss of peace you cracked two of my ribs. Man, you are too big."

The crowd roared with appreciation, for although Hereford was slight and pretty as a maid, he was as redoubtable a fighter as Lord Radnor and as well known. Hereford's blue eyes, so brilliant that they seemed lit by incandescent flames, flickered with merriment as he assured his friend that he would not for anything, including the assurance of admittance to heaven, have missed his wedding. As Radnor slowly unlaced and pushed back his mail hood to reveal hair plastered to his skull, rivulets of perspiration coursing down his cheeks and neck, and a face that looked like a death's head, however, the laughter gave way to an expression of concern.

"Good God, Radnor, what ails you? Are you sick too?"

The bloodshot, red-rimmed brown eyes suddenly fixed upon the blue ones in an agony of apprehension. "Too? What do you mean too? Who else is sick?" Radnor's hand closed on Hereford's arm in a grip that would have been excruciating had not his victim been made of bone and sinew like steel.

Hereford shrugged. "I hear that Philip of Gloucester is sick unto death."

"Philip? Why I saw him six months since hale and hearty. You must have heard amiss. I certainly hope you have. We can ill afford to lose such a man."

Hereford immediately took fire. "We? We can well afford it. Do not tell me, Radnor, that you have been buried so long in Wales that you have not heard that Philip is now the king's man."

Radnor smiled and shook his head. "So am I, Hereford, so am I. In any case, he is my foster brother and I must love him."

"That is different, and well you know it. Philip has betrayed his father as well as—"

"Hereford, Hereford, let us not become embroiled in politics here. Let me greet my godson." This from the Earl of Chester, an older man, slightly balding, with a face that could have been noble except for its weak mouth and chin. "Allow Radnor to come in out of the heat, at least, and disarm." He held out his hand to Cain, who kissed it affectionately. "I am sorry to see you looking so worn, my boy."

"I knew you would not fail me, sir." Radnor smiled. "Do you see if you can keep our little firebrand quenched enough so that he does not burst into flame." He put his arm across Hereford's shoulders, both for support and to quiet the impatient young man, and began to make his way toward the keep, murmuring greetings.

"Mortimer." A handclasp and they parted.

"Shrewsbury." A bow, a little distant.

"Leicester." A deeper bow of respect. "I am honored that you have come so far."

"Father-in-law." Another brief handclasp.

The group now began to break up as the men returned to their talk and amusements. Only Hereford and the Earl of Chester accompanied Cain up the stairs to the main hall of the keep. Edwina, who had effaced herself while Radnor greeted his friends, now fell in discreetly behind them. Radnor listened a little absently to a tirade by Hereford on the latest iniquities of Stephen while his eyes searched the hall. Leah was not there. His arm dropped from Hereford's shoulder as he saw Edwina.

"My lords, may I have a word with my mother-in-law?"

There was, of course, no place to be really private, but Hereford and Chester politely turned their backs and engaged each other in conversation while Radnor went up to Edwina.

"Leah? Is she well? Where is she?"

"Very well. I pray you, my lord, let me unarm you and bathe you. You can speak to your friends while you bathe."

"She does not come to greet me?"

"It is not fitting."

Radnor sat down heavily on a bench against the wall. "Yes. I know, but I would have three words with her. In your presence if you will."

"If it is your command, Lord Radnor, of course Leah will honor it, but I beg you to bathe and change your garments at least before you see her." Edwina's voice was icy although her words were deferential. "May I order your bath?"

Realizing that unless he issued a direct order Edwina would not permit Leah out of the women's quarters, Radnor gave up. He was not sure whether this was Leah's wish or Edwina's, and he might well have demanded his betrothed's presence to settle the question except that he was virtually sure he could not rid himself of Hereford and Chester without offense. They were obviously full of some news which they wished to impart. Cain's mouth set in a hard line.

"Of course I will not ask anything so improper. You can never tell what harm can befall a girl to whom I am only pledged in marriage at my hands in a room full of people."

67

Edwina's countenance remained perfectly immobile. "Your bath?" she repeated.

Radnor passed his hand across his face as if to wipe away his fatigue and stood up again. "Yes, of course, but in the tower room. I like to bathe in private." Edwina curtsied low. "Stay. Send a servant to find my saddlebags. I have something I would like to give your daughter." He moved away. "My lords, I beg your pardon for the delay."

"Radnor, you have been in the hills these months past. Do you know that Henry of Anjou will be arriving any day in England? He is—"

"Hereford, for God's sake, keep your voice down. There are men enough here who would be glad to carry the news to anxious ears." Chester's voice was steady, but his eyes moved uneasily around the hall. "Nonetheless it is true. Come to the window where there is less chance of being overheard."

Radnor sat down in the embrasure with a sigh that seemed to come from his gut. "Oh God," he muttered, "it is too late. It begins anew." He set his lips, but a voice inside him cried that he could bear no more just now. Now, until he was sure, at least, that he was still a man, he wanted to lie down in the dark with Leah and not concern himself with this rising; not concern himself with the ungarnered crops, the starving people, the wretches who screamed for mercy or watched hopelessly as their miserable possessions were completely destroyed by a barony drunk with lawlessness.

"I tell you, Radnor," Hereford was saying, his eyes blazing, "that this is our best chance yet. Matilda has already gone and will not return in the immediate future. That removes the sticking point for many who hate Stephen but hate her more. And Chester has a plan—." He stopped suddenly at Chester's raised hand and quickly shaken head, and Radnor turned his tired eyes to the older man.

"Godfather, godfather. I thought you had decided once and for all to make your peace with Stephen. Only last year—not even a year—you gave each other the kiss of peace—"

"My boy, I have tried damned hard, but a man can swallow only so many insults. I am so watched, so slighted—. Did you know that my nephew Fitz Richard is actually held at court almost as a prisoner, because he offered to stand hostage for me? Did you know that his estates—"

Cain bit his lip. "Have you spoken with my father?"

It was Hereford who replied. "Radnor, you must forgive me, but your father is the damnedest, stubbornest, pig-headedest—every ass I have ever met had a more tractable disposition." Hereford's voice had risen again with excitement, and Radnor could not help smiling.

"Yes, I know. He is my father after all. But I beg you, do not tell the whole castle of my shame. I gather he did not receive your notions kindly."

"Kindly? He did not receive them at all! He would not listen to a word I said, but told me that as you were representing him at council he trusted you could make up your own mind."

"Softly, Hereford, softly. You should not believe that because a man does not answer he does not listen. I—oh, Giles, find that worked gold necklet set with emeralds for me. It is somewhere in that mess of stuff. Now, what was I saying? Oh, yes. I really think that this is not the time or the place—"

"But—"

"Hereford, please! A day or two—yes, that is it. All right, Giles, I am sorry I broke your rest. Look, my lords." He held up a chain of heavy gold links chased into the form of serpents with highly polished emerald eyes.

"Very pretty, very costly. What are you going to do with it?"

"My wedding present to my bride. But you are wrong, Chester, for it cost nothing." He looked up and saw Edwina approaching with the maidservarnts. "We do not seem to have a moment's peace, but some day I will tell you how I came by it. Madam," he continued, rising and turning to Edwina, "I take it my bath is ready. I thank you. You need not trouble yourself further about me; I will go up and serve myself. I know the way. Do me the favor, instead, to take this to Leah. It is her wedding gift from me. I hope she will wear it tomorrow."

"A rich gift for a maid so young."

Cain opened his mouth to say something, remembered the listening ears, and shut it again. Edwina's animosity puzzled him. "It cost nothing except a little of my blood, and that is cheap enough. Bid her wear it."

"She will be wearing silver, my lord, the gold will not be—"

"Madam, enough! Do you see that Leah obeys my command without more ado." Radnor turned away, his face flushed with anger. "Women," he said to Hereford and Chester, "if you say a gentle word, they will have mastery in everything."

Hereford laughed loud and long. "The pains of being an only son. I may have troubles with my brothers, but I marry as I choose—and when. At least there are brothers to follow if I do not choose. You, alas, must father an heir; therefore, lo, the bridegroom cometh."

Radnor flushed hotly. Hereford's sally had pricked him on the raw. To father a son was indeed the crux of his problem. He hitched at his sword belt impatiently and pulled at the armhole of his mail shirt.

"How this armor binds! My lord of Chester, give me leave to go and unarm and bathe. Hereford, let me be or—or I will set Gloucester on to press for your marraige and make you sing another tune."

"Go, child, by all means." Chester said kindly. "Nay, I can never seem to remember, you are long since a man, Radnor. How inconsiderate of us to keep you. Are you well? You are red one moment, pale the next, and you look like death."

"To speak the truth, I am so weary I know not how I am. Godfather, on this matter of Henry of Anjou, I pray you to do nothing until we can speak together in a better place and when my mind is clear. Hereford, I promise you that I, at least, will listen to anything you have to say. Indeed, I must leave you. My bath will be cold. We rode through last night for I was fearful of missing my day, and I am asleep on my feet."

Radnor kissed Chester's hand again and shook his head at Hereford's offer to accompany him. When they left he limped wearily up the stairs clinging to the rough stone walls of the narrow circular staircase for support. Memories were so strong in the tower room that he stopped, short of breath. Everything was familiar—the chair before the now dead fire, the scent of herbs in the room; only what Radnor longed for most was missing. He undressed and slipped into the tub,

70

nearly fainting as the odorous warmth encompassed him. For a while he lay, half conscious in the water, but finally roused himself sufficiently to bathe.

No beds had yet been made up in the room, but Radnor found rugs in one of the chests which he threw on the floor. Wrapping his naked body in still another rug, he lay down on the floor and was instantly asleep. It was true that he had not reached the goal of his desiring, but its nearness soothed him instead of making him more eager and restless. For the first time in months, Lord Radnor slid into an absolutely dreamless sleep.

He slept through all the noise and flurry of receiving last-minute guests, wakening quietly when dinner was long over. He stretched luxuriously in his first sleep-dazed moments, filled with a blissful ease, a feeling of being at home, but soon enough sat up and looked for his clothes because he was cold. Even on a hot June day the earth-filled stone walls of the tower sweated moisture and the room was damp. Someone had been at work while he slept; the bath was gone as were the filthy garments he had dropped on the floor. Instead, neatly laid over the chair were the clothes his father had brought from Painscastle except that they had obviously received some recent attention. The linen shirt had been scoured to a whiteness it had not had since new, and the red tunic, red chausses, gray serge gown and gray cross-garters were carefully matched. Radnor smiled. So neatly arrayed he would be a shock to his friends who were accustomed to seeing him in garments that were ill-matched and ill cared for. He was feeling better but was conscious of a great weariness not due to physical causes, a weariness of the soul. What was it that was so unpleasant that he had to do—good Lord, Chester and Hereford, that was it; but first he had to see Philip of Gloucester. A sudden qualm of anxiety seized him. Had not Hereford told him that Philip was sick? Did that mean that Philip had not come?

At the entrance to the hall, Lord Radnor looked cautiously about. He had no desire to be seized upon by his godfather or his hotheaded young friend. No, they were out, it seemed, but Pembroke was in conversation with Shrewsbury. Radnor felt distaste, even knowing he should have expected it. It was wonderful how old saws always were true, and here were two birds of a feather flocking together. If it were not for the greater dower, he never would have consented to the alliance. But then he had not known Leah. One had to take the bitter with the better and father went with daughter. Radnor moved forward to accost his father-in-law.

"Pembroke—. No, no, Shrewsbury, do not let me interrupt your talk," Radnor said as Shrewsbury started to turn away, "I only wished to inquire whether Philip of Gloucester has come, and if so, where he is lodged. I have heard that he is unwell, and I would ask after my foster brother's welfare."

"I know he is come because Edwina had planned to house him with his brother William in the hall and I had to tell her they were not presently on speaking terms with each other. Since Philip joined Stephen, deserting his father and his cause for the bribes and land the king gave him, those of his blood have turned their backs to him. I believe he has a separate pavilion across the moat because he said he wanted quiet."

"Thank you. His colors will be up or I will recognize his servants. I will find it."

A little while later Radnor was gripping Philip's hand between both of his own. It was actually hard to recognize the man who had been his closest friend for many years even though he had seen him only a few months previously.

"My God, Philip, what has befallen you? How is it with you?"

A wasted hand made a gesture of hopelessness. "Never mind that now. Our time is short, let us use it well. I have bad news for you, very bad."

"I know it. You mean that Henry is coming. A pox take him. Nay, I do not mean that, but there could be a better time. Wales is on the boil, although I think I have quenched the flames under the pot a little, and there are still enough men who stand behind Stephen—for one reason or another. It is too much for a boy barely turned sixteen. I know he is wise beyond his years, but this country is like a stallion in rut. It needs a more experienced rider." He made a sharp gesture. "I do not know what ails me, Philip. I speak to you of Wales and England, but I scarcely know what I say. My mind wanders."

"Another woman. What a fool you are over women!" Philip frowned suddenly. "Do not tell me it is the little bride." Radnor nodded, flushing. "Oh, God! I hope you have more joy of this encounter than you had of the last. What is she like?"

"Nothing, no great beauty. She is small and fair. Gentle. I——. No, it is not that she is unwilling. It is myself. I fear I cannot——"

Nervously, Radnor got up and sat down, ran a hand through his hair, opened his mouth and shut it. Philip watched him attentively. Now Radnor had turned away slightly and was looking out of the doorway while he spoke, his voice so clogged with emotion that Philip could hardly make out the words. It did not matter. New fears, old fears, and the terrible struggle against fear itself and against the need to repress that fear because no one would listen or understand. Philip remembered the tortured, inarticulate youth who had come to fosterage with the Gloucesters, the young man with suspicious eyes who had so slowly become his friend, so slowly been induced to confide his dreams and his terrors. He could say nothing to help. What was important was that Radnor trusted him and could reason aloud, sure of sympathy in his presence. Philip's attention was focused by Radnor's sudden, anguished grip on his hand.

"In God's name, Philip, do not leave me. You are the only living soul to whom I can open my heart. Sometimes I forget what it is to talk without a guard on my tongue. When Hereford told me you were sick, I——I did not think. I was taken up with my own trouble and I did not believe it." He dropped his head onto the hand he was holding and Philip could feel his tears.

"Cain," he said gently, "you must believe it, for I am dying."

"No! You cannot know what. Such things are in the hands of God."

"He has given me warning. Nay, do not struggle so. It will be easier for you if you believe me. I grieve to leave so much undone, but it is lighter for me to bear in that I have so little time to think of it. Come now, bear up. You know I would indulge your sorrow, but there is so little time—so little time." There was a long pause before Philip continued. "And I have more trouble to add to what you bear."

73

In the past Philip had often been disturbed by the violence of his friend's emotions and by the influence those emotions had over his behavior, but now he made no effort to take his cold hand from Radnor's warm clasp. It was good to have someone who cared so much whether he lived or died, for Radnor's tears were the sweat of a heart overburdened beyond bearing. Philip had never seen Cain weep before. How infinite was the goodness of God. Radnor's desire to keep him on earth was completely selfish—the generous impulse would be to wish the suffering friend release. Yet it was the selfish desire that warmed Philip's heart and gave him strength. He was so infinitely weary, and the pain that racked him grew more constant and severe day by day. He would have prayed for death, had it not been for Radnor pulling on his heartstrings and for the necessity of striving on toward the crowning of Henry of Anjou. Radnor was in danger and a new outbreak of the civil war now might damage beyond repair Henry's chances of being crowned.

The choking sobs had quieted. "Can you listen now, Radnor?"

Cain wiped his face on his gown. "Yes, I am together again."

"Chester and Hereford are up to some new devilment. What it—"

"Save your breath. I know all about that or, at least, I will know all soon enough."

"They came to you then?"

"Before I had dismounted from my horse they were upon me."

"Do what you can to stop them. If you do not, I will have to betray them, for the time is not ripe. There must be no war! Cain," Philip drew a painful breath, "I wish I did not have to say this, but your father-in-law has some hand in this also."

"Nonsense. Pembroke cares nothing for Stephen or for Henry. He cares only for his skin."

"And his purse. You know that Chester's sister married Pembroke's brother—to bind the families in love! Well, Chester was a loving uncle enough, you know his affections are strong, and was so kind to his nephew Fitz Richard that the fool of a boy offered himself and his land as hostage—." Cain made an impatient gesture of acknowledgment. "Think, Radnor. Pembroke is his

74

uncle too. If the lands fall forfeit because of some folly of Chester's, who so likely to receive them as Pembroke?"

"But Stephen could not be such a fool as to—." Radnor sighed. "Who knows how much a fool Stephen can be. Nay, Maud would never permit it."

"So I think also, but Pembroke cannot or will not understand the power Maud wields and he thinks he can bend Stephen to his will. Radnor, forgive me, but you must not permit yourself to—to—"

"To what?"

"To fall into the power of your wife. You are like to do it, and I believe Pembroke plans to control you through her."

The flash of anger that had lit in Cain's eyes dissipated. "Now, Philip," he remonstrated, "you cannot have it both ways. If Pembroke sets Maud's power at naught, certainly he could not believe that a girl scarce more than a babe could make of me what she will."

A worried frown knitted Philip's brows. "I know, and yet the thing is too perfect. No sooner had you agreed to consummate this marriage than he began to incite Chester with talk of the slights put upon him and the harsh treatment Fitz Richard receives from Stephen and Maud—which, I must say, is nonsense for Fitz Richard is well treated although closely watched. I swear that it was Pembroke who put the Empress Matilda into the madness which has made her wish to send Henry here. Before she left, she swore to my father that she would do nothing until he told her we had a chance of winning our purpose. My father knows for a fact that messengers from Pembroke have gone to Matilda. He cannot prove this nor, unfortunately, bring it to Henry's attention. No messenger of ours has been permitted nigh Henry. We do not know whether our letters reach the boy at all, and we dare not trust certain things to writing."

"But what could Pembroke have said to the empress that should make her void her promise to your father?"

"Probably Pembroke told her that he would lend Henry support and perhaps even that you would too, since you were contracted to his girl. Do not trouble to protest, Radnor, these are my guesses. What is certain is that my father has finally determined to send Henry no help. How bitter a draught for both to drink, you

75

may imagine, but a rebellion now is hopeless. We cannot overcome Stephen at this time. Nevertheless, some profit may be had of Henry's coming. Since few will know how little money or support Henry has, it may be possible to wring from the king another affirmation of an Angevin succession. That will be your work, Radnor."

"No! I do not like this lying and crawling about. I will speak out in council for it, if you desire, but I will not cozen Stephen."

"Who likes it? Because of that creature, neither man nor king, my father and brother must pretend not to speak to me, my erstwhile friends turn faces of ice in my direction. Will I die without a smile from all whom I hold dear? Without a look or a word of sympathy from the men with whom I have shed so much blood, for whom I have humbled my pride? You are the only one left. I told you nothing of what my father and I had planned."

"I know your constancy, Philip. I could not doubt you. I knew that if you swore to Stephen and took money from him it was by your father's bidding because he needed you in court. But William is already there—surely he may serve your father's purposes alone. This lies to too heavy on your heart. By the ten fingers of Christ, I will not have it. Everyone shall be told. No gain can be worth your unhappiness at such a time."

"Do not be foolish. It is only the weakness speaking. I have not done all this to throw it away for a look or a smile. The barons must believe that Stephen has paid my price and I am his man. William is known to be my father's spy and is suffered because they cannot trap him. I am taken at face value, and I have some influence among the barons. In truth, I do not spy. What they tell me goes no further and I use my weight only to keep the peace. Just now, war is no answer; we cannot win and must not fight. This is why I cannot broach the matter of Henry's succession myself. There are still doubts. To show myself interested in his cause would raise so much suspicion as to make these last months' labors worthless."

"Is there no one else?"

"Who else could there be? Those to whom Stephen listens have joy of him. Why should they not? Their people lie still without even a groan. What need have they of succor from a king? We who fight for the peace of the kingdom, he will not attend to because we urge him to be strong or to yield to someone in the true line who is strong. Why do we sweat and moil and toil and bleed?" Philip cried with sudden passion. "We should lay down our arms and let the Welsh and the Scots flood across on them. Let them cry in vain to that—that image of a man." He stopped suddenly and began to cough.

"For heaven's sake, Philip, do not put yourself into a passion." Radnor bent over and lifted him to a sitting position so that he could catch his breath. "I will do anything you like, only be calm. Philip, I cannot bear it. I care nothing for all this. Your father must be suffering the torments of the damned, knowing you so sick, and unable to be near you. I will do your part too—anything. Go home. If you have rest and the heart and mind at peace, mayhap your health—"

"How could I be at rest and leave the task undone? Do you not know me better than that? My father loves me, yes, and suffers, but he would be the first to say my work must be finished before I lay down my tools. Sometimes"—a faint, wry smile pulled at Philip's lips—"I think you will never make a successful man of affairs, Radnor. You are too soft. You can never permit those you love to do what you would do yourself without question. Peace," he continued sharply as Cain was about to reply, "you have been here too long already. Kiss me and go. God go with you."

At the entrance to the great hall, a mass of noble retainers, but not of Radnor's generation and in much awe of him, fell back to clear a path. Gaunt, at the side of the room, was attracted by their movement and looked up from making a point to Leicester with clenched fist. "Ah, here is my son and he can probably tell us. Cain, come here. What is Walter of Hereford up to now? I saw you in close talk with his brother."

"I do not know. Hereford did not mention Walter to me. He knows that his brother and I do not—agree." Radnor spoke dully. He did not care two pins what Walter of Hereford was doing.

"You have been weeping. You have been to see Philip

of Gloucester, hey?" Gaunt said in his hard voice. "It is a shame he will not last this half—"

"What joy it gives you to unman me before company, I do not know, but tonight I will not bear it. I have borne enough. Make what excuses for me you can or will—make none at all—I care not. I am going to bed." Cain had turned a countenance completely distorted by rage and pain on his father. Leicester, startled, stepped back out of the reach of Radnor's working hands, although he was no coward.

Gaunt looked at Leicester after Radnor had passed between them almost at a run, with the blankest astonishment. He closed his mouth, which had been hanging slightly open displaying his broken and missing teeth. "Now what maggot is in that boy's brain? I did but say I was sorry his friend, and mine too if it comes to that, was so near death. What is there in that to enrage him? If ever a man was cursed with an ugly-tempered devil for a son, I am he."

"He was fostered there," Leicester replied with ponderous gravity. "It may be that the bond between them is close. Mayhap the wound of seeing Philip is still green. A man may flinch, even under the kindly hand, when a green wound is handled."

Gaunt did not reply to that, but a look that Leicester, no fool in spite of his heavy appearance and slow ways, would have put down to surprise and an angry chagrin had it not seemed unreasonable came into Gaunt's face. He had no time to consider why a father should so little understand his son, however, because Shrewsbury and Pembroke had hurried over to ask about the cause of the excitement and his thoughts were taken up with further surprise at the reasons Gaunt assigned to Radnor's hasty departure. Why any man should wish to display his son as evil-tempered to the point of madness was more puzzling than why he misunderstood him. There was some point in it though, Leicester soon realized, for the more Gaunt spoke of Radnor's unreasonable vindictiveness the more thoughtful the expressions he could read on the faces of the listeners.

Meanwhile, Radnor stopped the first maidservant he found and ordered her to tell her mistress to make up his bed. He spoke with such ferociousness that the girl was nearly incoherent when she found Edwina. Once the message became plain, other women servants were hurried off to fulfill the order. Poor Alison, Leah's personal maid, crept into a corner and sat trembling. Her fears were not all for herself, although she was one of the servants who would accompany Leah; she was also terrified of what awaited her little mistress for she was fond of her. To be bedded with that distorted face, those hard, angry eyes, that harsh voice—Alison bitterly regretted ever having envied Leah her high station.

CHAPTER 6

EDWINA LOOKED DOWN on the restless sleep of her daughter's future husband with close attention. If her life had depended upon it, she could not see anything in that face or body to tempt even the ignorant and sheltered girl that Leah was. True, Leah had seen few men, so few that Edwina had feared, fed as the girl was on romantic tales, that she could not be brought to accept any real man with complaisance. There could be no doubt that she had accepted Radnor, however, more than accepted him. Edwina leaned over and touched the man gently.

"You must get up now, Lord Radnor."

"Good God!" He started upright and saw the sun blazing outside an arrow slit. "Am I late? I have slept the day through."

"Not quite, and I must suppose you needed it sorely." He had a gentle way with him in spite of his appearance. It was a shame that he should be slaughtered like a sheep. "Your bath is ready and the barber waits. Here are your wedding garments."

Radnor's gaze followed the direction of her gesture. "Nay, madam, your housekeeping is at last at fault, for you have confused some other man's clothes with mine. I have nothing like that."

"The clothes are yours, my lord. More, perhaps, than any others. Those are my daughter's wedding gift to you. The thought was hers, and every stitch was set by her hand alone."

Frozen by the antagonism in his mother-in-law's eyes, Radnor made no acknowledgment of her information other than a low grunt and an invitation to her to leave so that he could bathe in peace. When she was gone, however, he went over to touch the velvet gently. It smelled of lavender and the odor brought with it a flood of passion and a flood of fear.

Leah, who had been ready for hours, had no fear at all. In spite of her excitement, she had sat quietly so as not to disarrange the perfect folds of the green brocade bliaut, the sheer wimple which, floating down under a chaplet of silver flowers, concealed not a bit of her fresh face or her loose-flowing hair. Her cheeks were flushed by eagerness, her eyes, brightened by their color, flashed a green brilliant enough to match the gems in Radnor's necklet which circled her full young throat. To Radnor, waiting on the steps of the church, her appearance brought such an intensification of his emotions that he felt he would choke on his terror and his desire.

Whatever admonition or prayers the priest who came out onto the steps facing them offered on their behalf were lost on the bridal couple. Radnor filled his eyes with the features so nearly forgotten; Leah's pleasure became mixed with anxiety at her husband's appeararnce. Bound up in their own emotions, neither heard the end of the ceremony nor the priest's permission to the groom to kiss the bride, so that he had to repeat himself and drew a laugh from the crowd of witnesses. The touch of Leah's lips destroyed any hope Radnor had of controlling himself. Above all other needs his need to know whether he was still a man was paramount. He took his wife's hand into a painful grip.

"I must speak five words to you alone. Soon—now! Where can we go?"

Leah looked blindly around at the crowd surrounding them. She knew quite well that her mother had planned every instant of her wedding day. She was due in moments to be formally introduced to the guests and to receive their good wishes for she had beeen kept in partial seclusion. It seemed impossible to escape. Not only would her mother be furious if she upset the well-ordered plans but it would be rude to the guests. It never occurred to Leah to try to expostulate or explain this to Cain. Whatever her husband requested, she must try to perform. If he had bidden her move the keep singlehanded, she would have strained every muscle and nerve to obey him without regard to the insanity of the command. She quickened her step.

"I will go to remove my chaplet and braid my hair. I will tell my mother that the silver flowers hurt my head. Do you on a pretext follow me."

Easier to say than to do. When Leah murmured her excuse to her mother, Edwina did not even trouble to reply except for an angry shake of her head.

"Mother, please. I am so uncomfortable I can hardly speak."

"You were so eager to dress early—now you must bear it. Stand here, they are coming."

With a low cry Leah wrenched herself free of her mother's grip. It did not matter what Edwina thought; it did not matter what the guests thought; her lord had looked across the room at her with what she took to be an impatient frown. In her own small closet she turned to greet him with a smile of success for a difficult deed well done. There was no answering smile, no look even of recognition as he seized her and threw her roughly on the bed, no word of love or apology as he took her with a brutality only equaled by his fear and his need. Leah's agony was intense, but very brief; in a few short moments Radnor was moaning and shuddering in the grip of his climax. Through her pain and her terror Leah heard him and dimly, through that pain and terror, she felt his need and his pleasure, his excuse for using her so roughly.

Now Cain lay like a log upon her. Leah dared not move, not even when, after a few minutes more, he rolled away and, turning his back, began to make himself decent. He glanced at her over his shoulder.

"Pull down your skirt, in God's name." His voice drew a whimper from Leah that no pain could wring. The sound made Cain turn on her sharply. "By Christ, you must not weep now. We must go down and make merry with our guests."

Obediently Leah swallowed her tears, but merriment or even comprehension was beyond her. She was so torn between her fear and her joy that she could hardly understand what was said to her during the hours of formal introductions to the guests in the hall below. Some thought her simple-minded, so vague were her replies to them; some merely assumed that she had a great distaste for the match. In either case, her youth and gentleness were so appealing, especially to the men and older women, that they were willing to treat her with sympathy.

When the formalities were finally completed the group separated as it usally did, the men gravitating together and the women forming small chattering groups. Little by little, as various women fingered her dress and commented upon her jewels, Leah recovered from her panic. She began to distinguish between the great ladies. The Countess of Shrewsbury who had just come up to her was exceedingly handsome and dressed with great magnificence. Her bliaut was a soft coral velvet beaded with pearls over a pale beige tunic whose neck was also pearl-embroidered. Even her long blond braids were intertwined with pearls. Leah grew a little dizzy as she tried to think what such a display would cost. She dropped her eyes, however, and curtsied deeply as Lady Shrewsbury addressed her.

"Lord Radnor is fortunate to find such a pretty face connected with so rich a dowry. Are the lands definitely settled upon you already?"

Leah blushed a little at the compliment, but she felt that so direct an inquiry into the financial arrangements of her marriage was a little tasteless. "I do not know, madam. I know nothing of the arrangement between my lord and my father."

"Heavens, you are truly an innocent. You must find out at once." Joan of Shrewsbury's eyes of a clear and fathomless blue dwelt mercilessly on the child before her. It mattered not a bit what Leah suffered if Radnor would suffer too, and nothing could disgust him more than a mercenary woman. "Do you not even know the value of your bride price?"

"N-no." Leah dropped her eyes modestly as an imp entered her soul. "But I do know that my lord paid a great sum without complaint—after he had seen me. Before that, I heard, he was less willing."

"Then you hold him in the hollow of your hand?"

There was a hardness, a controlled hatred even, in the voice which asked the question that made Leah recoil mentally. What if Cain should hear of her boasting? Actually Leah had never even thought of what bride price Cain had paid. She had spoken merely to annoy Lady Shrewsbury and had accomplished her end better than she had intended.

"I did not say that, my lady."

"Oh, you are young and pretty, and Lord Radnor—" Lady Shrewsbury's eyes moved around the hall until they rested on Radnor—"is not so pretty any more." Her voice faltered a little, and it seemed to Leah that that was not what she had intended to say. "For a while you may well hold him, but not for long. I knew him very well," Lady Shrewsbury continued, her eyes fixed upon Leah's with an expression that even the girl's innocence could not mistake, "both before and after he was so marked. You would not, perhaps, believe it, but he was excessively handsome at one time, well worth knowing."

Blood rushed to Leah's face, and she pressed her hands into the folds of her bliaut to hide the fact that the fingers had curled into claws. As if a man's face was what a decent woman loved him for! She wanted to say it, to tell the beautiful whore—for so Leah immediately classed her—what she thought of her. Self-control, however, was Leah's strong suit, and she said nothing.

"For goodness sake, Joan, what are you saying to the child to make her such a color?" The Countess of Leicester's kind voice saved Leah from the necessity of reply.

Irritation flashed in Lady Shrewsbury's cold eyes. "I was only telling her something about Lord Radnor that I thought she should know. I did not mean to embarrass her but to show her a good reason why she should settle her rights and allowances with him now, while he is still disposed to generosity."

"Joan is right about that. It is good to have such matters plainly declared and settled in some definite way. Then you know what you may spend, and your husband is not continually accusing you of being extravagant. Just so long as you understand, my dear, that what your husband did before your marriage is none of your affair."

"Oh, no," Leah murmured, "I should never think of—anyhow, I should not know if he did not tell me."

"You will find plenty of other people to tell you things," the countess replied dryly. "Some of them might even be true. Nonetheless, it is wisest not to hear, not to understand, or, if such things are forced upon you, to have a very poor memory. Do you expect to live at Painscastle?"

"I believe so, madam, but I shall live, of course, where my lord bids."

"That sounds very nice," Joan of Shrewsbury interjected, "but if I were you I would find out which was my dower castle, get on terms with the castellan, and put it in order. You might not find it convenient to continue to live with a man of such uncertain disposition as Lord Radnor."

"Now, Joan, is that the sort of thing to say to the child when she has not been four hours married? Besides, I never found Radnor to be hasty of temper unless his father was tormenting him."

Leah dropped her eyes, which had been moving anxiously from face to face. She had seen the Duke of Gaunt bait his son. Perhaps it would not be pleasant to live at Painscastle between two angry men. She felt a faint chill of fear at the thought. Certainly Cain had been rough and angry, with none of the tenderness and half-hidden amusement he had previously displayed with her. Was it because they were married now and he had her to do with as he pleased? Be it so or not, she thought, a tremendous inner pride welling up to stiffen her, no one would ever know. For good or for ill, her lord was her good lord.

"Perhaps I know his lordship better than you do," Lady Shrewsbury was saying. "Now here is Lady William. She should be able to settle this for us. Lord Radnor was fostered with Robert of Gloucester and has always been close to them."

Lord Radnor, absorbed into the male group, was no less roughly handled. True, no one discussed his wife with him, but he had to stand a plethora of crude jokes on his appearance. Armed with the consciousness that his fears of impotence were groundless, he was able to take the humor of his companions in good part and he was grateful that while they teased him about becoming an uxurious husband they were forced to leave political problems alone. Truly enough he was in no mood for serious thought of any kind and had deliberately surrounded himself with the younger men so that he was surprised to see Mortimer breaking into their group and bearing down upon him purposefully. Generally speaking, the Mortimers were even more aloof from national politics than the Gaunts. They sat grimly on their own lands, repelling advances or attacks from either side, but more and more of late the turns of fortune in England affected the peace of Wales.

Mortimer was a valuable ally and could be a dangerous enemy. Radnor knew also that the family was a little put out because they had expected him to unite with them, so he smiled as pleasantly as he could and walked aside with the older man as he was urged to do.

"Is Chester about to start this accursed war over again?"

"I certainly hope not."

"That is no answer. My people tell me that the other Marcher lords will call the young pretender from France and raise the Angevin standard."

Cain threw out a deprecating hand. "Certainly you may believe that I am not involved in such a scheme, nor is my father."

"I do not speak of you, although I am glad to hear that you do not hold with such a foolish idea. Who is to hold Fitz Richard's lands?"

"Are his lands forfeit?" Radnor parried.

Mortimer studied the face before him. "You are a liar—oh, not in your words but in your intentions. Do not trouble yourself to protest, for I do not care one way or another about these things except that I wish to know whether to build more keeps and arm more men."

"It can never hurt to be well armed against future trouble."

"Good, you have at least answered that question. Now to something to me more important. Will you give me the promise of your first-born for a son or daughter of my house? I can tell you right now what I am prepared to offer for a daughter or yield with one of my girls to your son."

To the details of the proposal Lord Radnor listened with great interest. In Wales, if not in the country as a whole, the Mortimers were nearly equal in power to the Gaunts, and to Radnor's mind they were good stock— Welsh and Norman like himself. He certainly wished to make a blood bond between Mortimer and himself, but he did not wish to commit his first-born because there might be even better opportunities. He fingered the scar near his mouth, irritated at the generosity of Mortimer's offer because it precluded obejctions on that score.

"You are most liberal, but I cannot close with such an offer now."

"You have something better in mind, Radnor? Are my girls not handsome enough, my boys not strong enough?"

The truth was that the girls were not handsome, but that was a matter of small account. Radnor laughed and disclaimed any other advances and any other intentions. Merely, he explained, a child might be long in coming and he did not want to bind Mortimer to a promise that he would not wish to keep.

"When I am willing to take the chance," Mortimer replied stubbornly, "why should you be concerned? Surely I am old enough to care properly for my own interests. I will give you my eldest son, if it is a daughter, and any girl you wish if it be a boy. If you do not wish me to be bound, give me the right of first refusal without oaths taken on either side."

Out of the corner of his eye, Cain saw the tables were ready set for dinner. In a moment they would be summoned to eat and he permitted himself to laugh heartily. "Well, that is something to make a note of. On my wedding day, I could have married off my eldest born—do you suspect me of dishonoring my wife before we were wed? Nay, Mortimer, I will not permit you to bind me by oaths or oathless. God send me sufficient children to fulfill all the offers and I assure you that you will not have to wait long before we are bound in blood. I am most willing, but this is no time for long or serious talk—there is the call to table."

They ate and ate—in the hall, in pavilions on the field, in the kitchens and passages. Whole deer, boars stuffed with rabbits, swans stuffed with geese, the geese with chickens, the chickens with pheasants, and the pheasants with doves. Myriads of sauces, jellies, and condiments were provided to grace the meats which were less elaborately prepared. Mountains of bread disappeared as did barrel after barrel of wine and beer. In the open spaces between the tables jugglers and acrobats, clad in the pied red and yellow of their trade, performed their feats and their women danced, rattling tambourines. When the roasts were removed to make place for the ragouts and stews, the jugglers withdrew and the musicians came forward so that the guests could dance. As the wine in the huge casks sank lower, the men grew more quarrelsome; fighting began to break out, personal and political grievances alike being aired and the language which was used showing the truth and directness lent by the wine. The soberer members of the party, including the bridegroom, leapt up to separate the combatants and calm them with the information that the matter could be fought out on the tourney field in the morning.

"Madam," Lord Radnor said to Edwina, "gather your ladies and let the bedding ceremony begin. If we do not rise from the tables soon and give the men something else to think about, there will be blood shed in earnest."

Edwina made no protest although she cast an anguished glance at Leah who was toying absently with food she had not eaten. This thing, to her the greatest horror of all, had to be, and delay would change nothing. She collected the highest-born ladies with her eye and they gathered around Leah. The men's attention was immediately withdrawn from their quarrels; each tried to outdo the other in raucous applause and coarse jokes, and much advice decent and indecent followed the women out of the hall. The bride was led to the tower room where Cain had slept, now furnished with a magnificent bed, Leah's parents' wedding gift to her. The ladies removed Leah's beautiful bliaut, her tunic, her shift, her shoes and stockings; they unbraided her hair and helped her into the bed. Radnor, apparently eager and not hiding it, arrived with his guard of honor so quickly that the women could not straighten out her clothing, and in his disrobing ceremony and the accompanying jests the garments were forgotten.

To Leah it seemed as if the crowd of noisy, joking people would never leave. She was frightened by the knowledge that their departure would herald a resumption of her painful experience of the forenoon, but she was more distressed by the appreciative glances of the men and by the pain and fear imperfectly concealed in her mother's eyes. Radnor was proving recalcitrant. He had stripped willingly enough down to his chausses and shoes, but these he refused to remove. This naturally enough brought forth a hail of chaff. All would have passed off easily enough, however, for every man there knew of his lameness and his reluctance to expose it, had not Gaunt interfered. Hereford was proposing some particularly indelicate reasons for Radnor's shyness when the duke's harsh voice cut across the merriment.

"Let him be. He has, in truth, something to conceal."

Radnor's face whitened; Hereford's voice was suspended mid-jest. A few uneasy glances passed from eye to eye in the unpleasant silence. Philip of Gloucester, who had been leaning breathlessly against the wall after making the climb up the stairs, came forward to kiss his friend defensively. Hereford followed. Chester embraced his godson's shoulders. Nothing could cover the suspicion renewed in all minds, however, and the spontaneity was gone so that only a few moments later the room was clear.

Afraid to meet Leah's eyes, Cain sat down on the bed with his back to her to remove the rest of his clothes. He dallied, unwinding his cross-garters slowly and allowing his eyes to wander aimlessly about the room. They fell on Leah's shift, passed, suddenly returned. The tunic and shift were stained with blood.

"What? Leah, how did you get blood all over your clothes?" No answer, but the bed shook as her shudder communicated itself to him through the mattresses. He turned to look at her. "Why do you fear me?" he questioned furiously. He associated her fear with his father's remark which could, indeed, have been taken as acknowledgment that he was a demon. The matter of the bloodstained shift was insignificant in comparison and had already slipped from his mind.

Leah shrank from him slightly and put up her hands as if to hold him off. "I fear because you hurt me." She heard the tone of reproach and resentment in her own voice and was appalled. That was no way to speak to a husband; he would be furious with her.

Cain did not even notice. His only emotion was a wave of relief that she was not afraid he was a supernatural monster. "I did not mean to hurt you," he said softly. "I did with you as a man does with a woman." His voice was uncertain. His experience had not been with innocent, virginal women. Radnor frowned thoughtfully at his wife.

Leah was terrified by that frown. It would be bad for her indeed if she had made him angry so early in their marriage. The fear showed in her face and in her trembling voice as she spoke to him. "Come, my lord, lie down. Let me darken the room."

He lay beside her as bidden, remembering that the fear in her eyes now was the same as the look she had given him earlier and that both glances were akin to the way the women whom he seized in the fields regarded him. He heard again the whimper she had given when he left her. Was this the same then? Had he lied to himself about her warmth, about her affection for him? His pleasure he had had, but it was bitter in his mouth as was the frightened stillness of the girl who lay beside him.

"My lord?" Her voice was a thin, trembling whisper.

"Yes."

"Alas, do not be angry with me. Do with me as you will."

"I am not angry."

He did not sound angry, his soft voice carried no threat. Leah spoke more surely, but still with caution. "You are my very good lord. You will be patient with me, I know." Emboldened further by his passive acceptance of that statement, Leah stroked her husband's arm gently and turned toward him. Cain did not want the response of fear. "Oh, do not turn away," she cried, and he realized that he had frightened her more and took her in his arms.

That was nice, very nice. He could not be angry and hold her so gently. After a little pause Leah sighed and pressed closer. "You are so warm and I so cold. My lord?"

"Yes."

"Were you angry at my boldness when I wrote to you?"

"No, I was well pleased." Cain swallowed. Holding her so close without going further was not easy, for her cool, pliant body awakened his passion. Leah moved her head on his shoulder and laughed softly. "What is it?"

"The hair on your chest is so harsh. It tickles my face with little pricks." Leah stroked his face. She would have begged him to kiss her, but his assurance that one type of boldness was not offensive to him gave her no guarantee that he would accept another type.

"Do not do that!" Her hand stopped and Cain felt her body stiffen. "Nay, I did not mean to frighten you, but that makes me—. Your hair is like fine silk. Last night I dreamt of it, like a web over my hands."

Leah's hand, still against his cheek, trembled a little and then turned his face more toward her. "My lord?"

"What now?"

"Is it evil in a woman to desire to kiss her husband?"

"What?"

Leah was silent. Doubtless her mother was correct and her husband would now think she was a woman without virtue. Cain felt suddenly frustrated. It was necessary, of course, for girls to be kept pure, but he was beginning to think that too much innocence could be a fault. Explanation of these matters was a work for other women, he thought, realizing with a shock that how it was for a woman was a mystery to him. Leah's hand dropped from his face.

"Leah, it is good, not evil, for a woman to love her husband."

"Yes, but—"

"What did your mother tell you of marriage?"

Cain did not realize how fortunate he was that Edwina, unlike most mothers who explained carefully and fully, had been unable to bring herself to discuss the sexual aspects of marriage with her daughter. Leah had thus been saved her mother's warped views on the subject and had imbibed only hints from the servant women and certain practical information from the evidence of her eyes in seeing the mating of the beasts in the castle and on the demesne lands.

"That I must obey my husband. That I must allow him to do whatever he would with me. Indeed, my lord, I did wrong to speak in that tone to you before. It is your right to handle me as you will. That I must not hang upon you. That—"

"Enough. She told you nothing of what—what I did?"

"Oh no."

"That is the way children are begotten."

"So much I knew. I ask again for your pardon."

"There is nothing to pardon. I was too rough with
90

you." His voice faltered a little and his arms tightened around her. "And now what must I do?" he asked softly. "Must I wait? I—it is hard for me."

She could escape the repetition of that experience. All she needed to do was lie a little. In the dim light Leah saw the shine of the lashes over his beautiful eyes. What she had been about to say died in her throat. "Be gentle with me," she whispered instead.

He had his will of her, and it was sweeter than honey because she was willing and then, when he drifted up out of that red well of pleasure, there was more sweetness yet, for Leah was stroking his hair and kissing his face.

"I am sorry. I tried to be gentle, but I hurt you, I know."

He had hurt her, and not a little, but she cared nothing for that. She lifted his face and kissed his closed eyes and pressed him into her breast again to sleep. Leah had sipped the heady drink of deliberately giving the blinding pleasure of physical love to her husband; she could forgive him anything for the knowledge of that power.

Content with a contentment that comes only with relief from fear, Radnor thanked God for his manifold mercies and drifted from a heavenly languor into the depths of sleep.

Leah, awake in her pain, watched her husband's even breathing. She was not concerned with her physical discomfort because her shrewd mind and quick observation told her that it would grow less with time; after all the hints of the maidservants and the jests of the other women at the wedding indicated that love was a thing of great pleasure. What caused her brow to wrinkle into a frown and kept her eyes wakefully staring at the bed curtains was the problem of whether her husband had given himself in the same way to the other women—to Lady Shrewsbury. It was true that it was no business of hers what Cain had done before they were married, but how was she to keep him from going back to the old stewpots? If he did, and her mother said he would, how could she bear it? What could she do to win him back? Round and round went her mind spinning like a wheel around the central hub of fact that could make her life a heaven or a hell—her husband's affection. Radnor sighed and stirred and she clasped him closer. Somehow she would hold him, she thought, as her eyes closed. With meekness and willingness and obedience all things were possible.

CHAPTER 7

MORNING BROUGHT THE SOUND of the ladies and gentlemen coming to wake the bride and groom. The guests were still heavy-eyed from their carousal, but they had recovered their good spirits and they greeted the fact that Leah was still abed while her husband was up and dressed with shrieks of glee.

"That does it," Hereford exclaimed. "He never went to bed at all. The whole thing has been a great hoax. I think he cannot mate with a woman and has lied to us all these years about being a man."

"No, no," Philip of Gloucester replied in his breathless voice. "Pembroke, at least, would never perpetrate such an expensive joke. Lord Radnor is only showing us who will be master of his household." The words were obviously meant to be a joke, but there was an undernote of warning. "Look you, he is up first. Will he summon her maids? Bring her her washing water? Run her errands?"

Radnor turned, smiling, from the arrow slit out of which he had been watching the preparations for the tourney. "A good morning to you all. It was the rattle of arms that woke me. It looks a fair green field. I am almost sorry I will not be upon it."

Hereford came up and landed a blow with his fist in Radnor's midsection that would have done credit to a horse. "For shame! What an admission! What sort of a man finds more attraction in the rattle of harness than in his bed on his wedding morning?"

Radnor grunted at the blow and laughed. "An old soldier is the answer to your riddle. More especially one who has been drawing his weapons to that sound day and night for almost all the years of your life—

boy." His eyes, however, moved uneasily to the bed where the ladies were performing their part of the customary ceremony.

The covers had been drawn back so that Leah lay exposed on the bloody sheets. Radnor could feel the terrible sense of possession well up in him; he knew he was going to make a fool of himself, but he could do nothing to prevent it. The eyes of the other men on what he now considered peculiarly his own were intolerable. He flung himself across the room, jerked the girl out of bed, and draped his own gown around her. The women stared in surprise; the men doubled up with mirth, Hereford sinking to the floor where he remained laughing weakly.

"Our Radnor, our Radnor," he gasped when he was able to command his voice. "Do you think," he crowed, drawing himself upright by climbing up William of Gloucester who was laughing more quietly, "that he will veil her altogether, like a Saracen?"

Edwina, quickly gathering fresh garments for Leah and handing them to her, was more surprised by her daughter's behavior than her son-in-law's; she had seen Radnor's reaction to infringement of his property right in Leah before. Edwina would have expected that the girl would shrink away from a man who had used her so hardly, but except for one startled glance at Cain's sudden movement, Leah gave no sign of fear. Her body lay with the relaxation of perfect trust against his, and, although she dressed in trembling haste, it was plain that it was only to please him and escape the examining eyes of the other men.

The sound of the herald's trumpets calling the first "To arms" finally broke up the group. Hereford dashed for the field with a yelp of dismay, and even Leicester quickened his usually deliberate pace. As the other men moved toward the stairwell, however, the Earl of Chester touched Radnor and drew him back.

"Take my arm, Radnor. It is as good an excuse as any to walk slowly together. I hope you are fed full enough now to think a little on some other matters."

"Yes, but speak low. In truth, I would be easier if we were without the walls. Here there are ears, many and long, and equally long tongues, I fear. But if the matter needs haste, you had better tell me now. We are so well entertained that there is little chance that we may be private unless we can lose ourselves at the hunt tomorrow."

"Well, the matter is important, but the hunt—. You know, Radnor, I am inordinately fond of hunting."

Radnor set his teeth to bite back an acid retort. His marriage was not important enough to delay discussion, but a hunt was. It was also more important than state affairs, it seemed. Chester had continued speaking, however, and Radnor wrenched his attention away from his own thoughts to attend to him.

"My boy, I know your opinion on these matters, but I have more experience of statecraft than you do and I think that you must consider seriously a new method of going about things. Stephen of Blois is not an old man and is in good health. It may be many years before he dies, and if we are to wait so long for a better man to come to the throne—and the true line at that—the entire country may well be in ruins." Chester held up his hand to stop Cain from interjecting a remark. "I know, I know, you have given your oath and you will not break it. But how would it be if Stephen were to renounce the throne in favor of Henry?"

"Chester, we are talking treason. You know how unlikely such a thing is. Why should Stephen renounce the throne? Many men stand by him still. He has hopes even that he can force his son upon us. He would be mad to commit such an act, and, since we are talking treason anyway I may as well speak my mind, though he is stupid as a pigeon, he is not that mad."

"But if he were in such a position that it would be his life or the renunciation—"

"In God's name, Chester, hold your tongue! Forgive me, that is no way for me to speak to you, but I have your interest at heart when I say this. To threaten the life of the king—"

"No, no. There need be no direct threat, but if he were in such a position that he must understand—"

"Chester, Stephen is a brave man. He has no fear for his life, and well you know it. You must remember how he carried himself when the Duke of Gloucester had him in close prison. He feared nothing, and then Eustace was but a child. Now Eustace is nearly a man. Do you think that he and Maud will sit idly by and let this happen? That Maud is worth ten of her husband and her son together. She saved him from death or permanent confinement once and may do so again or, if she cannot do that, she may well set Eustace on the throne. Where would be your profit then?"

"I have thought of that already. Eustace alone we may discount. Pembroke says—"

"Pembroke! You have not broached this matter to him! You know he will run posthaste to the king with the tale. I will not hear a word more—"

"Now, Radnor, I thought you would be less set against Pembroke now that you are his son-in-law. He is weak, but I believe he will be firm in this. He suggested that Shrewsbury's wife—"

"Joan!" Lord Radnor almost shouted with exasperation. "She is worse even than her husband who is a slimy toad—"

"Radnor, be quiet. If you interrupt me every moment I can tell you nothing. Do you think I am a child not to know that these men are not to be trusted? Both will do anything for the sake of their purses, however, and there is great profit to be had out of this—either from Queen Maud or from the establishment of a young boy as king. Moreover," Chester said with a sly smile, "there can be no profit Pembroke's running to the king. All he could get out of that would be the reversion of my nephew Fitz Richard's lands—and you will not let him keep those. He knows it."

"I will let him keep them sooner than be dragged into any plot against the king," Radnor snarled.

"You are in a rage, but I know you. Besides, your part in it will be very simple. We have had what passes for peace on the Marches for several years. Pembroke has planted a few seeds here and there on Fitz Richard's land to grow into a small flower of rebellion."

Radnor turned pale. "You could not be so mad! Godfather, you could not!"

"Why not? You will hasten to the borders to keep them quiet. I will raise an army to aid my godson and tell Stephen that if he comes with me to quell the Welsh, the Marcher lords will grow to love him better than they do now. Look you, Cain, you have nothing to do but hold your tongue and do your duty in keeping the peace in Wales as you have ever done. Once I have Stephen in Wales, who knows what may happen? It might not be necessary to hold him treasonably. A Welsh arrow—a dark night—"

Cain faced Chester, taking his wrists. "Godfather, you must not do this. You do not know the Welsh as I do. A small flower of rebellion does not remain small among them. Oh God, I looked for a month or two of peace with my wife. Now I must fly to fight in Wales."

"The more fool you if you do it too soon. I tell you, Radnor, that even if you put down the rebellion it will not stop my plan. Pembroke, Shrewsbury, Hereford, and I will all swear that the tribes are still restless—which will doubtless be true even if you have beaten them into submission—and Stephen will merely think you do not want him to come to Wales and be more eager for it if you gainsay us."

"At least do not drag Hereford into this," Radnor cried in an anguished voice. "He is so fine and young. He does not understand. Oh, God, they are coming to see what has become of us. I must speak further with you, but not here or now. Tomorrow—"

"Tomorrow I hunt," Chester replied with sudden coldness, and his face set with a weak man's stubbornness. "If you cannot see how good a chance—"

"What black looks, Lord Radnor. I hope my daughter did nothing to displease you." Pembroke's eyes were hard and speculative as they slid from one face to another. Beside him Shrewsbury snickered.

Whatever Chester did, Radnor would make no admission that he knew anything about the plot being hatched. Clear of it himself, he might still be able to save the others from their own folly. "I hear from my lord Chester that he is much slighted and mistrusted. The peace between him and the king was of my father's making. I would not have urged my godfather to such an act if I had not thought it for the best for him as well as for others. Now I hear that he is ill-treated. Why should I not look black?"

"Come," Pembroke said, "this is no day for such matters. "The second call to arms has sounded. If we do not make haste, you will have no time to eat before the opening jousts."

They moved down into the hall, Radnor stopping just beyond the doorway to wash his face and hands in a basin held by a servant. He started to walk to the long tables where white bread, wine, and early fruit were laid out for a morning repast when he was hailed by Leah's excited voice from a window embrasure.

"My lord, oh, my lord, come and look."

"Coming." Cain took a flagon of wine and a large piece of bread and went to her, his eyes abstracted with worry.

"Look at the pennons! Look how the armor shines! Oh look, Cain, look at the men with trumpets at the ends of the field! What are they doing? Look! Tell me!" Leah tugged at Cain's sleeve in her excitement and the wine slopped over his hand.

"Be careful, you little goose," he snapped, and Leah recoiled, the animation dying out of her face. Cain was instantly contrite. It was not the poor child's fault that he was harassed by irresponsible men who further complicated an already bitter political situation. It was a shame to spoil her pleasure. "Nay, I did not mean that. I am troubled by matters of state, Leah. What is it that you wish to know?"

"Indeed, my lord, I will not trouble you with my questions. You have greater affairs to attend to."

"Not today, Leah. I have attended enough to things which only sour my stomach and anger me. Today is yours." As he said the words, however, he knew he would have to find time for some serious planning with Philip. A painful contraction in the region of his heart gave him warning of what that visit would cost him, and he pulled his mind back to the far pleasanter task of contemplating his wife.

Leah had turned back to the window. Her spirits were dampened and she was silent while her husband began to eat. He was looking over her head now, stirred in spite of himself by the martial proceedings. It was a thin field, mostly made up of younger men, knights errant and squires, for the great magnates were saving themselves for Stephen's great tourney later that month. It was just as well that, as bridegroom, he was excluded from fighting; it would have been like stealing from a child to take the prize from those boys, and Radnor had no need of tourney prizes either to add to his wealth or to prove his valor. Nonetheless, the feel of the twelve-foot lance—well, there was the king's tourney to look forward to. Radnor laughed silently at himself as he realized that part, at least, of his desire to get onto the field was an urge to show off his fighting form to the girl beside him. It was really very amusing because the feeling persisted even though he knew perfectly well that she would comprehend no more about what he was doing than a pet dog.

"Will we watch from here, my lord?" Leah's voice was flat and cautious.

Her husband smiled down at her, relaxed now that he had literally stated his intention of idleness. "No, we are the guests of honor. We will watch from the very center of those benches they have set up—the lodges—where the shocks will take place directly before us."

"Oh, how exciting." Color was back in Leah's cheeks and vivacity in her voice under the influence of Cain's smile. "How is it decided who will fight against whom?"

"It depends on the type of tourney. At a small one like this it is often a matter of individual challenge and arrangement. For the initial jousts, those men who wish tell the heralds their names and conditions and say they will take all comers. Then those who desire to fight them arrange through the heralds. In the king's tourney, there is a king's champion appointed—me—and he must fight all who challenge him."

"You! Ah, yes, you told us before. But why?"

Radnor's mouth grew hard. "I do not know, but no doubt I will learn."

Leah was enormously proud of the fact that her husband had been chosen to be the king's champion out of all the warriors of the kingdom, but since he did not seem overly pleased by it she held her tongue on that subject. "Look, look!" she cried next. "Why are they forming in large parties? Have we missed something? Can we go now?" The girl was dancing with impatience and her quick movements jogged Radnor's arm again. Most of the rest of his wine spilled on the floor. This time he laughed aloud. Apparently he was not to have any breakfast today.

"Yes, yes," he said, mimicking Leah's excited tone. "If you will only give me leave to put down this wine I have not drunk and swallow a bit of bread. Calm yourself, do. We have missed nothing. The men are gathering to choose sides for the melee. Do you see that there is a red banner at one end and a blue at the other? The reds will fight against the blues, thereby eliminating county or other more personal designations so that there will be less chance of hard feelings between the sides. When each side has about an equal number of men, they will come together and fight, just as in a war, only without killing each other—or trying to kill each other—I hope."

"But you spoke before of the jousts—"

"Yes, well those come first. Sometimes when there are many men to joust, the melee is fought on the following day, but here there is no need." He laughed. "Very well, come then, you wish to see, not to be told."

Just before they reached their seats, Hereford stopped them.

"I say, Radnor, I am going to joust. Keep an eye on my form, will you?"

Cain nodded. "You can certainly use the practice. Remember what I am always telling you about carrying your shield too low. You expose your head too much. And do not count so much on your quickness and your wit. There are others with quick eyes and hands also."

"I have cause enough to know," Hereford laughed. "How many times have you laid me in the dirt for all my dodging?"

"Ay, but I lay you down gently. Others may not love you so well. Leah, you have met Lord Hereford, of course, but let him take your hand again. He is one of my closest friends."

Leah curtsied, smiling. "Now I will have someone I really know to wish success for. The best of good fortune go with you, my lord."

Cain swallowed an unreasonable jealousy as Hereford kissed Leah's hand lingeringly before he left them. "I hope the boy does not get hurt," he said irritably. "He is no famous jouster, although with a sword in his hand there are few who can match him."

Harry Beaufort, a knight who had come for the jousting, found his path blocked by Leah and her husband, and felt a twinge of envy at Lord Radnor's station in life. A man only found a wife like that when he could afford to pick and choose; so pretty and so kind and gentle. She had great estates, for Pembroke's daughter must, but knights errant did not look at pretty girls with great estates. The herald's trumpets blared out the notes that called for the beginning of combat. Sir Harry ran off toward his end of the lists and Lord and Lady Radnor quickened their steps toward their seats.

The first two jousters rode into position. Their names were called, both signaled readiness, set spurs to their horses, and came together with an ear-splitting crash. Leah squealed with excitement and clutched Cain's arm. With unconscious tension he pressed her hand against his side, and Leah could feel the heavy pounding of his heart through tunic and gown. This distracted her from the combatants, who were both slowly picking themselves up while esquires of the field caught their horses and led them back, and she looked attentively at her husband. His breath was coming rather quickly, and a fanatical light gave red glimmers to the dark brown eyes. When the next course was run, Leah, attending now to him rather than the joust, could feel Cain's muscles responding to the gait of the horses, could see his shoulders brace and twitch as the lances met.

"Look, Cain, there is Lord Hereford. He is next. Oh, I wish him well, indeed I do."

"Then sit down and do not distract his attention. You are more like to get him killed than to bring him good fortune by leaping to your feet and calling his name."

Again a slight uneasiness swept over Radnor although it disappeared almost instantaneously as he saw Hereford go into action. He swelled with the pride of vicarious accomplishment as he watched his pupil's perfect form and he offered no criticism when Leah leapt to her feet again with a pleased cry as Hereford kept his seat and sent his opponent flying over the horse's croup.

Six more courses were run. Leah subsided from the fever of excitement into a calmer enjoyment. At the seventh run, however, an improperly held shield and old, worn harness concerted to cause a common enough accident. The dull jousting lance, driven by the full force of two heavy horses' gallops, pierced and ripped open one rider. Bowels and blood spilled over the saddle; the knight screamed and fell; attendants rushed forward to see what could be done.

Radnor winced instinctively but showed no other reaction; indeed he had none, for these things always happened at tourneys. That was what lent the sport its charm. Leah, however, turned deathly pale. It was her husband's form she saw toppling from the horse, dead in a few hours if not dead already. The strength that held her upright in her seat voiceless and motionless came to her without volition. The course was cleared and the eighth, ninth, and tenth jousts took place before the mist which obscured her vision cleared; Radnor, completely absorbed in the sport, noticed nothing.

"There now," Cain said, turning to Leah and pointing, "that man with the shield barred *gules et or* will be Hereford's only real competition. His seat is excellent and his technique beautiful. It will depend on the eagerness of the jouster and the strength of the horse. See, it is as I said, he has unhorsed his opponent. He carries his shield inward a little, though. If Hereford hits him slightly on the far side to his body, the point may hold."

"Will Lord Hereford notice that too, my lord?" With immense effort Leah's voice was steady and her expression one of quiet interest.

"I hope so. He deserves a fall if he does not notice, for I have told him often enough that he must take account of every quirk of behavior no matter how small or insignificant."

The event took place just as Radnor predicted when Hereford and Sir Harry Beaufort were the only two remaining jousters. The first shock was inconclusive, both lances shattering on impact; the second shattered Sir Harry's lance, Hereford missing his point so that his weapon slid harmlessly off the slightly concave shield. For the third and last encounter, Sir Harry determined to try the difficult and dangerous helmet point; if he hit, his opponent would certainly be unhorsed and might very likely be killed. It went a little against the grain, but Sir Harry was desperate.

He was a knight errant, a younger son of a minor baron who could give him nothing except a good training in the use of arms, good armor, a good horse, a little money, and his best wishes. From then on the young man was on his own. He had only three choices for keeping alive: he could, if he was fortunate, take service with one of the great lords of the land; he could travel from tournament to tournament living on the ransom money and prizes collected from each opponent unhorsed in the jousts or downed in the melee;

he could turn robber, and prey on travelers or on the poor. He had found no great lord to favor him, and he had been unlucky of late. The last two tourneys had been similar to this one—he had ridden successfully to the last fall and then been unhorsed himself. Unfortunately his opponents had not been generous and had taken from him all that he won in previous jousts. He was tired; he wanted to go home for a while, but not penniless as a beggar and he had not yet sunk so low as to steal. It sat ill with him to try to kill so good a jouster, but he had no choice; he could not take the chance of a fall or a draw with the decision against him.

Radnor saw the slightly raised lance point and grew rigid. He could hardly prevent himself from calling a warning although he knew nothing could be more dangerous than to distract Hereford's attention. He had scarcely time to pray that Hereford too would see the aim of the lance before the run was completed. All over. Radnor's work had been well done, and Sir Harry was rolling himself painfully to his knees as Hereford turned his tired horse back to the judges' benches to make a final salute.

Radnor rose and walked as quickly as was possible for him toward Sir Harry who was dejectedly about to mount the horse that had been returned to him.

"Sir—I did not catch your name—wait. I would have a word with you."

"Yes?"

"What is your name and condition?"

Ordinarily Sir Harry would have questioned a stranger's right to demand such information, but he knew Radnor by reputation. "Sir Harry Beaufort, youngest brother of Miles Beaufort of Warwickshire."

"Did you mean to kill Lord Hereford in that last encounter?" Radnor continued.

Sir Harry looked into the dark angry face above him and answered with the courage of despair. "Yes."

"Why?"

"Because it is very likely that I will not have the ransom which will be asked of me."

"Oh." Lord Radnor was deflated. There was no plot against Hereford as he had feared. He had never had need for money himself, being as his mother's heir rich from birth, but he had come often enough into contact with knights errant at tournaments to understand their dire need. "Well, in that case—" he hesitated, somewhat at a loss while Sir Harry took off his helm and pushed back his mail hood. The face that looked into his was engaging, plain and freckled with sandy hair and blue eyes, hard now with anxiety. Radnor touched his scarred mouth as he often did when making a decision. "Let that not worry you, Sir Harry. You are a brave jouster. I will make good the ransom. Are you a good man in the melee also?"

For a stunned moment Harry Beaufort could not answer and leaned against his horse studying the severe countenance before him. "Tolerably good, my lord," he said finally.

"Well, do your best so that I may judge your worth. Come to me—hell and damnation, when will I find time? The best I can tell you is to come, if you are whole when this is over, to the great hall and stand within my sight and wait. When I am free, I will speak with you. There is always a need for strong fighters in my household. If you are looking for a place, perhaps we may suit each other."

Lord Radnor turned away and limped back toward his wife without waiting to be thanked. He did not ordinarily employ men with knighthood status, but it would be necessary now to form a household guard for Leah. Giles would be perfect, but in truth Radnor could not spare Giles, who was like an extension of himself. Of his other men, none had the habit of easy intercourse with gentlewomen. Sir Harry might do very will if after a period of personal service he appeared trustworthy.

At first Leah was more thrilled than her husband by the noise and rush of the afternoon's melee. In the beginning the fighting was good-humored enough, but this stage could not last and soon tempers rose. After a little more than an hour, as the odor of blood and dust became more and more overpowering, Leah found her excitement waning and her fear rising again. Every man who fell or cried out was her husband, and only the visual and aural evidence of his complete enjoyment of the sport kept her from bursting into tears and running away. Radnor was having a wonderful time. The harder the fighting grew, the higher his spirits rose. He spent at least half the time on his feet shouting advice, comment, and appreciation at the top of his lungs.

"My lady looks a little pale and tired." A silken male voice in Leah's ear startled her out of one more fearful dream, and she turned gladly to answer.

"It is so noisy and the—I am not used to so much excitement."

William of Gloucester leaned intimately nearer. "Some women love this, some men also. Lord Radnor never seems to grow tired of fighting; it is his greatest passion. You, I can see, are all womanly compassion. I can sympathize with you deeply for I too grow nauseated by so much useless bloodshed. My father, however, is like your husband and I have witnessed thousands of such spectacles."

"I am sure it is all very interesting," Leah said, firing up in Cain's defense, "only I do not perfectly understand what is happening and I am rather tired because—"

"You do not need to explain," William replied, possessing himself of her hand and patting it gently. "Radnor is a great man, but he has spent all his life in battle. I am sure he was rough with you, poor child."

Leah's face flamed and she snatched back her hand. The idea that she would discuss such a matter or complain of her husband to another man was utterly revolting to her. Lord William, wise in the ways of women, saw that he had trod amiss and began again.

"Tomorrow will be a quieter day for you, unless Lord Radnor insists that you hunt too."

Leah had averted her face, but this was an unexceptionable subject and anything was better than attending to the fighting and having her imagination torture her. "I do love the hunt," she confessed, "but I fear I am not up to the riding that will be done tomorrow. My mother has plans for the entertainment of the ladies who do not hunt also; I believe she counts upon my presence. Of course," she added hastily, not wishing Lord William to think that she placed her mother's commands above her husband's, "if my lord desires that I go, I will attend him."

"Spoken like a good wife," William said blandly, "but you need not exhaust yourself to satisfy Radnor's whim. Remember that his strength is greater than yours and if he asks for more than you can perform it is merely lack of understanding on his part, not deliberate unkindness."

The murmur of voices had slowly penetrated Radnor's concentration. He turned quickly, masking the hard, angry look on his face in a flash. "Sorry, William, I was enjoying the spectacle so much I did not notice you. Did you want me?"

"Not really. I saw that your lady was looking a little wary, and I thought I would entertain her in a less violent way for a while." There was a warning in William's voice.

Radnor looked at Leah anxiously. Certainly now that William of Gloucester had drawn his attention to it, he could see that her face was tired and seemed almost translucent with pallor. Leah herself, however, energetically disclaimed fatigue.

"I am not at all tired," she said, casting a reproachful glance at Lord William which shocked him because he totally misunderstood it. "I am only a little frightened by the noise and the violence and by not understanding what is taking place."

"Shall I take you back?"

"And spoil your pleasure, my lord? Certainly not. I am perfectly content to be here."

Lord William had risen and taken Leah's hand to kiss. He bowed his farewell and left without further words, but he was deeply concerned. That look Leah had given him was an indication that she did not wish to speak to him when her husband was attending. A most unhealthy indication in so fair-speaking and so newly married a lady. If Leah was so soon looking abroad for amusement, she might seek it in the wrong places at court. William's decision, made in a moment, cost him no pain; he had certain loyalties, but sexual loyalty was not among them, and although he trusted Lord Radnor, he did not like him. If Radnor's wife desired amusement, William would provide it for her, discreetly, safely, and with great pleasure. Lord Radnor, that mighty warrior, would be cuckolded before he was a month married—and none the wiser.

Innocently enough, Leah had not the faintest notion of the thoughts passing through the mind of the handsome man who had shown her such flattering attention. She could not help being pleased on the whole, although she was at the moment very much annoyed by Lord William's stupidity in bringing her uneasiness to her husband's attention. It took her ten minutes to convince Cain that she was happy to remain where she was and that she was not tired. Even then she could not relax and close her eyes because he would break off watching the fighting to look at her with a worried frown. When he did lead her back to the castle, directly after the trumpets sounded retreat, he took her to the room which had been given over to them for their short stay at Eardisley.

"I care not what you say, Leah, you are tired. You are as white as my shirt. Stay here and allow no one to trouble you. Lie down and rest. Where are your women? Shall I send someone to call them?"

"Oh no. Truly, I am well if a little tired."

"I must go out." His eyes shadowed over with the thought of what was coming. "Yet I do not like to leave you alone."

Leah's lips twitched. What did he think would happen to her in that room? "So please you, my lord, if you cannot stay, I desire no other company. I will be glad of a little time to myself."

"You are sure?" She nodded. Cain looked at her with knitted brows; he was not accustomed to such accommodating women. "Permit no one in here except your maids, if you want them."

"Yes, my lord."

"Let me see you lie down, and I will leave you in peace."

Obediently, Leah removed her shoes and lay down on the bed. Her husband took half a step toward her, smiled uncertainly, sighed, and went out. Leah closed her eyes and relaxed.

CHAPTER 8

For all her frail looks, Leah was actually about as delicate as one of her father's field oxen. Twenty minutes after Lord Radnor left she was up, completely refreshed. What she had wanted all along was a chance to get at Cain's clothing, of which she was desperately ashamed, and she now attacked with enthusiasm the load of baggage the Duke of Gaunt had brought with him which had been placed in their room. All of the garments were removed and examined and clucked over with frowns and headshakings. In her opinion every article Cain owned would have to be torn apart and resewn properly as well as trimmed and embroidered.

Radnor returned to find his wife on her knees amid a welter of clothing. He had just passed several of the most harrowing hours of his life. Philip of Gloucester had been in particularly bad condition, and his struggles to concentrate and communicate were horrible to witness. The litter in the room tore at Cain's jangled nerves and the suspicion that Leah had torn apart his baggage looking for jewels or money—it had happened to him in the past—brought a swift and violent reaction.

"What are you doing with my things?" Cain bellowed.

Leah whirled to face him. She opened her mouth to explain, but the impact of his appearance brought entirely different words. "Oh my God, what has happened? What is wrong?"

"Nothing," Radnor said bitterly. "Nothing is wrong. Is not God in His heaven? Does not that make all right with the world?"

A fit of trembling seized him. Leah stood frozen. What should she do? Would it be better to ignore what she saw and explain what she was doing? Dared she ask again what his trouble was and try to soothe him? Very slowly Leah approached her husband; his lips drew back from his teeth in a feral snarl. Leah stopped and clasped her hands before her in an attitude of prayer.

"Will you not sit down, my lord?" she asked in a trembling voice. "Will you not tell me how I have offended you so that I may try to amend it?"

But Leah knew she had done nothing wrong; she recognized the expression of impotent rage on her husband's face. It was the same expression her father wore when something he could not control went wrong, and it ordinarily preceded his most dreadful excesses of cruelty. To her amazement, for Leah had already braced herself in terrified expectation of a brutal beating, Cain covered his face with his hands for a moment and then looked blindly around the room as if he had never seen it before. He looked so stunned and confused that Leah took a good grip on her courage and approached him again.

"I pray you, sit down."

Cain allowed himself to be led to a chair and sat. Leah knelt before him and took his hands in hers. For a long time she said nothing; her knees began to ache on the hard stone floor and she moved almost imperceptibly trying to ease them. Radnor sighed heavily and focused his eyes which had been staring into space.

"What were you doing, Leah?" he asked quietly. If she was greedy, he had better know it.

"Sorting your clothes, my lord, so that I could tell what must be done to them and what more you will need." He looked puzzled. "The other men," she explained gently, "are dressed much differently. The cloth of your garments is so fine, it would be a shame upon me if it were not made as well and bedecked as well as theirs."

"I see. I thought—never mind." If the idea of money had not entered her head, he would not put it there.

"You are wringing wet. Let me bring you water to wash with and fresh clothing."

"Very well." Leah released Cain's hands and prepared to rise, but he suddenly pulled her back. "No. Stay with me just now."

There was another silence, short this time. Cain lifted Leah to his knees and pulled her close against him. There was nothing sexual about his desire for her now, only the desperate need to feel the warmth of her healthy, living body against his after the hours of contact with Philip's dying flesh. Leah put her cheek against her husband's neck. She could feel the quick pulse of his blood, a little uneven still. Not like my father, she thought, he is not like my father. He did not hurt me although he was mad with rage. He spoke the truth; I need not fear his frown. Her hand stole up from her lap to caress his cheek, to feel gently for his eyes and press them closed, to pull his head so that it rested against hers.

"My lord, I have been looking—oh, I beg your pardon." Edwina had come with an urgent message directed to Radnor's attention, but Leah's attire, her position in Radnor's lap, the mussed bed, all led to one conclusion. Edwina was

108

embarrassed by her intrusion and prepared to back out of the room.

"Come in, madam, I pray you." Radnor read her expression quite right and his face was suddenly ruddy with the rush of his blood. "Did you want me, or your daughter, or both?"

"I have a message for you, my lord. A courier from your estates, I believe." Edwina stared as she handed the scroll of parchment to him, but not at Radnor. Leah had to be pushed to make her get off his lap! Not only had the girl seemed perfectly content to continue as she was, but now she had moved behind his chair and was lifting his hair, still wet with perspiration, off his forehead.

Radnor for his part seemed neither angry nor impatient at Leah's fussing over him. He had broken the seal of the letter and started to read, but he reached up with his free hand to stroke his wife's arm. Edwina watched them with bitterness. She had not been prepared for the pain of losing her daughter so completely. She had been so sure that her own daughter could not be like the coarse maidservants and "enjoy love," that she had not feared that Leah would truly mourn her husband.

"When you have time, Leah, I would like a few words with you." Edwina could not keep the coldness from her voice.

Cain had finished reading and was staring straight ahead with a totally expressionless face. At Leah's gentle touch, however, he twisted to look at her. She repeated her mother's request and Edwina's lips tightened. Cain nodded. Permission received, Leah turned to her mother.

"Very well," she said softly, "I will come straightaway." Instead of following Edwina when she left, however, Leah shook her head gently. "I wonder what makes my mother so strange? Well, it is no great matter. Come, dear lord, let me bring you washing water and fresh clothes."

"Never mind that," Cain snapped. "Send a servant for the water and just lay out what you want me to wear. I am accustomed to caring for myself."

"I know, my lord." Leah, still behind Radnor's chair, pressed his head back until it rested against her breast. "But now it is not fitting. I am here only to serve you."

Radnor closed his eyes. After what he had just read, how could he believe in Pembroke's daughter? The seeds had been sown, not in Fitz Richard's land but in his own, and already they were full-grown and bearing fruit. It was so sweet to lie thus. Her arms were sweet, her lips, her eyes so innocent. Surely Philip must be wrong. Pembroke was involved in something, yes, but Cain could not bear to think the girl knew anything of it. He lifted his head finally and squared his shoulders.

"It is nearly time for the evening meal, Leah. You had better go to your mother." He twisted around to face her, smiling faintly. "My trouble has passed," he lied. "You may go."

"Yes, my lord, I will. After I have seen to your needs."

Shortly after the servants removed the broken meats from the groaning tables, Radnor crossed the hall to seek out a quiet spot. His castellan at Penybont, Owen of Wells, had written to say that the tribes of Rhayader on the border of his holding were restless. If Rhayader rose, that rebellion might easily spread east and set the whole land on fire. No doubt Pembroke and Chester did not believe this to be true, but they had not spent their lives fighting the Welsh. Blank-faced and blank-eyed, Cain fought his battle with desire. No matter how much he wanted to ignore Owen's warning, he could not do it. He would have to leave his own wedding feast and attend to the Welsh. They had done it deliberately, Cain realized, stopping stock-still in his pain. Pembroke and Chester, his father-in-law and his godfather, had chosen this moment because they believed he would not leave his new-wed wife and his wedding guests to go to war.

The price of Radnor's abstraction was that he was snatched by Hereford into the wild romp of "Hoodman Blind" because rough games had taken the place of eating and drinking for amusement. Cain might well have refused to play because romping hurt his crippled foot, but his bitter decision had been made and he wanted relief. Moreover, Leah was already engaged in the game. Forgotten were her womanly dignity, her new cares and joys. Skirts lifted to show very pretty ankles, braids flying, she was shrieking with laughter, running and jumping like a ten-year-old. Cain was enchanted. He was so enchanted that he forgot to duck and was caught by the hoodman whose vision was obscured by having part of his tunic drawn forward over his face. Now the hoodman needed only to guess whom he had caught, and the victim became in turn the hoodman blind. Guessing in Radnor's case was no feat at all. His size and facial scarring were distinctive. Moments later, he himself was blinded and groping about for a victim. He heard Hereford laughing and protesting.

"No, no, Lady Radnor, you must stand well back. There are parts of you his lordship knows entirely too well, and you have a look in your eye that bodes the sport no good. You will let him catch you out of sympathy."

Radnor swung his blinded head about, listening. His ears were well trained, but the hall was so noisy they did him little good. His step was too slow; he could only depend upon his immense reach and the lightning-swift hand action that years under arms had given him.

Someone was very close—a woman, by the suppressed titter that he heard. Just as he lunged, a ravishing scent that was horribly familiar assailed him, but his physical action was quicker than his mental recoil. His hand had fallen on a shoulder and breast all too well known; he had Joan of Shrewsbury. She pushed him, very lightly and obviously with no intent to free herself, for she had no objection at all to the rude handling that was customary when a man seized a woman. It was all Radnor needed, though. For the first and only time in his life, he thanked God for his lameness and stumbled. His hand, which could easily have held her, fell away. He spun about and began to grope in the wrong direction to a chorus of howling laughter, but it was better to be a fool than a dupe.

He would have liked to catch Leah. To run his hands over her under the eyes of a room full of people would lend spice to what was his, but he could hear by a confused murmur that she was being kept out of his way. The rushes rustled softly and gave another victim to him. Radnor threw his arms wide and grappled like a bear before the person who was near could land a blow or trip him up, a customary proceeding in that rough game. The push he received this time was not at all gentle and rocked him on his heels, sending a searing pain up his left leg, but now he laughed and held on because he could feel the short-cropped hair of a man under his chin.

"Hereford," he chortled, knowing the slight form with the strength of a wild horse.

When he was freed of his hood, he stood watching for a while longer well out of reach. Hereford caught Elizabeth, Chester's eldest daughter, not entirely by chance. He felt her hair and face and shook his head sadly; he slid his hand over her hip and thigh murmuring, but loudly enough for all to hear, that those parts were not familiar

111

to him. Then he gripped her about the waist so that she could not wrench herself free and felt her breasts.

"No," he said, "I have never touched these before."

The crowd roared appreciation and ribald jests. Radnor looked down, tensed to move away, as someone nestled to his side, and then relaxed when he saw Leah. They watched together as Hereford lifted Elizabeth's face and kissed her lingeringly on the lips.

"Ah—Elizabeth Chester," he cried, "with the sweetest lips this side of heaven."

Cain smiled down at his laughing, pink-cheeked wife. "Do not let them catch you, or they will make that pretty white face as red as a beet." He tweaked a braid, treating her like the child she still partially was. "Have a good time. This sport is too rough for me."

Later, when they were in bed, Leah held him off gently with one hand. "Cain, why does the Countess of Shrewsbury interest herself so greatly in her husband's affairs when she cares nothing for him?"

"What?"

"Have I said something wrong, my lord? She makes no secret of it, so I thought it no harm to ask." This, thought Leah, needled into action by the obvious byplay between her husband and Joan of Shrewsbury, was going to put a fine light on Joan's character. Maybe Cain would think twice about having ado with such a blabbermouth.

"What do you mean, she makes no secret of it?"

Leah looked a little apprehensive, an emotion she did not feel just then. "Well, I do not know if it be fit—she spoke as a woman among women and I think to me—because I was a young bride—perhaps she thought I needed to be warned that men are sometimes harsh because she knew nothing of my father. She told me—private matters."

"About Shrewsbury? About me?"

"A little about each, but that was not what she really wished to speak about. It seemed to me that she wished to know if you had told me aught of your plans."

"Ohhhh. And what gave you such a thought?"

"Because she asked me in passing, as if it were a matter of no moment, about your affairs."

"And what did you reply?" Cain was startled by the intelligence in his wife's eyes.

"That I knew nothing. Which was true, but I would have said the same in any case. Your affairs are no

112

business of hers. It could be that she did not speak the truth about—about the matters of her bed and only wished to draw my confidence because it was my first time and she thought—like my mother—that I would be angry because you hurt me. I would swear though that it was truth and that though she loathes him, she would have run posthaste to him with anything I told her. Mayhap I do her an unjustice, my lord, and she was only a little talkative because of the wine."

Cain was watching openmouthed and made no reply, so Leah continued after a little pause. "I almost thought that she wished to make trouble between us—but that could not be so. It must be that she wishes to know where you will next move for Shrewsbury's sake. Therefore, I should have something to tell her, my lord."

"Tell her! What would you tell her?"

"Anything you wished me to say, but I would not say that you had given permission. I would say that I heard you speak of these things with my father and yours."

Pembroke's daughter, born a liar and a cheat! "Even so," Cain said coldly, "why should Lady Shrewsbury, or any other person, believe you?"

"My lord, I do not say she will believe, but indeed she may. In any case she will talk and much can be learned from lies. And, if I am skillful in reply, hesitating as if the confidence was drawn from me unaware—have I spoken amiss, my lord?"

"My God, I would never have believed it. I have read it, but I could not credit—"

"What? How have I erred?"

Cain laughed a short bitter laugh. "Not even Pembroke could have taught you so much. I believe you have spoken the truth of your heart, if there is truth in the heart of a woman. But fifteen years old, and wise as the serpent—and as evil."

"Evil!"

"Ay, they say women are born with the knowledge of evil in their bodies, and that they save this to give their daughters to use as a weapon against men. The men children they bring strong, but unknowing, into the world. Man must learn evil—to his bitter cost—mostly from women, but sometimes from other men who have learned. Have you learned this from your father to use against me?"

Leah cried out in protest against this injustice. "But it

113

was for you, my lord. For myself I care nothing about such matters. You said before you left when we were betrothed that I should listen in the women's quarters, and I have thought much over every word you said to me—"

"So Eve spoke when she bade Adam eat the apple of sin—for you, my lord, for you. Nay, Leah, do no weep. It is no fault in you that you are as God made you."

He took her ito his arms, knowing that he should try to impress upon her the idea that her father was no good guide to follow, knowing that he should tell her that he was leaving in the morning to put down the rebellion that her father had started in Wales. While he was seeking for words, her appearance warmed his blood. She must be ignorant of Pembroke's tainted plans and in a way innocent too, he thought. She would not show the turnings of her mind if she wished to use them against him. He leaned over and, with his lips, touched her breast where it began to swell near the armpit; he breathed her light lavender scent.

Leah lay staring into the unsnuffed candles and thinking that it had been easier this time. The trouble was that now Cain was through with her she found herself wakeful and tense. She wanted something more of him. Cain had turned onto his side, away from her, as was his custom, and Leah touched him gently. He shrugged his shoulders impatiently.

"Are you asleep, Cain?"

"How can a man sleep when you hiss in his ear. Let me be!" Leah moved away at once, but she felt alone and sad and began to weep softly. "Curse you woman, what ails you? If I hurt you, I could not help it. It will grow easier for you in time."

Leah buried her face in the pillow to smother her sobs. After a while she stopped crying and lay listening to Radnor's even breathing, broken every so often by a low moan. She could see the moonlight shift on the floor.

"Leah." It was spoken so low it could not have wakened her if she slept.

"Yes, my lord?" Cain did not answer at once, and Leah felt him shift his position in the bed. "What is it?" she asked anxiously. "Is there something wrong?"

"No." He sounded hesitant, and, weakly putting off the moment of revelation, said, "I am hungry."

Leah sat up and began to feel for her shoes. "I will fetch something for you. I pray you, do not be impatient, it will take me time to find the way with all the sleepers in the passage."

By the time Leah returned, Cain had found flint and tinder and had lighted some new candles to replace those which had burned out. He was sitting up, a robe thrown over his bare shoulders, and when Leah entered he pulled the bedclothes so that they covered his feet. Leah hesitated infinitesimally, her throat closing with fear. Was one leg shaggier than the other? Could that dark, rounded shadow glimpsed for an instant be a horn hoof? A half-frown brought her hurriedly to the bed. He was already cross with her; if she showed fear or consciousness of what he was hiding, the worst might befall her at once.

"I could not find a goblet in the dark, but if this does not please you, there are other meats."

The trembling voice made Cain more ashamed of his earlier severity. "Anything will do," he said gently.

Leah slipped off her gown and lay down again, the kindness of his tone already soothing her terror. Radnor began to eat slowly, cracking the bones of a wing. He turned his body to glance at Leah sidelong; her face had no particular expression, but her eyelids were still a little reddened.

"I thank you," he said even more softly. "You are very kind."

"It was nothing."

Cain found his mouthful unaccountably hard to swallow. "I am sorry if I was sharp. To trouble a man with talk after he has made love is no wise thing. That is a time for sleeping."

So that was why he was angry! The logical explanation lifted Leah's spirits. "If you do not correct me, my lord, I cannot know. I will not do so again."

"You are a good girl, Leah, and most obedient to me. I wish—. I have news for you, and not good news. I must go into Wales again." Surprisingly she made no answer, and new doubts tore at Cain. "Your father has aroused my own men against me," he added softly, wanting to hurt her, wanting to see her fear.

It was apparent even in the candlelight that she had paled. "Is that true, my lord?"

"Is it like that I would tell such a lie?" Would she deny complicity in her father's schemes or beg him not to go?

Leah lay mute, paralyzed. She did not dare speak out against her father. If she had no loyalty to her father, her

115

husband would think she could have no loyalty to any man. Cain could not know how cruel Pembroke was to her, and even if he knew, he would not accept that as an excuse for disloyalty. Cain himself would expect his wife to be loyal even if he were cruel to her. Tears stung Leah's eyes, but she forced them back. She did not even dare cling to Cain and beg him not to leave her. He had told her that her tears unmanned him; her mother had told her that clinging to a man disgusted him.

"You do not seem to care," Cain said in a deceptively gentle voice.

"I—I hope it is some mistake," Leah faltered, "but you know all things best and you must do what is right."

"And what will you do when I am gone?"

Leah could master her sobs, but now the tears could be held back no longer. "I will do as you bid me do, my lord."

"Even if I bid you go to Painscastle alone and bide my coming there?"

She had been staring straight ahead, but now she faced him, the tears drying on her cheeks. "Yes, my lord. Oh yes. Even if you bid me come with you to Wales. I would come gladly."

Life had come back into her voice. Cain bit his lip in an agony of indecision. She sounded as if she cared nothing for him in one moment, yet in the next she wept and offered to endure the miseries of camp and dangers of war to be with him. It could be that Philip was right, that Pembroke had told Leah to stay with her husband at all times and bind him to her will.

"I cannot take a woman to battle with me. I must leave at dawn tomorrow. You could not be ready and, even if you could, the forests of Wales are no place for a frail girl."

"You will not leave me here, my lord! Pray, pray, do not!"

"No," Cain said coldly. "If I have not returned before my father leaves this place, he will take you with him and set you safe at Painscastle so that you may begin your work as a wife."

Now would come the flood of tears, the hysterical protests. Leah must know she could be no use to her father shut up in Painscastle alone. But there was no protest. Leah merely sighed as if some weight of fear had been taken from her. Perhaps she was not false; perhaps she was only afraid of Pembroke and wished to be out of his power. It was a comforting thought, and Cain clung to it. That thought made it possible for him to return warmly her farewell embraces in the dawn and to reply encouragingly to her trembling pleas that he care well for himself. He would try to believe her innocent until she proved she was Pembroke's ally or dupe.

Lord Radnor pulled at the lacings of his mail hood. He wished that he were lying with his head in Leah's lap, and his eyes had started to cloud when a peculiar sound snapped his mind into the present. An owl was calling. An owl? At midmorning? Cain pulled his horse to the side and motioned the men following him to proceed. The troop continued past him until Giles was in sight. Directly in front of the master-of-arms, where he could watch them, rode two men who were dressed in ragged clothing and completely unarmed. Radnor pulled his horse into line just in front of them and, as soon as he came to a slightly open stretch, gestured them forward. He addressed them in Welsh because they spoke no French or English.

"Bring me the man who hooted like an owl, and the partner to whom he cried. Do not lose yourselves. Remember that your wives and children are hostage to me. If there are more than those two in the wood, I wish to know it."

Pwyll and Cei slipped from their horses which were only moving at a slow walk because the troop in front had reached a section of heavy undergrowth. They did not even trouble to look their hate at Radnor because he would not care. All he cared about was that they would follow his orders faithfully, and that they would surely do, for Lord Radnor had proved in the past that he could be perfectly merciless to hostages. Pwyll handed a lead rein to the trooper ahead of him and Cei attached his lead rein to the saddle loop of the preceding horse. Then they moved quietly into the underbrush, the sounds of their passing completely concealed by the heavy tread of the horses. Lord Radnor had fallen back further now and, first pointing to his ear, motioned Giles ahead to lead the men. Usually the Welsh attacked from the rear, trying to pick off a man at a time or to throw the entire group into confusion, but sometimes they would make a direct frontal attack and Radnor wanted a responsible man at the head of the column.

Cain pulled his helmet around from his back where it hung from a thong, and put it on, pulling down the strip of mail that made a double shield for his neck over the mail hood. In spite of this protection, the hair on his nape prickled and his breath came a little short. He knew perfectly well that the situation was not good; his men were forced by the vegetation to travel in single file which left them singularly open to attack. What would be best was to look for open ground and form into a defensive position, but what if there were none but the watcher and the man to whom the signal was given? How foolish they would look, and what a tale to be carried to the Welsh encampments—that the Marcher lords were frightened of one Welshman or even less, an owl's hoot. Besides, Radnor could feel his fingers itch to grip the hilt of his sword. He almost willed the flight of that first arrow which would signal the beginning of the fight.

There was, however, no flight of arrows, and Radnor Castle was reached without further incident. In view of what had occurred in the forest, Lord Radnor stopped at the castle; they had nothing to tell—there were rumors, the people were restless, but when was it not so? Sir Robert, the castellan, said that Owen of Wells was a young fool and afraid of his own shadow. Lord Radnor blandly agreed with Sir Robert and, saying he wished to empty his bladder, called Giles aside.

"Choose now a faithful man and send him posthaste to my father. One message he will carry in his purse, another in his head. For his head, he is to tell my father to come to Radnor Keep without delay. If men are available, he should bring them, otherwise his own guard will be sufficient, I believe, but haste is most necessary."

Giles nodded. "Something is rotten at the top of this heap of rock. The bottom is sound enough. I have been idly talking here and there, and I warrant my ears that the men know nothing. Do we stay until the duke comes, or go, my lord?"

"We must go to Owen at Penybont. He is not a man to call me from my own wedding lightly. Also, send Cedric and someone else out to watch and stop the Welshmen. It will be better to question them away from here because doubtless the trapped birds will not sing well if Sir Robert be their trainer. I do not like it any way it is turned, for once out of the gates who knows whether we will come in so easily again?"

Giles turned his head and spat; Radnor shrugged in agreement. He felt slightly sick at what he had discovered because he would have sworn, until that day, that the men who governed the Gaunt strongholds would be faithful. What could have been offered the castellan of Radnor to make him plot treason was a puzzle; if he was fortunate, Cain thought, he would soon know, and if he was not, he would care nothing about any earthly matter. He paused on his way to the hall, repressing a faint qualm. Whatever he had expected, rebellion in his own keeps was a complete surprise to him. Possibly he was not meant to return; possibly he was accursed, as his father had told him when he was a child, and the Gaunt line would end with him.

With a slight bitter laugh, Lord Radnor shook off both qualm and anxiety. He strode purposefully into the hall and ordered that men and horses be fed and a meal prepared early for himself. He queried Sir Robert about supplies and made a note of what was needed. Innocently, he told the castellan that he was sending a man to arrange that the supplies be forwarded and that his father had been warned to expect a messenger the following day. Displaying open indifference to Sir Robert's seeing what he did, Cain wrote the letter in the hall with materials supplied by the castle scribe. As he poured the hot wax and pressed his seal into it, he added fretfully that in these disturbed times his work was doubled because his father would accept as genuine no message except one in his own hand. Finally he sat down to eat and drink, apparently quite relaxed and ready to make small talk about his marriage. He spoke of the youth of his bride, regretting that Lady Robert was so far removed from Painscastle that it would be impossible for her to advise and help his Leah. There was no awareness of tension in his eyes as he watched Sir Robert playing nervously with the poniard which hung around his neck. He even commented softly on the beauty of the worked gold chain while the thought crossed his mind that one way or another it would very soon be his.

Giles came in shortly to say that the men were ready and the horses rested. Lord Radnor nodded and rose to his feet with a sigh. He thanked the castellan and his wife for their hospitality.

"It seems that I never become comfortable but I must leave that place forthwith. Well, well, such is my life. Since there seems no need, I should not be back for a

119

month or more, perhaps not at all. If my father passes this way because he must go to Shrewsbury, he may stay a night. Please be so kind as to entertain him and take the cost from my share of the manor yield. I expect to be at Penybont for a day or two to calm Owen, so if you hear anything of interest or need me, a rider may find me there."

Sir Robert saw them down to their horses and wished them Godspeed politely enough. He hoped his relief did not show in his face. Curse Pembroke for not holding Lord Radnor as he said he would until Penybont had been taken and Lord Radnor could be entrapped. Now he would have to accept Gaunt's visit too because he really would need the supplies the duke would bring. Young fool, he thought, arrogant young fool, talking and talking in that soft voice of his instead of questioning and listening. Had he guessed, he might have saved his own neck. He laughed, but the laugh turned sour. Gaunt would not be so easy to fool.

There was a bitter taste in Sir Robert's mouth. He had been an honorable man all his life, faithful to his trust, and first Gaunt and then Lord Radnor, when he came of age, had been good masters. Now he was getting old, his fighting days were nearing their end, and he knew that Lord Radnor did not like his son and would not promise to pass the possession of the keep into his hands. Perhaps his son was not perfect, but if he did not become castellan of Radnor Keep, there would be no provision at all for his own old age. Pembroke had promised Sir Robert that when Lord Radnor was dead he could hold the keep and its demesne lands as a true vassal. Then his son would inherit the keep by right; no man could put him off the land. Sir Robert watched the column of men as they were gradually hidden by trees at a bend in the track. He wanted Radnor Keep more than he wanted his life, but it was bitter to purchase it at the price of dishonor.

About one quarter of a mile past the bend in the road where trees shielded the view from the castle, Lord Radnor halted his troop again. He beckoned Harry Beaufort to follow and the two men made for the edge of the woods. Here five others waited their coming: Pwyll and Cei, who had been ordered to catch the caller in the forest; Cedric and Odo, who had been detailed to stop the Welshmen short of the castle; and one who was called a man only by courtesy, being in truth no more than a boy.

120

Cain dismounted with his usual grimace of pain, but his expression was completely indifferent when he turned to his men.

"Where is the other?"

Pwyll shook his head. "We could not find him. There were signs, but they ended in a false trail."

Lord Radnor's expression did not change, but something behind his eyes did. Even Odo, who did not know his master well and had never seen him close up in a cold rage, was frightened. Cedric hissed gently between his teeth; he had been long in Lord Radnor's service and could see what was coming, even if he could not understand what had been said.

"A tracker who cannot see has blind children, Pwyll, and a tracker who cannot track has no need of feet, Cei." The men gazed back at him gray-faced, but they did not plead for mercy. There was no mercy in those black eyes just touched with red. "Stretch your bow, Cedric, and see that these useless dogs do not leave us. If they run, bring them down, but do not kill them; the sweet death that comes from the yard shaft is too good for such as these."

The last statements were made in English so that Cedric could follow the command, but Cedric's action made clear to the others what was coming. The most horrible thing of all, Odo thought, was the unmoved expression and the gentle voice.

"What is your name and your tribe?"

The question was addressed in the same quiet tone to the prisoner. The child was trembling so that he could hardly speak, but he finally answered in a spate of words. He was from these parts, he told Lord Radnor, and it was true that he was watching the troop, but he had meant no harm. They had been told at the village that the lords would come no more into these parts and that the men from the west would destroy Radnor Castle. Others had come also and told them that it was true that the Norman lords would come no more, but that Radnor Castle would remain and they would pay only Radnor tax and no more lord's share. The village had doubted at first, then as the weeks passed the regular early plowing, when the great lords usually came, and no one came, they had wondered whether to believe the men from the west or those from the castle. So the boys of the village had been set to watch to see if the men from the west would come. The boy

121

would have continued his protestations of innocence, but Radnor silenced him with a gesture.

"If you meant no harm, why did your companion run away? I think it might be well to lift your hide a little with the birch. No doubt you will sing another tune. You"— Radnor switched to English and turned so suddenly upon Odo that the young man jumped—"cut yourself a good pliable switch, strip off his rags, and lay to until I bid you stop."

The boy flung himself on the ground at Radnor's feet. "Mercy lord, mercy. I speak the truth. There is no more. I do not know why Llwellyn ran away. He was afraid. I ran because I was afraid too. Ask me anything and I will tell you."

Cain swallowed to still the fluttering in his stomach. How he hated it, the screams and the pleading, and how they drove him to greater and greater ferocity, as if to prove that he could bear it. He envied his father who seemed totally unmoved by the pain he inflicted. As for himself, although he had learned to control both expression and voice, the screaming of a tortured man brought him to the edge of hysteria. One inner voice cried "More," the other "Stop," and between the two Radnor himself was so racked apart that he often missed the right time to put the questions. He stepped back to allow Odo a freer swing and unconsciously set his jaw as if the birch were to fall on his own back.

Cedric hissed softly through his teeth again. A glance had brought Odo's face clearly in view. The young man exhibited a greenish pallor that augured very ill with regard to his ability to carry out his orders. Cedric's eyes did not waver again from his charges, but his mind was occupied with Odo. He was sorry he had chosen the lad for this little jaunt. He had wanted to harden him somewhat, but he had not expected that it would be Odo who had to lay on the birch. Cedric himself was used to it and considered it a mild form of persuasion. He was a free man and a mercenary and had served with other fighting groups; he had seen things which made flaying alive seem merciful.

The birch cracked, the boy screamed, Odo swallowed his rising gorge and, in reaction against his own sickness and terror, struck harder and faster. Incoherently, over and over, the Welsh boy screamed that he could tell nothing more. Radnor, frozen in his own conflict, watched without expression. After a score or more strokes, the rod drew blood and Odo's resistance broke. With a gasp he abandoned the switch and ran for the bracken where he retched uncontrollably. At the cessation of the action, Radnor woke from his trance with a shock of rage. Even before Cedric could consider whether it was worth risking his neck to explain that Odo was on his first expedition, however, the rage passed. Odo's reaction was so akin to his own that Radnor could not help but understand and appreciate it.

Sir Harry had indifferently turned his back on the entire proceeding. Now he turned swiftly back again to touch Cain's arm. "Look!"

Radnor spun on his heels, his sword half out. "Llwellyn! For God's sweet sake, why did not the boy say it was you he was with—or was it you?"

"It was."

"I did say it was Llwellyn," the boy whimpered.

"You little fool," Radnor snarled, "did you not consider it needful to say it was the Bard of Radnor? Is there only one Llwellyn in the Welsh woods? Never mind. You are lucky you came to no harm. A good beating is good pay for stupidity. But what in the name of heaven ails you, Llwellyn, to take to your heels? Surely you saw my blazon."

Clear blue eyes looked gravely from the elderly man's austere face. "I had pressing matters to attend to. Call off your dogs, my lord, for I have a song to sing for you."

"A song? Now?"

"A song of great men, of great fools, and of great fears. And these are the Three Great Troubles of Wales."

That was clear enough. Llwellyn's song concerned the present unrest in Wales. Even in his anxiety to get to the heart of the matter, Radnor could not help smiling as he turned to Cedric.

"Gather up that person of compassionate bowels, Cedric, and take him back to his horse—what is his name, by the way? He is new among my men."

"Odo, lord, and what of these?" Cedric gestured with his bow toward the two Welsh trackers from whom he had not taken his eyes.

"They are remitted their pains. It would need a magician, not a tracker, to catch Llwellyn in Radnor Forest. Also see that the boy's hurts are dressed."

Calmly and with great dignity Llwellyn leaned forward

on the long staff he carried. His long white hair stirred gently in the breeze and he regarded his master for a long moment before he began to speak in a voice so musical that he might have been singing.

"I will sing you a song of a king careless of custom, of lords careless of reverence, and of subjects careless of life. And these are the Three Carelessnesses that bring Grief."

"God's truth," Cain muttered, but not loud enough to interrupt the bard.

"In years past Richard Fitz Gilbert was the first lord of Wales. He was a man of great desires and greatly he desired a kingdom. Therefore he made peace in the mountains. That peace was hard and bitter, for Richard swallowed alive the first-born of every man, and he was a great plague upon the Welsh, and he set great tasks upon them, and they builded for him a great and impregnable fortress. But he was a man careless of reverence to them to whom it was due, and this carelessness wrought him great harm, for the colors of his horses and his dogs changed from silver to red, and still he took no heed."

Sir Harry had gone to the baggage animals, returned with a low camp stool, and set it up. Radnor glanced at him keenly, but grasped his forearm for support and eased himself down without comment. Sir Harry was right, of course, this tale would take some time in the telling, and Cain glanced uneasily at the sun, knowing that if Llwellyn took very long they would never come to Penybont in daylight. It was hard to believe that Llwellyn was using delaying tactics, even though the news he was relating was ten years old, because bards sang the glories of a particular family and would usually cling faithfully as long as there was a man of the family to sing to and to sing of.

Llwellyn's voice had continued elaborating on the signs and portents that Richard had ignored and come finally to the denouement in which Richard had been ambushed and killed. "Thus Gilbert Fitz Richard, who was son to Richard Fitz Gilbert took the land and ruled it as was becoming to the heir, and still there was peace of a kind in the mountain kingdom. The peace was less quiet, for this plague was lighter and so the men groaned more and gave more thought to old wounds since there were few new ones to lick. Yet it is custom that the son shall inherit from the father, and they might have been still, had not the king who was careless of custom found him a man who was careless of reverence for the bond of blood. Thus

124

Gilbert Fitz Gilbert, brother to Richard Fitz Gilbert, also desired a kingdom in Wales, caring naught for what he owed his brother's son.

"Now it could be seen that on the hills many trees grew without tops, only the side branches flourishing, and those not greatly. Then a great fear overcame the men of the mountains, and he that was careless of reverence for the bond of blood fed that fear, that instead of losing only the first-born, the tribes themselves might become headless. Thus they were plunged straightway into madness. Others saw the signs differently, however, and said it was the bringers of the plague who would die, and the tribes, like the side branches would grow, although thinly, because of the sacrifices of war. So between fear and hope these became careless of life, thinking that it were better to bring matters to the proof than to live in uncertainty of what would next befall."

Radnor grunted softly. This was recent information, and though he had heard it before, he would like to know how the Welsh tribes found out Pembroke was trying to grab Fitz Richard's lands. Even more puzzling was why Llewellyn was telling him this. The bard knew of his marriage to Pembroke's daughter and might guess that Pembroke's plans were familiar to him. Radnor's body tensed with the conflict between the urgency to go and the need to hear Llewellyn out. It was impossible to hurry the old man, for any interruption was an insult and he would merely stop speaking and leave. The thought of applying the same inducement to speak to Llewellyn that had been applied to the boy never entered Cain's mind. For one thing it would be useless, for another Llewellyn was an old and trusted friend. He would as soon put Giles on the rack.

"Look not at the sky, my lord, but listen." Radnor started and found Llewellyn's piercing eyes, which had been fixed upon a point immeasurably distant, now upon his.

"My friend, I listen, but it grows late and I would keep my men from needless hurt. It is sometimes dangerous to travel in the Welsh woods at night."

"Listen, I say," Llewellyn replied with calm assurance. "You will not travel this night."

Lord Radnor started to rise, incensed at the idea that Llewellyn should give him orders, but the old man's eyes remained fixed upon his, and the dignity of a profession that had once caused the greatest chieftains in Wales to tremble gave him pause. He sat back, frowning slightly but reassured.

"It was even said," the melodious voice went on, taking up the tale again, "that these matters would spread beyond the lands of the bringer of the plague, and that in certain other places in the Marches all matters would be changed from the straight path. Look you, my lord, to see if your own black horse is not spattered with red where no blood but yours could run."

Again Cain half rose from his seat, then sank back tensely because the story had hit home but had not come to an end. Coupled with the previous tales of Pembroke's desire to rule Wales, the warning of an attempt on Radnor's own life could only mean that the attempt would be arranged by Pembroke. As if to make the accusation against Radnor's father-in-law clear, Llwellyn took a step forward and grasped Cain's arm. He bent forward before he spoke again, his pale eyes boring into Radnor's startled brown ones.

"Some say that the sins of the fathers shall be visited on the sons for many generations. By the sin of a father, the lands of Radnor passed through the soft white hands of a maiden away from her father who was their rightful lord and into the hard grasp of a stranger. Now it is said that the sin will be redeemed, and the lands shall pass again—again through the sin of a father and through the hands of a maiden, but this time back to the hands of the maiden's father."

"I thank you," Radnor said quietly, but his eyes were empty as if to feel anything at all would be dangerous. The girl he could not help loving—did she know of this? He got painfully to his feet. "It is good to know what the winds whisper to the wise men of Wales. But why do you say I will not travel tonight?"

"Not only winds whisper, Lord of Radnor. Men whisper too. We have had two whisperers in the village, and it was to tell the people to hold them straitly that I took to my heels when I saw you come. So well had they done their work that I too believed you would come here no more—and for other reasons."

"Truly, I suppose you had your reasons, but what, now it comes to my mind to ask, were you doing in the village, and why are you dressed in the clothing of a serf?"

"Sir Robert bade me go. He said he had no need for my caterwauling. I believed then that there were no more

126

Lords of Radnor Forest, and that you would come no more to Wales, for else he had not dared."

Lord Radnor's scars flamed suddenly in a face gone white with rage. "Another score I have then to even with him, and with——." He bit that off. "You need not fear, Llwellyn, your revenge will be complete, and you may spit in his face before he dies if it will ease your heart." A satisfaction I will never have, Cain thought, as he paused to get voice and temper under control. "For now it does not matter. I would like you to come with me to aid my trackers in any event. One moment, I want to tell Giles to give orders for camping and get you a horse."

"It is quicker to go through the forest," said Llwellyn.

"Ay, but easier to go on a horse by the road. Your paths through the woods are for a mountain goat, not for such as I."

The false dawn was lighting the sky before Radnor and his party returned to camp. Of the group, Llwellyn, although the eldest, was the least tired; he had not been present at the questioning of the two men held by the villagers. Radnor went to his own tent and collapsed on the cot. Out of the sight of his men, he could relax the iron control he kept over himself for their edification. He buried his face in the bedclothes to muffle the sounds he was making and shook and shook until he thought he would jar his bones apart. It had been worth it, for he had a good deal of information now, but the information had not been easy to get. In mercy he had ordered the throats of the quivering lumps of raw flesh that had remained when he had finished with them to be cut. The eyes had thanked him when they saw the knife coming, for the voices had long since been screamed away.

CHAPTER 9

WHEN HIS BODY WAS EXHAUSTED, Lord Radnor at last lay quiet. His mind, however, found no rest, squirming away from the remembrance of the physical agonies of his prisoners only to meet his own emotional pain at the treachery of his father-in-law. Not that Pembroke had ever been a favorite with Cain, but that he should have a blood bond with a man so steeped in depravity and greed disgusted him. He did not dare think of Leah's position in this tangle. Every time her name crossed his mind, Cain broke out into a sweat with fear. At last he slid from his cot with a groan to seek Giles.

"Send someone along to the village and have him bring me a woman," he said to his master-of-arms. "I cannot sleep."

Giles dressed to do as he was told without comment. Usually he would have had a few caustic remarks to make, but he had seen the haunted look of his master's eyes, and would not add to the trouble he was already bearing. He did not think that a woman would bring Lord Radnor sleep that night, but she would at least give him something pleasant to think about. He was irritated, too, because he had no time for the usual evening council on what was to be done the next day, and when Lord Radnor had a woman with him it was impossible to enter his tent before the first light as was his custom to ask for orders.

His problem solved itself, however, for when he went yawning to wash, there was Lord Radnor sitting on a camp stool with the remains of his breakfast before him and his eyes fixed upon the first streaks of dawn in the sky. He had not changed his position and his expression was forbidding, but when Giles returned he squatted down and muttered a morning greeting. From the look of his lordship's face, Giles thought that his guess had been right. If Radnor had slept for ten minutes in the night, he would swallow his bow without gagging.

"I sometimes think," Radnor said, suddenly breaking a long silence in which he had not acknowledged Giles' greeting or presence in any way, "that if I see or smell any more blood I will go mad. You have been a soldier for more years than my whole life, Giles, does this never happen to you?"

"I don't remember any more, my lord. These days I don't seem to notice the blood at all, except to wash it off when I get sticky, if I have the chance."

Radnor burst out laughing. "That is why you are the best lieutenant in England, Giles. You are absolutely literal and nothing at all can surprise you."

"I wouldn't say that. The Welsh surprise me all the

time. I wouldn't hardly credit it when I first came to serve your father what they would do, and after all these years, by God's eyes, I still don't believe what I know about them."

"I am more than half Welsh, Giles," Radnor said slyly.

"Yes. I know," replied the older man with his usual wooden expression. "That's what I meant. Half the time I wouldn't credit the asswise things you do if someone just told me. Why didn't you send me to question those men last night? You know you have no taste for minced meat. Now you won't be sleeping for a week and you'll be keeping me awake half the night fetching whores for you."

For a moment Radnor was openmouthed with surprise—it had been quite some time since Giles had administered a tongue-lashing to him—then he laughed again. "Your tongue grows no kinder with the years. The next thing I know, you will have my chausses down to paddle me."

"It couldn't do you any harm, but I never noticed that it did you any good either. Any notion that gets into your head is in for good. That's enough of your nonsense now, my lord. What's next to do?"

It was impossible to take offense at a man who had paddled your behind for your own good twenty years ago, so Radnor laughed again, more easily, and outlined what he knew and guessed. Pembroke had spread the word that Fitz Richard was in prison. The Welsh, as usual, had decided to make hay while the sun shone. Envoys had been sent from Fitz Richard's territories in all directions to arouse the tribes so that there would be rebellion all over at once and the Norman forces, already weakened by the lack of or change of overlord, would have to spread thin and be unable to concentrate to crush the rebels. An attack was planned on Penybont within the next few days. Of Pembroke's part in Sir Robert's plans, Cain said nothing. It was not necessary for Giles to know, and until he was sure that Leah had no part in the plot, he could not bring himself to speak of it.

It was likely, Lord Radnor pointed out and Giles agreed, that the force around Penybont was large and growing larger, since they planned to take the castle by assault. No pressure—and every form of torture that several active and desperate minds could devise had been applied—had been able to draw from the captives the expected size of the attacking force or the exact day of attack.

129

Radnor could only assume that the wretches truly did not know, but he was faced with the problem of deciding whether to attack the rebels at once or wait until he could marshal a larger army of his own. His mercenary troop was large and well trained, but it was not competent to take on a full scale army.

"It seems to me, Giles," he said after they had discussed the matter for a while, "that we would do best to fall upon them at the dinner hour when their belts are loosened. If the force is too large, we can make off without much hurt to ourselves, particularly since a few hours will bring darkness. We will do some damage and put the fear of further retribution into them. We might even take some prisoners and discover thereby what more is planned."

"Ay, my lord. If the force is still small we can disband them. Even if it be large and we can put them into suffi- cient disorder, Penybont may be able to send out men to help us or we may delay the major attack on the keep."

"If Penybont is still ours."

"If it is not, we will have our work cut out for us. We had better send to your father again, my lord, and tell him to bide at Pembroke's keep until this battle is over. May- hap he will need to summon the vassals."

"More than that, even. I must make haste to be at the king's council in the very beginning now. Above all, Pem- broke must not have Fitz Richard's land and Stephen is such a fool that he might be persuaded thereto. Pray God we can put them down at Penybont and my father can hold them quiet until I can free Fitz Richard. Curse Ches- ter for leading the boy into this when he should be guard- ing his lands."

"Well, I always said your godfather was caper-witted, but he means you no harm—which is more than I can say for that father-in-law of yours. Curse them both, if you will, but let us set about our part of the business." Giles shrugged off future problems and went to give orders to the squad captains.

Radnor stretched his legs which had been folded under him and leaned against the tent pole staring at the slowly reddening sky. He rubbed his hand over his burning eyes and, as he dropped it, brushed the crucifix which Leah had again fastened around his neck. It had hung forgotten out- side of his clothing, and now he slipped it into the neck of his garments where it lay cold against his skin. Cold com- fort, he thought. Leah herself seemed so warm when she lay against the same place. Was the warmth, like that which the cross was now taking on from his own flesh, spurious and ephemeral? If she knew of this plot, he would kill her. Even as Cain thought it, he knew he would do no such thing. She was so—not beautiful, but the hair like honey, the wide greenish eyes, and above all, the expression of trust on her face. Perhaps she had meant to warn him against Pembroke but had been afraid. Perhaps that was why she had begged to be set at Painscastle.

"Now what ails you, my lord?"

Radnor lifted his head to look at Giles. "Nothing. Why?"

"You have been sitting for ten minutes looking at nothing. Your servant is waiting to take down your tent, and the men are assembled and waiting for you to speak to them."

"Very well, I am coming," Radnor snapped. He mounted his horse which was waiting saddled beside the tent and followed Giles' disapproving back into the crowd of waiting soldiers. They made way for him to reach the center of the group and then stood silent, pressing close as possible to hear because Lord Radnor's husky voice did not carry well. He looked around for a moment with an expression that was almost tender as his glance traveled from one familiar face to another.

"Many of you, indeed most, have fought often with me before. To you it is not needful to say that I lead you into battle not to gain power or plunder but to keep peace. I have had news of uprising beyond Rhayader, and already Penybont is threatened. You know that if the Welsh descend upon us they will raze the land and we will starve; they will take your women and your children into slavery. It is necessary to destroy them before they do this harm, for if we wait we may be too weak to defend ourselves. Then we too will die. I know not how large a force lies before Castle Penybont; therefore listen well, for our plans of battle are changeable. We must go with great silence. Pad your scabbards and your bows so that they do not rattle; keep your horses on the turf, avoiding stones; above all do not speak, even in whispers, to one another. Nothing travels through the midday hush of the woods like a man's whisper. You know all these things; I do but tell you once again so that you will be reminded. We form in a wide line in the last shelter we may find and ride down upon the camp in the hour of the evening meal. If the force is too large, we will retreat to save ourselves. Your captains know the place to re-form. Watch well my standard. If I retreat, leave what you are about—even if success seems within our grasp—and follow me. I need not tell you to have courage, for I know you have it. God keep you well, my men."

There was a raucous laugh from the center of the group, and a coarse voice cried out, "If we must wait until we see the Gaunt blazon in retreat, we'll win or die. I've never yet seen your standard going backward, my lord."

Radnor swung his horse a little to the left, laughing. "William Tanner, I know your voice. You are not yet so old that you will not see things more strange than my banner in strategic retreat. It was well said long ago that 'he who fights and runs away, lives to fight another day.' I've a pretty young bride waiting for me, and with what you take in plunder on this trip, if you don't drink it all, you can buy one for yourself. If I say run, you run—like a scared rabbit. But if you run before I say so, I'll have your ears."

"You can only have one of them, my lord. I lost the other when you got that pretty smile you wear."

"Ay, I had forgot, you bloody devil. Guard yourself well. Pretty brides like at least one ear to bite. Mount up now, men, our hour draws upon us."

The rays of the sun indicated about four o'clock when Lord Radnor received word that his troop was ready and in position. Through the trees and across the intervening fields, sounds of human occupation came faintly to the waiting men. Radnor fingered the scars near his mouth and on his forehead with an unconscious gesture, and his lips began to move, although he made no sound.

Odo and Cedric, sitting tensely in their saddles nearby could see their master. Cedric watched with amusement and pleasure, because watching gestures he knew well from hundreds of preludes to battle reduced his own nervous tension. His lordship always did the same. At first Cedric had thought Lord Radnor was praying, but he had asked one of the priests and he had been told, disapprovingly, that it was pagan, heretic poetry written when the Romans were still in England, that Radnor recited. If that wasn't like his lordship, to be flying in the face of Providence by mouthing heresies before battle, Cedric had thought then, and he thought it again now. Cedric's own pre-battle gestures, as familiar to his comrades as Lord

Radnor's were to him, went unnoticed by himself. He ran his fingers along the blade of his already drawn sword and bit his lips, then licked them, then bit them again.

Odo, watching the silent fidgeting of the veterans around him, was overcome by a desire to relieve himself so intense that tears came into his eyes. He did not dare break silence; Cedric had told him in no uncertain terms what could happen to a man who fouled his lordship's battle plans. He pressed his knees against his horse, his body against the saddle pommel. He could not move. He knew he would not be able to move when the charge was called. He was a coward, and it was true that the serfs were made of lesser stuff than the lords. He wished he were back on the farm, that he had never said or thought anything to distinguish him from his fellow serfs. The tears rolled down his cheeks, but he no longer cared what the other men thought of him. There was death across that field of stubble, lying so quiet in the afternoon sun.

Lord Radnor pressed his hands against his thighs. He listened intently while his lips moved without sound in Allecto's speech from the Seventh Book of the *Aeneid*. "Lo, discord is ripened at thy desire into baleful war: bid them now mix in amity and join alliance! Insomuch as I have stained the Trojans with Ausonian blood, this likewise will I add, if I have assurance of thy will. With my rumours I will sweep the bordering towns into war, and kindle their spirit with furious desire for battle, that from all quarters help may come; I will sow the land with arms."

Faintly a metallic clangor drifted from the Welsh camp. Soup was being ladled from huge cauldrons into individual bowls. Radnor drew his sword and lifted it. He raised his voice, clear and loud, as his men heard it only in battle.

"A Gaunt, à Gaunt. Le droit est à moi."

Spurs clapped suddenly to his horse's side made the beast leap forward, and the whole troop surged after its leader in a shallow V, each man charging a split second after his more central neighbor. They rode into the disordered camp like a band of the furies Radnor had been describing a few moments previously. The noise of their charge had heralded their arrival and men were mounting, mounted, armed, searching for arms, fighting, and running all at once. In the first few moments many of the Welsh were slaughtered like sheep, but the others soon recovered and began to fight back.

Cedric hissed through his teeth with each breath and

133

paused momentarily to roll the body of a richly armed chieftain into the shelter of a tent. He wanted that armor as plunder, and he expected to be too busy for a while to strip the corpse. He turned quickly to help Odo who was barely holding his own against three unmounted men.

"Back your horse," he screamed. "They will broach him." And he cleaved the nearest man's head with a direct down-blow. The sword was caught in the bone of the skull, and Cedric wrenched at it, making the soft brain tissue ooze out and using his long shield to hold off another man who had run up.

Giles fought his way steadily from the right wing toward the center of the camp where the thickest press of men were. He could see the Gaunt blazon staggering back and forth as Sir Harry struggled to keep his horse directly behind and to the right of Lord Radnor. Giles smiled grimly although his breath was coming a little short. Beaufort was doing well in his first experience as standard-bearer and Radnor was still safe. Old Giles had fought so long that he worked like a machine, scarcely conscious of his sword arm darting forward to slice at an oncoming Welsh horseman. He twisted the blade hard as he withdrew it. These he wanted dead, not with clean wounds that would heal; dead, they would fight no more. He could see the group he was heading toward now. Radnor's sword arm moved up and down like a pump handle, the blade gleaming red and wet each time the weapon rose. The great painted shield made a sharp downward thrust and another cry rang out as a footman fell, brained, under the ironshod hooves of the war horse.

The Welsh fought with the stubborn courage for which they were famous. Actually, man for man, they were no match for Lord Radnor's well-disciplined troop, but even the best-disciplined veteran fighters can only fight so long and kill so much. The very weight of the Welsh army, which outnumbered his men at about five to one, was forcing Radnor slowly backward. He gasped as the point of a blade slipped under his shield from the back and gashed his ribs through the mail, but in the same instant he heard his attacker cry out as Beaufort's shield bludgeoned the footman's face to pulp. The press of Welsh moved ever closer. Radnor was enjoying himself, but a flickering glance up and down the field showed him that great pressure was being exerted all along the line. Another footman appeared at his right, sword held ready to broach his horse. Dropping his sword point because there was not room enough to use the weapon in the normal way, he thrust forward with the pommel. Blood sprayed over his gauntlet and leg as the teeth fell out of the face so near him and an eye bulged slowly from its socket. Radnor backed his horse, about to signal retreat, when a new cry came from the other end of the camp.

"*A Gaunt, à Gaunt.* For Owen, *à Gaunt.*"

At first the Welsh drove forward even more frantically because of the pressure of this new attack on their rear, but Radnor's men had new heart. Castle Penybont was still theirs and Owen of Wells had men enough and strength enough to help in the fight. Lord Radnor grinned, his teeth flashing in his unshaven face, and addressed himself with satisfaction to decimating his enemies.

William Tanner laughed aloud and said to the man fighting beside him, "I told you that you wouldn't see the Gaunt blazon going backward." But the last word finished in a bubbling sound as he crumpled up with a faint look of surprise on his face and his chest bathed in the blood that gushed from his slit throat.

The twilight was now darkening into true night, and Lord Radnor found that he could not see well. He lifted his shield so that he could wipe the perspiration from his eyes with the leather inside of his gauntlet. A blow that numbed his sword arm made him lower the shield precipitately, but Beaufort had knocked the man aside. A little while longer and one could not tell friend from foe. Well, there could be no harm in trying a trick that had worked before. Radnor raised his voice.

"*A Gaunt, à Gaunt.* Hold hard. They break. They run."

The cry was picked up by the men closest who had breath enough to cry aloud and soon rang from every quarter of the field. Radnor's men set their tired jaws; now they had them. Soon there would be rest and plunder, no running through the woods with pursuers close behind.

"*Le droit est à moi.* They break. They run." Radnor's voice rang out again. It was getting very dark and a frightened boy did run. He was not a Welsh fighter; he was no more than a cook's helper who had been trapped in the melee, and a boy at that, not a man, but it was too dark to tell man from boy now and that note of panic caught and spread like wildfire. Half an hour longer saw the end of it, and Radnor's men, prewarned not to pursue a group still larger than themselves into forest they did not

135

know well, straggled together to count up their gains and losses.

Lord Radnor sagged forward against the high pommel of his saddle after he had unstrapped his shield and slung it in its usual place across his shoulder. He roused himself briefly to pull the cloak from a prisoner passing with one of his men to wipe his sword and sheathe it. A reaction to battle that he had not had for a long time was taking possession of him. He could feel his tired horse trembling and he thought dully how strange it was that a war horse would press forward in the thick of a fight almost without urging, would not shy even when blood spattered its face, yet when the battle was over that same horse would tremble with fear and even bolt because of the smell of blood. The horse's reactions made no connection in Radnor's mind with those of their riders, but he turned and took the lose reins of Beaufort's mount as the destrier laid back his ears and showed the whites of his eyes. Radnor watched the young man retch.

"My lord," a strong voice called. "Fifty men are dead; forty-three are like to die of their wounds and certainly cannot travel with us on a near day. Of the rest, about half are hurt, but not badly."

Lord Radnor lifted his head; his eyes had misted over at the sound of those matter-of-fact tones. "Giles! I am not used to be separated from you in a fight. I am glad you are here safe."

The master-of-arms wiped at his mouth to hide his surprise, and his voice came even harsher than usual to conceal his own emotion. "And it's just as well I am too. How many years have I told you that after a battle you must count your dead and put your wounded in a safe place? What if the Welsh were to come down upon us again? And you sit like a bump on a log, as usual, looking at nothing." The old man's words were sharp, but his hand touched Radnor's neck and shoulder in a gesture that was certainly a caress. "Look at yourself, bleeding in half a dozen places and too stupid to call for a leech."

"Not too stupid, Giles, too tired."

"Beaufort," Giles called sharply.

"Let him be," Radnor murmured. "The sickness of battle is upon him. I have known it myself. Let him be."

"Good greeting to you, my lord," Owen of Wells called cheerfully as he rode up on a blood-spattered gray horse.

"I thank you for coming so soon. Had you delayed longer we might not have been able to issue out to help you."

"Greetings, Owen." Radnor removed a gauntlet and held out his hand which Owen kissed. "Have you fresh men enough in the castle to guard this camp and collect the plunder?"

"Yes, and enough to bury the dead too," Owen replied. "Most of the serfs are in the castle. I did not think we would be starved out; it did not look to me as if they planned a siege, so I took them in."

"Well, then, I suppose—" Radnor rubbed his forehead and eyes with the gloveless hand. He was now almost dropping with desire for sleep.

"Go to. Go to." Giles interrupted. "Go into the castle and have your hurts tended. Will you teach your grandfather to suck eggs?"

Lord Radnor looked at his master-of-arms in patent amazement. Never before had Giles interrupted him when he was about to give an order—although in his youth he had frequently countermanded his orders—nor did he usually exhibit in public the familiarity with which he treated his lord in private. Cain's mind flashed back over the last few minutes—nor had Giles ever touched him with a caress like that before. Or had he? Was it possible that he had never noticed the old man's affection? In any event he was too tired to argue or to seek explanations.

"All right, grandfather," he said with a gleam of humor, "suck eggs for me and see how much nourishment I get from them. One moment you tell me not to sit and look at nothing and the next you send me off to do just that. And while you are offering me wise saws, do not forget to have your own hurts seen to." Radnor touched his horse and moved over to Beaufort. "Enough, Harry. Wipe your mouth and swallow your gorge and come with us." The young man was shaking with dry sobs. "It will pass. Harry, I have been there and I tell you it will pass."

"Will you eat with us, my lord? I confess I am sharp set. We heard your battle cry just as we sat down to meat. Needless to say we did not wait to finish but came at once." Owen was irrepressibly cheerful and, loving a good fight, rather exhilarated by the victory.

At the mention of food, Lord Radnor had to swallow his own nausea before he could reply. "No. I want only to sleep, and a leech for my wounds. In God's name, man, ask me nothing and tell me nothing, but show me a bed."

Several hours later Lord Radnor woke. Beaufort was asleep on the floor on the other side of the fireplace where embers still glowed, lighting the room with a dull red. Radnor considered waking him and sending him for food, then changed his mind, belted on his sword again, and went down to the great hall. Except for one woman servant puttering about and men sleeping on the floor, the hall was deserted. Radnor grasped the woman by the arm.

"Go find me something to eat."

"My lord, there is nothing fitting for you," she cried.

"Anything will do, I care not what. The broken meats and bread." As he sent her off, he noticed that she was young and not ugly. That would complete his needs. All women were alike, and if Pembroke's daughter was a snake like her father, there would be others. When the maid returned carrying a platter heaped with meat and bread, he told her roughly to wait and set to with real appetite. A good fight, a good meal, a good tumble, and a good sleep—a good day.

Radnor pushed the platter away and drew the girl to him. Under his hands, her body was rigid with revulsion. That was nothing new to him and usually did not affect him, but this time he was astonished once again to find that his body would not obey his desire. He looked around at the men in the hall—this was not the place for it anyway; if the girl cried out he would have an audience. Dragging her with him, he returned to the tower. Beaufort was still asleep and so heavily that Radnor thought nothing would wake him.

"Be silent," he said to the trembling girl. "Whatever I do, be silent. If you cry out and wake my man, I will cut your tongue out." He drew her down on to the pallet with him, undid her bodice, pulled up her skirt, and lay for a while fondling her breasts and hips. Her skin was young and smooth and pleasant even though her whole body protested against his caress silently, the back arched and the limbs rigid. What had been an idle thought before, now was an insistent desire. He would have her! But still his body would not obey and, in spite of his inflamed mind, he was cold as ice. Radnor shoved the girl away. Was he doomed to be capable only with the daughter of his worst enemy?

"Wait!"

Dim as it was, Radnor could read the terror in the maid's stance, could sense the revulsion she felt in the way she clutched the open bodice across her breasts. He knew what he was and what he looked like in her eyes and wondered abstractly if even her fear could keep her still if he touched her again. He made no attempt to try the experiment, reaching for a purse he had dropped by the side of the bed.

"Take this." A couple of coins chinked into her free hand. "Go. Get out," he snarled at her, and she fled to the safety of the kitchens.

No sooner was Radnor alone, however, when Leah's image rose into his mind. To this his body responded with such promptness that he cursed aloud, and with such fluency and vehemence, that Sir Harry woke with a start.

"What is it, my lord?"

"Nothing," Radnor replied, "go to sleep."

CHAPTER 10

———◆———◆———◆———

IN THE MISTY DAWN of another hot day, Lord Radnor levered himself to a sitting position. Beaufort was gone and, free of the restraint of his presence, Radnor groaned aloud at the thought of the duties of the coming days. Stiff and sore as he was, the Welsh camp had to be broken up immediately, the plunder divided and distributed, and a plan of action against those who had escaped roughly formulated. The prisoners would have to be tortured for the names of the tribes involved and siding with the rebellion so that his father would know where to strike next.

At least Owen could see to the torturing of the prisoners, and, with the addition of all Radnor's men except his personal guard, would have a large enough force to protect this area until Gaunt and the vassals arrived. Nonetheless there was enough for him to do, some of it very unpleasant. He began to dress, wincing as he moved at first and wincing again as he pulled on his left boot. The pain in his body was almost welcome for it occupied his thoughts, at least for a little while. Then there was breakfast to busy himself with, then the council with Owen. At last there was no more good reason for delay, and Cain sat down to write his letters. One went to Leah, ordering her to remain in her father's keep. The letter began very sternly, but her sweet face hung before him with tears trembling on the lashes of her wide, innocent eyes. "Be sure," he had written, "to do as I bid you," and now he added, "for I hope to be with you before the wedding guests depart. My labors here have so prospered," Cain continued after careful consideration, "that it is more needful for me to hasten to speak with the king than to quell the Welsh."

He had said what he had to say, and if Leah was in league with Pembroke, those last words would be a pretty trap for them both. The letter, however, lay open and unsealed while Cain wrote to Chester and Hereford and to his own father describing what had happened and the Welsh rumors regarding Pembroke's intentions. To no one, not even Gaunt, did Cain mention what Llwellyn had told him about his personal involvement in Pembroke's plans. His father would discover the facts soon enough from Sir Robert, if they were facts and not rumors, and from the rest of the world Cain had every desire to hide the facts. Pembroke's shame, now that a blood bond existed between them, was his as well through Leah. Leah—his eyes slid back to the open letter and he reached for it, reread it, made a gesture of casting it aside, and then hastily rolled and sealed it and thrust it into the bag with the others.

Four days later, Lord Radnor rode once again across the drawbridge and into the keep that held his wife. All the way from Penybont, he had wondered how much of his message Leah would have transmitted to her father. The stunned face which Pembroke turned to him when they met in the courtyard gave the answer. Obviously Leah had told her father nothing—not even that her husband was on his way back.

"Where have you been?" Pembroke gasped. "To where did you go? Your father would say nothing except that you were mad and given to such disappearances."

Momentarily Cain could make no answer because his wife was hanging on his neck and he was fully occupied with soothing her. Leah's slight body trembled pathetically, and she pressed herself frantically against her husband, shying sidelong as her father approached them.

"Gently, gently, dear heart," Cain protested, wincing as Leah squeezed his hurt side. "I am battle-sore. How now,

140

what a greeting for a week's absence. If I am gone two weeks, I shall be afraid to come home lest I should be hugged to death. Look up. Come, do. I swore I would come soon and safely, and here I am."

"So the little bitch knew where you were," Pembroke snarled, unwisely laying a hand on Leah's shoulder.

In the next moment he was picking himself up from the ground five feet away. Gaunt, who had entered through the bailey gate, began to help Pembroke dust himself off. "Restrain your ebullience in greeting, Cain," he said dryly. "I am forever telling you that you do not know your own strength. If you wish to pat a man, do so. Do not knock him down."

"I am very sorry," Radnor said stiffly. "I do forget. I have been known to kill a man with kindness."

It was impossible that Pembroke should accept such an excuse or miss the warning in the last statement, yet he certainly seemed to do so. He returned to clasp Radnor's hand warmly, ignoring his shuddering daughter, and to press him to come in to dinner which was just being laid on the tables. Cain's nostrils flared as if he were seeking the scent of an unclean beast, but he followed readily and even sat down beside Pembroke to eat. He began to describe his sojourn in Wales with genuine pleasure, watching for the signs of discomfiture he was sure Pembroke could not completely conceal. The effort, however, was totally unrewarded. Pembroke nodded unqualified approval.

"The only thing I cannot like," he said, "is your leaving so many of your men behind you. You have not a large enough troop now to guard yourself properly. I would advise you to wait until they can be returned to you before you go to London."

"No," Radnor replied softly, his eyes flickering with amusement under their fringe of lashes. Pembroke was a fool to lay such an open snare. "My business with the king is most urgent, concerning as it does the peace of Wales."

"Then why do you not take some of my men with you? I do not go to this council. I am growing old and find such jaunts too much for me. You, I know, will guard my interests, since they are also yours now. But you should not take Leah with you. Nay, do not frown at me. Do but think of how that girl acted today. She is simple! She will blab all your business to everyone who exchanges a word with her."

"She will not know my business."

"Oh, very well. I am not going to quarrel with you over a chit of a girl, but if you take her with you, you will need a house in London. You cannot camp with a woman in your train."

Cain frowned. He had not thought of that, but it was perfectly true. "She will have to put up with a camp, or perhaps she can stay with Leicester until I have a place."

"Nonsense," Pembroke said. "I have a house in London and there is no reason at all why you should not stay there."

"I thought you had sold that house to Oxford."

"No, I rented it to him, but for my own son-in-law he cannot refuse to give the place up. You will, of course, have to return the rental to him, but that cannot signify to you."

The hair at the nape of Radnor's neck prickled as if he were expecting to be ambushed from behind. To give himself thinking space he choked on the roast venison he was eating, reached for his wine, and drank, coughing occasionally. Surely Pembroke could not be so mad as to attack him during a baronial conference; he had too many powerful friends. What was the purpose of this sudden burst of friendliness? What benefit could accrue to Pembroke from placing him in any particular house in London?

"If there is time," Radnor agreed warily, "and you would be so good, it would save my looking about."

"No trouble at all. I will send a messenger to Oxford tonight. You will no doubt come in to London by the Oxford road so that you will pass his keep. If you stay the night there, Oxford can give you the keys and tell you how to find the place and you will have but two easy days' journey into London."

Radnor closed his eyes altogether at this statement. Ambush on the road? Very possible, but Pembroke knew what route he would take since it was the only one possible without all this elaborate arrangement. Murder at Oxford Castle? That too was possible. How interesting! This was going to change a dull trip into a battle of nerves and wits. Radnor opened his eyes very wide as he heard Pembroke ask sympathetically if he felt unwell.

"Not at all, not at all."

"That is very good. I thought you had grown faint suddenly."

"No," Radnor replied, smiling broadly, "I was but considering how kind all men are to me."

Oddly enough he was speaking the literal truth, for Pembroke had told him, unintentionally, something which was far more important to him than information concerning the time or place of his own assassination. If Pembroke still did not wish Leah to go to London, then she was no part of his plan except as the heir to his estates. His assumption was confirmed when Edwina bore down upon him shortly after dinner.

"You are scarcely ever to be found alone, Lord Radnor." Cain's brows rose. What need had Edwina to find him alone? "I wished to speak to you about Leah," she continued.

Radnor had little desire to be told how to manage his affairs by his mother-in-law, but he was much interested in what she had to say. "I am here now," he said encouragingly.

"Gilbert says you are still determined to take Leah to London tomorrow."

"Yes."

"Do you think that is wise? She—"

"Yes."

"Forgive me, Lord Radnor, but she will be perfectly safe here, while at court—she is so young. Her head has already been turned by these festivities."

"I had not noticed."

"Again I ask your pardon for differing with you, but you must acknowledge that I know Leah longer and perhaps better than you do. She was used to be a docile, sweet-tempered girl, but of late she is grown very willful and disobliging."

"Not to me."

"No, not yet, of course, but if you indulge her—"

"You should be pleased."

"I look to the future. Now when she is young these tricks and quirks are charming. You may not find them so later. There is something more important. If she is already with child, such a trip will likely destroy it, and if she is not she may get ideas that are bad for your succession."

Radnor's eyes shifted. He had not thought that Leah might be breeding yet, and there was now no woman he could ask for advice. Well, if she conceived so readily, she would conceive again. Surely it was too soon and the mother knew it. Pembroke had put her up to this, no doubt, but Cain was tired of listening.

"Madam," he said, "her training would be sadly at fault if the court could teach her such lewdness in a few short weeks. Moreover, I intend to guard her well and use her well. She will have neither the chance nor the strength." He laughed coarsely. "I do not take Leah for her convenience, but for my own."

In the dim light of the one shaded candle, Leah's face looked pinched and pale as she peered around the room. She did not think there was anything that remained to be done. All of her new clothes and other scanty possessions were packed in wicker baskets suitable for the portage animals. Her husband's clothing was similarly disposed. The garments he would wear for traveling were laid out—the inevitable shirt and chausses, rough homespuns in the grayish tan common to unbleached wool, a tunic, also homespun, the mail shirt that was essential protection for everyday travel in England in these times, and the old worn brown velvet surcoat. The mail shirt had been brought to her by a courteous young knight with pleasant, easy manners who had introduced himself as Harry Beaufort. He had stayed to talk for a time, telling her about the battle at Penybont which Cain had shrugged off when she asked. Helmet, shield, and other minor armor were still in Sir Harry's care and would be delivered to Radnor just before they mounted up to leave. That was all then. Leah looked around as another restless movement made the bed creak.

Cain had slept very heavily for a time right after their lovemaking, leaving Leah trembling, near tears, and wide awake. He had been very slow, deliberately holding back to savor his own sensations and Leah's response, playing and playing with her until she had been driven to scratch him and bite the hard, scarred mouth that tormented her so pleasantly. Too soon after that, however, he had rolled away. Leah had been almost frantic with desire to keep him with her. What she wanted, she did not know, but the feeling which possessed her could not keep mounting and mounting. At some point the tension and passion had to burst. The bursting might kill her, Leah thought, so intense was the sensation becoming, but at the moment that death would have been welcome compared with being left as she was. Forbidden to touch Cain lest she disturb him, afraid

144

to weep for the same reason, Leah had crept softly out of bed to work off her nervous energy by finishing her packing for the next day's trip.

Now her husband was restless, moving uneasily back and forth across the bed. Leah blew out the candle and returned to him. She was tired and quiet now and could sleep the few remaining hours until morning. A groping hand seized her and drew her close.

"Lord," Cain's voice was thick with sleep, "what a nightmare. I dreamt you were lost and I could not find you."

Leah pulled Radnor's heavy head on to her shoulder. His beard, thickly grown, scraped her tender skin, but the sleepy words had assuaged some indefinable hurt and Leah was happy again.

"Get up, you little slut," said a husky, friendly voice, and Leah sat up with a start, pushing her hair out of her face. Her husband was smiling broadly. "I never saw such a lazy, naughty chit. You mauled me worse than a bear last night. And now I have called you three times and all you do is bury your head deeper in the pillow." Awkward with tenderness, he sat down beside her to play with her hair and touch her sleepy face with his fingertips. "If you are not up, washed, and dressed quicker than a lamb can shake its tail, I will leave you behind." Unfortunately for his husbandly discipline he immediately destroyed any effect his statement might have had by kissing her.

"Oh, Cain," Leah said, disengaging her lips, "do you have needles and thread?"

"What?"

"Needles and thread, my lord. If we stay above a few days in London, I must have the wherewithal to sew."

"Now what would I do with needles and thread?" he laughed. "Ask your mother."

Leah blushed and Cain was diverted by watching the color dye her throat just stopping short of her white breasts. "I—I cannot. Needles are so expensive and my father—. It would be so hard for her to replace them."

"Oh." Cain's face had become carefully expressionless. "Very well. I will see what can be done. Get up now." He turned to the maids who had slept in a little separate area just outside the door and had come into the room when they heard the sound of his stirring. Leah had made it plain to them that their duties had begun and if either she

145

or his lordship had to send for them she would skin them alive. They had been waiting quietly in a corner since they had finished attending to Radnor's needs.

"Get your mistress dressed, and quickly too." He started to walk away, looked at the maids again, and turned back to Leah. "What ails those girls of yours that they leap like scared rabbits every time I look at them or speak to them?"

Leah smothered a giggle. "They are afraid of you, my lord."

"That is plain enough, but why? What have I done to them?"

Could she tell her husband that her maids feared he was the devil incarnate? Leah dropped her eyes to hide her own sudden resurgence of fear and said slowly, "A woman does not need a particular reason to be wary of a man in this house."

"Well, tell them to stop it," Cain replied crossly. "It makes me feel like jumping myself when they jerk about so." Leah's fleeting terror vanished but the poor maids' terror increased manyfold.

By the time he reached the great hall, however, he was smiling faintly once more. The room was relatively empty, for he had chosen to leave earlier than the remaining guests, but his father was waiting for him as arranged on the previous evening. As they walked aside to be as private as possible, the duke covertly studied his son. Radnor was still dreadfully thin, but there was a relaxation in his expression that changed his face. Gaunt saw that the large dark eyes with a lingering smile in them were hers, now nearly thirty years dead, and Radnor's mouth, softened by some inner joy and security where it was not marred by battle scars, was also his mother's. In the harsh, angular planes of the face, Gaunt saw his own heritage to his son. Why did he torment this man, flesh of his flesh? His legs went weak with a sudden memory of his own father and a pang of regret for that relationship not repeated with his child. Cain caught his arm.

"Father!"

"The lame are now supporting the old rather than leading the blind?" The bitter words were habit. Gaunt himself was surprised by them.

Radnor's fingers tightened brutally on his father's elbow and then relaxed. "Ay, I am lame and you are old, and yet it may be that the well-doing of our country rests upon

146

us. Let's do it, father, and spare me today your tongue—nay, spare yourself. Today your tongue touches me not. First, you had my letter about Sir Robert of Radnor?"

"Ay. I am glad you had sense enough not to drive him out at once. He holds an important place and many plans must have been opened to him before he agreed to betray us. I will squeeze what he knows out of him, never fear."

"I do not fear for that. Spare his lady, she is—"

"How you grow soft! Nay, do not fear for that either. I do not make war upon women unless it be needful."

"You have heard Chester, father? Have you tried to reason with him? The matter—"

"Neither heard nor tried the impossible, but I heard Hereford at great length. Cain, I can see no way to stop them. They must fall into the pit of their own digging."

"No, they must not. Hereford I will save because I love him, but with Chester, Fitz Richard falls—and the Welsh rumor that his lands will go to Pembroke. How they know of these things is a mystery to me, but they are too often right to doubt."

"I bid you stand clear. Do you think me a fool? I have been listening. Pembroke has, I can guess, a promise—mayhap even written—from Stephen to cede him the lands, but Maud will not let Stephen do it. Philip says—." Gaunt's voice hesitated as a spasm crossed his son's face, spoiling for a moment the repose that had made the eyes beautiful. "I have no intent to fret you, my son, but I must speak of him."

Cain nodded and leaned his massive shoulders against the roughhewn stones of the huge, empty fireplace. If Philip were dead, he could have borne it better; it was the hopeless slipping away that tore his heart. Then his eyes took on a softer expression. The last time his father had called him son was when his face had been laid open a few years before and the pain, which would not let him eat or sleep, had finally set wide the door to madness. It had been then that his father, struggling to hold him whom no one else dared touch for fear of his strength, had said over and over, "Be quiet, my son," and once, perhaps, "my dear son."

"Philip says," Gaunt was continuing, "that Maud has been turning her eyes toward Wales. What I fear is that she seeks to trap Pembroke and, through him, us, into this treason of Chester's. If we all fall she thinks, not knowing the Welsh, that she may set whom she wills in our places,

147

surround and destroy Gloucester, and destroy all hopes of the Angevin succeeding. That is why I say if it comes to open treason you must stand clear. If you can stop Hereford privately, suit yourself. Nothing will stop Chester. I know his stubbornness, but if we remain safe mayhap we can save him later. It can do neither Hereford nor Chester any good if their last powerful friends fall too."

"Very well. Your will falls with mine in all matters except that of Hereford. To the limit of my ableness, I will do as you say."

"Cain, Pembroke must be kept out of this. What smirches him, smirches our name too. If it were not for the dower—. We have won our way up from nothing on great dowers, but he is worse than I thought." Anxiety filled the old man's eyes, but he turned them to the ground so that his son might not see. "The more I think on it, the more I wonder why he offered so much."

Again Cain's lips parted to tell what he was coming to believe was really true, that Pembroke intended to seize the Gaunt estates through Leah. A new consideration held him silent. His father's father had been the holder of a small barony in William the Bastard's time. He had taken to wife a Welshwoman and, through a set of fortuitous circumstances which had robbed her of every male relative, had inherited the entire property of the family. So much had been chance, but the first Gaunt, not yet a duke, had not needed a second lesson. In turn he arranged that his son too be married to a Welshwoman, and this time there was no need for fortuitous circumstances. With great deliberation, that first Gaunt had murdered his son's father-in-law and brothers-in-law. Thus Radnor Forest and the adjoining properties had come undivided and uncontested into the family. Moreover for his great work in subduing the Welsh, he had been made a duke. Cain assumed that his father knew what had been done, although he had never spoken of it. If he had connived at it, perhaps he had already been punished or perhaps his punishment was yet to come. In any case, Cain would not torment the man who had just called him son by recalling that old shame.

"One thing more," Gaunt said.

"Yes?"

"Let not that pretty piece of a wife distract you from this affair. Her head hangs on it as much as yours."

Radnor lowered his voice and fixed his father's eyes with his. "Do you too advise me to leave her here?"

"Certainly not. If I were going to Painscastle as was first intended, I would take her and set her there, but I cannot now spare the time. Watch her close, very close."

"It must be as you say, I am besotted." Tension crept back into Radnor's eyes, changing their shape. "I cannot help it, I believe her to have no part in her father's plans—be they what they are."

"For the love of heaven," Gaunt said in a disgusted voice, "how I ever came to have a son so softheaded and softhearted, I will never know. Only an idiot like yourself could think of employing such a simple babe for any purpose beyond warming a bed and breeding an heir. He did not offer that dower for nothing, I say, and somehow he looks to make a profit of her. Perhaps the bride price you paid for her has whetted his taste and he thinks to have another or even to have back the dower by keeping her from you. It needs no great mind to see that you would sell your soul to have her near. Cain, you are a greater fool about money than about friendship, and that is saying enough. I tried to tell you that you should not make yourself look so soft a mark when you came to his terms for the sake of the girl's bright eyes."

Lord Radnor scowled, furious with himself for being a gullible fool and listening to Llwellyn's tales. Of course that was what Pembroke wanted. He knew that neither Cain nor Gaunt really cared much about money, so it was safe to bleed them. Surely Pembroke was too lily-livered to plan Radnor's death, especially while his father still lived. Perhaps he believed that there was little love between Gaunt and his son, but the loss of his only heir would be reason enough for Gaunt to tear Pembroke and his property to little pieces, and in no quick or merciful way.

"Well, Cain, that is all. Have you money enough for your purposes? There may be some buying of men and voices to be done to bail Chester out of his trouble or if the question of promising the succession to Henry comes up."

"Yes, and I can draw on the moneylenders if I need more. You have reminded me, though—have you a box of silver?"

"Silver—yes, to pay for field forage. What is your need for silver?"

Radnor looked a little shamefaced. "My wife would have needles and thread. These she asks for from me as if

149

I were used to carry them or conjure them from the air. She is young. Let her have the pleasure of buying them for herself."

Gaunt burst out laughing. "You are ten times a great fool, but this I will let you learn for yourself, you can afford it. Oh, madman, to give money to a woman! How much do you want?"

"About two pounds. For more I can break gold at a moneylender's."

Gaunt laughed again and nodded, dismissing his son with a friendly blow on the shoulder. Why he was presently in charity with Cain, he did not know. Usually his son's pleasure aroused him to protective brutality. He should have reminded him that about half of all young brides, his own mother included, died in childbearing. Well, let him learn that the hard way too, if learn it he must.

Leah had come into the great hall flushed and flustered. Her delay had been caused by Edwina who had come to say goodbye in a more private spot than the hall or courtyard. Leah loved her mother deeply, in spite of their recent differences, and was greatly moved by Edwina's obvious distress, but the back of her mind kept urging her to hurry because Lord Radnor wanted her. She was not yet of an age which would permit her to mask her feelings from her intimates, although she was rapidly perfecting her ability to do so in public, and her mother read the divided attention in her transparent face.

Tears rose to Edwina's eyes. Nothing she had said or Radnor had done seemed able to alter Leah's love. Plainly the girl doted on her husband; plainly she would suffer when he was killed. Edwina was coming to a desperate decision because her love for her daughter was stronger than her pride or her fear, but she wished to test Leah's bond to Radnor. Perhaps a hint of permanent separation from her mother would show where her real affections lay.

"How can you be so unfeeling?" Edwina asked. "How many blows have I taken for you? Who has loved you so long and so well? Child, we may never see each other again."

"Oh, mama," Leah cried, startled into giving her mother the name she had used most tenderly in childhood, "never say so." Now she ran to Edwina to be hugged and kissed. "Mama, mama, that cannot be true. Not even father could be so cruel, and my lord is so kind. He would never forbid me to visit you. Painscastle is so very near, not more than a day's ride. I am sure we will be together again soon. I could not bear it." And Leah was also in tears.

For a long moment Edwina held her daughter in her arms, silently struggling with her fears. She had not heard from Leah what she wanted to hear. She could not bear to see Leah hurt without having tried to help her, yet if Pembroke discovered that she had divulged his plans her punishment would be terrible. And if she told Leah and Pembroke was foiled through her, there was truly little chance she would ever see her again. Her decision wrenched her very being awry, and in the final moment her courage failed so that she compromised.

"Do not become involved in your husband's affairs; seek to know nothing of them. Try to wean your affection from him. Moreover, never come here alone, and if a messenger should come from your father or from me and ask you to go aside with him, by the Holy Name, do not do it. To seem to know anything of your father's doings will be death to you, for he purports to bring you here and keep you from your lord."

"No, he could not. For pride alone Cain would have down the castle, even if he had no care for me, and, mother, in spite of what you have said, I am sure he has a kindness for me."

"As a breeder of young. Hush, quietly. There is no need for the maids to hear. How could Lord Radnor have down the castle if you are in it? He will pay what is asked, for he must breed an heir, but he would hate you for this. I have told you only so that you can show yourself innocent—so that you will not be punished for your father's faults."

"Oh heaven, he will punish me for father's fault anyway. He will be fit to tear me apart when I tell him."

"Tell him! You are mad! This is for your ears alone so that you may take care. If Radnor hears this he will take vengeance and your father will either murder me or set me in the deepest dungeon of the keep to rot."

"Nay, mother, it will not be so. It is your care that has given us warning. I will pray my lord that you may come to Painscastle. You will be safe there and we may be together always."

"To be a handmaiden to my own daughter. Do not be foolish, child," she said sharply as Leah shook her head and started to protest. "It must be that way if I am a second woman in your home. Even if you would suffer me to be the lady of the house, and I do not think from what I have seen of late that it would be so, your husband would not suffer it. I will not do it, Leah. Only hold your tongue. This habit you have of telling your lord everything will bring you to grief."

They had parted with more tears and kisses on that, and when Leah reached the hall and found Cain still engaged with his father, she was grateful for the respite from her problem. To tell or not to tell, and it was a bitter choice. When they mounted up to leave and Leah kissed her mother for the last time, she wept again and so bitterly that for some time she could not have spoken even if she wished to. Her husband rode by her side without interference. He felt her emotion to be natural and was, moreover, occupied with issuing instructions for the order of march. These were so detailed and cautious that Giles looked questioningly at his master. Cain met his eyes steadily and shook his head.

"For now just look sharp."

"But for what?"

Radnor shifted his eyes briefly to his wife. There was no sense in frightening her or making her sadder than she already was. "Later, Giles," he said. It was not likely that Pembroke's men would attack so close to the keep with the other guests leaving sporadically.

For the first few miles the territory they rode over was familiar to Leah who had been hawking and hunting over it. There was nothing new in the low green hills and sparkling streams to assuage her grief or divert her mind from her troubles. If only she had the faintest notion when her father planned this thing; if only she could wait until they were abed. She could tell Cain anything then. Leah was not experienced, but there was no mistaking the effect she had upon her husband in bed. He would not be angry then, at least not with her. She could make him promise anything then, too, and he would hold to his word so that her mother would be safe. But if her father made his try that day and her husband were caught unawares he might be hurt in the fight. Leah was so sunk in her own thoughts that she never noticed the preparations against attack which Radnor was making. Was it more likely that Pembroke would try close to home or further away? Close, Leah thought, because he could use his own men, because it would be easier to get her home, and because there was less chance that Radnor would overtake his attackers and win her back again. But if they were prepared her father would know that her mother had confessed; if they were not prepared, Cain might be hurt. Scenes from the tourney rose in her mind. Come what might, she had to speak now. Above all, Cain must not be hurt.

"My lord."

"Have you had your fill of weeping?"

"I pray you, be not offended. I have never parted from my mother for so much as a day, before this."

"I am not offended," Radnor replied. He was not really attending to her. His eyes followed the meeting of the low hills with the sky on either side of the rough track, and his forefinger ran up and down the puckered mark that drew up his mouth.

"I have something to tell you, my lord." Leah's voice trembled so noticeably that Cain turned to look at her with attention.

"Well?"

"No, it is not at all well."

"I know," he said in a resigned tone which struggled to conceal its amusement. "You have left all of my clothes behind, or yours, or the bed, or something else from which you cannot be parted—we must return."

"Oh no, my lord, I am not so careless. Indeed, the matter is of greater moment. Do not be angry with me, for it is none of my doing or desire."

"Of greater moment than my clothes?" Radnor laughed heartily. "I cannot believe it." Then, seeing the tears in his wife's eyes, he became serious. "Very well, I will not be angry. But suppose you tell me about what I am to keep my temper."

"My father," Leah faltered, "my father sometimes does strange things."

"This once, at least, a woman has spoken less than the truth," her husband muttered. Leah, however, was so encompassed by her own fears that she scarcely heard him and did not understand him at all.

"I have heard that he proposes to take me by force or guile and hold me to ransom." She gasped out the words as quickly as possible and held her breath, waiting for the storm to break.

The silence, however, was only broken by the sound of the horses's hooves, and after a minute or two Leah dared to breathe easily and look sidelong at her lord's face. He looked, instead of shocked or angry, smilingly interested, as well he might since his hope of Leah's innocence was more than confirmed.

"Who told you?"

"You are not angry? You do not care?"

"You did not answer my question. I suppose, if I think about it, I am a little angry, but certainly not with you. Who told you?"

Men were utterly incomprehensible, thought Leah. A decision about who would be crowned in a faraway city at some unspecified time in the future could throw them into an ungovernable rage, but treachery at home, among their own relations, moved them not a whit.

"My mother told me," Leah replied with more assurance. "She must have overheard my father making his plans."

"She has courage. If your father knew he would make matters most unpleasant. Ay, well, you may be easy on that head. I will do nothing to inform him and I will keep you safe."

Leah's spirits rose. She was not to be blamed for what was no fault of hers after all, and if Cain was not troubled and furthermore understood her mother's position, why should she be worried? They were now out of the area familiar to her, and she looked about with bright eyes. The countryside was changing. The low hills were in the background now and they were traveling through a fertile valley where the fields gave promise of plenty in spite of the settled drought. The people of the small hamlet they had passed were not like the people on her father's land either. There had been a flurry of fright when the armed cavalcade came into view, men and women running from their labor in the fields toward the houses, but it had subsided when Radnor called out something in a language Leah did not understand. When they passed through the straggling dusty street with low mud and wattle cottages thatched with straw on either side, the people had come out to stare and exchange comments with the members of Radnor's troop who spoke their tongue. One old man, toothless, bald, and dressed in a sheepskin so matted with grease and dirt as to look almost smooth and black, hobbled to Radnor's side and passed a remark which made her lord laugh and throw some copper coins. That had been only an hour ago, and now they were coming to an even larger village.

Here the people were even less frightened. Lord Radnor stopped and asked Leah if she were thirsty or hungry, since it was nearly midday. Thirsty, Leah replied. She would be grateful for a drink, the road was so dusty. But even before Cedric, accustomed to doing the lord's buying in English villages, had dismounted, a rather pretty young woman with a year-old baby on one hip had come out of a nearby hut carrying a wooden bowl of milk. This she had offered wordlessly, but with a smiling, clumsy curtsy to the bright vision on the gray gelding. Other women came up shyly to look at Leah's wonderful clothes—wonderful to them, although the pale gray tunic and darker, dusty green gown were among the simplest and hardiest Leah now owned. They were even more fascinated when Leah stripped off her gloves to take the milk and exposed her white hands with their long, shining, buffed nails and the great betrothal ruby winking on her finger. One even made so bold as to touch one of Leah's braids with a grimy, broken-nailed finger. Many of the village girls had fair hair too, but none of them had the time or knowledge to care for it, and it soon became matted and scraggly. To them the braids seemed like the spun gold hair of the fairy princesses occasional minstrels sang of in the village in exchange for food and a night's lodging.

Radnor was at first surprised when the women came out, because ordinarily they did not venture forth even when peaceful troops passed for fear of being carried off. He realized that it was Leah's presence that made them show themselves. First of all her appearance and clothing were an almost irresistible draw, and secondly her presence virtually guaranteed the proper behavior of the men escorting her. He was pleased too with Leah's manner, which showed neither revulsion at the dirt and odor of these people nor any friendliness or compassion toward them. She nodded kindly at the woman who had given her the milk and allowed the others to touch her without really acknowledging their presence. Radnor had just flung another handful of copper coins wide and was trying to pick out a small enough piece of silver to pay for the milk—or rather to reward the woman for her free offer of it, for in itself the drink was not worth even the smallest of the copper coins—when the warning he had been half expecting came.

"Ware! Arms!"

Instantly Leah was surrounded by a group of hard-faced veterans who cleared the other women away rapidly, if not kindly, with the butts of their spears. Radnor, slapping on his helmet and lifting the great shield which had been strapped across his back to cover him, was moving to the front center with Giles coming up hurriedly from the right. Before Leah could shame herself by crying out to ask what was happening, a firm hand clasped a lead rein to her horse and the cheerful voice of Harry Beaufort reassured her.

"It is nothing, madam. Be of good cheer. Probably no more than a single messenger going from one place to another, but in these hard times it is well to be sure."

Leah did not like that lead rein on her horse, but as Sir Harry made no move to use it, she remained silent, looking anxiously toward her husband. The sound of hooves came closer at full gallop; plainly it was a single messenger, but he might be the forerunner of an armed band. A second or two later, Leah heard what must have been the messenger's breathless voice and then Cain's laugh. The group surrounding her disappeared as quickly as it had formed and Cain was coming back, pushing off his helm and shifting his shield back over his shoulder. Radnor himself unhooked the lead rein and Sir Harry fell back.

"Is that needful, my lord?"

"What? Oh, the rein? Yes, I believe so."

"Why? Do you have so little faith in me?"

Radnor was surprised by the question and looked at his wife. He answered honestly, "No, I think you would stand well enough. I do not like your father, but there's good blood in him and as good on your mother's side. It was more that lily-livered creature you are riding. I think at the first shout or smell of blood he would bolt. Your heart I honor, but I greatly fear that those lovely white hands are not strong enough to hold a bolting horse."

"It is true that Cold Dawn has never seen or smelled blood, but I could not ride my hunting mare for such a trip, could I?"

"Of course not, you did right to take your hack. I will buy you some riding mares at Smithfield the first Friday we are in London. I do not like geldings. When you take the manhood away—even from a beast—you cut the heartstrings too."

There seemed to be nothing to stay for, yet they did not move and Radnor, even as he spoke to Leah, looked back along the road on which they had come.

"May I ask for what we wait, my lord?" Leah's voice was steady because she willed it so. She was really afraid there might be a fight, and she had changed her mind about wanting to see men fight.

"Oh yes, did I forget to say? We wait for Hereford, who is not ten minutes behind us, according to the messenger. He was to go north with Chester, but some matter has changed his plans and now he proposes to ride with us. As well, actually. With two of us together, no one would be mad enough to attack. We will stay this night at Hereford Castle, and you can—no, I will tell you of that later."

CHAPTER 11

LORD RADNOR COULD NOT HAVE CONTINUED his conversation with his wife even if he had intended to do so, for the Earl of Hereford was coming down the road at a spanking pace. Once he pulled his horse up beside Cain's all had to yield to him.

"If I ever heard of such a muttonheaded idiot as you. You ride off with a quarter of the number of men you usually have, carrying a woman with you, and with intentions of staying at Oxford's keep. I thought you were jesting, but Pembroke told me you meant it."

"Of course I meant it. Oxford must needs give me the keys and the direction of Pembroke's house in London. I must stay somewhere, and that will be most satisfactory to my purpose."

"Yes, but there is no need to spend the night with Oxford. You have not been to court this past year, so perhaps the news has not come to you. Joan of Shrewsbury has fixed her talons on Oxford, and she loves you not."

With Leah present, there was nothing that Radnor could do but ignore the last part of Hereford's remark. "I cannot believe that she would have him. What pleasure or profit could Oxford give Joan? She likes her men to be men."

"Perhaps she has had enough of *men*. There are things, mayhap, that half-men know that big oxen do not. Look at William of Gloucester and see how he holds a woman in thrall."

Radnor was accustomed to Hereford's jibes and took this in good part, although it seemed to be more serious than usual. He replied only, "Or Hereford?" laughing and refusing to be drawn.

The young earl colored slightly. "That is neither here nor there. What is the point is that Joan has also heard that you intend to visit Oxford. Do you think she is likely to miss this chance to be revenged on you for casting her—"

"Hereford," Cain said sharply, glancing at Leah. "If we are talking of foolishnesses, let us speak of serious ones. Joan will not be at Oxford Keep when we are there and need not concern us. This business of Chester's is bound to fail. I will tell you straight out that it is no longer a secret. Philip of Gloucester knows, and he suspects—"

"Then Robert of Gloucester is more a fool than I thought him, to be telling that traitor of a son—"

"Hold your tongue! Do not missay Philip to me, and do not tell me that Robert approved of this madness."

Hereford looked aside sullenly. "I did not say that Robert has approved. I said the matter had been broached to him."

Leah, not much interested in plots and counterplots and also rather unsure of whether she was meant to hear these things, dropped behind and found herself beside Harry Beaufort. He smiled pleasantly at her and Leah smiled back.

"Have you ever been this way before, Sir Harry?"

"Oh yes. I come from Warwickshire and I have passed through Hereford often in following the tourneys."

"What is it like?"

"The keep or the town, my lady?"

"Oh," Leah replied, laughing, "both. I am very ignorant, for I have never been away from home before."

Sir Harry laughed too, but he was uncomfortably aware of Leah's warmth, and he looked away, unwilling to be tempted. It was impossible to be rude to his lord's lady, however, and he tried to answer her eager questions until, as they were topping a slight rise, Leah interrupted him, crying, "Oh, look!"

Instantly alert, with sword half drawn, Beaufort did look—ahead, behind, and to both sides—but he saw nothing except the church spires and huddle of houses that made up the town of Hereford. The cry had attracted Radnor's attention too, and he turned in time to see Leah point ahead with the hand not holding the reins and ask an excited question of Beaufort. Suddenly Cain felt that it was senseless to continue a conversation in which it was plain that he had made no headway. The only real lever he had to use was that of Pembroke's perfidy, a subject which he could not broach anyway until he was sure that there was no other way to save Hereford. In the meantime mere talk would not change Hereford's mind and he might as well spare his own digestion by occupying himself pleasantly. Hereford, who was tired of being scolded, excused Radnor readily and said he would ride ahead to inform his mother of their imminent arrival. Radnor nodded and pulled his horse to a slower pace; Sir Harry fell away from Leah's side to make room for his master, and Leah flashed her husband a brilliant smile which showed the small, sharp teeth that had left their mark on him the previous night.

"I am so glad you have finished your talk with Lord Hereford. Have you time to speak with me? Sir Harry is very kind, but he knows nothing to the point. I ask about markets and he speaks of fortifications."

Cain laughed at the type of information she thought important and thought him capable of giving her. "I am in much the same case, Leah. It is the misfortune of men to be always thinking of fortifications, but I will try. What is it that Beaufort could not tell you."

"First whether there was a fair in town—is there?"

"I have no idea." Leah's face fell so ludicrously and there was so much surprise in her eyes that Cain laughed heartily. "But Leah, there are many things I do not know—I am not God."

"Then what are all those booths with guild pennons that I see?"

"That is Hereford Market—oh, I understand what you want to know. Hereford is not like your home. It is so large a town that they have a market for buying, selling, and bartering twice a week, every week. London has a market that is open every day. A fair does come here, perhaps twice or thrice in a year, but that is for special goods—cloth and spices from the East, fine riding horses, foreign women—and other things," Radnor concluded hastily, his tongue having run away with him.

Leah tactfully ignored the last statement. Perhaps it was just as well the fair was not in town. Besides, she wanted something and this was no time to start an argument about

159

other women. She began a little hesitantly. "Do they dine very late at Hereford? Will there be time and light after we eat to go to the market?" Her husband made no reply; he had looked away toward the keep. "Would it be possible for me to go look—only to look, my lord?"

Radnor turned back to her, his face perfectly expressionless. "We will see," he said repressively.

Leah did not sigh or let her disappointment show. Experience had taught her that such behavior accomplished nothing; perhaps when they were alone dressing for dinner she could try again. She asked some further inconsequential question to make her husband talk and lapsed into thoughtful silence.

Entrance into Hereford Castle drove all thought of the market from Leah's mind. The keep was much larger than that of Eardisley, having eight towers connected by battlements set on the curtain walls rather than four, but this was not what took Leah's breath away. It was the interior of the manor house and the furnishing of the private sleeping quarters which Hereford had temporarily ceded to Radnor in honor of his nuptial. Even though Beaufort had described the manor house, Leah had expected the interior to be dim. In the blaze of early afternoon sunlight, for three large windows with their shutters pushed all the way back faced due west, the hall was as bright—and more marvelous yet, as warm and dry—as the outdoors. But the private bedroom—Leah had stopped in the doorway, to which she was escorted by the friendly, maternal, clucking dowager Countess of Hereford, with a sigh of pure pleasure. Here one large window each faced east and west while the fireplace took up part of the north wall; the room was very light, but it was also a blaze of color. On each side of the hearth, well away from heat or sparks, hung great tapestries worked in brilliant shades. One depicted Charlemagne and the twelve peers of the realm, the other a hunting scene. These were the work of Lady Hereford and her women. On the floor lay carpets in wools soft as silk. Great flowers unknown to Leah, strange birds and beasts foreign to the French or Celtic pattern were interwoven in deep reds and blues with touches of brilliant yellow that glowed like patches of true gold.

The countess, noting her young guest's awe and pleasure, explained that the rugs were prizes of war that her late husband, Miles of Gloucester, had won. They had originally come to France with knights who had returned from the First Crusade, then across the sea with some baron of William the Bastard's. Leah knelt to touch their surface reverently and showed a disposition to avoid stepping on them which made Lady Hereford laugh and assure her that they had withstood many years of wear and would bear many, many more.

"But the tapestries—you say you made them?"

"Yes, child."

"It must be terribly difficult."

"Not at all, only slow, for the design must be drawn so that it may be divided into long strips, and the colors planned. Then the joining must be made so skillfully that no seam may be seen and no break in the pattern."

"Oh how I wish—." Leah stopped, fearful of being rude or presumptuous.

The countess smiled and patted the small hand she was holding. "What do you wish?"

"Could you—would you—do you think I am too stupid to learn how to make something like that? I am clever with my fingers, my mother says, but she loves me and might flatter. Is the working a secret?"

Lady Hereford was delighted with this child who showed interests of which she approved highly and smiled again. "I can teach you, and there is no secret involved but hard work. Only I cannot give you a design unless you are able to copy these. The patterns were worked for me by a lay brother of the monastery not far from here. He painted the books for the monks, but he is long dead now. Still, if you would like to learn, I will teach you when the men are at their talk tonight. It may well be that there is a man similarly skilled on your husband's estate. Now, here is your lord, and I will leave you."

The countess greeted Cain kindly a second time, giving him her hand to kiss and asking after his father. She did not linger many minutes after that, merely naming the dinner hour, which would be rather late because of the extra preparations caused by the unexpected arrival of her son. She had hardly closed the door, when Leah literally flew to Cain, stuttering in her eagerness to point out the beauties around them. He bore her tugging patiently with a quiet smile, but finally he touched her face gently and put her aside.

"Yes, I know. I have seen them many times before and we have such stuffs at Painscastle, although they are not used. You may have them all to amuse yourself with when

161

we go home. Just now, take this." He handed Leah a rather heavy purse which she held quietly, expecting that Cain wanted his hands free for some purpose. Instead, he stood looking at her as if waiting for something.

After a little silence, Leah asked, "What must I do with it, my lord?"

"What you like. It is yours, as are its contents. There is no pleasure in looking at what you cannot have, so if you intend to go to the market, you must needs have the wherewithal to purchase what you see."

Down went the purse on the floor and up went Leah's arms about her husband's neck. Tiptoe to reach his face, which she still fell an inch or so short of, she pulled energetically at him until he lowered his head so that she could kiss him, on his chin and cheek and nose before she reached his lips. Aware that the danger into which such thanks might lead them would keep them from getting to the market at all, Radnor disengaged himself.

"You have not even looked to see what coin is there," he chuckled, well pleased. "Mayhap I have given you but coppers worth nothing."

"Then I will buy sweets for us both. I care not for the coin, only that you are so kind as to grant my wish to see the market." She opened the purse then and looked with wonder at the silver pieces. "Cain?" she said shyly.

"Yes?" There was caution in the question. One way or another, every woman he had ever known had been mercenary. Had she expected gold in spite of the pretense of indifference?

"What are they worth? How does one count money?"

Radnor roared with laughter and sat down in the nearest chair. The girl was one continual delight to him, her warmth, her innocence, and her wisdom being always exhibited in the most unexpected ways. He pulled her down on the rug beside him and spread the money out in his lap to explain.

In the market Leah recalled her mother's behavior and showed not a bit of her newly cast-off ignorance. She wandered about for a while just enjoying the sights and taking her bearings before she instructed her groom in gentle but lofty tones to find the booths of the sellers of needles, pins, and thread. Radnor rode beside her, his lips twitching now and again as he strove to maintain his gravity. The contrast between his wife's public dignity and her hoydenish behavior in private was nearly too much for him, and he would not for the world hurt her feelings by seeming to laugh at her. Preceded by her groom and attended not only by her husband but by Giles, Cedric, and Odo, all well armed, Leah decorously rode to the section of the market indicated. When she entered the booth, Cain lounged in his saddle just outside and the armed men watched the crowd narrowly. Even in the town of a friendly lord like Hereford there were dangers from thieves, bands of market-day drunks, and personal enemies, and it was well to be prepared.

The merchant laid out his wares. Leah took from her purse three squares of cloth—fine silk, linen, and wool. Through these she passed the appropriate needles, noting the holes they made, whether they caught in the cloth or pulled the threads, and whether a piece of thread went smoothly and ran easily through the eye without catching. Radnor watched from his saddle with surprise and pleasure as his wife chose six needles and twelve pins which suited her.

Thus far, all had gone smoothly, but when the merchant, not blind to the youth of the girl and the doting looks of the man, named his price, the moments of harmony were over. Leah lifted her brows coldly in simulated surprise. She said that she was not purchasing golden needles or silver pins but inferior stuff which the merchant should be glad to give away. She made a counter offer of less than half the merchant's demand and the man, recognizing his mistake, settled down to chaffer in earnest. Radnor was still amused, but not so well pleased at this display of his lady's shrewdness. When Leah, heated out exultant in a good bargain, mounted up to leave, he protested.

"Leah, it is beneath the dignity of a great lady to chaffer. I am a very rich man. A few pennies more or less are of no account to me."

His wife, usually so docile to him, now faced him with surprising determination. "But, my lord, it is not a question of a few pennies. That much I might throw in charity to the crowd on a feast day. If a thief were to try to steal your purse, you would defend yourself even if it contained but a few pennies, would you not? Why then should you be robbed by a merchant who sets the price of his goods far above their value?"

"I do not know," Radnor said, struck more by his wife's ability to see clearly and state clearly such a point than by the argument itself. "In that way, perhaps you are right. Nonetheless, I do not like to see you arguing about money."

"Of course, if that is your wish, I shall never do so again." Leah submitted immediately, but she sighed a little for she enjoyed chaffering. "I shall have to teach one of my maids straightaway."

That innocent statement destroyed not only Radnor's gravity, but also his resistance. The subtleness of the thought combined with the naïveté which spoke it aloud was priceless. Leah was surprised by her husband's sudden laughter, more surprised when he leaned from his mount to embrace her and give her a quick kiss, and totally puzzled when he urged her to get as good a price as she might in the thread-seller's booth. She did not know what had brought about the reversal in Cain's opinion, but she had not a cloud in her serene sky, and she was positive that of all women living she had the best, kindest, and most indulgent husband.

Leah's happiness persisted for the next two days as they traveled slowly southeast toward London. On the surface, everything was the same at Oxford as it had been elsewhere, for to Oxford they went in spite of Hereford's repeated protests that it was as foolish to stay there as to put one's head into the maw of a half-trained bear. Radnor only laughed, saying that if a man did not come face to face with a bear he would never know whether it was dangerous. Leah had held her peace, relying on her husband's assurance that all would be well, but once in the keep, it seemed to her that Lady Oxford could not meet her eyes and that the talk of the men was too lighthearted and inconsequent. Her husband, dressed in orange and brown, looked unusually well, and laughed a great deal more than he commonly did. Unfortunately these facts gave Leah little comfort, for she was beginning to understand Cain's arrogance in the face of danger and beginning to understand too that the danger was great. How great was indicated by the fact that Cain's eyes glowed with a feral light and he wore a wonderful garment made of links of metal as fine as thread underneath his tunic.

In spite of Leah's growing fears, all ran smoothly enough at first, except that she felt too much wine was poured and drunk all over the hall. Cain kept taking his lower lip between his teeth and biting it as if it were slightly numb, and, by the time the roast meats were removed, his speech was slurring a trifle over difficult words.

It was in the middle of a discussion on tapestry making that the peace was broken. The men seemed to have run out of small talk, Hereford looking anxious, Oxford looking worried, and Radnor looking drunk, and the women alone were speaking, raising their voices steadily to combat the rising noise from the lower tables where the men-at-arms ate. Suddenly Leah and Lady Oxford were drowned out completely as the voices of the men reached a new pitch and a dozen of them leapt to their feet, poniards drawn. Hereford, Oxford, and Radnor all bellowed at once for their men to sit still and keep the peace, but by now all were too hot with wine and temper to hear or care. More joined the combatants, and the three leaders rose quickly to go down and pull them apart before lives were lost. Instead of falling away under the hammerlike blows of their masters' fists, the mass congealed. Radnor was the first to go down; never easy on his feet, he was cleverly tripped and disappeared under a battling crowd of men. Hereford struggled like a madman to reach his friend, but every time he broke a hold, others seized him to draw him back, and then he went down too. Oxford, less encumbered, also seemed to be struggling to reach the fighting men and he shouted from time to time for them to hold their hands. The swarm above Radnor heaved as he exerted his strength to throw them off, flattened as the effort proved unsuccessful, and heaved again.

In the end it was the newest servant rather than the old retainers who freed his lord. Harry Beaufort, unlike Giles who had thrown himself into the struggling group at once, at first remained seated at the very end of the high table with a faint frown on his face. A few minutes after Lord Radnor went down, however, he calmly took a flaming torch from one of the wall holders and began applying it indiscriminately to backs, heads, and buttocks of the heaving group over his new master. In seconds Radnor was free and was surrounded by a wall of angry men while Giles helped him to his feet.

The rest of the fighting quieted as if by magic. Hereford's men helped him up and dusted him off. Oxford babbled apologies and excuses. Leah stood like a statue, unmoving and without a sound, her hand on her own small dagger. She had jumped to her feet and had begun to pull the knife when Cain went down, but she had been

165

seized from behind and after a brief struggle had frozen into immobility. Somewhere within her frozen faculties she heard Hereford's anxious voice and then her husband's husky, unshaken tones replying, but she could not make out the words because her ears buzzed so. She knew too when Radnor reached the table, although her misted eyes could not see clearly.

"I pray you, my lord, that you take me to our chamber. I should like to retire and rest. I find this entertainment a trifle too exciting after a day's travel." She could not believe, as she heard it, that the normal, quiet voice was her own.

They went out and up to the tower room assigned, protected by a hard-eyed group with murder in their hearts. In the same normal voice Leah bade her maids fetch water, and she helped Radnor undress with perfectly steady hands. With the same steady, gentle hands she bathed and anointed his wounds, mostly small cuts and tears from knife points that could not fully pierce the hidden mesh of steel. She wrung and folded the cloth she had been using, capped the ointment jars, handed both to Ailson.

"You may go. I will not need you again tonight." As the door closed, she crumpled to the floor, still silent, in a dead faint.

Leah knew nothing of the furor she caused, the excitement being very little less than that occasioned by the attempt on Radnor's life. His anguished cries brought nearly all his own men, Hereford and half of his, and, eventually, the only people of any use, the ladies of the castle, on the run. These last, when they could finally make their way through the crowd on the stairs and induce the men in the room to let them through, cleared the chamber and put the poor girl to bed. She began to revive naturally a few moments later, and, seeing her eyelids flutter, Lady Oxford assured Radnor that his wife would now be perfectly well and withdrew.

Cain had never been so shaken with fear in his whole hard life. "What did you do that for?" he asked in a low, vicious voice as soon as her eyes focused on his.

Leah dropped her lids and tears leaked out under her long fair lashes. "I am sorry," she faltered, "I was frightened."

He caught her into his arms then, smearing the bedclothes and her naked body with salve and blood, and held

166

her so tight she felt strangled. "Do not do it again. I do not like it."

The voice was hard and angry, but Leah could feel the pounding of her husband's heart against her breast and the tremor of his arm muscles. He had not been affected that way after the fight, so it had to be fear for her. Terror and weakness notwithstanding, Leah's sense of humor was tickled by Cain's ridiculous remark. She smiled feebly.

"I did not do it on purpose, I assure you."

"I did not say you did it on purpose," Radnor replied, his voice rising with the irritation of relief, "but I will not have it. I forbid you to do it again—absolutely forbid it. Now what is so funny about that?" he bellowed, for Leah was laughing openly at the silliness of commanding a frightened woman not to faint. She did not answer, however, only pulled his head down to kiss him until the level of his breathing slowed to normal.

When he disengaged his lips, Cain sat looking at his wife broodingly for some time. Now that he had a chance to think at all, his thoughts were not pleasant. In spite of the preparations he had made, he had not believed, since his talk with his father, that any attack would be made upon him. The events, however, had proved Gaunt wrong and Llwellyn right. Pembroke did plan to have him killed and expected to escape the ill consequences for the very reason that Radnor thought he would not dare. If one took the time to work out the tortuous path, it became clear enough. While Gaunt lived, no one could say that Pembroke would profit from Radnor's death; not even Gaunt would think of it, and Pembroke planned to cover himself additionally by thrusting the blame on Oxford, Lady Shrewsbury, and the king and queen. It would be normal, if her husband died, for Leah to return to her father's protection. Then Pembroke had to do no more than keep her unmarried and wait for Gaunt, who was old, to die.

The business with Chester was not only an attempt to get Fitz Richard's property but also to insure Pembroke the reversion of Gaunt's property. By betraying Chester and Hereford, Pembroke believed he would gain Stephen's and Maud's favor. And, Radnor thought, new light breaking in on him, Maud as well as Stephen had probably encouraged Pembroke to believe this was true. After the betrayal, Pembroke would have to come to court to be invested with the land rights. He would come, but he would never leave, and the king and queen would have in their hands to do with as they pleased very nearly all of Wales and western England. Radnor shrugged his heavy shoulders and smiled. They were all mad together to think such a complicated thing would not fall of its own weight. First, it would not be in the least easy to kill him, as both Maud and Pembroke should know. Second, it might yet be possible to turn Chester and Hereford from their plan.

But Leah had told him that Pembroke wanted her for ransom. Why? To keep him off guard? And when the attempt on him had failed she had fainted. She said she had fainted from fear—doubtless that was true enough, but from fear for him or from fear because her father's plan had miscarried? Then she had laughed, and cozened him with kisses. Cain slid one strong brown hand around his wife's slender throat. He would press no viper to his breast to sting him to death. Leah had closed her eyes, but at his touch she opened them. No fear misted them. The greenish irises were clear as glass, the expression as trusting as a child's. Radnor tightened his grip, but Leah only smiled and turned her head to kiss the fingers of his other hand which lay upon her shoulder.

Cain snatched both hands away, and Leah looked startled for the first time. A moment later she was crimson; she had been too bold again, bestowing kisses unasked. Still, when Cain rose from the bed her hands clung to him as he moved away.

She is very young, Cain told himself. She could not know, keep her counsel, and act in such a way. If she wished to betray me, she could have slipped a word abroad about the mail shirt I wore. The clinging hands nearly convinced him so that he turned back to her and leaned forward expecting to catch a whispered plea that he stay with her. The eyes seemed to plead, but the lips, trained to obey the dictates of duty, stayed mute. Cain was dissatisfied, but he knew now positively that he could not bring himself to hurt her. Since he could not leave her behind or send her away either, it was best to remain on good terms. If she was innocent, it would be foolish to give her a reason to hate him by harsh treatment for which she would know no cause. Cain patted Leah's cheek kindly.

"There is no need to fear. You are in no way endangered by this. No one wishes you any harm. Now I must go down to my men. I have a few things to say to them

168

that may well save us from similar broils another time. Oh, I will warm their ears for allowing themselves to be trapped into this."

Leah lay trembling and praying. She had thought that once she held her lord in her arms she would be at peace, but she saw that her mother had been right and that to love a man was to live from moment to moment in a torment of fear. The minutes crawled by slowly. Now it was growing dark, and still Cain had not returned. Leah drew on a robe and stole to the door. At the faint click of the latch, four men in the antechamber jumped up, their hands going automatically to their weapons. "Stay still, madam," one said gruffly, and Leah closed the door. Her fear could not be greater; instead a blessed numbness took hold of her. She took up Cain's gown and embroidered steadily, and even when, long after the watchmen had called midnight and she had once renewed the candles, the sound of footsteps and voices penetrated the door, her hand did not falter nor did she raise her eyes from her work. The door opened and closed and a halting step came across the room. Leah laid down her embroidery and closed her eyes to fight off the faintness which came with utter relief.

"You are still awake! I was sure you would be sleeping, so I sent no message fearing to disturb you. When I came down I found Hereford trying to discover the cause of the uproar. The only thing he found was that whoever planned this is clever as a snake. It seemed best to go back to the hall as if we believed it to be an accident. Get you to bed now, madam. The earlier the better away from this place."

"Let me help you disrobe."

Cain came up and rested a hand on her shoulder reassuringly. "I sit awake tonight. Nay, do not look so aghast, Leah, there is no cause to be afraid. I will keep you safe."

As her own safety was the last thing with which Leah was concerned just then, this scarcely gave her comfort, but there was nothing she could do. No sight could have been more welcome to the tired girl lying perfectly still with wide staring eyes than the coming of full daylight. Radnor stood up and stretched his somewhat cramped limbs. He had no need to dress or arm, having changed silently to his traveling costume soon after Leah had gone to bed. Hereford too was ready, showing faint bluish patches beneath his eyes, for his fair complexion was readily marked by every sign of strain. They breakfasted politely, but with all possible haste, and Leah began to breathe a little more freely as they made ready to leave in the courtyard.

Radnor watched Leah lifted into her saddle by her groom and prepared to mount his own horse, always a painful process because of the need of putting his full weight on his left foot in the stirrup. Ordinarily he eased the strain by grasping the pommel and pulling himself up. He was just about to do so when a blow on the shoulder and a scream of "Ware! Guard!" made him throw up mail-clad arms to protect his bare head and neck and leap back from his horse in a crouch. He heard Beaufort cry out as he was struck and whirled to cover them both with his shield. From the corner of his eye he could see his stallion rear and fall, screaming with the pain of three deep-driven arrows. Leah's groom struggled to hold her terrified gelding, and in moments the courtyard was a seething mass of infuriated men and kicking animals.

Sticky and warm, Beaufort's blood ran over the hand with which Cain was supporting him. More blood poured, dyeing the ground red as Giles grunted and cut the stallion's throat. Radnor went mad. Bareheaded and without the shield which he had left covering Sir Harry, he charged the inner door of the keep. It was shut and he flung himself against it again and again, calling his battle cry. His men rallied to the call; the door gave under the combined assault. The innocence of the greater part of Oxford's retainers was loudly proclaimed by the ease with which the keep was reduced to a shambles, but no evidence could halt the impetus of Radnor's rage. It did not matter that few of the retainers were armed and even fewer put up any fight at all. Radnor's men, well seconded by Hereford and his troop, raged through the castle led by their blazing-eyed master until battlements, stairways, and the great hall were awash with blood.

Nauseated with reaction but not yet sated, Radnor faced a trembling and unarmed Oxford. "Arm and fight," he choked.

"I am no match for you."

"Full armor for you, I will fight as I am."

"No!"

"I will fight you on foot as I am, if you will arm and fight."

For a split second Oxford hesitated, since on foot the

crippled Radnor was at a huge disadvantage. Then, "No."

"Yield, then, for the craven you are or I cut your throat before the faces of your wife and children."

"I am innocent of this," cried Oxford, bursting into tears. "I have done you no harm and wished you no harm. You cannot do this to me."

"Can I not?" Radnor snarled, and lifted his sword.

"Hold your hand, Radnor," Hereford intervened, arriving blood-stained and gasping from the courtyard. "Those arrows belong to your own men."

"What!"

"Ay, the feathering and crests are those of Gaunt, but I will lay my life against a copper mil that no man of yours loosed the string that sped them. However, six of your men are missing."

"I know nothing of it—nothing—nothing," Oxford sobbed, and went down on the floor and embraced Radnor's knees.

"You must let him be, for all that he deserves hanging," Hereford continued, his mouth twisted with revulsion. "There is no proof against him. I doubt not that the bodies are buried or concealed or the pieces of them down the waste-fall, but who can prove that the men were not bought by someone else and fled on the failure of the plan? His men are one thing, but if you harm him personally, we will be arraigned for murder."

"Dead men do not bring complaints," Radnor insisted, his eyes still red with anger.

"Do you mean to put every soul in the castle—women and children—to the sword? There will always be someone to bring complaint."

"Before God," wept the man clinging to Radnor's legs, "before God I had no part in this. Whether they were bought or slain—I had no part in it, no knowledge of it."

"Radnor, for heaven's sake, you have taken vengeance enough for a mare's son. Give over. Let us go. Mayhap he even speaks the truth. His men were unarmed and unaware, without defense. Nothing stood between us and the keep but one door, and that only hastily locked, as one traitor might have done, not barred or bolted. This is a dreadful sin we have committed, to kill men unarmed and unaware."

"A mare's son only? Is my man's life worth nothing?"

Hereford came forward, wiping his bloody sword and sheathing it. Once Radnor stopped fighting and began to talk he was always reasonable. "Beaufort is hardly hurt. A wound in the flesh of the shoulder. He will mend quicker than your rage will abate."

Without another word or glance, Radnor pried Oxford free of his legs and left the keep. Another horse was ready saddled for him, and the courtyard was regaining some semblance of order under Giles' direction. Harry Beaufort was on his feet, and, though he had a bloodstained cloth round his shoulder, he stood sword in hand guarding Leah.

"How much are you hurt?" Radnor asked him.

"Nothing, my lord. A scratch that let a little blood."

Radnor nodded acceptance and turned to his wife. "Are you all right, Leah? You are so pale. You were not hurt?"

"I am perfectly well, but for God's sake, my lord, let us go from here before worse befall us."

"As quickly as we may. I stay only to gather my men, and Hereford the same. Giles!"

"Coming, my lord."

"What is the count?"

"Six missing—did my lord Hereford tell you?"

"Yes."

"Half a dozen scratches that a cat could do better, and a broken arm."

"A broken arm?"

"The fool slipped in the blood on the stairs and must needs come down on one arm. He can ride."

"Let us go then. Hereford I see is also ready. My belly crawls in this place."

"Ay, you were always one with an uneasy stomach for such work," Giles remarked. "Mayhap it would be better not to go to a place where you expect blood pudding to be served, especially when you do not intend to finish the portion. Have you never faced a flight of arrows before or a knife in the ribs that you need run mad?"

"Very well, very well," Cain replied irritably. "I know it was not well done. Were you so cool last night? Then you were crying out for blood."

"It was not my head they were after. There are things I love better than my own skin."

Radnor turned eyes filled equally with pain and disbelief on his old tutor. "You have known me for nearly thirty years," he said finally with an effort, "can you say this to me? Can you call me a coward? In all these years, you, at least, have never missaid me before—"

"What made you commit this folly, then? How are we to win home again? Is there a man between here and London to whom Oxford is not tied by blood and marriage? If you were not mad with fear, why did you do it?"

Cain rubbed his forehead, leaving bloody streaks across it. "It was the blood, the way the horse screamed and Beaufort bled," he answered slowly. "I must suppose I *was* mad. Well, there is no help for it; we must make London tonight. I do not believe we return by this path in any case, but it will be time enough to ford that river when we come to it."

"That spills readily enough from your tongue, but things are not as they were wont to be. Will your lady wife be able to ride so long and so far?"

Cain's eyes grew momentarily hard. "Needs must is a hard master, but one that is obeyed. I can carry her on the saddlebow if she grows too weary. Give the order to ride. To tarry longer is fruitless, and dangerous."

CHAPTER 12

LORD HEREFORD BROKE A LONG SILENCE when the tired troop reached the West Gate in London's wall. "Do we rouse the porters and demand entrance, or do we stay here until sunrise?"

Radnor shifted Leah, who was sleeping before him in the saddle, so that he could take the reins from his numb left hand. "I think we had better stay. I had not meant to come so far, but I have been so occupied in seeking a way out of this hideous coil that I did not see where we were. Let us withdraw a little way, make camp, and enter with dignity at a reasonable hour in the morning."

"At a reasonable hour? Do you not mean to win to the king on his first rising? Why have we ridden all night but to explain first and in our own way what happened at Oxford?"

"Nay, we rode to keep our skins whole. Oxford has too many relations between his home and London to make comfortable travel for those who have offended him. On the other matter, Hereford, you cannot have considered. If we run with all haste to the king, we tell the world that it is important which side of the tale he hears first. Innocence does not hasten to proclaim itself, but looks greatly surprised upon being questioned and then gives answer."

"Innocence! There is the blood of some hundred or two men on our hands. How do you mean to explain not mentioning that? A slight lapse of memory?"

"Nonsense," Radnor replied testily. "What need to mention a deserved chastisement except to make suitable apologies if the insult was not intended. Look you, Hereford, here is what I propose. I will go to Pembroke's house," he glanced at Leah but she slept soundly, her cheek nestled against the velvet of his surcoat, "and——"

"Oh, you are madder than a hornet—and to think I have known you all these years and never seen it before."

"Why should I not take the house? I have paid for it. You are the one who claims Pembroke is innocent. Anyway, will I not be better on my guard in his choice of a house than in my own which I might think, wrongly, safer?"

"Now you are making madness sound like good reason. Thus you cozened me into Oxford's keep and into this mess. You only talk around and around me. I know something is wrong, but I cannot lay my finger upon it."

"Hear me out, perhaps it will become clear. Tomorrow or rather today at the usual time and in the usual way I will present myself. I expect to be met with Oxford's accusation, to which I will reply that one attempt upon me might well be an accident, but two in the same place give good reason for suspicion and chastisement. For present safety I need only Stephen's verbal pardon in open court, and I believe I can have it, for the Marcher lords are here in strength to support me—and, no doubt, my innocence will shine forth."

"And what of me?"

"You? What have you to do with this matter? You were merely there by accident, and if a few of your men were carried away by the excitement and became embroiled, why you could not help that. Oxford owes his life to you."

"A few?" Hereford laughed, amused in spite of the gravity of their situation by the surprised and injured innocence of Radnor's voice and expression.

"Do not be a fool," Radnor replied, completely sober

again. "It is not you they want. You," he added with dry bitterness, "are in a fair way to hang yourself without their help. I doubt that Oxford will mention you at all except to praise."

"All right," Hereford agreed finally. "I like it, all except that accursed house. God knows how else you could explain what happened. After all, even if your men did turn on you, you can claim they were bought, and who more likely to buy them in Oxford's keep than Oxford."

When Radnor saw the house to which Oxford had given him the keys the previous night, he was well satisfied with the first portion of his plan. It was a reasonably large building, the lower half of stone and brick, the upper of wood. The gardens were overgrown and useless, but the stable sheds in the back yard seemed to be adequately roofed and in fair repair. There would be room for his men on the lower floor, and, best of all, the house stood alone and should be easily defensible.

Leah was more interested in the upper floor, for she would live there, and in the kitchens at the back of the lower floor of the house, for feeding the men was her responsibility. Before anything else was attempted, she realized, she must obtain servants. The men-at-arms might be willing to chop wood and draw water, although she doubted it, but they would be incapable of performing most other household tasks and unwilling to do so for fear of losing social status. But how did one obtain servants in a place like London? People were born into service on the estates or were chosen for training from the children of serfs or villeins. All were eager to become castle servants because the life was far easier than that eked from the land, and socially a castle servant was above the serf or even the free farmer. However, there were no serfs belonging to Radnor in London, as far as Leah knew. There was no use in asking her husband for help in this matter, for away from Hereford's presence he had given way to his emotions. He was dressing for his court appearance now in a black fury, kicking furniture about and cursing in three languages, using words even in French which Leah could not understand.

Leah knew she must manage this matter on her own. Of the people she had met at her wedding, who would be likely to be in London? Lady Shrewsbury—Leah shuddered. She certainly would be unwilling to help her, or entirely too helpful for reasons of her own. The Leicesters should be here by this time, and so should William of Gloucester and his wife. She would have to ask Cain where they would be staying and how to contact the ladies. Just as she reached that decision, however, he burst past her with such an expression on his face that even Leah, who had not been in the least frightened by his display of bad temper, would not dare speak to him.

"Sir Harry and the first fighting order will accompany me. Now! Quick! God damn you, move your filthy hides, you whoresons. Hurry!"

The men leapt to obey, having considerable experience of their master in this mood. One unfortunate who stumbled against Radnor in his rush was felled unconscious with a blow that would have stunned an ox. Giles pushed Odo, who happened to be nearest him.

"Take his place, quick, if you want us all to keep our heads. My lord, do I accompany you?"

Radnor looked around, his eyes blank with his inner tempest. To have to explain, to excuse himself, possibly to humble himself before Stephen and his court made him sick. To know that it was his own fault, that it would not have happened except for his loss of control, that except for that he might have had a weapon to use against one of the favorites of the king, nearly made him insane. Why had he done it? Was it fear? Hate? Pride? Just the lust to kill and kill and kill? He hardly heard the question addressed to him.

"What?"

"Do I go or stay?"

"You guard her ladyship and attend to her wants."

Another time Giles might have protested this order. It was inconceivable that anyone should wish to hurt Lady Radnor, and as long as she stayed in the house she was safe. On the other hand, Radnor was going into a hotbed of enemies in a mood that was scarcely calm or conciliatory. Nonetheless Giles knew his master. When Radnor's eyes turned in on his own soul, giving that blankness to his expression, it was a warning that even Giles must obey without question. Giles crossed himself as he turned away. He did not quite know why, but he had always done so. Even when Radnor was only a child, his periodic bouts of looking inward at himself had made Giles uneasy. The soul was God's business and His priests'; a man, in Giles' opinion, should leave his soul to those who understood it and not toy with it himself.

176

Upstairs, Leah folded and smoothed Radnor's cast-off clothing absently, wrinkling her brow over a new problem. Whom could she send to obtain the directions of Lady Leicester or Lady William? It was just as well that Cain had gone out, considering his mood. He would have been the greatest hindrance, for all her time would have necessarily been spent in soothing him. Her eyes smiled reminiscently —it was a great pleasure to do so, but it would not get the household running, the food cooked, or the bed set up. She opened a clothespress and shook her head—dust and broken twigs and leaves of old, scentless herbs. The dust, at least, could be attacked.

"Alison. Bess."

The girls appeared at once, both pale and tired. Neither could ride a horse, and they had, in consequence, been forced to travel in a heavy springless cart. The poor things had been so jolted and bruised that they could not sleep and were deeply regretting their previous desire for adventure and the sight of strange places. Leah was gentle and sympathetic to their complaints, but unrelenting in her demand that every chest be turned out and scoured clean. She would return to help them, she said, with a sudden look of decision, as soon as she had spoken to Giles.

"I hope there will soon be other maids and menservants to help you, and perhaps if you finish quickly we will go to the great market and buy rushes and herbs."

It sounded odd to speak of buying rushes and herbs, but what else could one do in a place where one owned no water and the garden was an overgrown mass of weeds? After seeing the girls set to work, Leah went down the stairs. Her first few steps were bold and firm, but as the clamor and confusion of the men's quarters became more apparent, her steps grew more hesitant. Would these hard men obey her? Her mother had guarded her carefully from her father's men-at-arms, but certain early memories of their cruelty to unprotected women lingered.

"Giles," she called. Her soft voice, softer even because of her uncertainty, could not carry over the noise. One man near the staircase heard a sound, however, and looked up. With horror in his eyes, he poked another. In a few minutes one could have heard a mouse walking on velvet in that huge room. Leah came down two steps more while the men watched suspended between confusion and terror. Lord Radnor would have every one of them drawn and quartered if he returned and found her there, yet who

177

would dare say her nay or stop her and risk her displeasure.

"Giles," Leah repeated, fear giving a rather peremptory note to her voice.

"Coming, my lady." The old warrior hurriedly pushed his way forward through the paralyzed mass of men and came up toward her. "You should not come here," he said in a low, angry voice. As the words came out, he wondered how the light of his master's eyes was going to take this criticism. If she were a proud one, there might be trouble between his lordship and himself.

"Oh!" Leah exclaimed with widening eyes. "Is it proper for you to come upstairs? I must ask you something."

Giles' lips twitched. "For me, yes. I am old enough to be your grandfather," he replied as he shepherded her up the stairs again. "For others, no, not unless your lord be with you." He was a fine one, he thought, to be giving lessons in etiquette.

"Oh." There was a little pause. "Then how may I let you know I want you if my lord is gone and I may not come down?"

Giles was jealous of this girl; he could not help it, for he loved his erratic lord and he felt that Radnor's affections were centered elsewhere now. Leah's gentle innocence, however, was having its usual effect on a man unaccustomed to dealing with women. "Send one of your maids out to the stables to your groom, and he will fetch me up. Now what did you want of me, madam?"

"There is so much to be done that I scarcely know where to begin asking. First and foremost, I must have servants. Cooks—the men and his lordship must eat; menservants to draw water and chop wood; maidservants to clean and sew. Someone must go to the market—myself, if you think Lord Radnor would permit. We must have food, rushes for the floors, herbs and salt and spices—"

There was a dawning respect in Giles' eyes as he looked down at the girl before him. "True enough. We have never kept house here before, but I will be little help to you. Protect you I can, but no more."

All men were alike, Leah thought disgustedly. Old or young, they had no sense. They could think only of fighting or killing, never of making life pleasant. "I believe that Lady Leicester or Lady William Gloucester would help me. Can you bring me to one of them?"

Lady William was ill, Giles reported after coming out of her house and swinging into the saddle again, but Lady Leicester lived near and they could try her next. Leah curtsied deeply when ushered into Lady Leicester's presence, but that good dame seemed delighted to see her. She motioned Leah to a seat and sat down herself in a manner indicative of her readiness for a long chat.

"Madam," Leah said urgently when the necessary civilities had passed, "I am afraid I have come here to impose upon you and ask you for a great favor."

Caution appeared in the older woman's eyes. She liked this child, but she was not going to embroil her husband with Lord Radnor over her. "If I can help you, child, I will."

"Well, I do hope you can, for I know not where else to turn."

"If there is trouble with your husband—." Lady Leicester hesitated, and the girl interrupted her hurriedly.

"No, no. Nothing of that sort. It is only that my lord has taken a house for us, and I know not how to find or employ servants in this strange place. Can you tell me—"

"Do you mean to say that Radnor is here without a retinue? That is impossible. Even he would not travel alone in these times."

"Of course not. He has his household guard with him, but they are not servants. I need men and maids to clean and serve and cook."

Lady Leicester looked stunned momentarily and then began to laugh. "Bless my heart and head, what a man! What does he expect to eat? Where does he expect to sleep?"

Leah could not help smiling too. Ordinarily she resented any criticism of her husband, but this time his disinterest in mundane matters had really gone too far; they were in an impossible situation. "I do not believe that he thinks about such things. He is not in the least particular about what is set before him and will eat the same dried meat and grain as the men have if there is nothing better. And I am sure if I told him that the bed could not be set up he would lie down on the floor without the slightest protest. Indeed, he did so once in my mother's house. But it is not fitting that he should be so served. If I had but a few menservants I could contrive, but I have only these two maids, and they are young and timid. I do not like to send them among the men-at-arms."

179

"If that is not like a man—to take a house and then let a child like you struggle to manage it without help. I will help you, my love, even if I must send you some of my own people. Only I am so shorthanded because—wait, I know what we must do. I will send to the Lord Mayor's steward. I am sure that he will be able to find suitable people for you."

A page was dispatched and Lady Leicester proceeded to question Leah about her supplies and furnishings. She was distracted between amusement and horror when she learned that they had come without making previous arrangement for the house to be stocked and that Leah intended to go to the market that morning. She offered, however, between gusts of laughter, excellent advice on prices and hints on how to judge quality, so that Leah was grateful in spite of the amusement at her husband's expense.

By the time the dinner hour was near, Leah was trembling with fatigue at the same time that she glowed with satisfaction. The house was stocked with food for a week and more was ordered; five cooks and three bakers were preparing dinner; all the floors were swept clean and new-laid with fresh rushes; and, finally, her own bed was set up and her room was in perfect order. Leah looked about. The brilliant red coverlet of the bed gave color to the rather dim room. Facing the one large window at the front of the house, a low-backed chair stood ready before her embroidery frame, and set to the other side was a high-backed chair, its seat and footstool also covered with red cloth cushions, all ready for her lord to take his ease.

The thing Leah wanted most now was a bath. The question was whether there was time. Lord Radnor had given her no indication of when he would return, and Giles could not help her since he had as little information as she. The best she could do was to tell the cooks to hold back the meat for the high table half-cooked and wait. Then she thought that it would not matter if Cain returned to find her bathing. Surely that would not displease him. It might even occupy him until dinner was ready. Almost hoping he would come in, for Leah was developing a taste for the pleasures of the marriage bed, she lingered in her bath until the water changed from hot to tepid. She nearly sent the maids for more hot water, but a glance at the woebegone faces awakened her pity and, besides, she did not wish her skin to grow wrinkled with long soaking. Dressed in the coral and gray outfit she had worn on her last day at home, Leah dismissed the girls to their dinner, and sat down to her embroidery, a seemingly endless task. She was very hungry, for the dinner hour was now long past, but she thought she would wait a little longer.

The next thing Leah knew was being startled awake by a hubbub in the front garden. She had fallen asleep, tired out with work and excitement, her head pillowed on the embroidery frame. It was now too dark to make out who had arrived, but Giles' voice, rising above the general clamor, was filled with welcome and relief. Leah hurried to the antechamber, a small room into which the stairs rose from below, to send a new little page scurrying off for lights.

Radnor passed through the men's quarters quickly, without a word. He was so tired that he was not even fully conscious of why he was in such a hurry to get upstairs. Simply, something promised rest and surcease from pain there. At his first sight of Leah, waiting in the antechamber with a branch of candles, the first wave of peace came. Not so for her. She had never seen Cain limp so badly or look so horrid. Deep lines were etched from his nose down to his mouth, and under the weatherbeaten brown his complexion was pasty. His eyes were dull with fatigue, red-rimmed from sixty hours without sleep, and the lid under the scarred brow twitched constantly with the nervousness of long-restrained emotion.

"How tired you are, my lord. Come and rest. Have you eaten?" Leah tested cautiously for the flash of temper that would make her efface herself as much as possible. The voice that answered her was so low she had to strain to hear it, but it was tired, not angry. The way was open to give comfort, and Leah slid her husband's arm over her shoulder in what might have been merely a gesture of affection but which also provided him help in walking.

"Eaten? No." Radnor sank into the red-cushioned chair, keeping his body rigid to prevent himself from crying out with relief. "I could not eat. I did not wish to eat there. I must break bread with Stephen sooner or later, but the later the better for me."

"I will go and order dinner at once."

"Thank you."

He closed his eyes and allowed his stiffened muscles to relax slowly. There was a cool sweet scent in the room from the fresh rushes on the floor and the odor of lavender which permeated Leah's clothing. Cool air and his men's voices, laughing and cursing as they gambled and talked, drifted through the window. He heard Leah returning and opened his eyes to find her offering a cup. The wine was hot and spiced; the sharp odor of aromatic herbs filled his nostrils and brought a new wave of well-being and comfort.

"Drink, my lord. It will refresh you and enable you to eat. Afterward you can sleep."

Cain sipped the wine and looked around. The candlelight was not bright, but he could not help noticing the excellent order of the room. Nor could he fail to notice the fact that the manservant who brought his dinner and the elderly maid who carried a small table to the side of his chair were strangers. Strangers could be spies—or worse.

"Who are these people, Leah?" he asked sharply.

"Our servants. I have such a great deal to tell you, Cain, but not now. You are too worn out to listen to my nonsense."

Since he made no move to serve himself but continued sipping his wine, Leah cut several slices of roast pork and divided a chicken in half. These she laid on a thick slice of freshly baked manchet bread and pushed within easy reach. Then she started to eat her own long delayed meal.

"I should like to hear. Tell me while I eat. What have you been doing? Where did all this food come from?"

So Leah laid down her barely touched food and recounted her adventures and misadventures until a faint smile touched her husband's lips.

"It always does me good to hear you, Leah. I have used you shockingly ill to set you down in a strange place without help. I am sorry, I never thought about it, but you have done very well." He leaned forward, his smile fading, pushed away the remains of his meal, and rubbed his left thigh surreptitiously.

"Will you eat no more, my lord?"

"I must go down and speak with Giles. There are things to be done and things to be planned—"

"Could you not send for him here?" Emboldened by her successful attempts at independent action and Cain's quiescence, Leah dared question his statement. Two days previously the idea of doing so would never have entered her mind.

"You permit? These are your quarters, Leah. My

182

stepmother would never allow the men-at-arms, not even Giles, to enter her chamber."

Leah's mind jumped to what she had heard among the women—that even their husbands asked permission to enter their quarters. Her father had never extended that courtesy to his wife, and Leah had not expected it, but apparently Cain did not know this and was prepared for her to demand the same privacy as the other women he knew had.

"Tonight, gladly." She had accomplished so much she now dared try for more. Watching Cain's expression, she said gently, "You have had enough standing and walking for today. I can see your foot hurts. I will send a page to summon Giles."

It was the first time since the day they met that she had mentioned his lameness. Leah wanted to see that foot. It was not mere morbid curiosity or superstition. She had to have Cain's permission—his request—to look. As long as he concealed his deformity from her, the darkest part of his soul would remain his own secret. When that secret was hers, he would be naked before her and Leah felt that she would then truly hold her husband in the hollow of her hand. Nor was her desire simply a selfish urge to have another, greater hold upon him. For his sake too she desired to share his fear and shame. And what if the fear is just, asked the voice of superstition. What if he shows you, and it is not a crippled foot but the horn hoof of Satan? Such things happened; the priests and holy books had tale after tale of women so deceived. If it was an ordinary crippled foot, of what was he afraid? Leah's eyes flew to her husband's face.

Cain had not answered his wife's remark, but it broke his peace. He was turned slightly away from the light of the candles, his lids drooping over tired eyes, trying to think through the haze of fatigue in his brain. Leah's insistent stare drew him to look at her, and he started to rise.

"What is it? Of what are you afraid?"

"Nothing. What is there to fear?"

They remained, eyes locked, and Cain reached out and drew his wife toward him. "To whom have you been speaking? First you mention my foot, and then there is fear in your face."

"No! Not for that!" There was too much emphasis, perhaps, which gave the lie to her words. The strained silence stretched tight with tension. The truth, thought Leah. It is

183

I who am naked now and he can read me. I must speak the truth. "The fear is yours, my lord, not mine. If you are afraid, must not I be so too? My eyes and heart are but a mirror for yours."

Very possibly it was so. Cain had noticed before that Leah seemed to feel what he felt even before he spoke. He sank back into his seat. "There is nothing to fear," he said dully. "Help me to take off this infernal steel shirt and send someone for Giles."

Temporarily delayed, but not defeated, Leah attended to her husband's needs. By the time Giles came up Cain was slumped in his chair again, wrapped only in a homespun robe. He acted toward his wife as if he had forgotten what had passed between them, but he placed his feet on the footstool before him now and he rubbed his painful leg openly, defiantly denying that he was afraid. Leah, busying herself to still her thrill of triumph, moved another branch of candles to light her embroidery and sat down to her work. The first breach in his defenses was made, for he had to prove to her that he did not care. The evidence was plain; whenever he sat in her presence previously, he had tucked his left leg under the chair, out of sight.

"Take that stool and sit down, Giles. I hate to have to twist my neck to look at you."

The master-of-arms looked uneasily at Leah as he obeyed. In spite of the morning they had spent together, his previous conditioning with the late Duchess of Gaunt had not led him to believe that women in her position would docilely accept what almost amounted to discourtesy. Leah, however, was as innocent of the knowledge that it was discourteous for Giles to sit in her presence as she would have been of resentment if she had known. Already Giles was not a servant, he was Giles. She did not even look up from the golden fleur-de-lis she was setting into the collar of a dark green serge gown.

"Well?" The old man asked the question in his usual hard tone, but he was filled with a triumph of his own. Not the young bride but the old friend was needed when important matters were at stake.

"Thus far, well enough. I was received as if I were the prodigal son. I did not even have to ask pardon—it was freely given with mournful headshakings over the sad misunderstanding."

"Something stinks to high heaven here."

"Oh, ay, but I cannot scent whether it be assault or

treachery. And I swear that Stephen himself has no part in it. Either it is Pembroke alone or Pembroke supported by the queen." Cain rubbed his forehead and eyes, attempting to brush away the webs of weariness that clogged his brain. He had forgotten the girl who sat with suspended needle and bated breath, her color fading. "I spent the live-long day in that place, bowing and smiling, talking and listening. The only thing I can smell there is fear. They know Henry of Anjou is coming, it seems, though no man spoke of it to me, but not where, nor when, nor how supported. So much is good, but there is bad in with it. They speak of Chester with sidelong looks that show that there is no secret in the secret. The king waits only for a hint of proof, a single move, one man's accusation—and Chester will be taken. But this is not the worst. I fear greatly the reasons for the delay in the finding of the proof or making the accusation. I think the queen waits until others—likely myself—can be drawn in. Giles, something you must do at once, is—"

"Wait up a bit, my lord. These may be matters of life and death. Do we well to speak here?"

"Why not? Oh well, close the window. It is not likely that anyone will be in the road, but as well be sure."

Giles closed the shutters seeking for a tactful way to explain that it was Leah's hearing and talking too much he was worried about. He knew how dear the girl was to Lord Radnor and did not wish to anger him, but finding no better way, he spoke directly to the point. "Your wife has ears too, and she is Pembroke's daughter."

Cain lifted his head sharply and both men looked measuringly at Leah, her head bent over the beautiful stitchery. She had had time to recover from her shock, however, and aside from a transparent pallor her face showed nothing but acceptance of what had been said. All in all, although he would have spared her if he could, Radnor was not sorry his revelation about Pembroke had slipped out. If she was innocent, she would be warned against speaking or writing openly to her mother about her husband's doings. If she were not innocent—Cain dismissed the thought with a painful tightening in his bowels.

"I am not deaf," Leah said quietly, "and I will gladly go and sit in the antechamber if that is your will, my lord. But you need not fear me for my father's sake. He has given me, except for marrying me to you, no reason to hold him in affection. From his cruelty I have learned

185

some things to your benefit. I have long practice in silence."

"There is no use in locking the stable door after the stealing of the cattle," Cain said at last. He realized he could not send her out of the house or down into the guardroom, and from the antechamber, she could hear if she wanted to. "She holds our heads in her hands anyway, for who knows whether I talk in my sleep or she is the kind that listens at doors. If she be not faithful, what matter how the blow falls?"

If I am not faithful, Leah thought bitterly, keeping her eyes on her golden flower with an effort. How can a woman prove her faith? If I speak a word against the beast that fathered me, I am disloyal and not to be trusted. If I sit silent, obeying my lord's command, I am doubted because I have not declared my loyalty to him. What path can there be between speaking and being silent? I may not offer a caress to prove my love because then I am bold and bold women are not faithful. I may not beg him to avoid danger because it is a woman's duty to strengthen, not weaken, her man. The resentment drew Leah's eyes to Cain's face and she met his anxious glance. The stake he was gambling on her good faith was his life; her face softened. Who could blame him for a little doubt?

Giles had shrugged and sat down. Radnor spoke the truth, for if his wife wished to destroy him nothing could be easier than a slit throat while he slept or poison in a cup. "Your orders?"

"First, the relay messengers to my father. Are they set? Trusted men?"

"Am I in my dotage yet that you ask such a question?"

"Good. And if I did not ask, no doubt you would have a few words for me, and not such pleasant ones either, about carelessness. Now for the heart of the matter. It may be necessary to find a road home for Chester and Fitz Richard, not to mention that idiot Hereford. We cannot take them north, so the southern way it must be. Make certain of a quick road with horses waiting."

"Through Surrey, Hampshire, Wiltshire, and Dorset? Wellaway, that is tough chewing. You will never get Chester home by that road."

"The way things are, I fear I will never get him home at all. You know not how black matters hang. Just now I can devise no better. This is more than nothing. Try, at least, for safe-conducts."

"What I can, I will do. What else?"

Radnor ran a forefinger down the scar to his lip and then back and forth across his mouth. Suddenly he shook his head and covered his eyes. "Giles, I cannot think. My head is full of fleeces."

"Oh, ay, and mine too. Three days and two nights without sleep—and we are getting older, my lord, both of us." Giles yawned hugely. "We do not leave tomorrow, praise God. Let it hang a day longer. I will do my part, but for now, let us get to bed." He rose without ceremony, forgetting Leah, and walked off as he would have in camp, without farewell.

Cain sat shielding his eyes from the light with one hand, the other automatically rubbing his thigh, too tired to go to bed. A few minutes later, Leah shook him awake.

"My lord, come to bed. You are asleep in your chair." He sat on the bed, dozing. "Let me undress you," Leah smiled, "you cannot see to undo the laces."

That jerked him awake. "No! Let me be. Get to bed yourself and put out the lights."

He was unconscious almost before he lay down. Leah, realizing that she had tried to push him too fast, sought to recoup lost ground by pressing herself against him, but she got nothing for her pains but a sodden snore. Nonetheless, out of the combination of Cain's exhaustion and the pressure of her body came a lesson about the relationships between men and women that Leah never forgot. After several hours of sleep, the consciousness of a female body beside him pierced Lord Radnor's weariness. He groped, pulled her close. That he had no idea who she was, was quite apparent, because he covered her mouth with his hand, growling, "Be still." The release of his passion was so quick and impersonal as to be an insult, and his push when he rolled off her was a cold brutality. "Get out," he mumbled thickly, "I am through with you for tonight. I'll pay you in the morning."

Leah had sense enough not to take those words to herself, but for a long time she could not sleep. Never before, even in that first urgent rape from which all tenderness had been absent, had Cain's caress been an insult to her body because, tender or harsh, he had always desired her personally even if only for breeding purposes. This time he had no more concern with the person he was using than he had for the waste-fall when he relieved his bladder or bowels. Leah's heart contracted and began to pound sickly.

187

Thus it was for wives whose husbands had no fondness for them. Thus it could be for her if she lost Cain's regard through his boredom, her own folly, or another woman's design.

There was no resentment or offense in Leah's mind connected with her husband's casual use of her. She knew that at present he was attached to her and saw what had happened only as the merciful intervention of an infinitely kind deity for her benefit. This had been a warning to preserve her alike from overconfidence and carelessness in her dealings with Cain and from falling a victim to the dissipation of the court. Cautiously, not desiring to wake him, Leah took her husband's hand and pressed it to her breast. Holding on to him, she regained her calm and slept.

CHAPTER 13

DROWSILY REPLETE, Lord Radnor lay with his arms behind his head watching Leah's maids dress her. Something about her clothing troubled him, and after she had gone into the antechamber to give the servants their instructions for the day, he lay with closed eyes puzzling about what it was. Something he had forgotten. He looked vaguely around the room until his eyes were caught by the bright design of Leah's gold embroidery. Gold! Jewelry—he had forgotten to give her the jewelry brought from Paniscastle for her. He had also forgotten to tell her that Maud had virtually commanded her presence at the White Tower that day. Staying only to draw on chausses and shoes, Cain flung open the door to the antechamber. Alison and Bess squeaked with alarm and drew together; the other servants present, head cook, steward, and several maids, drew back also, startled by the huge, half-naked apparition, unshaven and unkempt. Leah, too, rose, but smiling and with a hand extended in welcome.

"Good morning, my lord. You look better rested now. How can I serve you?"

"Come in here. I have something for you."

"Yes, my lord. You—er, Jennet, have the men bring up—. Will you bathe, my lord?"

"If it can be done quickly."

"If not, I will know why. I bade them keep water hot. Jennet, have the men bring up the bath and water and have the barber wait in readiness."

Radnor drew her impatiently into the solar and closed the door, setting his back against it and pulling her close to kiss. "You are fresh and sweet as new-ripe fruit."

"I thank you, but like fruit you will pulp me if you squeeze me so." Leah answered playfully, but she gasped in earnest.

He relaxed his grip a little and bent to bury his face in her breast. "You smell like a garden, too. Lavender and—and rose, and woman. Will you do me a favor, Leah?"

"A favor? You may command me in anything, my lord. You have no need to ask favors."

"Yes, but I do not wish to command you in this. I ask it as a favor. Do not use the scents the merchants sell. They are sweet, but I like the odor of fresh woman better."

Leah laughed and rubbed her face in the hair of his chest. "And you smell like horse and hard-worked man. Let the servants in with your bath."

He let her go, but reached out quickly as she moved away to pull her braid. "That was very unkind. Surely I deserve better after all my flattery. Have you seen a small black ironbound box that was packed with my clothes?"

"In the chest on the right of the bed. And I must say, my lord, that I am not nearly so rude as you are. Imagine telling a woman that you were flattering her when she believed you to be sincere. I am desolated. My heart is broken."

"You look it, you impertinent minx." He had taken out the box and opened it with one of two keys that hung with Leah's crucifix around his neck. "Where did you learn to be so saucy? Not from your father, I warrant. He swore to me that you were good and biddable. I can see that if I do not take a firm hand with you, you will soon be outrageous. Come here and take your punishment." Smoothing the covers with a quick motion, Cain emptied the contents of the box on the bed.

The hoard of nearly a hundred years of systematic robbery plus the dower jewels of several generations lay spread across the coverlet. Leah was dazzled and stood looking, leaning against her husband, but making no move to touch what he said was hers. Most of the jewels, wrested from the Welsh tribes the Gaunts battled continuously, were of Celtic design—golden birds with jeweled eyes sat atop long pins that could be affixed to garments; fabulous beasts, each scale a different flake of ruby, emerald, jasper, and chalcedony twisted sinuous tails of gold to form a necklet; unset stones from the freezing white diamond and the pure shining pearl through the ruby which glowed with the heat of the netherworld lay loose, winking back the light among the silver and gold chains which were worked and twisted into fantastic geometric and floral designs. Here and there an odd piece of far different pattern told of years on crusade, for while that ancestor of the Gaunts spilled his blood for God, he could see no reason why he should not fill his saddlebags at the infidel's cost. There lay, therefore, jade bracelets from a place so far away that no one could say with truth that it was real; earrings of lapis lazuli set in red gold; and a silver headband with red and blue stones which contained glowing silvery stars within them, set in a smooth pattern of flowing curves and bends foreign to the French or Celtic mold.

"Am I not to be thanked? They are yours."

"My lord! I am afraid to touch them. How will I dare wear them?"

Cain laughed. "Afraid or not, you must screw your courage to the sticking point and deck yourself out properly. If you do not, the women of the court will pity you for having so mean a husband, or such a poor one, and you will get me a bad name for lack of generosity. I am sorry, I forgot to tell you last night that the queen has expressed a great wish to meet you and we are invited to spend the afternoon and dine with Maud and Stephen."

There was a wry twist to Cain's mouth, and Leah knew that her husband was none too pleased with the invitation. For once, however, she did not care whether he liked something or not; she was both pleased and excited. She could ask no questions then, for Cain's bath had arrived and he maintained the habit of bathing alone. In the interim, Leah countermanded the orders for the high table dinner and spent some thought on outlining sufficient tasks to keep her maids busy while she was gone. For all their expressed timidity about the men-at-arms, Leah suspected that they would find themselves braver with no restraining eye upon them if they were idle. She was able to ask her husband while he was dressing whether the occasion was important enough to merit her wearing the green brocade dress, but she might as well have saved her breath. Cain replied with nothing but a blank stare and a shrug. All the women wore pretty dresses, he said finally, when the consternation on her face touched him—and a great many jewels, he added in an effort to be helpful. Leah could only laugh, even though she was exasperated. She should have known better.

All in all the entire period between then and the time they left was exasperating. Cain went out and came back in a foul humor. She had the devil's own time cajoling him into changing his clothes again, and, considering that she had worked like a slavey to finish restitching and embroidering the costume, she was dead set with her own gentle mulishness on having her way. Finally she succeeded, and, between kisses and pleadings, she even succeeded in getting several gold chains hung round his neck and spread across his great shoulders and breast, but neither with smiles nor tears could she cajole a ring onto his fingers. A ring, he pointed out, kissing away the tears, spoiled the grip of the hand on the sword; and when Leah protested that he would not, she hoped, be using his sword that night, he only laughed and said that in these times one could never tell.

When Leah and her husband walked down the immense hall of the White Tower, however, she was glad she had made the effort. Comments which she overheard on Radnor's new sartorial magnificence brought her a glow of satisfaction, although her pleasure was somewhat tempered when she intercepted a number of predatory glances from various ladies. Their progress was not rapid for they stopped continually, greeting and greeted by Radnor's large acquaintance. Everyone wanted to inspect the new Lady Radnor, and soon Leah felt that if she had to repeat another idiotic platitude her tongue would cleave to the roof of her mouth. She had just turned away so as not to seem to be attending to a pair of overdressed and bejeweled popinjays who were telling Lord Radnor that she was "a pretty little thing but looked simple" as if she were deaf, when Hereford accosted her. She fairly sparkled with relief and pleasure at his familiar face and a chance to loosen her cramped tongue.

"My dearest Lady Radnor, you look magnificent. I see that Radnor broke open the strongbox for you." He bowed low over the hand she extended and kissed it, a little lingeringly.

"My lord earl. Tell me how my husband looks."

"I had rather tell you how you look. You are lovely. I am much tempted to flirt with you."

"Well, I wish you will not. You know it puts my lord into a dreadful temper, and you teased him enough in that way upon the road here. I have better things to do this afternoon than to cajole him out of a black mood—especially when you do not mean a word of it."

"Now that is the most unprincipled thing I have ever heard you say. Does that mean I would have a chance if I were madly in love with you? And how do you know that I am not pining away secretly for passion."

"Because, Lord Hereford, no one could look as you do and be as merry-mad and be pining away for anything at all, much the less love."

They both began to laugh, drawing Cain's attention. "If you are through amusing my wife, Hereford, I want to take her on to see Maud," he said coldly. Hereford's violent guffaw and Leah's giggle did nothing to soothe the suspicion he had that Leah felt more attraction than she should for the handsome earl. "Now what have I said that you both think so damned funny?" he snarled, but neither frown nor question could extract anything beyond more laughter from either, and Cain could do no more than lead his wife away in a most dissatisfied mood.

Before a rather dumpy little woman with slightly graying hair and a ravaged complexion, Lord Radnor stopped and bowed low, "Madam, may I present to you my wife, Lady Radnor."

So this was Queen Maud. Leah sank to the ground with bowed head in the curtsy reserved for royalty. When she rose, Maud was holding out her hand and Leah kissed it, curtsying again.

"Such a pretty young bride. This is your first visit to court, I am sure, Lady Radnor. I could not fail to remember such a charming face."

"Yes, madam, my first visit."

"I am sure it is too soon to ask what you think of London. You can scarcely have had time to see any of it. Do not fail to make your husband take you to see the market. It is a sight rivaled only by the great markets of Paris. You need not stand waiting for us, Lord Radnor. You will forgive me if I steal your wife away for a while. You will not be interested in our talk. I promise to return her safe to you."

Cain's mouth hardened, but there was nothing more he could do than cast Leah an anxious and admonitory glance. He had not expected Maud to be so open and direct in her attempt to detach Leah from his side, and he could not, without great discourtesy, ignore such a plain dismissal. It was like throwing a babe to the wolves, he thought, leaving Leah with the queen and now he could only hope that Leah would remember what questions Maud asked so that he could guess what she had told. He was a fool to have brought her.

"Have you seen Painscastle yet, Lady Radnor?" Maud was asking, drawing the girl aside to a window seat and inviting her to sit down with a gesture.

"No, madam, we came direct from my home to London."

"Joan of Shrewsbury tells me that your wedding was a great affair and beautifully managed. I am very sorry the king and I could not attend, but I am sure your husband's friends were all there. He must have been proud to show you off to those he loves best, for a prettier girl I have seldom seen."

Leah blushed modestly at the compliments bestowed upon her, and could not help but be flattered by the kindness and interest the queen was showing. Nonetheless she noted how alive Maud's dark eyes were and how impenetrable.

"I—I—you will think me quite silly, but I can hardly say whom I spoke to and who was there. My mother and I had lived so very retired, you know. I was confused by all the excitement and"—her blush deepened—"and by marriage."

"Of course you were," Maud replied sympathetically, well pleased with this ingenuous reply. No wonder Radnor had looked so anguished. For all the girl was not too young to be married, she was truly a child. With proper handling she would tell everything she knew and never realize she had said anything of importance. "His lordship tore himself from his wedding to rush to Wales, I hear. I hope you were not offended or distressed. The trouble must have been great to drive him to leave his lovely bride."

Looking attentively at her fingertips as if she were suddenly seized by shyness, Leah considered that remark. Did the queen believe her to be playing her father's game?

Was Maud particularly interested in the Welsh situation for some reason? "I know nothing about such matters," she murmured. "My lord did not even tell me that he was in Wales." She caught Maud's dissatisfied glance and a faint movement of restlessness. To pretend to disinterested idiocy was the safe path, but if she did so the ladies would not talk to her or before her at all and she could bring no information to Cain to warn him or help him.

"You know, madam," she added in a slightly aggrieved tone, "it is shameful the way Lord Radnor never tells me anything. I know I am young and not very wise, but I am not a simpleton. If I am not told, how can I learn?" That was better, Maud was interested again. "I am resolved to teach myself, however, so I watch and I listen when he speaks to his men or his friends."

Maud smiled kindly. The girl was exactly what she said she was not—a simpleton—and Radnor had apparently been somewhat unguarded in his speech before her, either because he was in love or because he had arrogantly depended on his ability to control his wife. The queen almost felt guilty at using so unsuspecting a child and possibly making trouble between husband and wife, but her own husband and family came first and Radnor was a very dangerous man.

"It is a good thing for a wife to keep her eyes and ears open. Men often do not realize what a help a woman can be. For instance, if your husband should fall ill or be hurt in an accident, to whom would you send for help?"

"I should send to my father at once by fast courier. That is all arranged." Leah told that whopping lie without a blink or a hesitation.

That was useful to know, but not exactly what the queen wanted. "Surely there is someone closer at hand who could help you. It would be days or weeks before your father or even Lord Gaunt could come."

That was not so easy to answer. Leah dared not lie, because the queen would certainly know who Cain's friends were. What she wanted to find out, Leah realized, was who had been visiting them or whom Cain had been having close contact with recently. "Well," she began hesitantly, "we did ride here with Lord Hereford." That was perfectly safe. The entire court knew that Cain and Roger of Hereford had come together. "I do not know if he would help us though. He was very kind to me, but he and my lord quarreled all the time they rode together."

"My dear child, men always argue. No doubt they were talking of horses or hawks."

"Sometimes I know they spoke of those things, and very likely it was about that they argued." Leah suddenly looked very grave and lowered her voice. "But sometimes they spoke of more serious matters." Maud leaned forward to show her interest, not wishing to interrupt this fascinating confidence. "I could not hear much, but they spoke of—but, indeed, I should not tell tales, for I have no desire to make trouble for anyone." Leah sent up a silent prayer to be forgiven for this second thumping lie. She had a great desire to make great trouble for Joan of Shrewsbury.

"You may tell me," Maud soothed. "A queen is a safe repository for secrets. No one will ever know what you say here unless you tell of it."

"Are you sure it is not wrong, madam? My ears might be mistaken, you know."

"You are not swearing to anything, my dear."

Leah certainly was not, since she was fabricating the whole as she went along. "It was something about the Earl of Shrewsbury being in contact with a man called Henry of Anjou. I do not mean that Lord Hereford and my lord were arguing about that. They were both very angry and said it would break the peace. Radnor says—men talk about the oddest things in bed, do they not?—that a man must stand by his oath above all things. He was very excited that night we stayed at Oxford's castle—did you hear about the big fight there? I was so frightened that I thought I would die of fear—anyway, he did talk to me a little there. I could not understand it all, but I gathered that he had sworn to be the king's man and would not change and that caused trouble between Lord Oxford and himself." Leah's wide innocent eyes gazed steadfastly at Maud's, which had become more and more like black marbles throughout this burbling fairy tale.

"You are a very clever little girl," Maud said finally, patting the small hand she had taken. Could Radnor have put his wife up to this? It was possible, but it was also possible that Joan of Shrewsbury was playing a double game, and Oxford was no doubt her tool—it would not be the first time. "I hear that you paid a visit to Lady Leicester. She is a very pleasant woman, is she not? But your husband should have taken you to see the sights, not sent you on errands on your first day in the city."

"Oh, he did not send me. It was the most diverting

thing—only I did not think so at the time. Lady Leicester was so kind as to help me find servants."

"Find servants?" Maud exclaimed, shocked.

Leah laughed really happily for she was truly on safe ground now. This story could harm no one and would fill much time. She had been trembling inwardly with the tension of watching for slips of the tongue while seeming perfectly unconscious of what she was saying. She launched into the story of her housewifely activities at great length, sending up prayers of thanksgiving for so quick and easy a release. Maud for her part was perfectly satisfied to listen, partly because she was genuinely amused and partly because a discussion of household matters would lead her to other questions she wanted answered. At the conclusion of Leah's tale of her misadventures, Maud laughed heartily and promised that Radnor would be finely roasted for being such an idiot. About this, Leah did not care one pin, for the more she thought about it the more she realized that Cain had behaved like an idiot and deserved to be the butt of a few jests. Nevertheless, she widened her eyes to their fullest extent and pleaded with the queen not to betray her.

"He would be so angry. He is angry for so many things I do, and I know he would not like me to speak of him in this way," Leah said mendaciously, trembling with well-simulated fear. The last thing she wanted was for Maud to believe her to have influence with or importance to her husband.

"No, no. It will all seem to come from Lady Leicester as far as he is concerned. Is he harsh to you, poor child?" Maud earnestly hoped so. A young girl with a severe husband was easily played upon by sympathy and her loyalties could be confused.

"N-no. Often he laughs and is kind. I suppose it is because I am young and foolish that he is cross. He is used to women who know better how to manage." Leah had to hedge in case Maud should see Radnor in an affectionate mood before she could give him warning of what she had said. Besides she was not really certain that he would not object to being cast in the role of the cruel husband.

The talk went on, but now Leah wanted to escape very badly. Maud was back on dangerous ground. The queen seemed to be asking questions about household management, quantity of food ordered and consumed, and whether Lady Radnor planned to set up a sewing room, but Leah realized that truthful answers would tell a clever woman like Maud pretty exactly how many men Radnor had with him, how long they planned to stay, and other matters which she felt were Radnor's business alone. She was able to break off to say with startled pleasure, thanking her patron saint for answering her prayers, "Oh, there is Lord William Gloucester. He is so very—I do not quite know how to describe it—attractive."

"Yes, he is. But there are many attractive men at court." If that was what Lady Radnor wanted, thought Maud, it could be easily supplied. Lord William, of course, would be useless for her purposes, but there were others even younger and just as smooth who were court toadies. She tried a few more times to engage the girl in conversation, but Leah's attention was plainly wandering and she answered so much at random that Maud gave up. Summoning William with a nod, she consigned Leah to his care to be delivered back to Lord Radnor. All in all, Maud was very well pleased with Radnor's wife. She gave every sign of being a valuable asset to the queen's insatiable need for information until experience or her husband made her cautious.

Leah startled Lord William considerably, not by the obvious pleasure with which she greeted him or the urgent clasp of her hand on his—women very often pursued him, even women he had met only once or twice before—but by the deep sigh and tense murmur of, "Well, I hope that turns a few points elsewhere."

"What did you say?"

Turning her greenish eyes up to his with a sweep of long lashes and adding a smile of innocent vacuity, Leah murmured, "I have put a bug in her ladyship's ear that may buzz a tale or two, that is all." Then she frowned. "Have you seen my lord? I must speak with him as soon as may be."

William blinked at the first sentence and then put its meaning down to his own suspicious mind. Radnor's girl wife could not possibly have intended to say what that sounded like. "No, I have not seen him, but we can stroll about to look for him. Lady Radnor, your new life must agree with you. I have never seen you more beautiful. Truly roses bloom in your cheeks this day."

"If you mean I am flushed with anger, you are perfectly right. Roses indeed!"

William of Gloucester was Cain's foster brother and, al-

197

though Leah knew there was no special affection between them, she also knew she had no need to guard her tongue with him. Lord William jerked upright from his automatically armorous lean as if he had been pricked. He was only taken aback momentarily, however, before he realized that the poor girl must have been put out of sorts by Maud's prying. It was possible too that Maud had been giving Leah some details of Radnor's private life in an effort to make trouble between them and enlist the girl in the court's interest. He would have to warn Radnor of that when he had a chance, but just now the best thing would be to try to soothe Leah himself. He was just about to start on a new tack, when she took her hand from his hurriedly.

"Forgive me. There is your brother just come in. I know you will not wish to speak to him because you have quarreled, but Cain has a particular kindness for him, and I must do so."

Philip did not notice Leah until she took his hand in hers as she rose from her curtsy. Even then his clouded mind took a little time to fix her in memory—Radnor's new wife, that was the girl whose warm clasp was giving spurious life to his right hand. He noted that she looked different from the two or three times he had seen her at Pembroke's keep—not in dress or jewels, although she fairly glittered with the Gaunt collection now—but in her expression. Her face was alive with intelligence, the shrewdness of her glance contrasting strangely with the childishly flushed cheeks and innocent mouth. He murmured a conventional greeting, wondering what she wanted.

Leah, for her part, continued to hold Philip's hand while she answered with equally conventional words because she had the feeling that if she let him go his mind would slip away. She fought a sensation of revulsion, thinking that she had never touched a corpse before but now knew what it was like. The flesh was cold, flaccid, and clammy, and absorbed her warmth without return; only the eyes lived in a face that was no longer capable of changing its expression.

"Lord Philip, you cannot stand here. Let me help you to the window seat."

Philip tried without success to steady his shallow breathing. He was very nearly at the end of his endurance. "I could use an arm to steady me. I fear you are right. I

198

must sit down." His voice was hardly above a whisper and his eyes had started to glaze over.

Leah glanced at the crowd which bustled about them, but those close by had turned their backs politely so as not to intrude on a private conversation. In any case, Leah realized instantly, she could not call on a stranger for help. It might just happen that that person was an enemy to Philip and that he would not wish it known how desperately sick he was. She pulled his arm over her shoulder and stiffened under his weight, which fortunately was not great. Fortunately, too, the window embrasure was not far, and she eased him down and back against the wall. Screening him with her own body, Leah looked wildly into the crowd. She could see no one that she could trust, but she heard a light, pleasant laugh that was hearteningly familiar.

"Are you all right? Can I leave you for a moment?"

Philip nodded faintly in answer to Leah's questions, and she plunged off in the direction of the laugh. Hereford was merrily engaged with a group of about his own age, one of which was a startlingly beautiful dark girl who looked familiar. Leah neither saw nor cared what Hereford was doing. She grasped his arm and pulled him aside.

"My lord, you must obtain some aqua vit for me at once."

"Aqua vit?"

"Strong waters—usquebaugh—I know not what you call it. Oh hurry, please."

"Is something wrong with Radnor?"

"For pity's sake, do not waste time with questions, but do as I ask." He was back very quickly, holding a flask, no trace of laughter in face or voice. "Now," Leah added, reaching for the drink, "find Lord Radnor for me, I pray you, and tell him that Philip of Gloucester is here and is very ill."

"Philip! You mean I have been swallowing my heart for that traitor?"

"Hush, oh hush, Lord Hereford. I know very little of such matters, but he is dear to my lord. I do only what I think Cain would desire. And you should not speak so loud of such things in this place. I beg you to bring my husband to that window seat."

After Leah held the flask for Philip, almost forcing him to take several healthy swallows of the fiery liquid, he began to recover and asked anxiously where Lord Radnor was. Before Leah could reply, Cain reached them with a scowling Hereford in his wake. By then Philip was perfectly capable of talking, but he knew that the flash of strength lent by the drink would be ephemeral and that when it passed he would be worse than ever. There was no time for consideration or caution.

"Cain—"

"What are you doing here? I did not expect you for two or three days longer. Why did you travel in such haste?"

"Because Pembroke will be in London tonight or tomorrow morning."

Now Cain scowled as blackly as Hereford had done before. "Curse him!" he said briefly. "He swore he would not come, but we guessed he would not keep his word."

Philip wiped sweat from his face with a shaking hand. "I heard on the road that he rides with a very small force for the sake of secrecy. If we could take him, there is a chance of delaying or even preventing the accusation against Chester. I took to my horse thinking to beat him out by some days, but my accursed body failed me. For Christ's sake, Radnor, do what you can to stop him."

"You took to your horse? Have you taken leave of your senses? Are you trying to kill yourself?"

"Radnor, for once in your life, let your head rule your heart. I know you love me, but great matters are at stake. Pembroke, as you say, swore to us all he would not come to this council. He comes so secretly only to betray Chester and gain Fitz Richard's lands in person. If we keep him from court, perhaps we can yet save Chester and all those with him."

"I cannot believe it!" Hereford gasped.

Lord Radnor appeared to have heard neither Philip nor Hereford. His unstable temper had disintegrated with a crash, for he had been reasoning hopelessly with Chester on that very subject when Hereford had found him. "To hell with Pembroke and Chester too. May the devil fly away with this damned country and its idiot ruler and everyone connected with him. I will tell you what I will do. I will take you and put you to bed, and if you move a muscle, I will end your agony and mine also by throttling you."

Hereford gripped Radnor's shoulder so hard that the big man winced. "Wait. There must be some mistake in this. Philip, God forgive me, I may have wronged you, but this is no time to talk of that. I know that Pembroke's swearing he would not come and then doing so looks ill, but I am sure he means no harm. In any case, Radnor can do little enough about stopping him because he may not offer violence to his father-in-law. If Pembroke plans to betray us, I am not so bound. I will go."

"Is that you, Hereford?" Philip squinted in an effort to see better. "My eyes are not good. Come closer. Take a warning. Stop Chester if you can. If not, save yourself. The whole country knows your so-called secret plan."

Hereford laughed bitterly. "Apparently. God knows I would give much to be clear of it. When known, such a plan can be nothing but disaster. I have given my word, though, and I will not betray it. You may rest assured that I will do my uttermost to save what can be saved while keeping faith." He turned and departed briskly.

"That was the most urgent matter," Philip said, wiping the cold sweat from his face again. "You had better go now that Hereford has left us. The less we are seen together the better."

"How did you come here?" Radnor asked, clinging stubbornly to his purpose.

"On horseback. It is only a little way. Do you think I wish to tell the whole world of my weakness?"

"Fool!"

"You are so wise!"

"I pray you, lower your voices," Leah interposed. "People are looking at us."

"Here, you, page," Radnor called. "Go down and order Lord and Lady Radnor's horses and men to make ready, and Lord Philip Gloucester's too."

"Radnor, you will ruin me!"

"I do not care."

"My lords, please! Cain, do not argue with him, you only make him worse. Can we support him between us in such a way as to hide his illness?"

"Not another move does he make. Look at his face. What is there to hide? I will carry him. Nay, Philip, it will not hurt me. You do not weigh what you once did. My step will be steady enough for this small distance."

Lord and Lady Radnor arrived back at the White Tower barely in time to sit down to dine. Having seen Philip into bed and somewhat recovered, Cain began to use his head again. In an attempt to remove any doubts which his intimacy with Philip might have raised, he answered the few questions on his absence with equal truth and indifference. Philip of Gloucester had been taken ill, he said calmly, and he had seen him safe home. His manner was sufficiently unconcerned so that those who heard him had little doubt that he too disapproved of Philip's new loyalties. Radnor was apparently prepared to do his duty punctiliously, but no longer cared for a closer association than that duty required. He was serious enough with those who approached him to discuss political matters but a trifle impatient, quite plainly preferring the antics of the jugglers and dancers.

He was quite impatient with his pretty little wife too, William of Gloucester noticed as he took his seat. William gave no sign of his irritation at Radnor's stupidity, but he touched Lady William who moved down at a glance from him, and he slid in beside Leah. It would be well to sweeten her somewhat until he could get her husband alone and point out the dangers of snubbing his wife as he had just done.

"You have had an exciting day, Lady Leah—I may call you so, may I not? We are in some sense related, since Lord Radnor is my foster brother."

Leah looked up quickly with a tentative smile. It seemed to her that Maud's eyes were fixed on their table across the smoky room.

"Oh yes, that is, if my lord does not object. I could not."

"But you do not like rudeness or familiarites, I know. You were very angry with me for saying that you bloomed like a rose."

Leah's pretty laugh trilled out. "Well, I was very angry, but not with you, Lord William. The queen showed such a kind interest in all my lord's doings that I was hard put to answer her."

Was that a warning? William did not know, but he was sure that the need to talk to Radnor about his wife was very pressing. He continued to flatter Leah, but when the roasts were being removed he leaned behind her to tap Radnor's shoulder.

"We have both had enough to drink, Cain. Come with me to ease yourself and make room for more." Near the garderobe he put out a hand to stop his companion. "I hope your wife knows not too much of your private affairs," he said softly, looking over his shoulder to make sure they were alone. When he looked back at Radnor, he was stunned to see that he was shaking with laughter. "Man, you are drunk. This is serious. That girl is not as stupid as you think. You snarl at her. Maud offers her sympathy. She will spill everything she sees and hears if you do not have a care. Why did you bring here a babe that does not know that her advantage lies with her husband even if she hates him? It is no laughing matter. You may think you tell her nothing, but if she be a sly one she can learn."

"Nay, William, I am sober still. Some men say I was born of the devil. If so, my wife and I are well matched, for that chit is surely a spawn of the serpent. Pembroke's daughter! You should hear the pack of lies that sweet babe poured into the queen's ears, and all with those eyes as wide as they could stare and those sweet lips trembling a little with fear, I doubt not." Radnor's expression sobered. "I laugh now, thinking on it, but I was not so merry earlier. She told Maud that she overheard Hereford and myself condemning Shrewsbury for playing with Henry of Anjou."

"She did what?" William gasped, and then, clinging to a straw, "Did you?"

"Of course not. If he has had dealings with Henry—and it would in no way surprise me because Joan likes to keep one foot in each camp and he does her bidding in all—he has kept it very close. I know nothing of it and, though I do not love him, it is not my way to tell lies, even of my enemies. Come, since we are here, let us accomplish what we came for. It would look strange if we went out again later. She also filled Maud with some cock-and-bull story about Oxford trying to shake my homage oath."

The earth seemed to heave under William's feet. He had flattered himself that he knew all there was to know about women. It was inconceivable that such an innocent bit of fluff could have so tortuous a mind—unless Pembroke had schooled her well in advance.

"Did he?"

"Who? Oxford? No. He was too busy trying to kill me—or trying to escape the consequences of someone else's attempt."

"Are you sure that was what she told Maud—or is this a tale for your ears?"

There was a short pause while both men rearranged their clothing. When Radnor turned back to William his face was set in troubled lines. "I am no longer sure of anything. This morning I would have said that the girl was as pure as the rain that falls from heaven, but she is like all women. What I do not know is whether she be false to me or false to Pembroke. I think she told me the truth," he added slowly. "She has a fondness for me—at least—well, I think so."

"Then you had better smile on her a little more and growl at her a little less. An unhappy woman is fruit ripe for the picking by anyone—unless she be afraid, and one who lies so readily to queens is not easily frightened, or with child, or better, both."

Radnor began to laugh again at that. "You should know, but the growls were her idea, not mine. I will have you know that her ladyship has so ordered me that in the public eye I am to look upon her kindly but seldom. It seems she also told Maud that I was a severe husband, impatient with her youth and folly."

"She told—are you?"

"I wish you would stop asking stupid questions. I told you she made whole cloth out of lies. No, I am not impatient. I find her more amusing than traveling players."

Nonetheless Lord Radnor did not look in the least amused. He could not quarrel with Leah, for what she had done was in his best interests. In spite of the assurance he had displayed to William, he was uneasy and rather resentful of the way in which she was assuming independence. William was not much deceived by Cain's light tone, but he had done his best to warn him and would only irritate him by insistence. When they turned back toward the hall, therefore, he changed the subject, and by the time they were again seated at the table their conversation was innocent enough for anyone to hear. Radnor was maintaining that the finest falcon a man could fly was a white gerfalcon, and Lord William was insisting that the brown peregrine, although smaller, was fiercer and gave better sport.

Suddenly Radnor's voice drifted away, and Lord William became aware of his fixed gaze on the dancer who had just come to their side of the room. Then the eyes of both were riveted on the writhing, sinuous form before them. Brown arms, brown legs, hairless and gleaming with oil, shone and retreated into shadow in the uncertain flare of the torches. Smooth and shining, the body dipped and swayed, its even glow broken by the glittering of jewels set in the oddest places.

"What is she?" William murmured on a note of awe.

At first Radnor did not answer. The girl was certainly aware of their attention for she had not moved on. Her body moved ceaselessly, hypnotically, and the strange music beat against the watching men giving even more meaning to the girl's already obvious gestures. There was a wail to that music, a beat, a sensual hesitation that sent the blood up.

"From all I have heard and read," Cain said at last, "no Saracen ever dressed his women like that, but books may lie."

"All I can think of," William murmured avidly, "is Salome."

"You cannot count—or else she has dropped a few veils along the way."

Radnor kept running his tongue across his lips, his eyes fixed in an unblinking stare. His words were light, but his face was rigid and his utterance choked with lust. William, equally responsive, had permitted his mouth to drop open. He was all for relaxing and enjoying the titillation of his senses, but Lord Radnor's reactions were more direct. Somewhat relieved that he could respond to any woman besides Leah and thinking that he would show her that she needed to tread warily with him, Cain got to his feet. Leah stopped mid-sentence in her conversation with Lady William as she saw her husband sweep food and wine out of his way and slide across the table in his haste. The trestles nearly gave way under his weight, but he made it safely. With unbelieving eyes she watched him accost the dancer, exchange a few words with her, laugh, point to one of the gold chains which she herself had hung around his neck, and start toward the door, steering his prize with a hand on her shoulder.

Leah turned again to Lady William, and she must have continued to behave in a normal fashion for no one paid any exceptional attention to her. If her life depended on it, however, she could not have recounted another thing that happened that night except for two facts which stood out with the brilliance of suns against the pervading darkness. One was that Harry Beaufort came to take her home, and the other that her husband smelled of a strange, musky odor when he fell into bed hours later.

The next morning Radnor left to accompany the royal

205

hunt before Leah got up. She had been conscious of his rising and leaving, but she pretended sleep and, to her great chagrin, he did not disturb her. Leah went to church and spent two hours on her knees praying for patience and circumspection, but it did her little good. Another insult arrived via Giles after she had held dinner back two hours waiting for her lord. This was a hurried note in Radnor's own hand to say, without excuse, that he was dining with the hunt and did not know when he would arrive at home. "Tell Lady Radnor not to worry," was scrawled across the bottom. Leah was so frozen with fury because he had not the courtesy to write to her direct that she had to try three times to speak before she was able to whisper, "Thank you, that is all," to the master-of-arms.

She was still awake and fully dressed when Radnor finally came in, even though the false dawn was already lighting the sky. His voice reached her first as he paused halfway up the stairs to answer a ribald jest about his late return made by one of the men he had awakened, and he was still laughing when he entered the room. He stopped when he saw Leah, and the laughter changed to a gentler smile.

"You had no need to wait up for me. I remembered this time to send you word I was safe." He came forward, reaching out for her. "But I am glad you did. I have missed you in this long day."

"Do not touch me!" Leah shrank back, pressing herself into her chair.

"What?"

"Do not touch me. Do not come near me."

Radnor stood still, one hand still extended toward his wife, his expression one of genuine puzzlement. In the dim light he could not see Leah's face, but it was apparent there was something seriously wrong. "What is the matter, Leah? I know I must stink to heaven after a day's hunt, but yesterday you were not so nice."

"It is the smell of lechery I cannot bear, not the odor of honest sweat." Cain stood perfectly still, too stunned by what his wife had dared to say to him to be angry, and Leah jumped from her chair to seize and throw the box of Gaunt jewels on the bed. "Here, take them back," she cried, tugging at her betrothal ring, "and take this too, and go and buy what you want. Mayhap I am with child already and you need not trouble yourself with me any more."

So many conflicting emotions whirled about in Cain that he continued to stand like a statue for another minute. Then he laughed, picked Leah's ring from the bed, and held it out to her. Amusement, relief, and pride had come out as the uppermost emotions. He was relieved because her jealous rage was so sincere, proud that she cared enough for him to be jealous, and amused that her jealousy could so enrage her gentle nature.

"Put this ring back on, and do not act like a silly goose." She slapped his hand away. Still laughing, Cain attempted to take her into his arms, and she struck out at him, her hands beating harmlessly against his mailed strength. "Be careful," he said, laughing harder, "you will hurt yourself." He bent to kiss her and Leah scratched his face and bit him; exasperation began to temper his amusement. "Leah, do not be so foolish. It was nothing. I cared nothing for that woman."

"Nor for me either," she shrieked. "How do you think I felt? Not two weeks married and you rise from my side to go with a whore—before my very face!—in the sight of my eyes!" Leah gasped for breath but continued before Cain could answer her. "You can have her or those like her, or me. I, for one, will not be coupled in harness. I will not lie with you to take the leavings of every slut in the street."

At that he hit her. It was barely a tap from his great strength, but it sent Leah crashing to the floor several feet away. Pain and humiliation broke her rage, and a storm of tears swept over her.

"I, no more than your father, will be said nay in my own household. You have taken one too many liberties with me. Now get up and come over here or I will break every bone in your body. Help me out of these clothes, and keep your tongue between your teeth while you do it."

Wrapped in his old homespun robe, Cain went to the sideboard and poured wine to drink. Leah stood with her head buried in her arms, leaning on the high-backed armchair, sobbing and shuddering. He looked at the pitiful figure she made, and remorse overwhelmed him. He had been wrong to go after that dancer right in front of her; she was only a child and did not understand such things.

"Leah—." She started and cowered at hearing his voice so close. "I pray you," Cain said softly, "weep no more. I am sorry I struck you." He put a hand on her shoulder and she shook convulsively. The hand dropped away, and

207

Lord Radnor looked at his wife helplessly. The tears were a weapon against which he had no defenses; he could not bear them. "Leah, come and sit beside me. I will do you no more hurt. I only wish to speak to you."

Her obedience was prompt; she would not tempt his anger again. They sat together on the bed, and when he put his arm around her she made no move, but her body, swayed against his, was lifeless, lacking its usual warm yielding.

"Look you, you are my wife, I must needs care for you," Cain began, making matters worse by implying that it was only because she was his wife that he thought of her. He turned her face up to his with a hand under her chin. There was blood on her mouth, and her lip had begun to swell where her teeth had cut it when the blow fell. Cain swallowed to relieve the constriction in his throat.

"Truly, I cared nothing for her. I was only curious because of her dark skin, and because of the music." He stroked Leah's hair and her unbruised cheek. "Do not weep so, my love. I did wrong. I should not have gone to her in that hall while you were watching. I did not think. I am not used to being married." If it was a lie, it was in a good cause.

Mute and frigid, moved only by her occasional sobs, Leah sat unresponding in the circle of her husband's arm. Cain rubbed his face. He understood now why so many men gave in to what he had previously felt were unreasonable demands by their wives. He had called them doting, but he was ready to do anything or say anything himself to win a spontaneous response from Leah. Any man could beat his wife into submission, but what good was what was left when the spirit fled? Truly a whore was as good as the lifeless doll that sat beside him and obeyed out of fear.

"Go, get you to bed," he sighed. "I will sleep elsewhere this night. If you feel the same tomorrow—well—I do not know—." Cain's voice was defeated and his shoulders had a discouraged slump which no fatigue could give them. He rose to go.

A pang of pure terror shot through Leah. Her madness had driven him away. If he left her, she would have no one in the whole world. "My lord." She could scarcely whisper, she was so choked with tears. "Wait, please wait. I have done wrong, not you. Or, at least, what you have done is between you and God. I have no right to check you. Do not leave me."

Radnor frowned. "Now what does this mean?"

"Do not frown at me any more," Leah cried, beginning to sob violently again. This time, however, she flung her arms around her husband's neck and hid her face in his shoulder. "I will do so no more, my lord. I am sorry, my lord."

"My love, dear heart, do not weep any longer. I am the one who will do so no more. I swear, I will never cast even my eyes upon another woman. The bitch was not worth one of your tears to me, no, nor is the greatest lady in the land. Leah—"

He sat down and took her on to his lap, leaning back on the headboard so that she lay against his breast. What a fool he had been to try such a trick upon an innocent, perhaps giving her the notion to pay him back in his own coin, perhaps shaking her faith in him so that she would seek other forms of revenge. He redoubled his attempts to soothe her, whispering assurances of future fidelity and present affection. Leah, regaining quiet in her husband's fond embrace, slowly realized that she had won the battle between them. True, she had started out with no specific purpose in mind. Driven only by her wounded pride and her jealousy, she had first lashed out blindly at what hurt her and then yielded to her fear. The rage had won her nothing—but the tears! From them came an assurance that she would be hurt thus no more, but far more important than that assurance was the knowledge that with this man tears and meek words could be both weapons and armor.

CHAPTER 14

———— ◆ ❯◆❮ ◆ ————

SOMETIME BEFORE Leah and Lord Radnor had exchanged their first angry words, Lord Hereford had reluctantly opened his eyes in response to being brutally shaken and slapped. His head ached abominably and his mouth tasted as if a cat had littered in it, but his strongest emotion was amazement—first at being slapped by anyone and then, before he could be angry, at the fact that his squire was weeping.

"Thank God! Thank God!"

The voice was that of Alan of Evesham, his master-of-arms, and it was choked with sobs. Still more incomprehensible and even revolting was the fact that Alan was hugging him in what appeared to be a passionate embrace. Hereford thrust him away and turned to his squire.

"William, pull this madman off me," he said thickly. "What ails you both?"

"We thought you were dying," William replied.

"Dying? You *are* mad. Why should I die when I am not ill?"

"My lord, we have been trying to waken you since yesterday dawn."

"Yesterday!" Hereford gasped, sitting bolt upright. "Where is Pembroke?"

"Gone, at dawn yesterday. That is why we tried to waken you," Alan said. "Lord Pembroke said you had drunk too much and should be left to sleep it off, but I knew you had come here with some purpose other than to welcome him and I tried to tell you."

Hereford's complexion was already green with nausea and could not change, but he got unsteadily to his feet as memory returned to him. He had found Pembroke late in the evening of the day he started from court and had ridden into his camp followed only by a few of his men. Pretending intense surprise, Hereford had confessed to an amorous assignation in the neighborhood and had inquired what brought Pembroke so close to London. Pembroke was not much disconcerted by Hereford's arrival; he was annoyed because he had intended to send for Radnor to try another method of disposing of him. Nonetheless the excuse prepared for Radnor would serve excellently for Hereford.

"What could bring me but trouble?" Pembroke asked in an aggrieved tone. "I came for two most excellent reasons. The first was to warn you and Chester that someone has betrayed us."

It could be true; Hereford wished it was true, but it was peculiar that Philip of Gloucester, who was surely a very sick man to whom traveling was a painful effort, had managed to come first with the warning. If the matter was so urgent that Pembroke would not trust it to a messenger, why was he comfortably camped not a day's ride from the town?

"I am very grateful," the young earl said, trying desperately to conceal his suspicion. "You show yourself most comfortably our friend by this care for our well-doing. I hope it is not too late, for Chester, as you know, has already spoken to the king. Nonetheless, perhaps Lord Radnor can convince Stephen that the betrayer lies. All may yet be well."

"You do not understand," Pembroke added impatiently. "Radnor will be no help to you at all. Philip has convinced him that Henry's cause is hopeless. You will see. Lord Radnor—and I shame to say it of my son-in-law—will lift no finger. I do not say he would betray you himself. To be sure, he loves you and Chester well and has probably done his uttermost to convince you to abandon this cause. If you are in danger of falling, however, he will turn his head aside from you and leave you to your fate."

For a moment Hereford's senses reeled. It was all so likely and so logical. As a matter of fact, it fitted perfectly with what Radnor had said to him.

"My dear Hereford," Pembroke murmured solicitously, "you look dreadfully pale. I will call for a cup of wine for you."

"Thank you. I cannot say it will come amiss."

Pembroke went out, pretending to call his servant, and Hereford was left alone with his thoughts. Logical or not, to say that Cain would let any friend of his be destroyed without making an effort to save him was nonsense. Perhaps that only showed that Pembroke did not understand his son-in-law, but the matter was too dangerous to gamble on. Whether he meant well or ill, Pembroke must go no further toward London until his purposes were absolutely clear. Hereford decided that after he had drunk his wine and talked for a while he would make some excuse to stay the night in Pembroke's camp.

"Here, my boy," Pembroke pressed a goblet into Hereford's hand. "Do not be so distressed. For you, at least, all is not lost. If you will but follow my advice, you will be safe no matter what befalls Chester."

"Safe!" Hurriedly Hereford took a swallow of wine to stop his own lips.

"Certainly." Pembroke had nothing to gain from Hereford's fall and nothing against the young man personally. If he could do Hereford a good turn and at the same time further his own plans, so much the better. "It will be no trouble to spread about the tale that you knew not Chester's true intentions, that you never believed he wished to depose the king and believed he really wanted Stephen to bring an army to fight the Welsh. You would not easily believe ill of Chester, no matter what others said against him—that is your defense for clinging to him so long. When, at last, you became convinced of his desire to commit treason, you can tell everyone you quarreled with him and parted company."

Hereford turned quite green with sickness. His hand closed over the hilt of his poniard so tight that the jeweled handle marked his fingers. Pembroke looked intently at him, but Hereford felt that if he opened his mouth to comment he would vomit. Perspiration beaded out on his temples with his effort to control himself, but strangely, in spite of his fixed attention, Pembroke did not seem to notice.

"I have thought of the perfect way for you to bring conviction to the minds of those who might doubt you also. On which side of the tourney do you fight?"

Determinedly Hereford swallowed his gorge. "I fight with the barons of the west and north, as I always have. Why do you ask what you know?"

"Because I think that under the circumstances you would do better to change sides. So bold a move would certainly convince everyone that you wished to be dissociated from any of Chester's plots."

"Perhaps," Hereford choked. "I can consider it at least."

"Drink up your wine, Hereford," Pembroke urged. "It will put heart into you."

Hereford choked again, bit his lip, and tried to lie. "Nay, my heart does not fail, for you have given me hope." He drank more wine to give himself a moment to marshal his thoughts, then said, "It would not be well for you to appear in this. Our meeting was most fortunate, for now I can carry the news of this betrayal to Chester. Perhaps he will be convinced and try to find some means to save himself, especially if I tell him that I will not stand by him in it." To conceal both his face and the fact that he had nearly strangled over the words, Hereford quickly drained the goblet to the dregs. "You too should consider your own safety, and remain as far from Chester as possible. Go, therefore, back to your own lands, and leave the rest to me."

"I wish I could," Pembroke sighed, "but I told you I came for two excellent reasons, and we have only talked of the first. I will be happy to leave warning Chester to you, but I must go to London anyway. I must have speech with my son-in-law. I have learned that the queen plans to steal my daughter from him and use her as a hostage for our doing of her will."

"What?" Hereford said stupidly, feeling very dizzy. "How could you learn such a thing? When does she plan this?"

"I have friends at court who send me word of this and that," Pembroke said caustically, "but Maud does not tell all to anyone. I would suppose she would try when Radnor's attention was completely diverted. For myself, I would guess that there can be no better time than while Radnor fights in the tourney. You know he can see and hear nothing when he is fighting. The Queen will take Leah then, for he came with such a small force of men that he will not have sufficient to protect her. I will be there, however, and hold her safe."

Those were the last words Hereford remembered clearly. It seemed to him now that he had attempted to get to his feet and that the ground had heaved beneath them. It seemed also, but very vaguely, that Pembroke had exclaimed with surprise on his inability to hold his wine and, when he could not rise, had come to help him with expressions of concern.

"Saddle our horses and let us go," Hereford now said bleaky to Alan. He and Chester were lost anyway, but perhaps there was time to warn Radnor.

The sodden sleep of emotional exhaustion was broken by the pounding of a sword hilt on the oak door. "Radnor, it is Hereford. Do not let fly at me, I'm coming in."

"Wait a minute."

"Cover your accursed wife. I will not rape her with my eyes. I have not got a minute." He burst in, muddied and disheveled.

"You fool, what has my wife to do with it? Get out and let me put my shoes on." Cain sheathed the drawn sword that was lying in his lap when he saw that the intruder was Hereford alone.

"There is no need. I want your head, not your sword arm. Stay where you are. Only tell the woman to go."

"My head is already forfeit to her—why not yours too?

Let her stay. You are damned already by her seeing you here in this case at this time of morning. Now, what the devil has happened?"

"As Philip said, the fat is in the fire. Chester is lost, and I with him. Pembroke slipped the leash."

"How?" Cain yawned and rubbed his head, ruffling his black hair until it stood on end. "I thought surely you had him safe when you did not return last night or early morning."

"Fool that I am! Dolt! Dunce!"

"What happened? Never mind what you are."

Hereford cast a glance at Leah. The man was her father and she must be hurt by hearing of his treachery. Well, if Radnor did not care, it was no business of his. "I went with my men, the whole fighting troop, and hid them in a bushment—well hid, I thought them, and I am no novice. I could not believe, however, what Philip said to be true, so I rode into Pembroke's camp to give him a chance to explain. He seemed right glad to see me; he spoke me sweet words and soft. Oh"—Hereford raised his arms and shook his fists at the ceiling—"let a man have but one drop of Welsh blood and he lies faster—"

"I know plenty without the drop who do the same. Hereford, my men will hold off whoever is pursuing you, but I have no stomach to be embroiled in this and my father bade me stand clear. For God's sake, tell me what happened without all these useless groans and complaints and let me think where to hide you so that you be not taken."

"No one pursues me."

"Then what is this haste for? If Pembroke has already slipped the leash, he is here. If he is here, what can I do but speak honeyed words to Stephen later? What need to wake me in the middle of the night and fright Leah into a fit?"

That last was unjust. For one thing it was well on into morning and for another Leah had not squeaked or moved a muscle since Hereford entered the room. She was sitting upright, clutching the bedclothes to her breasts to conceal them, her hair down over her back and shoulders. At the first alarm she had repressed the frantic urge to cling to her husband—which could easily have destroyed them both by hampering his sword arm if the emergency had been a real one—and had withdrawn to a corner of the bed to be clear of his swing or thrust. Now she was almost relaxed. The conversation of the men was serious enough, but it entailed no immediate physical emergency, for Leah could see the pulse in Radnor's throat beating slowly and steadily without excitement and the huge muscles lay smooth under the skin, not tensed and knotted for action.

"Nay, my lord, I am not frightened." Leah felt it necessary to add a third voice to the conversation because she could see the offense in Hereford's face and she wanted to give her husband, who was sleepy and annoyed, time to collect himself.

"I am very sorry to have disturbed your sleep and exposed you to royal disapproval. In future I will know enough to take my problems elsewhere."

"Hereford, come back here. Come back, I say, you know I cannot follow you. Be not so thin-skinned for a gibe from a sleepy man. You and Giles are alike. Yesterday I was too bold; today I am too timid—make up your mind. Now, sit down and tell me what happened since you are already here and I am already awake. When you stride around the room like that, you make me dizzy and half the time I cannot hear you. Do you want something to eat or drink?"

"Wine, if you have it to hand."

Leah turned her back and pulled a robe on under the bedclothes. She bade the little page bring cold meat and bread from the kitchen and poured wine herself.

"Anyway," Hereford was concluding his tale, "he slipped off at dawn yesterday and either has hidden himself in the city or Stephen has taken him."

"Dawn yesterday! Where have you been until now?"

"Sleeping."

"Wenching, more likely."

"Sleeping, I tell you. He drugged my wine. My men could not wake me."

Randor's jaw tightened. "He might have killed you with a draught so potent."

"I wish he had. Do you think it lighter to sit in prison—or to lose one's head? But why is Stephen hiding him? Why is he not here or known to be at court?"

"I told you and you would not believe. He comes to accuse Chester"—and to kill me, Cain thought, but he could not bring himself to say that aloud. "The king, or more like, the queen keeps him hid for two reasons. One, so that none can make him change his mind before the council, and, two, so that she can, after the council, imprison him or destroy him to change the succession in Wales."

"In Wales? How can that help her?"

"Hereford, you do not think!" Radnor swallowed his exasperation hastily. He was being vastly unfair, for Hereford, although a redoubtable fighter, was little more than a boy, had little experience of court policy, and was of an honest and open nature. "Look you," he began patiently, "are not the Welsh lords ever opposed to Stephen and in favor of Henry? Maud will find evidence that Pembroke was involved in the rebellion after he has betrayed Chester in council. Then she will be able to keep or kill Pembroke also so that his lands, Fitz Richard's, Chester's, and yours may all be sequestered and put into hands loyal to the king. Who does that leave to aid Gloucester or fight for Henry?"

"Oh God! But what of you? As long as Gaunt is in your father's hands, Gloucester cannot be attacked from behind."

"Ay, what of me?" Radnor said very slowly. "My father is not to the point. He is very old, and Maud is not really impatient. She would be willing to wait until nature solved that problem for her, but what of me?" A slow smile spread across his face, making the increasing coldness and hardness of the expression in his eyes really ugly. "Perhaps it was not all in sweet compliment to me that I was chosen king's champion. Perhaps—"

"No!" Hereford choked.

"No." Radnor readily agreed, but not to comfort Hereford. His eyes had caught the frozen figure of his wife, and he could have bit out his tongue for so carelessly frightening her. "It is but my own evil mind that invents such treacheries. You know how suspicious I am. In any case," he said briskly, "they will not take you, nor Chester either if we can but bring him to see reason. Not while I have a trick or two in my head, and if you and Chester are not to fall there will be little use in tampering with the rest of Wales. You are too close to Gloucester and will too readily go to his aid. Listen to me. Since Stephen has done nothing yet, it is plain that he wishes to make his move in full council and the council does not meet until the day after the tourney. Until then you are safe. Doubtless you will need some excuse for your absence from court for the past two days. Make up a tale of an assignation with a woman. It has been true often enough in the past to lend

216

credence to the story. If you do not hear from me that I have obtained a pardon for you, ride full armed as you are from the melee to the south gate. There you will be met, and I have planned a route of escape—"

"Stop." Hereford's face worked and then assumed an unnatural but beautiful graven stillness. "I do not want to hear. You do but tempt me to dishonor. If I can reason Chester into abandoning his purpose, mayhap we can save ourselves. If we cannot, we will come to the south gate together and you may do what you will with us. But if Chester holds his purpose, for good or ill, I am with him. He has my oath on it. I will not be foresworn."

"God keep you." With the sentiment Hereford had just uttered, Radnor would not argue. He too regarded his given word as sacred. "In any case, do not despair. Trouble there may well be, but somehow I will find a way to keep you from permanent harm. Between Gloucester and myself there will be a way."

Hereford had risen to go, but at the name Gloucester he stopped. "But one thing more I have to say." His blue eyes were hard as agates. "Some bird sang a song in Pembroke's ear before ever I could reach him that if sweet words would not convince him to go home I would use force. Who knew of this save you, I, she, and Lord Philip? Who sent the bird that sang?"

Radnor opened his mouth to make a sharp reply and then shut it; to be angry at Hereford or suspicious of Leah was useless. "Leah at least had no chance," he said calmly. "She was under my eye from the moment you left us until long after you were safe in Pembroke's camp. Philip could not, for I had to carry him in my arms like a child to his bed. That leaves me—well?"

"The whole thing could have been planned before Philip came to speak to you. If you had gone as he asked instead of I—what a weapon in Stephen's hands. Dear Philip! And I said I had wronged him. You would have been ruined."

No, Radnor thought, seeing it clearly, not ruined, killed, and if there was a plot, not Philip but Leah was involved. "Perhaps, but what profit is there for Philip in my ruin? We are known to be foster brothers and close companions too. He would be tarred with the same brush. No, Philip's only fault is in the sickness that has clouded his mind and prevented him from seeing the trap. Well, I am as much a fool, for I was so taken up with his pain that I saw it not myself. And you were no better either. Did it not seem strange to you that Pembroke should camp so near London instead of riding straight in?"

"Of course I saw it. That was what made me suspicious enough to ask questions so that my wine had to be drugged. But what good was the trap if there was no bait to bring you?"

"If Philip had not come, someone else would have. Such traps lack not for bait but, fortunately, the wrong mouse went."

"You may be right," Hereford sighed. "Radnor, do I go to court tomorrow?"

"Assuredly. To hide is to proclaim guilt. What else can you do but face the matter out boldly? Be of good heart. I swear I will have you out of this with whole lands and a whole skin."

The young man smiled wanly. "No blame to you if you do not. It was my own judgment that took me in, you ever spoke against it."

"Yes, well, never mind that. Do not worry more than you must, and do not show that long face in public. It is not like you to be sad and will tell the tale to all who do not know it."

At that Hereford smiled more naturally and came back to kiss Radnor's cheek. "You need not school me like a child. I know better than that even if I am a fool. I will see you tomorrow—no, it will be today, of course. Fare you well."

"God speed you."

Radnor sat and watched the closed door for a while after Hereford left. "He is so clean and good, it is a sin to dip him in this mud. For all he says, he is little more than a child. Not but what he is a man and more on the field of battle, but he thinks the skies would fall if he broke his word."

"I have heard that you were ever one to hold by your given promise." Leah's throat ached with unshed tears. If Cain were not so bound by his honor, perhaps she could have induced him to run away before the tourney, not to risk his life. How foolish. If he were such a man, she would not love him and would not care whether he lived or died. Leah laid her lips against her husband's shoulder as she slipped into bed. He pulled her close absently, still staring at the door, his mouth a bitter line.

"There is a difference, Leah. I keep my oath in bitterness and pride, knowing full well that others will betray me. He keeps his in hope and trust. Each new betrayal is a new pain to him."

He fell silent. It was easy enough to say that he would bring Hereford scatheless out of this situation, but not so easy to do. What he needed and needed desperately was a lever to use on the queen. If he had but one tittle of proof of what he thought to be true or if he could somehow twist Pembroke's intentions to destroy him so that they seemed to be Maud's also, he could count on the Marcher lords to support him.

"My lord." Leah's voice broke into his train of thought and he turned to her impatiently.

"What now?"

"I did but think that if there was truly use in convincing the court that Lord Hereford had been with—with a woman last night and yesterday, in this I might be able to help you."

"What? How?"

"Elizabeth of Chester—"

"How do you know Elizabeth Chester?"

"She was at our wedding, Cain. I met her there and she is one of the queen's ladies, so I have had some talk with her."

"I hope you will take no notions from Elizabeth Chester. She is my godsister, and loyal and helpful to her father, but her ways are bold and her manner to her menfolk—I will not have you think that you may do the same."

Leah lay silent through this lecture with dropped eyes. She would not argue with Cain on any matter again for quite a while, but she wondered with a little impatience how he could wander from such an important subject as Hereford's fate to such a slight one as Elizabeth Chester's behavior.

"No, my lord. Of course not, my lord. But on the matter of Lord Hereford, Elizabeth Chester can—"

"What has Hereford to do with Elizabeth?"

"My lord, if you would only allow me to finish one sentence, I will tell you. Nay, it would be better to use fewer words and see the thing done."

"What thing?" Radnor's voice went sharp with anxiety.

"Perhaps it were better for you not to know. There are other women involved—"

Radnor grasped his wife's arm brutally. "Are you inti-

219

mating that I cannot hold my tongue?" He was totally incredulous. All jest aside, this chit was getting out of hand.

The mistake she had made was instantly clear to Leah, but there was no help for it now. "No, no. Only that what is life and death to a woman is often a light matter to men."

"Look you here, Leah, my dogs do not go to hunt on their own for their own pleasure, and my wife will not play politics without my approval. Your little jest with Maud was one thing—you had no time to talk to me—but if you move in a matter in which I could have been consulted without my knowledge, I—I will beat you witless and lock you in Painscastle for your lifetime."

"I only wished to help Lord Hereford," Leah whispered timidly.

"Why?" Cain's jealousy was alive on the instant. Hereford and Leah seemed to be very friendly.

"Because you seemed to wish it."

"Then out with it."

"Elizaeth Chester knows Hereford's mistress—"

"Which one?" Radnor asked dryly before he started to wonder how his innocent bride came to be speaking glibly about such matters.

"Nay, my lord, this is Lady Gertrude, not a—a woman of the streets. But she is not so young as he and very jealous."

"She has need," Lord Radnor laughed, forgetting for the moment that he had just tripped over that stone himself.

"Elizabeth, I am sure, will carry this tale of still another woman to Lady Gertrude, pretending to be hurt and angry at Hereford. No doubt Elizabeth can choose such a time and place that Lady Gertrude will be certain to meet Hereford soon after. From what Elizabeth says, Lady Gertrude will not be able to contain her wrath. A few wellborn witnesses with loose tongues can easily be provided, and they will soon spread the tale which Hereford will not dare deny. In this manner, backwards as it were, not coming from him and in a manner making a fool of him, there will be weight enough to carry it as truth."

"It may well be. But why should Elizabeth Chester be willing to so demean herself? It will not help her father. And why should she seem angry at anything Hereford does?"

"I pray you, my lord, do not use this as matter for jest—do not. Elizabeth will have Hereford, if she can get him, to husband. It is common talk among the women and Lady Gertrude knows this. Lady Gertrude does not know, however, that Elizabeth knows she is Hereford's mistress."

"Elizabeth—and Hereford? There was talk of a dispensation once so that she could be proposed to me, but—." Suddenly Radnor started to laugh. "Oh, they will make a merry pair. I can hear the crash of the crockery now."

Leah's hand, pleading, touched her husband's. "Do not let him, above all, hear of this. I think she has a lust to him and he to her, but he says to all the world that he will not marry, and she, for all her light tongue, will have him no other way. I think it is to torment her that he has taken a mistress at court, and a stupid slut at that."

Radnor was still laughing at the thought of those two living together. "Very well, I swear I will say nothing, but I would love to warn him. Nonetheless it would do no good. If Elizabeth says she will have him, I have no doubt she will. God, she is beautiful." Cain's eyes lit suddenly with the sensual fires never far from the surface, but the interest died out in a flash. "I would not have a hellcat like that in my house for anything you could name. There are beauties other than that type. I think I should tire quickly of that opulence always displayed. Nay, I have what is better in this unfolding, petal by petal."

He turned and bent over Leah, gazing avidly at the way her loose hair made a transparent golden screen between his eyes and her body. It was late and he should rise, but their quarrel the night before still hung heavily on his spirits and Leah's appearance behind that shimmering screen was irresistible. Cain slid his fingers through the shining mesh of hair, watching for a sign of renewed anger or reluctance. Leah lay still, paralyzed by his caress, her mind going blank, her eyes closing slowly, every sense concentrating on her feeling. Cain's fear that he had destroyed her love made his own passion slow to rise. By the time he drew his wife to him, Leah was nearly insensible with a pleasure terribly akin to pain.

It was nearly breakfast time when Bess entered the room to open the shutters and wake her master and mistress. She cast a quick, alarmed look at the bed. Both occupants were soundly asleep, but she could see nothing of her mistress except a blanket of golden hair which hid her back and strayed over Lord Radnor's shoulders. Why had her mistress cried out in that dreadful way? There had been no sound of argument or blows. Perhaps this one had other ways of hurting a woman—ways that did not show. Bess shuddered as she realized that she had made a sound which had disturbed Lord Radnor. His right hand reached down automatically, even before he wakened, to the long sword by the bed. Let them wake of their own accord, Bess thought, and with a little gasp, she was out the door.

The feminine gasp reassured some unconscious mechanism in Radnor, and he sank again into sleep; it had, however, the opposite effect on Leah who sat up cautiously and stared at her husband. The room smelled faintly of burnt wax, for they had allowed the candles to gutter out, and a fresh breeze blew in at the open window. Feeling slightly chilled herself, Leah drew the coverlet higher over Cain's shoulders. The sensation disturbed him, and he turned flat on his back and pushed the covers all the way off with an impatient gesture. Leah smiled at her sleeping lord. He was always much warmer than she, and she could never remember it. Her eyes ran over him affectionately; then their expression grew fixed and she began to study his body with an awareness of it that she had not had before.

"Have I turned green of a sudden?"

"No, oh no. I was only looking at you."

"So I see, and I at you. But why?"

"I do not know. Because you are, all of a sudden, so—" she paused seeking for words, looking into his face and then down at his body again, "so—beautiful."

It was the wrong word, singularly inappropriate for that powerful masculine frame so marred with the scars of war, and yet no other word could describe her feeling. Cain stared in amazement, thinking it an unkind joke, but it was so unlike Leah to taunt him that he could almost believe she meant it. Could it be true that for her, just now anyway, he was beautiful?

"Before," he began hesitantly, and watched Leah blush, "what did I do?"

She dropped her head so that her face was hidden by her falling hair. "I do not know."

"Were you hurt or pleased—or unwilling? I heard you cry out, but I could do nothing then."

"I do not know," she repeated stubbornly.

"Look at me."

Her eyes were strange under heavy lids, filled with a sort of wondering recollection. Cain's tension began to dissolve although she did not return his questioning look for

222

long. Her eyes returned to his body, irresistibly drawn, and he felt drained by that gaze, as if he would turn all to fluid.

"I wish—" Leah murmured dreamily, slowly lifting her hand, "may I touch you?"

Cain released a shuddering sigh. "As you will, so do with me."

It was a complete novelty for him to lie still under her exploring hands, a novelty and a revelation to them both, for he learned something from her surprise and she learned much from his reactions. In the end his reticence was broken, and he groaned and writhed. Leah did not smile, for her face was rigid with her own rising passion, but a deep sense of power grew within her. So might a man be tamed. So. And so. She had pushed him too far, however, and he was finished almost before he started, leaving her, for she now knew what culmination was, dissatisfied.

"You did not wait for me," she cried, and he heard her through a numbness of his satisfaction.

Leah's protest was unintentional; she hardly knew she uttered it. Indeed, had she thought about what that instinctive cry should teach her husband, she would have bitten out her tongue before she gave vent to it. In the first instant of hearing, the words had no meaning to Radnor, but as he lifted himself, he caught a glance at his wife's face. Her fleeing expression of frustration recalled to him others, and her words suddenly gained significance.

Cain's relationships with women had always been largely unsatisfactory, and he had a secret envy of men like Hereford who seemed to be able to hold the most avaricious women in thrall with nothing but their persons. He had blamed the women for dishonesty of purpose and dismissed the matter with the belief that none of them had ever cared for him. It had needed a woman with an innocence equal to his ignorance in this matter to put into plain words the explanation for his repeated failures as a lover. Cain blinked, drew in his breath sharply, and allowed himself to sink down on Leah's breast. He would not make that mistake again, and he could rectify it this time, but how did Leah know a man could wait? Had she looked abroad for someone else to fill her craving?

Leah understood very quickly what she had gained and what she had lost. She would not again need to suffer the misery of unfulfilled desire; she had learned ways to tempt

Cain and increase his pleasure, and that would help her hold him, but she had taught him what a woman desired. Would he now be tempted himself to try his power upon others? Not yet, certainly not while he still desired to breed with her. For the present, at least, all his attention would be bent upon providing himself with an heir. Leah sighed and shifted her husband's heavy head on her shoulder.

Leah's plan to establish Hereford's innocence functioned as if charmed. Hereford walked into the trap all unaware, and amidst the ravings of Lady Gertrude, the icy-eyed affront of Elizabeth, the ill-concealed amusement of the watching ladies and gentlemen, and his own inability to explain or deny, he gave as genuine an exhibition of chagrin and embarrassment as could be desired. Leah went home from the White Tower, where she had stayed to see the outcome of her plotting, to relate the whole graphically to Lord Radnor. She was rewarded by his smile and nod of satisfaction.

"You were right," he said. "It is better this way than for Hereford to make the excuse." Suddenly he began to laugh, realizing that Hereford, who was so often guilty of seduction and infidelity and so clever at soothing women and wriggling out of situations, was finally being brought to account. It was only just that he should be found guilty on the one occasion when he was actually innocent. "I will roast him. My God, how I will roast him."

"No, you cannot, my lord," Leah protested. "How could you hear about it? Remember he did not see me for fear he should guess."

"It does not matter. I will seek out someone at court who will tell me the story anew. I could not meet his eye now without—." Then he collapsed, bent double in his chair, laughing until he hiccupped. "But the cream of the jest is still coming. I am sorry you will miss it, Leah, for you certainly deserve to see the flowering of the seed you sowed. Briefly, it is this. At council they will ask him to name the woman so as to give witness, and he will refuse—nobly risking his life to shield her honor. Then the eyes of those lords will turn inward and from side to side. 'My wife?' they will think, 'his?' Every man living within a day's ride who was not in his own bed that night—and with the feast, how many were?—will burn with the torments of the damned, and not a few will look cross-eyed at blond child-

224

ren born nine moons from now. Oh, merrily we go along—merrily, merrily. By the time this is done there will be as many knives out for Hereford's ribs as for mine." Cain glanced at his wife and added hastily, "For a different reason, Leah."

He bent again, still chuckling occasionally, over the task that had occupied him all that afternoon. He was setting the edge on his long-sword. Technically this was a task for the armorer, but Cain loved the weapon, a remarkably fine one which had been his father's gift to him upon his knighting, and he allowed no one else to touch it. The room was warm and he sat in the full light of the window, naked to the waist. Sunlight flickered through now and again as the June breeze moved the leaves of the shade trees outside. It gleamed in little flashes on the sweat-shining skin covering biceps knotting and relaxing in the regular rhythm of drawing stone against steel. Head bowed, thickening the strong column of the neck, shoulders hunched a little, Cain was the living image of quiescent power. With his scarred face hidden, he was a sight to stir any woman's blood, and his wife was no exception.

Made restless by her steadfast stare, Cain looked up. "For the tourney," he said, pointing the sharpening stone at the sword. "I will do you proud, Leah. I have ordered a new hauberk and helm to be beautiful as well as successful, and my shield is to be all new-painted. Thus will I grace the new surcoat you were kind enough to prepare."

A mixture of pride and fear, liberally salted with desire, shook her. Leah came up behind Radnor and laid her hands on his back to feel the play of the muscles under her fingers. "You look forward to the tournament, my lord?"

"Yes and no. Mayhap I will learn more of the queen's purposes, but taking that necessity away, sometimes I think that a man who fights in earnest as much as I should have a lighter sport. All we do for pleasure means killing—hunting, hawking—. The jousting is but practice for the same with man." He sat up and leaned back against his wife; her hands slid down over his shoulders to comb through the hair on his chest. "But what else can a man do? To sit too long over the chess board or draughts makes the muscles twitch to be up and doing. At Painscastle I read—the monks of the abbey are kind enough to lend me their books and some I have had copied myself—but that too is restless work for a strong young man."

"But my father and the queen——. Are you not like to be hurt in this rough play?"

Cain stared ahead. Was Leah trying to warn him? Did she know and wish to speak openly but fear to do so? "No doubt I will be bruised and banged about. The more I think on it the more I cannot believe that anyone does more than hope for an accident." Perhaps his seeming carelessness would make her speak out. "I only pray I have not forgot my skill with the lance. It is long and long, nigh on a year, since I have truly used one. You are, I suppose, in better favor up Above than I, being more innocent. Send up a few prayers that I may not be ignominiously laid in the dust on the first course."

"I wish I were as sure you would come to no harm as I am that your skill is unimpaired. Oh, Cain," her hands tightened, the sharp nails scratching his bare breast a little, "for all you say, my heart misgives me about this tourney."

"You are too fearful, Leah. Such are life's chances. Where would be the sport if there were no danger? Would you rather I were like William of Gloucester, scented and oiled with hands as soft and white as a woman's?"

"No, oh no. I must be proud of my lord. Only—is it needful to go beyond the jousts for which you are champion and fight in the melee?"

Cain laughed. "Not needful, no. I doubt my ability to stop, though, once the heat of fighting is upon me. It is like drink, Leah. The more you take the more you want, until at last a sickness overcomes you." He paused, but she still said nothing. Suddenly Cain did not want her to speak. "In any case it is not something I could give over because of your fears. Next you would be afraid for me to go into battle to guard my lands. What would become of us then?"

"I would be afraid. Indeed, I am afraid of everything you do, of every minute you are out of my sight, but I would not say a word against your duty. I would rather urge you to it, in spite of my fear, than keep you from it. But is this tourney your duty?"

Why would she not leave the subject? Would she be so insistent if she did not know there was a plot to kill him? It was natural for a woman to be timid, and Leah was afraid of her father. Did the warnings mean that she knew but was not party to the plot?

"Ay," Cain said, "I can just see you with the stern ex-

226

pression of Athena—a pagan goddess of whom you know nothing—urging me—I the meanwhile all trembling with fear—out to fall upon my enemies."

The words were totally unrelated to his thoughts, spoken because he had planned to say them as a further diversion. In another revulsion of feeling he grasped her hands to pull her further forward and turned his head over his shoulder to ask outright what she knew. There were tears sparkling on Leah's lashes, and all Cain could do was kiss her. Now he would never ask because he did not want to know. Leah was a little surprised at the tightness of his grip. She was not at all reluctant; Cain had no need to hold her to make her mouth cling to his.

CHAPTER 15

THE EARL OF PEMBROKE bowed low over Maud's hand in a quiet, well-guarded little house very near the White Tower. "I am most comfortable here, madam, thank you, and I am grateful for the guard you set about me, but I do not completely understand it."

"You do not understand?" Maud sounded surprised. "You told me that you had met Hereford, warned him that Chester would be betrayed, and you are surprised that I guard you. Can you not guess that Hereford will run straight to Radnor, and that Radnor will convince him that you, and not Philip, are to speak out against the traitor? I can easily arrange that Philip will back your accusation of Chester so that you need not fear to bear the blame alone, but for now if Hereford and Chester believe you guilty, doubtless they will try to find you and kill you."

Pembroke turned pale and Maud dropped her eyes to hide the laughter she was afraid might show in them. "I am sure they will never suspect," Pembroke replied. "It is true that I dosed Hereford's drink, but it was only a drop and should do no more than give him a sound night's sleep." A worried frown crossed Pembroke's face. "It did

227

act too quickly though, I hope——." The frown cleared. "At worst it will kill him, and since no man can say that Hereford ate or drank aught with me—I went for the wine and dosed it myself—no harm can come of that."

As annoyed as she was with Pembroke—for Hereford's all, not his death, was an integral part of her plans—Maud's voice was smooth and unconcerned. "In any case, you will be safe here. Nonetheless it is most unfortunate that Radnor will not go to you as planned. I begin to believe that he is of the devil's brood. Nothing seems to harm him. He came clean away at Oxford, and now this escape——. You know that without his lands it will be impossible for the king to go through Wales in peace and knock on Gloucester's back door. If my husband cannot do that, there is little profit for us in giving Fitz Richard's lands to you."

"You need not concern yourself, madam. My plan for the tourney cannot fail. He would naturally be on his guard in Oxford's keep. We both knew that and I tried because there was nothing to lose. It was ill luck that Hereford heard of my coming and met me first. I had a message so prepared that Radnor would not have failed to come to me. I could not send it, of course, because he might well have known that Hereford intended to go. Curse that boy's long tongue."

"But Oxford has a long tongue too, and he is acting for you in the arrangements for the tourney."

"Yes," Pembroke laughed, "and who will believe his long tongue no matter what he tells the men he hires? All know what Radnor did in Oxford's keep. Think how foolish Oxford will seem if he says that I, Radnor's father-in-law, gave him gold to hire assassins. What purpose could I have for so mad an act when Radnor's father is yet alive?"

"That is true, but this plan *must* work. We must be rid of him before the council. I fear his influence with the Marcher lords, and I greatly fear that he has a plan to steal Hereford and Chester away from the court if there is an accusation. Once they reach their own lands, there will be no holding them. I hope you are sure of what you do, for your danger will be greater than mine if they are not taken."

"It cannot fail."

Pembroke smiled his assurance at her, and Maud offered her hand again to be kissed and left. The smile began to fade from Pembroke's face, and then grew

228

broader. Radnor would die in the tourney most certainly, but Maud might not approve of the manner of his going. Did she think him such a fool as to put himself completely in her power? He too needed a weapon in reserve, and he had it in the way his plans were laid. First he had sent a warning to Oxford that the queen had bribed some of Oxford's men to murder Radnor, pleading that his son-in-law be kept safe. Then, pretending to be terrified by the queen's threats and grief-stricken at what he was forced to do, he had come to Oxford to arrange Radnor's death in the tourney. Oxford was very happy to make the arrangements, hating Radnor, but if the queen had not tried to use his keep as a place to assassinate her enemy he would have been saved much hurt. He did not mind keeping Pembroke's name out of it and hinting to the men he hired that when they accomplished their purpose they would find favor in high places. Maud will play no tricks on me, Pembroke said to himself, having already arranged both the kidnapping of Leah and a way out of the well-guarded little house, and went to his dinner with excellent appetite.

The Duke of Gaunt was also thinking of the royal tourney, but he was not eating his dinner with appetite. He was staring sightlessly across the great hall of Radnor Castle. Sir Robert had died that morning. He had not died easily or quickly, but he had told all he knew of Pembroke's plans before he was granted that merciful oblivion. It was true that Sir Robert could not, or would not, give any details; it did not matter. Gaunt did not need to be told that the easiest way to murder a man and conceal the fact of murder was during a tourney. His messenger had been sent off some hours before, carrying all that he knew or guessed to warn Cain, but Gaunt's mind would not clear. He sat toying with his food, telling himself that Cain was old enough to care for his own interests and could be trusted to take adequate precautions.

"Old fool," he muttered angrily, paring a sliver of meat from the roast before him and putting it into his mouth, "what is there to consider? He has faced worse danger on the field before. He managed that business at Oxford Castle well—if a little too thoroughly. It is more needful to keep the land quiet than to worry over one man's life in any case."

For whom do I keep the land quiet, he wondered, the

well-flavored meat sticking like dry dust in his throat. I am almost three-score years, and except for him there is no one, not even a cousin of Welsh blood. So the estate, whole and peaceful, will pass to his murderer or to the king. Nonsense! Cain will return as he always has. He will find some excuse not to fight or he will find some way to guard himself—he is no fool. The old man laughed aloud harshly. To think of Cain trying to find an excuse not to fight was as ridiculous as thinking of his trying to fly. Besides, what excuse could he find? To say that his father-in-law was conspiring to assassinate him would make him a laughingstock, and to admit that he would not fight for that reason would brand him a coward. I alone could stop him, Gaunt thought.

He rose restlessly and paced to the nearest window, noting the position of the sun and counting the hours that remained. Sending another messenger would be useless. Probably Cain would pay no atention since only his own safety was at stake. Even if Cain should wish to obey, he had not sufficient men with him to fight his way free of the city, and to leave it peacefully at such a time was impossible. With Chester's plot widely known and Henry rumored to be coming, Maud was not likely to leave unwatched any man who was not devoted to her heart and soul. Cain could not even approach one of the London gates without giving warning of his intentions.

Gaunt tapped his knuckles against the frame of the window. The sky was serenely blue, investing the turbid waters of the moat with a wholly false appearance of clarity. The meadows, cleared from the surrounding forest, sloped gently away from the walls and cattle fed peacefully upon the good grass. Along the track leading to the drawbridge, a carter urged his oxen in a monotonous singsong. A rich land, a good land, a land worth defending. The tapping fist came down with a crash which brought blood to Gaunt's knuckles and startled the men-at-arms.

"Let every man able arm and provision himself to ride to London," Gaunt roared.

I will not let them eat my son. He will not fight without his men around him to be surely slain. I will cry defiance to the king if need be, and if that is being forsworn, then forsworn I will be. He is flesh of my flesh, blood of my blood, and they shall not have him.

The day before the tourney, in the women's quarters of

the White Tower, Maud and Joan of Shrewsbury were exchanging half-confidences.

"Oxford tells me that Hereford may change sides at the tourney," Joan commented when the other ladies were out of earshot.

"The more fool Oxford," Maud replied tartly, for her temper was on edge with waiting for events to move. "The only thing Hereford could change for is to separate himself from Chester, and he would never do that. There is no such thing as political expedience to a man raised in the principles of Miles of Gloucester and so young as Roger of Hereford."

"Oh? Oxford thought that Pembroke had warned him to change because he hoped to separate him from Lord Radnor. If Hereford fights on Radnor's right hand, it will increase the difficulty of pricking Radnor hard enough to keep him abed."

"If that was intended, it would indeed. For that type of wound—bad enough, but not too bad—care and consideration are needed."

The bright color in Joan's cheeks faded appreciably. "Madam, you cannot mean to have him slain!"

"What else? Why, Joan, you are distressed. If I had known you still had a lust to that particular piece of manhood, I would not have told you. It would have been easier for you to have believed it to be an accident. My dear, I am truly sorry, but you have spoken of him with such cold disdain for the past year that—"

"I assure you my distress is for no such reason. I have not now, and never did have any feeling at all except—oh, perhaps, a little pity—for Lord Radnor. I did only what we decided would be best. Shrewsbury felt it to be an object of the first importance to block his betrothal to Elizabeth of Chester. That accomplished, I was finished with him. Still, I knew him well. To snuff out such a life deliberately—I am distressed for a pet dog that dies."

Maud knew that Joan was really upset because it was not like her to make foolish statements, and at the time she had been leading Lord Radnor on a string he had already been contracted for Leah. The business with Elizabeth had been years earlier. She did not appear to notice the slip, but went on sweetly. "I must say that this surprises me. What exactly was between you two was always a puzzle, but I must compliment you, and Shrewsbury too, upon your powers of dissimulation. I would have sworn,

231

and I am no fool, that you were in love and that your lord knew nothing. Radnor, it was plain, was hard hit, but he is like glass in matters regarding women. I wish it were so in other matters; things then might not have come to this pass. I am a little sorry for his silly bride, but she is plainly simple." Of this, Maud was not at all sure, but she wished to enrage Joan. "She will forget him in a month or two. Speaking of that, and since you say it is not a tender subject, I have heard that he is completely besotted about her. I have set my servants upon his and they talk."

"About what?"

"Everything. Is that not the way with servants? Imagine, he could not summon sufficient resolution to leave her behind with her parents—and she told me in ten minutes everything she had seen and heard. I scarcely needed to ask a question; it poured from her. Her eyes are already wandering too. You should see how she looks at William of Gloucester. Radnor will be spared the grief of being cuckolded at least."

"I can scarcely believe that Lord Radnor could care for such a woman. He took her, I know, because of the dower lands—and he was none too eager to fulfill the contract."

"Yes, he was mooning over you like a sick calf then. It is true that he is mad for her now, nonetheless. He has changed. It is a matter of jest with his men that he cannot wait to get up the stairs to her solar—and for all he speaks sharply to her and she does not know her power, the servants say that he is ever kissing and pawing her. They are afraid to enter the room for he always must break an embrace and looks black as night at them. He is so mad for her," Maud laughed, "that he discusses business with his master-of-arms in her presence. I know some things which will cost Lord Radnor dear—or would if he lived."

Maud knew what she was doing. The color had returned, higher than ever, to Joan's face and her blue eyes fairly shot sparks. Whatever momentary softness she had felt for her old love, for Maud believed not a word of that nonsense about not caring for him, she felt only hate now.

Maud had miscalculated again, however. She had set Leah's worth and Joan's intelligence both too low and had, all unintentionally, given Joan reason to believe she might win Cain back and a weapon to use for that purpose. Joan was willing to accept the fact that Cain was presently enamored of his wife's physical charms—after all they had only been married for about three weeks. She had always thought, and now was sure, that Leah was not equal to him. As soon as he discovered this, he would be bored and might easily be brought to appreciate a woman who had more to offer than a mere body—especially when the body was well worth having too. Lord Radnor had left her— Joan faced the fact—because she had betrayed him. How bitterly she regretted it now, not the betrayal, which was necessary, but the crude way she had told him and laughed at him. She had been so sure that he was too much her slave, too much in love to resent anything. Now, however, it was his wife who had betrayed him, and Joan was in a position to save his life and warn him that Leah was a fool and was carrying tales to Maud.

In her own apartments at home, Joan bit her lips over the wording of her message. She had no fear that Leah would read it, for she was sure that the girl was too ignorant to read. What was more, she cared not a fig how jealous Leah became. Her difficulty was that she wished to communicate the idea that she was risking her safety and her husband's prosperity to do Radnor this service. Neither was true, of course, for although Joan desired Radnor, she did not care enough for him or for any living soul except herself to risk anything. Even with a warning, Radnor would probably be badly enough hurt to be incapacitated, and that was all that was necessary for Joan's purposes. She only wanted to keep him from seeing Henry of Anjou until Shrewsbury had a chance to conclude his business with the young pretender. About Maud's plans for Wales she knew and cared nothing.

Leah laid aside the message when it arrived with a sinking heart. Like everything else she kept about her, the parchment Joan used was permeated with her scent and Leah was coming to recognize the odor as readily as her husband would. She silently handed the note to him when he came in from his conference with Philip. Cain had no need to smell the parchment; the hand was perfectly familiar to him. His first impulse was to fling the missive into the fire, but for one thing there was no fire and for another his curiosity was awakened. He glanced at Leah who was looking out of the window, her back to him, and then broke the seal.

"My lord: I dare not sign this, but you cannot fail to know the sender. If you do not take great care, the prize your wife will have for the tourney is your body laid upon your shield. Mayhap she deserves this, for she has betrayed your secrets to the queen out of spite of your harshness, but you should die a nobler death. I hope you understand, for I dare write no more and risk all by even so much for your sake."

"I hope Lady Shrewsbury has not bad news for you." Leah's voice was totally without inflection and she had not turned around.

Cain looked at his wife's lance-straight back. He certainly did not want another scene like the one last night. On the other hand, he dared not show Leah the note because of the warning in it. She would have hysterics, he thought, if she were frightened any more. He could not help, moreover, being distracted by a burning curiosity about Joan's purposes. Surely she would rather have him dead than alive after what had passed between them. He was ashamed even now of what he had said in parting from her, but Radnor merely showed his ignorance of the fact that his death could bring Joan no satisfaction. Only two things could ease her heart—to see him humbled and to have him sue once more for her love.

"I wish," Radnor said finally with magnificent *non sequitur*, "that I had not laughed so heartily at Hereford's dismay yesterday. I am now in almost the same position, except, praise God, I have no witnesses of my discomfiture. I cannot deny that this is Joan of Shrewsbury's hand, nor that there is something here that I would not have you see. I swear, however, that it is no matter of a private nature between Joan and myself. For the rest I care not—she warns me that you have betrayed me to the queen."

"You need tell me nothing. I ask out of concern for your well-being alone," Leah replied mendaciously. "I am not like to question your behavior again, my lord."

"I hope not, but I would not have you distressed for nothing. Of all women on earth, you need concern yourself least with Joan of Shrewsbury. Are you not even interested in how you have betrayed me?"

"If you do not believe that I am faithful to you in word and deed, what could I do to convince you? I know I have betrayed nothing. If you choose to believe Lady Shrewsbury—"

Radnor laughed and gave his wife an affectionate hug with one arm. Whatever Leah's knowledge of her father's doings, he was sure she had told Maud nothing. "She does not name any particular thing. What lies have you been spreading now? Leah, Leah, you will never go to heaven if you speak so many untruths."

"I will go to heaven! God understands everything. Surely He will understand that it is needful for me to protect my husband's interests among those who wish him harm."

Covering his face in humorous despair, Radnor gave up the struggle. He replied, chuckling a little, that she must not forget to confess that she told lies and do her penance. He had to go out again to see what support he could muster for Hereford since there was no longer hope of saving Chester, but he hated to leave Leah while her mouth still drooped disconsolately. More and more her gaiety was his happiness, and her sorrow, no matter how small and foolish, wrung his heart.

"I must go out on business—nay, it is nothing to do with this letter, and you may believe me for I am not the prevaricator that you are. I must speak to William of Gloucester and Leicester and some others before the council meeting. Tomorrow I will have no time because of the tourney. What will you do until I return?"

"Nothing of which you would disapprove, my lord. There is always much to be done. I must talk of wines to the steward, of meat and flour and spices to the cooks, of sewing and cleaning to the maids—"

"Well, I do disapprove. You cannot always toil. It is Friday—oh, Lord, fish again—there seem to be five Fridays in every week. Why do you not go to the market, and not to buy wine and meat and flour, but to see the fairings? Giles will—. No, I need Giles. Beaufort can escort you and I will give you more money." That should cheer her up, he thought; above all women liked to buy things.

"You are very kind," Leah replied in a small, sad voice.

"Have you forgot how to smile this afternoon?" There was a short pause while Cain did some mental gymnastics. "Would it make you happier if I went with you, Leah?" He could not bear her unspoken depression and was now prepared to rearrange his own schedule to please her.

Having what she wanted, Leah did smile, turning her face up to his with brightening eyes. "Of course it would make me happy, but you must not do it. You are merely indulging me, and your affairs must come first. I will wait for you."

"That will take too much time. I do not want to be late in returning. Remember that I am to take the evening meal alone with the king tonight. I know what is best to be done. Go alone, and I will meet you at the Horse Market in Smithfield. I intended to buy you a riding mare or two and I need a replacement for my dead stallion. I will come as soon as possible, but do not look for me before the third hour after noon. Now kiss me quickly, and I must go. I am late already."

"Be careful, my lord. Oh, how I wish I might go with you."

"To watch me or to protect me? Go to, do not be such a goose. I would look something a little more than foolish explaining that I had brought my nursemaid along." He laughed at her, pushing away his doubts and telling himself that he should be flattered by her jealousy and her fear.

Radnor's first call was on William of Gloucester whom he found teasing a small dog with bits of meat prepared by a pretty boy. Radnor scowled at William's choice of company and William laughed. He did, however, gesture to the boy, who removed himself and the dog to the guardroom below.

"You have heard about Hereford's latest folly?"

"We have more similar senses of humor than I thought if you are going to class treason as a form of folly," William rejoined.

Cain snorted impatiently. "Well, so it is, in this case, but that was not what I meant. You know the tale that has been spread—give it what backing you can."

William smiled. "So be it, but no woman can save him if he failed to stop Pembroke. How could you send such a trusting child to fulfill such a duty? And do not ask me how I knew that Hereford had failed. I can read your face. Where is Pembroke?"

"I wish to God I knew. You know what it will mean to your father and your lands if Chester and Hereford are taken prisoner. Can you find where Pembroke is, William? Perhaps we can save the oats still. It would be worth— much—to all of us."

The heavy-lidded eyes flickered open and William's lips drew back further in a brief, vicious grimace that was no longer a smile. He would have allowed few other men to see that expression, but his trust in his foster brother was absolute—secure enough even to allow him to speak his true mind.

"If I can, you would be the last man I would tell of it. Fool that you are, you would try to save him for the sake of the blood bond that is between you. If I find him, he will die—and I do not desire to have you try to foil my purpose."

Radnor did not answer that remark. "Have you heard any more about Henry's movements?"

"Only what you know. That he will land in Devonshire. We receive his letters, but we still have been unable to reach him. How goes your part of that business?"

"I will see Stephen tonight—alone, without Maud. I am almost sure I can get from him letters in his own hand confirming Henry as his successor. To Stephen it will mean nothing; he is easy of promise who never intends to keep his word. I sadly fear I will not be able to have them stamped with the Great Seal. Maud controls that, but one cannot have everything. As it is, such letters will be of value if by some mischance Eustace is crowned during Stephen's lifetime and more argument arises on the king's death. With those letters in hand, I can get money—to send Henry home, to pay the troops he has brought, and for whatever else is needful. Thus we spare our own purses for that time when money will not be thrown away. I know Maud holds the purse strings, but she will see that it is better that Henry should go, even at her expense, than that he should stay holding those letters and fomenting continual unrest."

William nodded, his face impassive again but his eyes still showed his anger. "It is the best that can be done, I suppose. If it had not been for this idiocy of Chester's, we could have done more. I believe Stephen could have been forced to proclaim the true succession in council, before the whole court."

"Perhaps," Radnor replied, "but we must adjust our desires to what is possible."

"So I believe also, as you well know, and I think you should take your own advice. Have you asked your wife where her father lies hid?"

Cain took a step forward threateningly, but William did not move except to lift his eyes challengingly.

"It is well to hope, ill to believe, and disastrous to trust," William sneered. "If I were you, I would take neither food nor drink from my wife's hands before the tourney." Cain started to turn away, but with a movement swift as a striking snake's William caught his arm. "Have a care to yourself. When Henry is king, you may kill yourself in your own way, for all of me, but until that day it would suit my purposes very ill indeed if your father had no successor to his title other than Pembroke. What better place to have a fatal accident than a tourney? And what easier way to be sure of such an accident than a potion to make a man only a little drowsy?"

Shaking with fury, Radnor gripped Lord William and glared into his passionless face. He could have crushed William with a single blow, but he was not really angry with his foster brother; his fury was the impotent rage of insecurity. "Why do you missay Leah?"

Delicately, William freed his gown from the grip Radnor had taken on it. "I do not missay her. For all I know, she is as pure in heart as the Virgin. I only know that she is Pembroke's daughter and I urge caution on you because you have a look on your face these days that only a man besotted upon a woman wears."

"I am sure she is innocent."

"That is why I said my say. Think on it. Do not be so sure that you may be alive and more sure."

Radnor's mood was black as pitch when he left William, but fortunately the Earl of Leicester was of equable disposition and did not take offense. He agreed readily enough that it would be to no one's benefit that Hereford should be attainted, provided the young man would behave himself in the future.

"I believe he has learned his lesson," Radnor said shortly. "He will meddle no more with Chester's doings— if he comes scatheless out of this. He is hot-tempered, however, and if his property or his honor is touched, he will seek revenge. This is why I would have a free pardon for him."

Leicester nodded understandingly. "I will do nothing against it, I assure you—and for what my influence with Stephen may do you will have my voice for Hereford's support. The young are hotblooded and prone to mistake."

Cain bent his lips into a smile with an effort. "I thank you and I thank you for your patience with my bad temper."

"A man who faces what you do and yet troubles himself about others' well-doing may be forgiven much."

The remark stopped Cain in his tracks as he was preparing to take his leave. Apparently the whole court knew he was to be slaughtered. It did not sound like Pembroke's usual careful planning. What was more, it could not be suspicion of Pembroke's intentions, because Leicester gave no sign of knowing that Pembroke was in London. On the other hand, Leicester was close to the king. It was difficult to believe that Stephen would be party to such a thing; it was not his way, but it was certainly worth questioning further.

"Whence comes all this tender concern for my health, Leicester?"

The older man shook his head. "Not from where you might think. Stephen, good man that he is, loves you well. But I have heard a word here and seen a look there. My wife too has picked up a hint or two in the women's quarters. Since you have brought the matter out into the air, let me say this. You do not keep knights in your train and only knighted men may join in this combat. There are a surprising number of knights errant in the south and east party who are of a sudden very affluent and wear Oxford's colors. I know no more and desire to know no more. I have heard it said that you are the strongest man in England, and I doubt it not, but if you have influence with either the nether regions or the upper ones, you should whistle for help."

Cain's beautiful teeth showed in his broad grin. He could have kissed Leicester in his relief, for that remark about the rumors in the women's quarters indicated that Maud really was involved. Radnor was delighted because he would have no need to make evidence against her; he could with perfect justice turn her own plotting against her to force her to his will.

"Well, well, well. This promises fairly," he said to Leicester's astonishment. "I think I see a break in a very cloudy sky. I had not thought to find so much of real interest in a tourney. I thank you for your kind words and for your good wishes."

CHAPTER 16

THE SMITHFIELD HORSE MARKET had grown considerably in size since Lord Radnor had last visited it. Every type of animal was offered for sale or barter, from colts just weaned to creatures so long past their prime that their shrunken gums exposed the roots of their yellowed teeth from which the crowns had long since been ground by years of eating. Here and there an enterprising dealer even showed the small-headed, thick-bodied, thin-legged Arabian ponies, more beautiful than any other horse, to Radnor's mind. He stopped to look at each of these, stroking silken coats and gazing rather longingly into the large liquid eyes. When the dealers extolled the strength and fleetness of these mounts, however, Radnor laughed and exclaimed that they would never carry his weight, even unarmed, and that his legs would trail on the ground. "Wait until I have a son," he murmured, and rode away from a particularly beautiful mare, white as snow, her well-groomed mane and tail glinting like silver in the sunshine.

As he said the word "son" he realized that he had a wife whose weight was only a little more than a third of his own. He turned back and dismounted to question the merchant in earnest about breeding possibilities and price. The haggling was long, spirited, and involved, Radnor having forgotten all about the dignity of his position in his determination to have the mare for Leah at a reasonable price. Somewhere at the back of his mind, even as he bargained, Cain knew that Leah was rather late, but Joan of Shrewsbury had taught him the habit of waiting patiently for women at markets, and he assumed his wife had lost herself among the toys and gewgaws offered.

The deal closed, Radnor remounted and looked around again, this time a trifle impatiently. It was more than an hour past the appointed time and no wife was yet in sight. He was beginning to wonder whether he should send some of his men to look for her when Cedric appeared riding through the crowd, bloodied and pale as parchment.

"My lord! Thank God I have found you so quickly. Come home at once."

"Good heaven, what has befallen us now?" But Cain did not wait for a reply. "Arm and ride," he called to his men, and spurred his horse beside Cedric's.

"We have your lady safe," the man-at-arms said, shaking his head as if he was still slightly stunned, "but we greatly fear another attempt upon her. We are so few, we could not hold the house alone. Sir Harry was half frantic because he knew not where to find you earlier, and my lady was so terrified that at first she could tell us nothing."

Cain was incapable of either question or reply. He felt as if a huge cold hand had gripped his vital organs and was squeezing them so that he could not think or breathe. There was no consciousness of surprise or fear, nothing at all, until his men parted before him in the guardroom of his own house and he saw Leah seated, weeping, on a stool with Beaufort standing awkwardly behind her. She looked up, leapt up, and cast herself into his arms with nearly enough force to overset him, clinging and shuddering in spite of the interested attention of the retainers.

"All right, Leah, all right. No harm can befall you now. I am here. I will keep you safe," Cain soothed in a perfectly calm voice. "What happened, Beaufort?"

"I hardly know what to tell you, my lord, but it was thus." Sir Harry looked a trifle dazed and was bleeding from several small cuts. "We went to the market—myself and a dozen men, as you ordered, and rode about for a while. Her ladyship was rather uneasy about being behind her time, however, and could take no pleasure in the sights so we went very early to the Horse Market. That must have been not more than a quarter past the second hour. There we looked at the mounts and watched for you."

"Sit down, Beaufort, you look as if you may be hurt."

"Nay, my lord, I am more shocked than hurt. As we looked, a dealer came up leading a very beautiful black mare and began to show the animal's paces. He spoke much to her ladyship of the mare's merits and finally asked her to try the mount. I was at fault, I suppose, in permitting it, but I could see no harm and madam seemed eager to do so. It is here that I become a little confused. We rode, at the dealer's suggestion, to the edge of the market where there was more space. My lady mounted and rode a soft amble in a circle around us. Upon a sudden, and for no reason I could see, the mare broke into a full gallop straight away over the field."

Beaufort drew breath and there was a murmur of confirmation from the men who had been with him.

"We were taken by surprise, my lord. The mare seemed so docile and her ladyship rides well for a woman, so we did not think to guard against bolting. That was not the least of the surprises we were to have. In the few minutes before we gathered our wits, a group of armed men had appeared out of nowhere and surrounded my lady. She began to cry out for succor, and, of a truth, I knew not what to do. We were thirteen against many more."

"How were they dressed? What were their colors?"

"No colors, my lord, but I must tell you that even in

my hurry they seemed an ill-assorted group. I think that there were two parties of different minds about everything except the seizure of her ladyship. It was thus. I sent Cedric at the gallop back to the house for those at home and we prepared to engage or follow to the best of our ability. One group, those who seemed to me like the lowest type of hired assassins or men-at-arms, desired only to run. The other group was dressed no better, but I should judge them, nonetheless, to have been men like myself, knights errant in the pay of some great house. They wished to fight and they would not trust the others to take her ladyship away alone. That group, by God's mercy, was so engaged in watching the others and they so hindered each other that Cedric arrived with the men in time."

"And then? Did you manage to hold one of them?"

"No, my lord, they were too many still and, truly, I thought of nothing but having her ladyship safe again. Beyond what I have said there is little to tell. We wrested her from them, and I took her up before me, but she was so shaken, as you see, that I dared not stay. Also we feared that they might summon help and try again. I knew not where you had gone, and my lady could tell us nothing for weeping. I was also afraid that a force might be laid in wait on the direct route home or even in the house, for not a person was left behind but the women servants. We came very slowly by back streets. Then we wasted more time trying to calm her ladyship enough to tell us where you had gone, and by then we realized that you must have already come to the Horse Market, so Cedric went there to look for you."

"I thank you, Beaufort, you have done me good service. We will talk further when I have quieted my wife a little. Set a watch, Giles. I am almost certain that there is no need, but it is well to be safe."

Cain half carried Leah up the stairs and tried to lay her on the bed. She would not let him go, however, and cried so hard when he tried to loosen her hands from his surcoat that he finally sat down and took her on his lap. "You are safe now, sweet love, you are safe. Hush, be quiet. May I be damned if I ever let you out from under my eye again. Enough, Leah, you will make yourself sick with crying."

She quieted finally, resting against him, and with her increasing calm and the wearing away of his shock it was just as well that Leah was holding her husband. He kissed her hair, pressing his mouth against her head until he could control the trembling of his lips. The scars on his face stood out flaming red. It was one thing to try to destroy him; that was a legitimate move in the bitter political struggle, but if Cain could have laid hold upon the woman who had so frightened his darling—for he knew it must be the queen—he would have torn her apart with his hands and teeth. The minutes passed and Cain's mind began to function rationally again. The attackers did not mean to frighten her, they meant to have her. The lower class of men might have been thieves who wished to take a rich gentlewoman for ransom, but the knights errant? Would Maud dare hire men directly for the purpose of taking the wife of a vassal? Besides, why should she do so this day when she planned his death on the morrow?

"Leah, can you speak to me now?" A little nod and a sniff and a shudder. "You will not be frightened again if I ask you about what happened?"

"Only hold me tight," she whispered hoarsely.

"My love, my love, I will hold you as tight as you can bear. Among those men, did you see any face you knew, any horse you knew, any garment and color that was familiar?"

Leah shuddered. If she spoke she would be betraying her father and might give Cain a bad opinion of her; if she was silent, Pembroke might try again more successfully. With wits sharpened by terror, she temporized. "You must know. You must know already, if you ask. They had changed their horses and their garb, but I have known them long." Her whisper broke and she began to tremble and sob again. "I would not have spoken, but I thought I would never see you more."

His arms drew her tighter until Leah gasped with pain. "I am sorry, love. I did not mean to hurt you."

He was not angry at what she had said. Leah, really recovering now, permitted a very tremulous laugh, half sob, to escape her. "Better broken ribs than a broken heart. My lord, could it be that my mother was right? Could my father desire to take me for ransom and not mean to harm you?"

If Pembroke wanted Leah, he wanted her only because she was Radnor's heir. The suspicion which had almost died when she admitted that she had recognized Pembroke's men stung Radnor anew. "Perhaps it is so. It does not matter. You need not fear to be lost to me."

Leah did not need that assurance. She knew her husband would not give her up readily because she was his wife, the woman who would bear him sons to continue his line. She understood too that he was fond of her because of his gentle treatment and his readiness to do things which would please her. His passion she could not credit as a personal thing. Although she loved Cain for himself, not simply because he was her husband, she did not assume that feeling could be reciprocated, because she took it to be not only unusual but even a trifle sinful.

"In any case," Radnor continued, "there will be no second chance. I will send to the king to say I cannot come tonight. Do not fear, I will not leave you alone again."

Leah had clutched at Cain at the mention of the king, but in the time it takes for a deep sigh she had loosened her grip. "No, you must go. These are great matters. You would come to hate me if you failed in your duty on my account."

Her husband moved his head from side to side like a man in pain. She was right, of course, and there was no other time to see Stephen because Radnor knew he might be dead on the morrow. But why did Leah urge it? Did she wish to be taken by her father? Were the tears and terror because the abduction had failed? "It is true that much rests on tonight's meeting. But if I were to loose you—." Cain stopped abruptly. What ailed him, that he was about to confess his infatuation when he was not even sure of her good faith? "I will tell you how it can be. If I go alone, leaving Giles and the entire troop—"

"Oh, no!" Leah shrieked. She jumped off his lap to stand before him, her hands gripping his shoulders, her eyes level with his. "If you went unsupported into that nest of vipers, I would die of fear. You do not know. You cannot understand. When those men took me, I was afraid, but I could scream, and when I was safe, I could weep. You do not know the fear that freezes the very soul, that numbs the heart and tongue and brain until you are dead although your body lives. You do not know how I fear for you. I could have told where you were this afternoon. I only pretended to be hysterical so that I would not have to answer. I did not want the men to call you because I thought the attempt to take me might be a trap to draw you forth."

Cain turned his head aside. He was not brave enough or trusting enough any longer to allow Leah to see his eyes filled with tears. He wanted so much to believe her that it was like a physical sickness inside him. He knew too that he was tilting at shadows. Not even Pembroke would dare take her from the house when he was not ten minutes' ride away.

"Very well, Leah, you shall have your way. I will take half and leave half, and we will both fear half."

What a day, thought Lord Radnor, leaning against his horse and wiping his mouth. First Hereford, then Gloucester and Leicester, then the attack on Leah, and now a combination of Stephen and too much drink. No wonder his stomach was turned. He felt in his purse for the fiftieth time to make sure the precious letters were safe. They didn't mean a thing, though. Stephen didn't mean a thing. And since the whole world was spinning faster and faster, nothing meant anything because they would soon all fly off straight up to heaven. It would be fun to fly through the air, almost as much fun as trying to keep to his feet on the crazy, spinning world. But he could not fly away. There was something he had to do—the tournament. For an instant, Radnor was sober. Oh, God, the head he would have tomorrow. If he could see to hit a barn or had the strength to fight a mouse, he would be fortunate.

"Cedric," he said thickly, "I want to sleep in my own bed tonight. Do not let me stop and sleep midway." He raised his foot toward the stirrup and began to laugh again. "Help me to my horse. This damned animal—I will have to get rid of it—it keeps changing its size. Up and down, up and down."

"No, my lord. Yes, my lord," Cedric replied soothingly, and signaled sharply for help. His lordship was no light burden.

Once in the saddle Radnor was steady enough and gave his men no trouble, only beginning to sing and laugh helplessly from time to time. It took four of them, however, to get him up the stairs because he showed a stubborn inclination to sit down on each step, kicking at them and insisting they were tickling him when they tried to lift him up. Giles had the forethought when he first saw his master to send Beaufort up to explain to Leah so that she should not think that he needed help because he was hurt. She was rather frightened, because she had much experience with drunken men, but one look at her husband as he staggered in washed away her terror.

Radnor sober could be terrifying; drunk, he was charming and ridiculous. Leah could not help laughing both with Cain and at him. When she tried to undress him, he rolled across the bed on which his men had placed him and escaped, forcing her to pursue him and corner him before she could convince him that he would be more comfortable unarmed. Naked, except for shoes and chausses, which were untied and dangling loose around his hips, he conceived a desire to dance. If Radnor conceived a desire when drunk, there was nothing to do but to satisfy it. So they danced, not well, but with a great deal of merriment. She told him to take off his shoes and go to bed. He would have none of it. She begged him to allow her to take off his shoes and put him to bed. He would have none of it. He would sing.

Leah covered her ears and sank down on the rushes almost hysterical with emotion piled upon emotion throughout the day. Cain asked tearfully why she did not like his voice. Leah assured him, choking with laughter, that she did. Then they must sing duets. Leah ached between laughing and trying to sing. Finally in despair she sent the page to ask Giles to come up.

Giles looked at his master with fond disgust and shook his head. He gave it as his opinion that there was nothing to be done with him in that state except to wait until he got sleepy or hit him hard enough on the head to knock him unconscious. "And I don't like to do that, my lady," Giles said seriously. "He wouldn't mind; he'd understand, but his head will be sore enough without that, and tomorrow he must fight."

Cain watched them during this discussion with large, sorrowful eyes. "You do not love me," he protested.

"Ay, master, we love you well, but we would love you better if you stopped capering about like a half-plucked goose and went to bed."

"I care nothing for you both," Radnor exclaimed with great and tragic dignity, "I will sing alone."

Giles scratched his head and yawned. "He can go on like this all night sometimes. I will go down and get some food and hot wine. Mayhap that will send him off. Praise God he is not quarrelsome when he is drunk. If he wished to fight, he would be neither to hold nor to bind."

Unfortunately the next morning was not nearly so merry. Radnor was sick; the sound of the maids walking across the rushes and the motion of Leah rising from the

246

bed made him wince. When his wife slipped an arm beneath his head, he could not repress an anguished groan, but he made no other protest because he was quite sober and knew that he had to get up.

"Keep your eyes closed, my lord. If you open them, you will vomit again. I will just lift your head a bit so you can drink what is in this cup."

"No," Radnor gasped, vaguely aware that there was danger in drinking what Leah offered. "No, it will not stay down."

"This will, and it will make you much better. It is a remedy my mother used for my father who was often in the state you are now. Come, drink."

His lips parted to order her away angrily, but the words never came. In the depths of his sick depression, Cain no longer lied to himself. If there was something dangerous in the cup Leah offered him, he wanted to drink it. It would be better to die than to live with such knowledge, for he had fallen into the trap against which Philip had warned him. He was the slave of his love for Leah; even if he knew she wished him dead, he would not be able to hurt her to free himself.

Twenty minutes later, Radnor sat up gingerly. His head still ached, but his stomach was quiet and his mouth no longer tasted like an unswept barn. The drink was as she said; Leah would do him no harm nor conspire to harm him. Cain looked at his wife remorsefully, but he could not apologize for his suspicions without hurting her by naming them. Instead he laughed when Leah brought him his clothes and assured her that he did not drink to excess often. Helping him to dress, Leah forced herself to smile and reply that as long as he was so gentle and merry she cared not how often he was drunk. Her eyes were anxious, however, when she asked how he felt and whether it be safe for him to ride.

"Safe or not, it must be. Nay, I have been successful feeling worse than this. The first few shocks are hard, but when the blood rises the unease passes." He hesitated, passing his hand over his unshaven face. It would be better if she would stay behind so that if Pembroke were successful she would not need to remember seeing him die. "Will you not stay safe at home, my love, until I return to you?"

"A hundred times this night I have said just that to myself, that I should stay at home and not be tortured. I cannot, my lord. It would be worse torture by far to stay behind and not know what was happening. If harm comes to you—oh, God help me—I must be there."

There was no sense arguing. "Very well, then let me go. I must speak to Giles and arrange for your safekeeping."

Arrangements were very quickly made for guarding Leah in the viewing stands. Giles and one group would watch one end of the stands; Cedric and another would guard the other end, and a few trusted men were to be sprinkled through the crowd to keep their ears open and give warning. All were to be fully armed.

"We will have trouble getting through," Cedric protested. "The royal guards do not like full-armed men at these tourneys."

"You wear my blazon and I am king's champion. Tell the royal guards to protest to me. And I tell you all here and now," Radnor said, raising his voice, "that you are expendable. If any untoward circumstance other than that to do with the tourney affrights my lady, none of you will live to see Wales again. I will cut out your hearts and livers with my own hands and before your very eyes—and make you eat them raw and smoking."

"You are a little hoarse this morning, my lord. Have you lost your lust to sing?"

Cain turned his head sharply. "Let be, Giles. The head I have is punishment enough."

"No, it is not," Giles replied with sudden fierceness. "Before a grudge fight like this, only a moonling drinks more than he can hold."

"Keep your tongue between your teeth, old man. I did not do it apurpose nor willingly. These letters I had to have from Stephen, and the drink was a better convincer even than my golden tongue. Listen, Giles. There is some chance—. Bless me if I know how to say this or even what to say."

"If you mean to tell me that they will try for your head again—I know. Oxford's hired killers drink too."

"No, Giles, not that. I can still find courage to say straight out that death waits for me. First, send these letters to William of Gloucester, if that befall. Then, there is a matter closer to my heart. If I am slain, Pembroke must not profit from it. You must contrive to conceal my wife for a few weeks. There is some small chance that she may be with child. If so and you can take her to Painscastle, she will be safe. My father will protect her for the sake of the child who will be my heir and his. Nor will he press her into marriage because he will wish to keep her dower lands in our family. If she is not breeding—God help her! Will you try to gain the safety of her dower castle with her and hold her there for my sake? I could not die in peace, Giles, if I thought she would be her father's prisoner for he desires to gain the whole Gaunt estate through her. Maud too will want her to wed her with a man loyal to the king and thereby control our holdings. She might be forced at once into a new marriage with God alone knows what beast. The most brutal is like to be the most successful."

"If that is your order, my lord, it will be done. I am an old man, but while I live and can fight, I will guard her for you. There are some others too, younger, who would sell their lives dearly for her sake. Keep your mind on your business, and fear not for your wife. Her best safety is in your living."

Sir Harry Beaufort, following his lord to the lists, prayed silently with unmoving lips. He prayed for guidance and for strength to follow that guidance. On the previous night, after he had given Lord Radnor every detail he could remember about the party which had tried to make off with Lady Radnor, he had been offered a variety of rewards—a large sum of ready money, continued service at a higher stipend, or a position as castellan. He had gone to an alehouse to think this over away from the congratulations and jealous jests of the men-at-arms. There he had been approached by a weasel-faced creature who nonetheless had the manners and speech of a gentleman. Another very similar offer had been made, but for this one the task had yet to be performed. It was easy enough physically; he had simply to exert as little of his fighting skill to protect Lord Radnor in the melee as would allow him to continue to live in honor. He had laughed heartily at first, explaining why the offer had no attractions, but his conversant had not been taken aback at all. He knew that, he said, and his offer was a matter of pure generosity. Sir Harry could take what was offered or he could fight and die with Radnor. It was so sure a thing that Radnor would die that no guarantee would be asked from Beaufort; if he lived, the prize was his for the taking.

Sir Harry had gone back to the house as quickly as possible, but when he tried to speak with his lordship he was told that Radnor had already gone. A sleepless night and

Radnor's haggard morning-after appearance had given him furiously to think. If Radnor died, Lady Radnor would be free and very rich. She would be at the mercy of any man who could take her. If he could keep her safe, perhaps she would be grateful. Gratitude sometimes led to other things. If Radnor was not well enough because of a weakness for liquor to hold his own, was it incumbent upon Sir Harry to die for him? Strict honor did not leave the question in doubt. Harry had done homage to Radnor; it was his duty to die for him. Self-interest, the code by which Beaufort had lived since he left his brother's house, gave a totally different reply. Completely immersed in his own thoughts, Sir Harry did not notice that Radnor had run his first course until the roar of the crowd drew his attention to the fallen opponent.

"Oh my God, my God," Radnor groaned, reaching for his head as he handed his lance to Beaufort and accepted a new one. "I know I hit him fair because he went down, but I am damned if I can see what I am doing."

Beaufort's mouth hardened. He did not need to worry; Radnor would never last through the jousting. It had not rained for months, and the parched grass was slippery. Either the horse would fall because of poor management or Radnor would be so debilitated by the heat on top of his post-drunken weakness that he would fail. Even if he did survive the jousts—to hell with honor. Beaufort would not die for a fool who could not keep off the wineskin although his life depended on it.

An hour later, Sir Harry's opinion had undergone another change. Never in his life had he seen a jouster to equal Lord Radnor, and only a small part of Radnor's success was due to the accident of birth that had given him his physical strength. True, it was partly the immense power of the man that bore down the knight riding against him when the lance point held, but it was skill in jousting that made the point hold without breaking the shaft of the lance time after time on the first run. No mean exponent of work with the lance himself, Beaufort could not help marveling at his lord's skill. Opponent after opponent went down and the crowd roared louder and louder at each fall. In addition, Radnor himself, although breathing rather hard between each course and sometimes dropping his shield to rub his arm and shake his hand after a particularly powerful counterblow, looked immeasurably better than he had that morning. Sir Harry could not help but fill with pride. Before God, this was a master to serve!

A tenth knight arced rather gracefully over his horse's croup and Radnor rode across to the heralds rather than back to Sir Harry. He requested and received permission to change his horse. All were agreed that the beasts should not be subjected to the punishing shock of jousting for more than an hour. No such mercy, however, was shown to the king's champion; for every knight who fell, another seemed to appear at the challenger's list.

As Radnor returned, Sir Harry took stock of him. The helmet was brand new, undented steel polished to a high sheen. It was of the old style, a circular pot without panache that sat flat on the head with a nosepiece that dropped from the low forehead band. A brilliant surcoat of gold, lavishly embroidered with silver down the facings and around the hem, covered most of the mail shirt except the V at the breast, but this showed the close observer that the shirt was of the very latest fashion in contrast with the helm. Rare and costly, it was made of heavy rings of metal linked together rather than sewn into leather strips. Even Radnor's gloves had plates of metal sewn to the backs to protect his hands although he did not wear greaves. Greaves were considered effete, and most men did not use them because the long concave shield protected the leg on the left side and, for jousting, the horse's body protected the right leg. In swordplay, it was understood that a man's sword arm would protect his right leg if it needed more protection than that supplied by the long hauberk. The shield itself was of ordinary construction; a heavy frame of wood covered with hide hardened almost to the consistency of steel, bound and bossed with metal, it was painted with the chevrons of *noir et or* which were the Gaunt colors.

"Another horse, Beaufort," Radnor ordered a trifle breathlessly. "Also, while I run again, watch the lists. If many more men appear, ride over to Hereford's pavilion and see if you can borrow a mount up to my weight. If he has nothing, try Philip of Gloucester's men. I must save Satan for the melee, and I cannot trust the new horse."

"My lord, you cannot mean to break lances with as many men as would need three more mounts!"

"At one time, I did not mean to break lances at all, but since the king was so good as to name me his champion, I must answer whoever challenges. Oh, never fear. If Oxford thinks to kill me this way, he will fail. I can joust as long as he can find men to ride against me."

"All mortals tire, my lord."

"Do I look tired?"

"No, my lord, but—"

"Beaufort, you know perfectly well that there are ways and ways of hitting men. Thus far my opponents have been old friends who know nothing of what is planned against me or honest youths eager to try my strength, and I have set them down lightly. When hired men begin to try me, I can break bones and kill too, even with a dulled jousting lance. Soon they will see and no more will come. A man cannot spend the gold he is given when he is dead."

It was not necessary for Radnor to carry out his threat, however. Before the time came to change to another horse, William of Gloucester was complaining pettishly to Stephen that the spectators were growing restless. It was all very well, he said, to see one man down five or six opponents. It was even funny when the same man downed eleven or twelve, but to see the same thing endlessly over and over grew dull for men of educated tastes. The hour at which the melee was to start was already past, and the ladies and gentlemen were hungry and thirsty.

"Call a halt, Sire. This is all very well for the commons, but we are bored, and nothing can come of it. The man who unseats Lord Radnor now can win nothing but dishonor, and I think the commons will tear him apart. The giant in gold and black is their darling—not to mention that the Marcher lords are beginning to grumble that you owe them a grudge and therefore wish to see one of their number shamed."

Maud was of the same opinion and reinforced Gloucester's complaint. She had never really approved of Pembroke's notion of purchasing an endless stream of challengers for the joust. It was far too obvious a plan for her taste, leading to just the suspicion that Lord William had voiced. She was annoyed with Pembroke for trying to make too sure. That weaseling caution would ruin all! Her plans were laid for the melee, and although it was good to have Radnor tired from jousting, to tire him too much might make him withdraw from the big battle.

Oddly enough the person most displeased by Gloucester's intervention was Radnor. There had been nothing in the jousting which he could put his finger on, no man that he could pick as bought. Now he would need to continue to fight, taking the far greater chance that Pembroke's assassins would be successful under cover of the melee. He did not know why Stephen stopped the jousting, but he cursed the king under his breath when his protests that he was not tired and would like to continue were set aside as mere polite denials. By the time he reached the much-stained tent that served as his shelter on campaigns, the exhilaration which had sustained him during the jousting was dead and he was depressed by the notion that fate was against him. Silently he removed his helmet and unlaced his mail hood. Leah was there waiting, pale and quiet, but perfectly calm. She pushed back the hood and dried his face and hair which were soaked with sweat.

"I have dry undergarments for you, my lord, will you change?"

"To soak them anew? No. Only bring me something to eat and drink. I am faint with hunger and parched with dust."

He kept flexing his hands and rubbing his arms to relieve their numbness. Beaufort was right—men got tired. If only Leah would remain calm and not weep. Cain bit his lips. If she wept, he could not bear it. His talk with Giles had crystalized his fears for Leah's future and now he could not rid his mind of the image of her cowed, beaten into submissive negation, screaming with terror and pain. It was impossible to admit any longer that she might be willing, might show the same affection and warmth to someone else. At this point his passion for her had reached such proportions that he would have turned on her and killed her rather than believe she would accept another man.

Leah set food before him and he forced himself to eat. He knew that if he did not think about something else, he would die through his own inability to fight. If only he could contrive to scrape through this alive and take prisoner some of his attackers. Then he would have a weapon to use against his enemies. He would have a weapon that would save him from future plots of this kind by Maud because he could threaten to expose her to Stephen or to the neutral barons if she tried to harm him again. The same weapon could be employed to free Chester and Hereford because he could force Maud to urge Stephen to make peace with them. Radnor thrust aside his food and stood up, pulling the mail hood over his head again. Very gently Leah pushed away his hands and laced it herself.

Her face was turned up to Cain's so that she could see what she was doing and, slowly and very gravely, she smiled at him. "Do not fear for me, my lord. You will be preserved to me here, or I will follow very quickly wherever you go."

He had no voice and no heart to protest. It might be safest and best for her, if that was what she truly desired. He drew her close and he kissed her, her eyes, her forehead, her cheeks, her fingertips, but he kissed her as if he had parted from her already and caressed only a tender memory. After that neither spoke, neither smiled; there was no reason to speak or smile.

CHAPTER 17

THE SUN, as Lord Radnor stepped out of the gloom of his tent, cast light on both eyes and soul. It was only another battle, only that, no more. Hundreds of times, thousands perhaps, a whole army had seemed to seek his single life. Surely he knew every trick that could be played and a counter-trick for it. Surely, prepared as he was with knowledge of the treachery planned, he could save himself. He began to turn back to speak reassurance to his wife, and Beaufort called to him sharply.

"My lord, the trumpets have sounded once already. Why do you turn away?"

It did not matter. Leah would not believe him anyway, and very soon she would have him back safe. The field, made ready for the melee, stirred Lord Radnor's blood too. Before him as he rode were ranks and ranks of men, all in armor that glinted and sparkled in the sun. The great destriers snorted and stamped, raising dust from the drought-patched earth and causing the brilliant pennons blazoned with the colors of the great houses of England to quiver and flap in the breezeless air. There were the gold and red of Norfolk, the red, blue, and gold of Leicester, and on the opposite side the red and gold of Warwick dazzled the eyes. Between the colors of Hereford and

Chester there was a space which would be filled by Radnor's own black and gold. Shields still thrown over shoulders repeated the color scheme, and above all other sounds rose the buzz of excited voices as friend called advice and jest to friend across the field.

Radnor stopped behind Hereford. "Roger."

The young earl backed his horse with a frown. "If you must talk, be brief and look cross. There is a court rumor that we are at odds, which is good for us both right now."

"I will be brief. There will be, I think, a little trouble. If you hear me call for help, catch me a few of the carrion crows who will be attacking me and hold them safe. You might do well to conceal them quickly lest their masters win them back, and when you have them, put them to the question for me."

Hereford's face which had been flushed with excitement went dead white. So that was what Pembroke had been hinting at. "I will hold them full hard and question them most straitly," he said furiously.

"Ay, but I want them alive and talking when you are finished. Do not lose your head, Hereford, whatever happens."

The signal given, the lines of knights crashed together. The fighting at first was eager but not hard, and mixed with the cries and grunts of pain there were good-natured calls of, "There's for you." "Does that taste good, my buck?" "Watch, there's a horse down."

Sir Harry, a little to the left and behind Lord Radnor, had still not made up his mind. At present it was not necessary, since his master was cleaving the usual open space around himself with his tremendous reach. Beaufort did notice that the men before Hereford and Chester were holding their ground with every ounce of strength and skill, while those opposing Lord Radnor were giving way remarkably easily. Radnor saw it too, saw that he was faced with the problem of breaking through the opposing line or retreating to find new opponents. For a few seconds it was an agonizing decision; life and Leah tugged at him so strongly that he flashed a single glance backward to the safety of Chester's and Hereford's troops. Cain knew they would fight with him and for him, that he would be safe surrounded by their men. Unfortunately he knew also that every stroke they gave to defend him would hack away the chance he had to ensure their future freedom by capturing the assassins Maud and Pembroke had paid to kill him. With a violent thrust, Radnor disabled the last man opposing him and broke through, wheeling his horse as if to charge back and begin again.

There was, however, no way back now. All at once Radnor and Beaufort, who had been carried in the wake of his lord in his indecisiveness, were surrounded. The temper of the group opposing them had changed also. They drew closer, and instead of opposing single man to single man, the slashes and thrusts of a dozen swords at once took on a new deadly character. Plainly these men were fighting in earnest; there was no implication whatever in their behavior that they wished Radnor to yield as a prisoner for the sake of horse and armor ransom.

Radnor, now, was fighting in earnest too. One man went down with a choking cry as Radnor's sword caught him between neck and shoulder. Another toppled without a sound except for the clang and crunch as the same blade bit through helmet, hood, and brain. To Radnor's left a third fell away, his sword arm dangling uselessly, crushed by a blow from the edge of the black and gold shield. The lift of that shield was dangerous, however, and red began to dye the golden surcoat from a thrust that missed piercing Radnor's ribs and instead tore through mail and flesh at the waist. If his lord felt the thrust, he gave no sign, and Sir Harry, fighting well enough to protect himself but by no means at the peak of his ability, had time to wonder if the man was entirely human.

Now there were only seven men left in the group that separated Radnor from his friends, and a cry went up from these that was no known battle cry of any house engaged on the field. From several places knights disengaged hurriedly, sometimes from nearly successful encounters, and came to swell the ranks of the attackers. Of one thing Sir Harry became increasingly sure, that the weasel-faced man had neither been jesting nor speaking more than the truth. Still he hung undecided, his instinct driving him one way and his self-interest another. It was instinct, perhaps, that made him ward off a blow that would have severed Radnor's right leg, but his reason began to back his instinct as man after man fell to Radnor's attack. His lord was tireless, and admiration and enthusiasm began to stimulate him so that he fought harder, accounting in quick succession for a knight in green and gold and one in blue and silver.

Radnor thrust and drew, but his blade was stuck in

bone and mail and the dying victim fell forward almost into his lap, flooding his gauntlet with slippery blood. It was just as well, because in trying to free his weapon Radnor dropped his shield slightly, and a sword slid over its edge. The slash came right through mail and spine, severing the head of the dead man from his shoulders, and even after the head rolled clear across the bow of Radnor's saddle the sword continued downward cutting Cain's left leg above the knee.

Little by little, in spite of all the opposition could do, Lord Radnor and Sir Harry were winning back to their friends. Beaufort's breath was coming in painful gasps, his sword arm ached with the ferocity of its use, and the burning pain of several new wounds maddened him, but none of these things could still the exaltation in his heart. They would make it! He would not need to make the dreadful choice! "Into the valley of the shadow of death. Into the valley of the shadow of death." Over and over the phrase repeated itself in his mind like a rising paean of victory.

At that instant, Radnor's horse reared and screamed, split open from chest to groin. The beast went down, taking Radnor with him, tangling him in the now hanging entrails, and threatening to disable him completely with convulsively flailing hooves. In a single smooth movement, Radnor cut the stallion's throat and beat back the thrusts of several thousand men. Now was the moment of decision. Sir Harry could push his way through the ring of attackers and yield Radnor his own horse, the act which honor demanded, or he could pretend that it was impossible for him to break through to his lord. He raised his sword, wrenched with the agony of indecision because the man was worth dying for but life was sweet, and then, as his eyes took in what had happened in those few seconds of doubt they bulged with horror. There were foot soldiers on the field of mounted knights!

From some place of concealment on the edge of the crowd, footmen had appeared, and Lord Radnor had disappeared under their onslaught. All thought of self-interest gone, Beaufort howled the Gaunt battle cry again and again and began to hack his way through the mounted attackers. Why he called for help and why he fought he did not know; he knew only that, although he had done many things of which he was not proud in the past, he could not live with the memory of this shame. He had no hope of saving Radnor. Nothing could live under that mass of striking men even though it did seem as if the mound heaved from time to time and muffled cries came from it. It did not matter. Dead or alive he would have his master's body out of that heap or be dead himself. When a new band of horsemen rode down upon him, Beaufort did not even look up to attempt to protect himself. He had no interest in anything except the bloody mound of men on the ground, and nothing existed but the regular rise and fall of his sword arm.

Hereford and Chester had both been enjoying their own battles. No one had been seriously hurt; no one had been taken prisoner of their men; and they had four members of the opposing party as prisoners to their credit. Long experience had taught them to leave Radnor to his own very efficient devices, and what with his mild success and the violence with which the opposition was defending itself even Hereford was not troubled by his friend's disappearance until he heard the note of Beaufort's cry. Since there was not another man of Gaunt's on the field, that cry could not be meant to marshal forces; it could only be a desperate appeal for help. As men with a single mind, Hereford and Chester broke off their personal combat and organized their own forces. They met with surprisingly little resistance as they beat their way toward Beaufort's voice because Maud's men were not only sure their work was done but were appalled by the method used to accomplish it; they were only too willing to go. Hereford was not equally willing, however, and a group of knights who fought under his banner were told to engage and hold fast at least some of the retreating mounted group.

"Treachery!" Hereford screamed at the top of his lungs when he saw the bloody, heaving mass that Beaufort was striking at. "Treachery and murder. Take them alive for witness."

While Chester's men and his own dismounted to follow orders, Hereford wrenched his horse around and arrived wild-eyed before the lodges in which Stephen sat.

"I will bring charge against you, Stephen of Blois," he called, his words broken by sobs. "I will bring charge against you before your council that you did willfully try to murder or permit the murder of one of your faithful subjects. There are foot soldiers on the field of mounted knights. They have broached Lord Radnor's horse and dishonorably brought him down. Call off your curs, or I will shout your foul deeds to the high heavens until you stop my mouth with blood and earth also."

Stephen of Blois was on his feet and over the rail in an instant, his face flaming with shame. In another instant the recall was sounding from every herald's trumpet, and the noise of the fighting died down slowly. The king was on horseback now, as pale with rage as he had been red with shame before.

"Where, Hereford? Where? If there is one alive I will have the author of this outrage out of him if I must choke it out with my bare hands."

Even to Hereford, boiling with anger and grief, Stephen's sincerity was patently obvious. He was a weak man, often a foolish one, but generous and forgiving to a fault and genuinely aghast at the breach of the knightly code which had taken place. Moreover Stephen liked Lord Radnor personally in spite of their political differences. With a generosity seldom found in human relationships, the king admired in his subject many of the qualities he lacked himself.

The more knowing eyes of the court did not follow the king; they were fixed upon the queen. At Hereford's announcement Maud had first turned pale and then almost purple with fury. Now she was pale again, her eyes fixed on the rail before her, seeking, seeking a way to squirm out of this accusation. She had no illusions about Hereford's ability to squeeze information out of her adherents; right now he could probably squeeze it out of a stone, and there was no way in which, without exposing herself further, she could block him. How to twist the information to save herself and damn Pembroke was her problem. Tears of frustration rose to her eyes. How, knowing what she did, could she have been so stupid as to allow herself to become embroiled with that man? No matter how tempting the proposals Pembroke had made, she should have known better. In her wildest dreams, Maud would never have guessed that he could dare to arrange for foot soldiers to attack a knight at a tourney—a royal tourney.

By the time Stephen reached the scene, two of Chester's men were engaged in restraining and calming Beaufort. Most of Hereford's had disappeared with those assassins who could still talk, and the remainder were making sure that those who were not worth taking prisoner would not talk at all to anyone. The king dismounted and flung himself unarmed into the group of men, seeking for one who could tell him who had betrayed him, but neither Hereford nor Chester cared what Stephen did.

Hereford was beside himself. "How will I tell his wife?" he wept. "Merciful God, she will go mad."

"His father," Chester groaned in reply. "Gaunt's only son. How can I explain that his heir is dead and I was there and did nothing? If he tears me apart, I will not blame him."

"What would I not give to have him alive!" Hereford cried.

"Well, I am alive." Radnor's voice, considerably muffled and rather breathless but expressing irritation, came from the bleeding mound of men. "If you would get the rest of these bodies off me instead of indulging yourselves with useless lamentations I would better appreciate your display of affection."

"Praise God, a miracle," Hereford breathed, down on his knees in the slimy mixture of entrails, torn grass and earth, and horses' and men's blood.

"Gently, gently," Radnor gasped as Hereford pulled at him violently. "I think some of my ribs are gone, and there's a pike pinning my sword arm to the ground."

Once he was free, Radnor stubbornly rejected every offer of hospitality and attention from the king, Hereford, Chester, Gloucester, and everyone else. He insisted, more and more weakly, upon being carried home, until Hereford and Chester, afraid to excite him any more and terrified that he would bleed to death because they could not tell how badly he was wounded, acceded to his wishes. Away from the crowd of good Samaritans, Radnor seemed to recover a good deal of his strength.

"You have them, knights and foot soldiers, safe for me, Hereford?" His voice was low and speaking plainly caused him pain, but his eyes were clear and triumphant.

"Yes, yes—safe from the king and safe from Oxford, but be quiet."

"I am not so bad, I only wanted to be free of all those others and so pretended to fail. Can we go no faster? My poor Leah will be frantic, thinking me dead."

"She will soon recover. You cannot afford to be banged and jolted over these ruts. I dare not increase the pace lest you be dead in earnest. It is a miracle that you are alive."

"Nonsense! It is no miracle at all—"

The expression in the blue eyes that Hereford turned upon his friend stopped Radnor for a moment. "I tell

260

you," the young earl said, "that if it was no miracle of God's, I do not desire to know how you escaped. No mortal man could live in such case, and I—. How could you save yourself? Where were you when they fell on you?"

"Do not make me laugh, Hereford, it hurts me. If you would but think! I was half under and half inside the horse. Surely you do not think this was the first time I ever had a horse broached in battle. It is an old trick. Have you never played it yourself?"

It was just as well that they hit a particularly bad spot in the road at that point so that Radnor shut his eyes and gritted his teeth. He was spared the mingled expression of love and fear in Hereford's face; the desire to believe the explanation mixed with a brief terror that it was not true. The road grew worse and Radnor forgot Hereford's question, concentrating on maintaining his customary stoical attitude toward physical discomfort.

Mercifully Leah had lost sight of her husband soon after the melee began. She was very nervous, but William of Gloucester, who had found a position beside her, so irritated her by his assiduous attentions that the edge was taken from her fear. When Hereford galloped up to fling his distraught accusation at Stephen, however, Lord William had called to Giles, showing for an instant the steel of his will behind the softness of his face.

"Take your mistress home. That is my command and you may disregard anything she says. Use force if you must—the blame will be mine. My men will go with you. We will bring—him—as soon as possible."

He had gone off immediately, and Giles faced his mistress. Whether it was the note of command in Lord William's voice to which she responded automatically, or shock, or indifference, Giles could not decide, but she docilely left the field with him. Not only that, but once at home she did things that left him, as he guarded her from the doorway, agape with surprise.

First she had stripped the big bed and remade it with clean sheets—clean sheets for a dead man. She had made the bed with her own hands, rejecting offers of help from her maids in a courteous, indifferent tone of voice. Then she had ordered water to be heated for washing—why warm water to wash a corpse? Certainly, Giles thought, tears of grief rising to his old eyes, Lord Radnor would no longer feel the cold. Ignoring Giles' presence completely, she had changed her dove gray and blue clothing for a soft wool robe of grayish green and occupied herself with brushing and rebraiding her hair. Even now, when the sounds of the group bringing Radnor home were clear in the courtyard, she did not run to the window or to the stairs but stood calmly in the center of the room, looking about as if she were considering what household task to embark upon next. The only sign she gave that she was not deaf to the heavy treads on the stairs was a tremulous sigh.

"Even dead he shall lie nowhere but in his marriage bed," Leah was thinking, her eyes surveying the room and seeing that all was in its accustomed place. "Even dead he shall lie nowhere but in his marriage bed. Even dead—." Not another thought had crossed her mind in the entire period between seeing Hereford accuse the king of murder and this moment.

The task of conveying a man of Radnor's size and weight, who could not be overly bent or jostled, up a steep, winding flight of stairs was no light one, but his retainers nearly trampled each other down for the privilege, every man being sure that he alone would be sufficiently careful and sufficiently gentle. Their excitement was so great that none had a thought to spare for Leah, and it was only Giles, seeing their care in handling Radnor, who gave her a few seconds' warning by his cry, "He is alive!"

Then she ran to the antechamber to be brought up short by horror. There was not one spot from the helm to the shoes that was not dyed the sickening reddish brown of dried blood. Irrationally in that moment she thought, not of her husband, only that she would always hate Giles for awakening the hope that opened her dead emotions to pain. No man could bleed like that and live, not even Cain. She did not think he was conscious, although his eyes were open, and did not speak to him.

"Put him on the bed." The covers were already drawn back and now she swept the pillows to the floor so that he might lie flat. "Call the armorer—that mail must be cut off."

"No!"

Leah whirled to look at her husband who, stimulated by the fear that his precious mail shirt would be spoiled, had found the strength to protest even after the agony of that trip upstairs.

"Oh my love, oh my darling," she whispered, "but you bleed—"

The worst of the pain had passed again, and Radnor's

lips quivered in an attempt to smile. "Most of it is the horse's—and other men's."

The words unstuck her brain as hope had unfrozen her heart; she began to think and to function once more. It had to be as he said, of course. If it were he who bled, it would have been the bright, wet red she would have seen. Now tears stung her eyes and she kissed the filthy face very, very gently, once on the cheek and once on the lips before she turned her energies and resources completely to the task of keeping her lord alive.

The worst agony, the removal of the mail shirt, was fortunately over the soonest. When that was done and the extent of Radnor's injuries could be ascertained, Chester and Hereford, who had been waiting in anxious attendance, sighed with relief and left to undertake the pressing business of hiding their prisoners even more securely and squeezing information out of them. Unless the wounds putrefied or he was seized by the mysterious and greatly feared stiffening sickness, the hurts he had would do him no great harm.

Leah was glad to be rid of them. Their anxious questions distracted her from her single-minded concentration on treating the wounds. What she wanted and needed were silent, efficient helpers like Giles and Sir Harry who would do her bidding without asking why. She cut off Cain's undergarments and, after a little consideration, slit his chausses around the ankles and left his feet alone. The tear at his waist and the slash above his left knee were already clotted. Aside from washing the area gently, Leah did not disturb the work of nature, but the pike-thrust in his right arm was more serious. This was still bleeding sluggishly and would need to be sewn. Several leeches had been called, but Leah could not bear the way her husband winced under their rough ministrations and she dismissed them in a fury. Now she was a little sorry. How she wished for her mother! Edwina had treated hundreds of wounds, many worse than Cain's, and although Leah had watched attentively she had no practical experience and was terrified of hurting him unnecessarily.

"Dear love," she said gently. Cain opened his eyes and turned his head slightly toward her. "I must sew up your arm. I—it will hurt you."

"Yes, no doubt." His voice was very normal except for its breathless quality, and his calm communicated itself to her. "Do not look so worried. I have lived through much

263

worse. A little pain or a little weakness from blood-letting will do me no harm."

"Shall I call back the leech? Will you trust me to do it?"

"Whichever is easiest for you. So long as it be quickly done it makes no difference to me."

Radnor set his jaw and clenched his left hand on the bedclothes. He had endured this too often to fear it except that the pain might make him gasp and that would wake the nearly unendurable agony in his chest. Giles grasped his right wrist firmly so that he could not jerk his arm when the needle went in, and an elderly woman servant stood by to cut and tie thread. Sir Harry stood ready too—to hold his lord down, if need be, or to give him wine or aqua vit if he seemed to be failing. Leah, who had directed the arrangement, looked briefly at her hands to be sure that they were steady. She planned to use a special technique her mother had showed her because it would not cause the scar to pucker, a factor of importance not for appearance but for flexibility of the arm after healing. A loop was left at the end of the thread which Leah caught with the tip of her fingernail. After she pushed the needle through the lips of the wound, she slid it through the loop and knotted the thread over on itself. The maid cut the thread and handed her a second needle and thread with loop prepared. While Leah set the second stitch, the maid tied another loop and the process could be repeated. This style of sewing could not be used on body wounds or anywhere that pressure would be exerted on the stitches, because they were easily pulled loose; for an arm wound, however, it would do perfectly.

That over, Leah covered her husband tenderly and let him alone. She had sense enough not to ask how he felt or what she could do to make him comfortable. Nothing could make him comfortable, and he was perfectly capable of asking for anything he wanted—she hoped. He lay with closed eyes, taking fast shallow breaths which put the least strain on his broken ribs. About those, Leah could do nothing. If he had been unconscious, she would have bound him to prevent his breathing too deeply or driving the broken ends through his lungs by rolling over. As it was, he was best left in peace and handled as little as possible.

None of Cain's visible hurts was serious, although the ribs would keep him from any strenuous activity for several weeks, and only one thing caused Leah any anxiety. This was the simple fact that her husband was so quiet. Tears of pain had sparkled on his cheeks after she had stitched his arm, but not a groan nor a complaint had been wrung from him. Leah had no previous experience with a man who had been made ashamed to express physical anguish. Her father and his cohorts, like most other men, screamed for a splinter, bellowed for a hangover or a stomach ache, and had to be restrained from rolling about in agony when their wounds were dressed. Lord Radnor had been taught in a far different school. An abomination to his father in his childhood, he had been the unprotected butt of the servants. When he had been taught to fence afoot, an exercise completely unsuited to a child crippled as he was, and he wept with the pain, he had been called a coward and taunted and tormented doubly. Any confession of physical illness or discomfort had been taken by his stepmother, a woman who was unable to produce a son of her own and who had less use for him than his father, as a sign of poor spirit. The advent of Giles as his tutor had saved him from complete destruction by tempering with mercy what was necessary for him to learn to defend himself, but by that time the lesson of shame was too deeply ingrained. When Radnor was really hurt, he was silent.

Her ignorance of his background bred in Leah the terror that, although he did not look it, he was too weak to cry out. She sat, therefore, in a silence equal to his for hours, afraid to speak lest she disturb him and watching every breath in and out before she was convinced that he was not dying from some hidden injury. The room darkened steadily, and Leah finally rose with a sigh of relief to call for light. If any change in his condition had taken place, it was certainly for the better. He was breathing more easily and truly seemed to be resting. She set the candles she had called for so that Cain would not be disturbed by their glow and, with a little return toward normalcy, took up her sewing.

"Leah."

"Yes, love, I am here." She touched his right hand gently, secretly feeling for the dreaded cold that sometimes preceded putrefaction, but the fingers were warm and flexible and curled around to hold hers.

"Is it thoroughly dark outside?"

"Yes, my lord, it is night. Do not talk. Try to sleep. Does the light trouble you?"

"Is Giles here?"

"Downstairs."

"Tell him that I must speak with Philip of Gloucester at once. God send he will be well enough to come to me, for I cannot go to him."

"You mean now?"

"Yes, now. Do not fret me, Leah. You can only tire me with argument, and I will have my way." Leah put her lips to his forehead, but it was cool and moist. His pulse too affirmed that he had, as yet, no fever. It was perhaps a little faster than usual, but strong and steady. "I am not fevered. You may do my bidding in safety," he commented, recognizing the purpose behind her gestures. "I could eat too, if you could thrust a pillow behind me."

That was good. That was wonderful. Dying men do not ask for food, nor when it is brought do they eat with appetite. Leah put down the empty spoon.

"Will you lie down again, my lord?"

"Not yet. The moving up and down is the worst, and I must be able to see to speak with Philip."

Leah was silent for a while, sitting with the bowl in her lap. "Love," she said tentatively, "I have something to say to you." Cain's eyes opened quickly. It was most unusual for his wife to preface a casual remark in that way. "You will be abed for some time," she continued hesitantly, "and it is plain that you cannot bend." Cain's puzzled frown looked his enquiry. "You cannot lie all that time with your shoes on," she faltered. "Oh, do not look so black. I will not touch you unless you bid me. I will call anyone you desire to do it if you do not trust me—"

Radnor turned his head away without reply and stared at the black opening of the window. What his wife said was true. Sooner or later he had to have that boot off, and no effort of will would permit him to do it himself in a reasonable time. The terrors of his childhood, so far away and so vivid, made him so sick that perspiration beaded out all over his body. Through those early years the Duke of Gaunt had been like a madman. He could not kill his only son, for he could not seem to father another child, but he could try to release his own fury and grief and his frustration in his second marriage by tormenting the child. Goaded beyond endurance one time, Cain had torn off his left shoe exposing his foot and had cried out that he had only a crippled foot—not a cloven hoof, not a cloven hoof. The half-mad father had turned his back on the screaming child. "You see a crippled foot—I see a cloven

266

hoof," he said. He had not meant that literally, of course. He had been bitterly sorry for the words the instant they were out of his mouth; an atonement he had even bestowed a rare caress on his shuddering son, had even said he was sorry, but a seven-year-old could not understand the agonies of a lonely and embittered adult and took the mumbled apology to be remorse for bringing a monster into the world. Cain had never again allowed anyone to see his foot, and the words, after more than twenty years, were still seared into his memory.

Philip of Gloucester sat back in the red-cushioned, high-backed chair which had been drawn as close as possible to Radnor's bed and regarded his foster brother with a jaundiced eye. His voice, when he finally regained sufficient breath to speak held a mixture of tenderness and exasperation.

"If I ever saw such a great fool! Look at you."

Lord Radnor smiled mischievously. "But for once I was doing just as you are always bidding me. If my heart had ruled my head, I would not be lying here now."

"You mean if your lust to fight had not ruled both, you would not be lying here."

"Nay, Philip," Radnor replied seriously, "I swear I had little enough lust to fight this time. I knew what lay before me."

"Which, if I know you aright, would but lend spice to the meat."

"No longer. I have a wife to leave behind me now, and—but I waste breath of which, as you may see, I am short. How are you, Philip?"

"To ask after my health is not to waste breath?"

"Not this time. If you steel your will, could you sit in council this week? I would not ask you—I would be carried there myself, but—"

"Oh, you are mad—mad," Philip said disgustedly. "Nay, you are not mad, you are feeble-minded. Do you desire to finish the work so nobly begun? Be jostled around a little over the cobbles and down the stairs? Put one of those ribs through your lungs? That would end it, completely if not neatly."

"I had thought of that. I have no wish to die."

Philip gestured impatiently. "I had intended to go anyway. I am somewhat better of late. My sister knows best what to do for me and she does not disturb me with constant moanings and groanings. Do you have something special for me to use?"

"Two things or three. That business with Pembroke was a trap—you heard?"

A nod and a shrug. Philip had no energy to waste in regretting mistakes. "I am sorry. I slipped there."

"Hereford thinks that Pembroke will not accuse him directly, otherwise why the warning to change sides on the tourney? Perhaps. In any case Pembroke nearly killed Hereford with a sleeping draught; it is something if not much, for only Hereford's men know of it. Do what you can to keep the young fool free. I know Maud wants desperately to have him, but I think neither she nor Stephen will dare say a word against him after what happened at the tourney. If they do accuse him anyway—I do not know. I will find some other way to save him."

"How?" Philip asked bitterly. It had not been easy to sit idly watching Hereford and Chester bring about his father's destruction. Cain took his lip between his teeth and closed his eyes. Nervously blaming himself for asking unanswerable questions and distressing his friend, Philip leaned forward. "Cain! Lady Radnor, he faints."

Leah bent anxiously over her husband, almost hoping he had fainted so that she could send Philip away and insist that Cain rest, but his eyes opened immediately.

"I do not faint. It is nothing. Leah, go back to your needle. If I must I will stretch the weapon I have to cover him also, although I think it scarce enough to save Chester. In any case, before aught else is done I must have Pembroke out of the queen's hands."

"Why? If you think I will endanger my position at court for that—." Philip stopped in deference to Leah's presence. "Perhaps Pembroke guesses that you are such a fool that your blood bond will bind you even when you knew his falseness, but—"

"Nay, Philip, I cannot use the evidence I have against the queen until Pembroke is safe away, because it concerns him also. Can you not see that while he is in her hands she can twist matters so that he alone is at fault—and he is so lily-livered he will support what she says out of fear."

"Very well, do not waste your strength. I will do what I can for him, curse him. What evidence do you have against the queen?"

"Hereford holds certain prisoners who, under his handling, will no doubt sing of how Maud, through Oxford, planned to have me slain. Those prisoners are what I fought for. Probably they are paid carrion in Pembroke's service, but from the openness with which they were used I believe they thought they would be safe because of royal protection. If Hereford and Chester be taken at the council, those limed birds must be sent to Painscastle. With them in my father's hands, I am safe from Maud. From Pembroke alone, without her backing, I can protect myself."

"You are not such a great fool after all, but would it not be well worth Maud's risk to try to regain those prisoners before Hereford can apply the thumbscrews?"

"They are doubtless well hidden. Hereford knows their value and Chester is not new at this game. Moreover, Maud will not dare institute an open search. The one thing she fears on earth is Stephen's displeasure. You know, Philip, that whatever may be said against the king, treachery of this sort—in a game of knightly endeavor—would be abhorrent to him. She dare not confess by an attempt to regain those men that what they tell under torture of her being party to the plot is true."

"Yes. I think I will go and see if I can find a welcome to spend the night at Hereford's house. Those songs might be useful in successions other than those of Wales."

"So I thought." Cain moved his left hand restlessly across his abdomen, picking at the bedclothes. "I have also those letters of which we spoke. Do you desire—"

"That is enough, Cain. You can bear no more. I pray you, do not tell me that nothing ails you. I know you too well—ay, and God have mercy upon me, I know the feeling too well also. Whatever remains can keep until tomorrow. Henry is not here. Until that time it is as well for you to hold the letters as another."

"But if Stephen tells Maud that I have them, perhaps—"

"I will not listen. I too am tired."

The candles had guttered out and the room was dim with dawn when Leah rose quickly from her prie-dieu at a sound, or rather a cessation of sound, from the bed. Cain had been sleeping for some time, moaning softly with every exhaled breath, and it was the absence of those low moans that drew Leah's attention. She stepped very quietly to the bedside, not wishing to wake him if he still slept, but his eyes were open.

"Can I get you something, my lord?"

269

"A drink."

She brought him water laced with wine and raised his head. He drank avidly and Leah, feeling the heat of his neck against her arm, trembled. The fever was starting.

"Have you slept at all this night?" he asked irritably.

"Yes, certainly. You must not talk, Cain."

"Talk to me then." He rolled his head back and forth and his good hand pulled at the covers.

Leah was very much troubled. He should not be in such great pain now, not yet. The wounds had not yet inflamed. "Are you tired of lying on your back?" she soothed. "I can prop you on your side with pillows, love."

If he were on his side, what he wished to do might just be possible. "If you can." She shifted him and he waited patiently, trying not to gasp, until the pang of movement passed. "Why do you only call me 'love' when you are about to hurt me?" he asked, suddenly conscious of the endearments which she had been lavishing on him and which she had never used before.

"Do I? To put a little sugar in the bitter draught, I suppose. Nay, I would call you 'love' and 'dear' until you were sick of the words, but I know men do not like that."

"Do they not?" he asked. "And who told you that nonsense?"

"My mother told me, sweetheart. There, do you like it? I have no intent to hurt you now."

Cain did not reply. The tenderness of her love only made matters worse, for if he could not remove his own shoes and she saw what was under one of them and turned from him, it would make the pain of the rejection deeper. Leah got up to close the shutters because light was beginning to come into the room. Desperate, Radnor shifted his hips a little, edged his left elbow under him, set his teeth, and tried to lever himself up. This time he could not repress a faint groan, and, worst of all, began to cough. Leah rushed back to him, pulled the bedclothes tight over his chest, and held them firm until the paroxysm passed. She touched him; there was no doubt about it, he was even hotter than before.

"My lord, can you understand me?"

Cain opened his eyes in surprise, and Leah could see tears glitter on his lashes. "Why not?" he asked unsteadily.

"You are getting feverish. Just now you tried to get up. If you do that in your fever, you will hurt yourself. My strength is no match for yours, and it would do you great harm to struggle. I pray you, do not be angry with me, but I must bind you to the bed."

Nervously, Cain licked his lips, and Leah's heart was wrung by the expression of fear on his face. "That was not done in delirium, Leah. I wished to try—but it is hopeless." He paused, staring at her, the expression of terror growing and Leah hung over him murmuring endearments although she had no idea of what he was so afraid. He shifted his eyes from hers as if he was ashamed and muttered, "I must ask you, will I nill I, to take off my shoes."

"Yes, my love." It was a bitter triumph.

"Wait," he cried as she moved toward the foot of the bed. "Not now—I—oh, God have mercy on my soul. Whatever you see, I am a man, no more, no less."

Leah put out a hand to steady herself against the footpost of the bed. She sought for words of comfort and assurance, but there were none, only a deadly sickness. Only the sickness and the knowledge that if Lord Radnor were of Satan's brood, then the devil had succeeded and had her soul as well. Not even proof that her husband was a demon and not a man could wean her love from him now. She glanced briefly at the prie-dieu with its Christ hanging from the crucifix and then longer at Cain's sweating face, released the bedpost, and began to lift the covers.

"Wait!" he cried again.

"For what? Time will not change what is there."

Cain shoved his left hand hard against his mouth and bit it. Leah unlaced the boot and pulled it off together with the foot of the chausses. For a moment she stood staring, her body visibly shaken with uncontrollable shudders, and the great Lord Radnor whimpered like a hurt animal.

"Why did you frighten me like that?" Leah asked, indignation sharpening her voice. "Before God, you had me convinced that you were something unclean. What is there that distresses you so much in a twisted foot? I warrant you, it is no pretty sight—more especially all uncared for as you leave it—but you have borne it for thirty years. What need to make such a to-do and fright me half to death?" She was shaking and angry with relief and her voice rose to a shrewish scold. "What should I see but a crippled foot? Have you never looked at it in all these years?"

Slowly Lord Radnor took his hand from his mouth and his wife saw the blood on his lips. "God bless me," she cried, "if I ever saw such a man," and came back quickly toward the head of the bed. "You have bitten through your one good hand. You needed that—a few more festering sores." She began to cry and kiss him, pressing his head into her breast. "My love, what did you fear? Could you believe I would love you less if I saw you were not perfect?"

She felt the tremulous sigh of relief and then the total relaxation that meant unconsciousness. What pain and loss of blood had no power to do to Lord Radnor, this shock of release had accomplished—he fainted. Leah hung over him, sobbing softly and kissing his unresponsive lips.

"Is he dead?"

The harsh voice drew a terrified gasp from Leah, but she pulled her little knife from its sheath as she turned to face it. "Oh," she cried, dropping the pathetic weapon, "thank God it is you, my lord. I thought at first it was *my* father. No, he is not dead, but the fever is beginning and—"

"I will not trouble you with my presence, then," Gaunt said, but he came to the bed and stood looking down at his son.

He had been a fool to come, but at least there were some profits. Certainly his daughter-in-law was faithful; he need no longer wonder whether Cain had escaped sword and lance only to meet a slit throat in his own bed or poison in his food. Further, he could now deal with Pembroke in his own way, as soon as he could find him. And last, but not least, neither Maud nor Stephen would profit even a little by laying Cain low. It would be a great pleasure to see their faces in the council tomorrow—a great pleasure.

CHAPTER 18

FOR THE NEXT WEEK time merged into a nothingness. Radnor's wounds festered, and day after day he raved with fever. Leah tended him until she dropped and then

272

Giles took his turn. They fed him by force, washed his wounds by force, and cleaned his body by force. Once a day, busy as he was with political matters, Gaunt would come to stare with an impassive face at his son, but he offered neither help nor advice to his daughter-in-law, asked no questions, and never stayed long.

On the sixth day, Leah noted that dry brownish crusts were forming at the edges of the raw flesh instead of the pasty greenish yellow exudate, and that day when her husband had sunken into an exhausted stupor, she knelt to pray again. The prayers of the past week had been faint and doubting, if unceasing, but the thanks were full and fervent. That crust, plus the paling of the angry red ring around the wounds was the sign of true healing.

The seventh day was very quiet. Giles and Leah, close comrades now, spent most of the time just staring at each other, too tired to be grateful. Sir Harry, who had borne all the burden of receiving solicitous visitors and messages, sending replies, sending thanks for gifts, and answering inquiries, paced unceasingly across the short end of the room struggling with the conflicts brought to a head by the knowledge that his lord would definitely recover. So much contact with Leah had changed a vague longing to a burning desire, and time and again, Sir Harry found himself insanely envying Radnor's delirious ravings because he was attended by Leah.

The morning passed, and dinner was brought up. The three sat down together, as had become the custom. Giles ate out of habit; Beaufort forced himself to chew and swallow; Leah pushed food about, mashed it idly into her bread, and finally left it. She went again, for the twentieth time, to look at her husband, and Sir Harry turned to Giles.

"She eats nothing."

"She is tired."

"So are you, and you eat."

"I am older and more used to fatigue." Giles frowned and then spoke more softly than was his habit. "You should not watch so much nor care so much what she does."

Leah went to sit at her embroidery, but her hand lay still on the frame before her. The day wore slowly on. When the light began to fade, Lord Radnor shifted restlessly. Leah rose slowly from her chair, pushing herself out of it with her hands.

"Where do you go, madam?"

"To see if I must change the bedding, Giles. It is about his time."

"I will go. You are weary."

"And you are not? No, it makes you sick." She smiled wanly. "Do not deny it, I know it is so. How strange that is, that you should be able to rip out a man's bowels without a thought and yet be distressed for something so much less."

Cain's eyes were open, but Leah paid no attention for they often were. Before she could touch him, however, he smiled. "Leah?"

"Yes, my love, it is Leah. Are you yourself again?"

"I think so. Have I been much trouble?"

"No, no. You were always good and gentle."

Giles guffawed, coming quickly to the bedside. "Gentle as a lamb, you were, my lord. That is how come my eye is black and my face all swollen. You kissed me yester eve."

"Good God!"

"Ay, my lord. I wish you would arrange in the future when you are ill to abate some of your strength the while."

"But surely I could not have—I do not feel able to lift my hand."

"You were raving in a fever, sweetheart," Leah put in gently. "Giles, this is no time to tease him."

"Why not? If I know my lord aright, by tomorrow you will wish he were back in a delirium. A more pettish and unreasonable patient I have good cause not to wish to know. How now, madam, it was but a jest. Do not weep."

"Leah, do not cry. For God's sake, Giles—"

"Nay, my lady, he will be quiet with you, I am sure. You will have no more to bear from him."

"I do not weep for that," Leah said, sniffing and laughing. "I am only so happy, and perhaps a little tired."

"A little tired only!" Giles exclaimed, casting a warning glance at his master, for what he had said about Cain as a patient was perfectly true and the old man wished to spare the girl if he could.

"Giles, pray do not," Leah pleaded, afraid that Cain would send her away to rest. "Come, love, let me put these pillows behind you so that you can eat."

"You cannot lift me, Leah," Radnor said, misunderstanding Giles' expression.

The master-of-arms tried again. "Oh no, eh? And who

do you think has been lifting you, and shifting you, and wiping you—"

"Giles!"

"Black elves?" Giles concluded, ignoring Leah's interjection.

She could not help laughing. "Giles, go tell the page to bring up some broth and let your master be."

"I am not hungry."

"Ay," now Giles had the chance to make his point. "He begins already. When you ask him to eat, he is not hungry. When you ask him to sleep, he will play chess, or read a book, or—. Drunk or sick he is the same, contrary."

Now Cain took the hint and smiled. "Very well, I will try."

When candles were brought to the bedside so that Leah could see what she was doing, Giles' point was brought home even more sharply. Leah looked twenty years older; her hair was dull, her eyes red-rimmed, her lips and cheeks white, and she was not the only sufferer. Giles had made no light jest of his swollen face, but that was nothing. Cain could see his master-of-arms' hands tremble and his shoulders drooped with a weariness beyond what even his iron body could bear. This was no day or two that he had been helpless, Radnor realized.

"How long have I been like this?"

"This is the end of the seventh day," Giles replied.

"Good Lord!" All thought of Giles' and Leah's conditions disappeared in Cain's anxiety about the political situation.

"Cain," Leah said, "eat, do not talk."

He ignored her. "In God's name, Giles, what has happened? Is Hereford taken? Chester? What word about Pembroke?"

"Gently, my lord. You need trouble yourself about nothing. Your father is here."

"My father!" Cain half lifted himself off the pillows and Leah pushed him back. "But why?"

"Being in no sense related to a soothsayer, I do not know. He is here, and you need trouble your head no more." Usually that would have been true, but Cain and his father had differed about what they were willing to do for Chester and Hereford, and the trouble only deepened on Radnor's face. "Now you eat, my lord," Giles said soothingly. "I will give you the news, but if you fret your-

275

self, your lady will put me out, and I will not blame her. First, Hereford is perfectly safe, and, if you want my opinion, which doubtless you do not, he is a damned nuisance. Everything went at council as you could have desired, and every lady living in wide bounds between London and a day's ride is showing red eyes and bruises. In truth, I wish he would go out of town. He has been here every day but yesterday and today, clamoring for admittance and driving Beaufort wild with the craziest remedies. Sometimes I think that one's head is bolted on a little wrong."

Cain spluttered over a mouthful. "But his right arm is bolted on most correctly or perhaps I had not been here this day. Good God, I never asked about Beaufort. Assuredly if he had not so bedeviled those footmen they would have dragged me out. If any man saved my life, it is he. I hope—"

"Perfectly well. He has been helping to tend you, but something seems to weigh on his spirits."

"Giles." Leah had no idea what Giles was talking about, but she felt that no bad news which could be kept from Cain should be given him, and the note of warning in her voice was unmistakable.

Radnor's eyes moved uneasily from one face to another. "You will fret me more by making me think that you hold back something than by telling it."

Giles was furious with himself. This was scarcely the time for warnings about what most likely was harmless. "I hold back nothing of importance. Besides, if I told you nothing at all, it would make no difference. I speak only to spare you from worrying yourself into a fever again. In your state, what can you do?"

"I can think," Radnor replied irritably.

"An idea will come out of you now like a chick can breed from an addled egg. Eat. My lady will cast me out. Of Pembroke there is no news at all. His written deposition against Chester was read at council, but he himself did not appear. The silence is deafening. Philip of Gloucester was here yesterday—"

"How is he?" Cain asked quickly and anxiously.

Giles met his master's eyes squarely. "What do you want me to say? He was able to come. He told Beaufort that there was still no news of Pembroke. No one even knows whether he be alive or dead. There is no word, no sign, nothing. His men are loose in the town, but they

276

have not seen him since he entered the White Tower. They are fed and quartered by the king, as if Pembroke is his guest, but—"

There was no sense in worrying over what could not be helped. Cain glanced at Leah to see if she was worried, but she was silent, her eyes stubbornly downcast. She had a violent desire to say that she wished Pembroke were dead, but the fear that to rail against her father would appear as disloyalty in Cain's eyes sealed her lips. Cain was not troubled by her silence. He could no longer doubt her in any way. Never had any man been more at a woman's mercy, and never had any woman striven so to save him. He was not troubled about Pembroke himself at the moment either; he was sure that Pembroke was alive and equally sure that no harm would come to him because Maud needed him for a scapegoat. Somehow Pembroke would have to be wrested from her hands, but nothing could be done just yet.

"Chester?"

Giles hesitated, then said flatly, "In prison. Peverel of Nottingham holds him, but none knows where."

Cain licked his lips and turned his head away from another spoonful which Leah presented. She put down the spoon and bowl. "That is enough for now. Let me help you lie down, my lord. Giles, go and get some sleep, his lordship must sleep too."

"I am sleepy," Radnor said fretfully. "I am not a child to be told when to wake and when to sleep. Why should either of you watch me anyway? I will know when I am tired and speak no more. Why should I sleep when I am not sleepy?"

"Now, my lord," Giles began.

"Giles," Leah said peremptorily, "do not argue with him. Do not speak to him at all. I beg you, take those candles to the end of the room and go down."

"Damn you, Leah!" Radnor tried to shout, but his voice came out as a cracked whisper, shaking with fatigue. "You are too much in the habit of giving orders. Do not do so to my servants in my presence."

Leah burst into tears. Giles cast one thoroughly angry glance at his master, folded his lips tightly together with unaccustomed restraint, and went.

"Leah, Leah, forgive me. I am sorry. Do not weep. I will sleep. I will do whatever you like."

"Yes, my sweet lord, I know you will. Do not mind me.

I am only a little tired, so tears come easily. Indeed, if you cannot sleep, I will read to you. Philip was kind enough to find a book and sent it to amuse you while you mended. He knows your ways."

"No, I will not have you read to me. You must rest yourself. Are there no servants to sit up?" Cain's voice rose with weak irritability. "Can we not afford a leech that my wife and my master-of-arms must attend me like slaveys?"

Thus it went, from irritation to apology to complaint. Nonetheless Lord Radnor gained strength with amazing rapidity and his wounds healed well. Only his ribs remained sore, and that dull ache rubbed his temper more than the first agonies he had endured. Leah bore the brunt of this behavior because with the others he was totally outrageous. She, at least, had some weapons to use against him, and if she could not quiet him with kisses, she could always marshal up her tears. Sometimes even this last resort failed, and one day Gaunt arrived at just such a moment. He glanced quickly from Leah's face to his son, then told her harshly to go with his armed troop to buy five pounds of the finest eels for a gift to Stephen. When she returned, Radnor was sullen and silent, like a child that has been punished, but he was very well behaved for several hours. From then on, every time her husband became too obstreperous, Leah went out to amuse herself— to ride to market, to visit, or just to ride outside the city walls and breathe the bright summer air. The color came back to her cheeks and lips, the sheen to her hair, and her sense of humor returned too, enabling her to laugh at her irascible husband.

She was just so engaged, standing ready dressed to go out and laughing at her lord's angry warnings, when a tremendous noise of confusion came from the usually quiet courtyard. The warnings died on Cain's lips, and this time when he snapped, "Get me my shoes," Leah ran for them at once. He drew the sword always laid ready by the side of the bed, grimacing because his arm still hurt when used; but before he could don the shoes Leah brought, Giles and a royal guard burst through the doorway together. Radnor sat upright and raised his weapon. Even naked he was formidable enough to make the guard stop short.

"You are Lord Radnor?"

"Yes."

"Sheathe your sword, my lord," the guard said haughtily. "I am on royal business."

"I had some experience of royal business," Radnor replied with suspicious gentleness, pointing to the right side of his body, which was still horribly discolored with bruises.

The guard blinked with surprise at the tone and began again, much more pacifically. "We have no desire to disturb you, my lord. We only wish to search for an escaped prisoner."

"In my wife's bedchamber?" Lord Radnor laughed unpleasantly. "You may look for all I care, but tell your royal mistress that my temper is not good and grows steadily worse."

"No, my lord, of course not in your bedchamber, but in the guardroom below and in the outhouses."

Radnor frowned. "What prisoner?" Who would be likely to come to him? Hereford he hoped was not in trouble again. Chester?

"The Earl of Pembroke, my lord."

"So." The lids dropped over Radnor's eyes and his wooden face gave no sign of his satisfaction. "I have heard nothing from my father-in-law, certainly nothing of his being a prisoner. What is all this about, Giles?"

"I have no idea." An almost impreceptible shifting of the eyes indicated that Pembroke was not there.

"Very well. I have no objection to the search. If you ask politely, as a favor, you will be granted that favor. Now, get out of my wife's chamber, and thank God I am not a hasty man. I could have killed you within my rights in this place. You may spread the word that I will not be so soft another time to a man who enters unbidden into my wife's room."

The guard backed out hastily and Cain looked at Leah. "We move again, but I know not where. Do not go out today—that is an order, no jest."

"No, my lord, no jest. I will not stir from this room until you bid me."

"And now, also no jest, I must try my legs." He leaned forward to put on his shoes and straightened with a groan. "I cannot. Leah—"

She was already on her knees, slipping the chausses on and then the shoes. "Put your arm on my shoulder and stand so that I can pull these up." He swayed dizzily. "Can you stand without help?"

"In a minute, my head swims. For all I made your life a misery to you with demands to be out of bed, I had no desire to do it thus on a sudden. I can stand now. Go tell Giles to send out to my father at once, as soon as he is free of that hound of Maud's."

When Leah returned, her husband was pacing the length of the room unsteadily, grasping at the furniture to help him. In a short while he sat down. "I can do no more just now." He ran his hand through his hair and then began to finger the scars on his face. Automatically, Leah sat down at her embroidery frame, but she did not lift the needle. The look of thought on Cain's face was suddenly replaced by one of resolution. "Leah, can I ride?"

"Ride?" She turned pale. "You cannot even walk. Where should you want to ride?"

"I must have your father out of London and safe out of the queen's hands. Answer my question, will it kill me to ride hard for a day and a night perhaps?"

Loyal, disloyal—it did not matter any longer what Cain thought of her. Leah only knew that he was endangering himself for his most vicious enemy, that he was placing himself, weak and nearly helpless, in her father's hands. "You cannot mean to save him," she cried. "He is an evil man. He plots against your life. Will you free him from all restraint to make more plots?"

There was love, full measure and overflowing. Even her fear of Pembroke could still her tongue no longer. Cain drew his wife to him. "Have I any choice?" he asked gently. "He is bound in blood to me. Can I raise my hand against your father?"

"He has raised his against you!"

"Ay, and I make no jest to say I would gladly have him dead, for he would serve my purpose as well that way, but I am sufficiently blackened with sin. I cannot. Partly because I cannot take a man's life by stealth and he is too old to fight, and partly because—. You think you would not care, sweeting, but in the end you would. It is not good to lie abed with the man who spilled your father's blood."

"He is no father to me. His seed filled my mother's womb, but more than that, except to hurt me, he never did," Leah replied.

"Enough, my love. You do not know your own tenderness of heart. Now you hate because he has hurt me and you believe he will be able to hurt me again. That is not

280

true. Moreover, when he is dead, if you thought yourself to blame it would grow like a canker inside you. Tell me, can I ride?"

"It will not kill you, but if you take a fall—"

"I am not in the habit of falling off my horse," Cain replied dryly but with a smile. "Where is that man we sent to my father?" He rose and began to pace the room again, to be interrupted by Giles who ushered in a man garbed in the dress of a leper with only his vicious mouth showing beneath his drawn hood. Giles hit the staff so that it gave forth its hollow rattle, and Cain's mouth dropped open in surprise and amusement.

"Pembroke, by all that's holy!"

"I can see nothing to laugh at," Pembroke said in a voice quivering with fury. "I never thought, when I asked succor of Lord Hereford that he would dress me in this insane garb, laughing like a madman all the while. But that is no matter. I have a bone to pick with you, Radnor. How is it that you, my own son-in-law, did nothing in all these weeks when I was held by the queen? Hereford must have told you that I was here and meant to come to you. You must have known that I was held in restraint and that the deposition I made against Chester was forced from me by Maud. You could not think that I had willingly put down the words which were read out at the council table. If I wished to say those things, I would have gone to council myself and said them."

Radnor's lips tightened, but he managed to answer smoothly enough. "Perhaps I thought you did not wish for interference. Perhaps I did nothing because I was too close to death to do aught for anyone. You knew not that I was sorely injured in the tourney?"

"How could I know, being close confined?"

Leah gave a strangled cry. "He lies! He lies!"

"Viper!" Pembroke shrieked. "Do you wish to make bad blood between your father and your husband? It is your place to offer smooth words to make peace. I will teach you to hold your tongue!"

He raised the leper's staff to strike her. Leah shrank back; Radnor, in his weakness, stumbled and went down on his knees. Quite calmly, Giles wrenched the staff from Pembroke's hand and then went to lift his master.

"Where do you find such gall?" Radnor gasped, trembling. "How could you dare to go to Hereford after the trick you played him? How do you dare outface me, when—. What is the use of words! Let us understand each other. I will get you safe away, if it be in my power, but not for love of you or belief of your lies. I tell you too that you will not have Fitz Richard's lands, for I will free him and Chester also from this coil they are in. For the sake of this 'viper' alone, I will let you live, but—"

"Very well, very well. I understand you perfectly. You wish to blame me for what was no fault of mine, and no reasoning will alter your stubbornness. I played Hereford no trick. He was drunk already so that one cup of wine made him helpless. If I wished to harm him, why did I not do so then?"

"Your power to harm even a fly is gone, Gilbert. Hold your tongue."

All turned to face the voice which came from the doorway, and Pembroke went gray as ashes when he saw Gaunt. The old man shoved Leah's embroidery frame out of the way and sat down in her chair, casting a disapproving glance at his son. "You are a fool, Cain. I have always said so and always will. What is the use in arguing about something which cannot be mended? Yet you sit here crossing words when it cannot be unknown that a leper entered your house. Is there a reason for such a thing? Strip the garb off this fool, put it on someone else, and send him forth. Then, tonsure me this monk. My daughter-in-law has long needed a confessor. Here she has one to hand."

"Very good, father. He can stay here for a day or two, and then I will be ready to go."

"What brains you were born with, the fever must have addled. Where will you go?"

Cain answered without replying directly to the question, that since his father had finished his business in London it was reasonable that he should wish to go home. The following dawn he should do so, openly, allowing the royal guard to examine his men and search his baggage. After he rid himself of royal spies, Gaunt was to turn south and meet Radnor who would have smuggled Pembroke out. "Then I will return here, and you can see that Pembroke reaches Pevensey Castle, whence he can take ship for wherever he likes. Hell, I hope."

"Perhaps your brains are not so addled after all, although I have some matters to add. How will you cover your part in this, Cain?"

"Oh, Leah will say that I escaped from her keeping and

went drinking or whoring or what she will, and that I am fevered again. It will only be for one day and night. I could never hope that none will suspect, but it will need catching me to bring proof. Giles and Beaufort will have to remain behind, of course, to give credence to the tale, but Cedric will be enough for me."

"Ay, if you get past the gates at all, you will be safe enough. Giles, tell half a dozen of my men to come up here to me and do you see that the others make ready to go. Woman, go to market and buy openly provisions for my troop to carry to Wales."

In the quiet and enforced isolation that followed Cain's departure two days later, Leah had a chance to catch her breath. When it was sure that he was safe past the gates, she was able to consider a new factor in her situation which distracted her a good deal from her fears. She had a fluttering hope that she could not as yet believe in that she was pregnant. She calculated and recalculated and, though her flux had been delayed before when she was excited or frightened—and God knew she had been both since her marriage—it had never been this late. Still, she was puzzled because she had no other sign; no uneasy stomach, no headache, no spells of dizziness. On her knees before her prie-dieu, she counted the days again. It should have started near the day of the tourney, so it was more than three weeks late. If it were only true that she was already increasing. The joy of telling Cain! Surely no wife could do more for her lord than to bring him a child in the first year of their marriage. Surely the proof of her value as a breeder would bind him still closer.

At a discreet distance, Beaufort watched his mistress at her prayers. Hating himself, but unable to resist the temptation, Sir Harry was using the period of his lord's absence to bring himself to Leah's attention. He followed her constantly with his eyes; he leapt to help her up from her prie-dieu when she was ready to rise; he brought flowers to brighten the dark room; he pressed wine on her because he said she was pale. And Leah smiled upon him readily, and held out her hand to him warmly, seeing in his actions nothing beyond the proper attention of a vassal to his lord's lady. Partly she was blind because she was innocent, and partly because all her real attention was concentrated on her inner hopes and fears.

If he took her, Beaufort thought, he would deserve to

die, and if he did not, he would surely be slain by the madness that was tearing him apart. Giles came up from the guardroom to sit with Leah, and Sir Harry went out into the antechamber. His expression was one of such deep grief when Hereford came bounding up the stairs that the impetuous young earl stood stock still.

"I must speak with Lord Radnor."

"It is impossible."

"Beaufort, do not block me. I care not what he is doing. I will go in to him even if I must cut you down."

"I care not for that, but it would do you and him no good. You could jump up and down on him and scream in his ear. He will not hear you. He is raving again. If you do not believe me, I will call Lady Radnor or Giles. They will tell the same tale."

"My God, my God," Hereford groaned. "At such a time, when we need him so badly."

"If you will tell me what it is—mayhap he will come to his senses and we can tell him." After all, Radnor would be back that night or early the next day, and if anything important had happened he would want to know.

"Where is Pembroke?"

"I do not know. He came here, but my master was out of his wits and the guards were searching. The duke thought it best to send him to Arundel. This much we did. We have heard nothing further."

"You did wrong. If Radnor knew——. He will have a fit. Do you know what has happened? The king and his vassals have pursued Pembroke and are besieging Petworth."

"Petworth?" Sir Harry gasped, "but—"

"But what?"

Beaufort managed to stop before his tongue betrayed him. "But why?"

"Because that is where they came upon him. And Stephen has taken with him every armed man he could muster—the Gloucesters, Leicester—. There is not a nobleman's house with anything in it but women. Are you sure you cannot bring Radnor to realize what is happening? I am willing to move in this myself at any risk—I understand that if Pembroke is convicted of treason Maud will put men loyal to her on his lands and all the Marcher lords will have enemies both back and front as well as the Welsh to fight—but I know not what to do. I have only these few men with me. To fight is hopeless, and the king will listen to no word of mine for he knows me to be no good friend to him."

Somehow Beaufort managed to convince Hereford that Radnor could not possibly be approached, and Hereford went off grumbling bitterly.

CHAPTER 19

SEVERAL DAYS LATER, legs stretched before him, belt loosened, and replete with food and wine, Lord Radnor smiled patiently at Giles' insistent question.

"Very well," he said with a soft laugh, "I see that you are angry, being neither blind nor deaf, but I cannot think why. You ask what I was doing at Petworth and how I escaped—I can only tell you again that I was never there. Nor, as you well know, did I ever have any intention of going there." He listened to his master-of-arms splutter with rage for a moment. "But why are you angry with me because you took some harebrained notion from Roger of Hereford? It was you who told me his head was not bolted on right. Why, knowing what you do, did you listen to him?"

"My lord," Leah interposed, "Giles will take a stroke. Pray do not tease him any more. Truly, we would be glad to know what really did occur if you are not too tired to talk."

"It is briefly told. Pembroke and I left as arranged without let or hindrance. We rode due south as was planned and made a fair distance that night. No thanks for that was due to Pembroke either. His chest hurt him; his arms hurt him. He was forever tired or cold or hungry or thirsty—you would think that he was wounded in the tourney and I was the fugitive from the reluctance he showed to swift retreat. I do not think I have wailed in my whole life as much as he did in that one night. In any case, we did drag him forward, and early the next morning Philip of Gloucester sent a warning to the king that Pembroke was on his way south."

"Philip?" Leah gasped, "Philip told—"

Cain patted the hand that clutched his arm. "It was by our arrangement, my love."

"I suppose you did not think us trustworthy enough to keep the secret," Giles growled.

"It is easier to look surprised when one is surprised," Radnor laughed. "It was simple enough. My father gathered some of Pembroke's men who were loose in the town and, when Stephen was in sight, bade them flee into Petworth."

"Well," Giles muttered grudgingly, "it is not so mad as I thought. What went forward then?"

"My father and Pembroke, of course," Cain said with mischievous solemnity.

"Pah!" was Giles' only rejoinder to that piece of nonsense, and Leah giggled and pulled her husband's ear.

"We parted at Cocksfield," Radnor said more soberly. "I hope that my father and Pembroke made Pevensey before moonrise the next night, and I came home." He laughed softly again. "I was full sorry to miss the siege at Petworth. I would have loved to see the king's face when the castle gates were opened, as it were in fear and trembling, and Stephen entered in triumph—to find nothing."

"Then is the king still at Petworth?" Leah asked. She had not released a grip on some part of Cain's body since she had first embraced him. It was as if she could not believe him to be back safe without physical contact.

"I cannot think so, although it would be all to the good. Soon as they enter, Stephen must learn the truth and go on to Pevensey, but by then my father will be safe away."

"Nay," Giles grunted, "Pevensey is impregnable and fronts on the sea so that Gaunt may go whenever it suits him best, or not go at all. Stephen will never take him there."

"I still think it dangerous," Leah said. "You do not know my father. In anger or spite, he could open the gates to the king."

Radnor frowned at his wife. "Treason could open the gates, but he would be mad to do it."

"If the water should fail in this dreadful drought or he should be hungered by a long siege—"

"There can be no want at Pevensey. Springs flow in the bailey so there is always water, and the serfs go down by leather ladders to the sea to fish. Moreover they can even unload small boats that stand in under the cliffs and are

286

therefore safe from the attackers. No, Pevensey will not be taken, unless——. In any case, we have taken precautions against any length of siege. Why do you think William of Gloucester, Leicester, and the other neutral lords rode with Stephen? Only to convince him that a siege was hopeless. Even Philip—my poor Philip! If I had known he would be so mad as to go, I had never confided these plans to him."

"We must all die," Giles said. "Mayhap you have done him a mercy."

Leah said nothing, only tightened her grip on her husband's shoulders, knowing that he could have no comfort on this subject until he accepted the fact that Philip was lost to him. Lord Radnor set his jaw for a moment and then continued speaking as though there had been no interruption to his tale.

"Those lords rode, not to make war, but to make talk. In a week Stephen himself will be returned, convinced that Pembroke has fled." Cain closed his eyes and sighed deeply. "Pembroke will be in Wales; I will be abed. All this rushing and riding and shouting and whispering will be as if it had never been. What a waste. What a waste. We are just where we were when we first arrived in London."

"Not quite, my lord," Giles said bitterly. "Pembroke is free to make more trouble, indeed, but Chester is in prison and Fitz Richard's estates forfeit. You had best bestir yourself a little to think of some remedy for that."

"Oh, Giles, may he not rest even for an hour in peace? Do not forget, my sweet lord, that good has come of this too. Roger of Hereford is not only free, but has learned a bitter lesson. He will look twice before he sets his foot in another trap."

"Speaking of Hereford," Giles grinned, "had we not better send him word that you may be spoken to again before he leaps headlong into more trouble?"

"Yes. As a matter of fact, I need him. I have thought much on the subject of Chester and I see light, but I must have Roger's help in this." Cain bent his head forward as a warm caress touched his neck. Leah had been fooling with his hair and tickling his ears for some time; now she had put her lips just above the collar of his gown and nipped him gently. It was immediately apparent to Lord Radnor that he had done enough for his country that morning. "Do not send for him now, or if you think it necessary, send and say I have just dropped asleep again. I have a sudden and great desire to do some more riding."

Giles looked startled. "To where? Will you need me, my lord?"

"Oh, I do not intend to get anywhere in particular, and I certainly hope I will not need you." Lord Radnor lowered his lids and laughed suggestively. "I only need you when I have trouble, and I hope to have no trouble in mounting this mare."

Laughing, Giles shook his head. "Ay, there are some things a man must do without help from others—being born is one of them, and making children is another. Mind your sore ribs if you cannot wait."

Leah had walked away to cool her hot face in the breeze from the window. It was bad enough for her husband to inform the entire room of his intentions, but she wished he would not speak of her to others in terms of her purpose in life as a brood mare. Usually Cain was thoughtful about not making a point of the one real use he had for her. Usually, Leah thought, he exhibited a genuine or pretended pleasure in her company that nearly obscured the reason for his lovemaking, nearly made her believe that it was his desire for her alone that initiated his caresses. A burning resentment filled her. Why should she love him and he desire her only for the fruit of her womb? She wished to cry out that she was real, a person as much as he was, that she could think and feel and should be valued for more than the children she would bear. Some day she would find the courage and tell him; then Leah sighed. So she would tell him, and either he would laugh good-naturedly at her foolishness—as if a dog had tried to speak—or he would be surprised and disgusted.

Meanwhile Lord Radnor had come up behind his wife. He pushed her braids apart and kissed the nape of her neck. Leah bent her head forward to accommodate him, the warmth of his lips flooding her until she thought her bones would melt. Vaguely, a last coherent thought before her whole being was taken up by her physical response was that it did not matter what a woman thought within herself. She had no power to enforce her will because she could not even remain angry under the male touch.

Unconscious of the pain he had caused her, Radnor slid his hands under Leah's arms to cup her breasts and pull her back against his body. Through her clothes and his Leah could feel him quiver with desire, and she sighed, so dizzy she would have fallen if not for his supporting arms. Suddenly he let her go, pushed her behind him viciously, and turned so swiftly that the thrust of his hip threw her to her knees. Fifteen years of guarding his life and others from sudden death made for sharp ears even when all of his senses were concentrated elsewhere. The soft click of a door latch had often enough been the only warning he had of an enemy's approach, and Radnor had responded to it instantaneously.

"Hell and damnation!" he roared. "Is there no time when those cursed women of yours do not come creeping in and out of your room?"

Alison backed out with a cry of terror, but her place was instantly taken by Hereford, his beautiful skin bright red with wrath, his eyes the blue of a flame too hot to burn red.

"Yesterday you were dying—dying were you? Would it not have been kinder to speak the truth and say you would be bothered with me no more or that I was too dangerous to know or not important enough to know."

"Hereford, wait!" Lord Radnor glanced distractedly from his wife, still on her knees and leaning her head against the window ledge, to the young man who was just disappearing through the antechamber.

"Go," Leah gasped, "go after him. I am unhurt."

"Stop him!" Radnor called from the head of the stairs, knowing he could never get down them in time and desiring nothing less than a chase through the streets of London. "Hold him unhurt, curse you," he shouted to the men-at-arms as they fell upon Hereford. "If he bears one bruise or one scratch, I'll tear the man who did it limb from limb."

Radnor came down the steps as quickly as possible, watching approvingly the beating Hereford was handing out to the men who restrained him, but forbore, in fear of their master, from striking back. "Hereford, Hereford," he cried, "let me speak." He had reached the group and was about to speak with or without permission, but for several moments he was silent, listening with awed approval to the startling string of obscenities his fair young friend was mouthing. They were something exceptional even in his wide experience. When Hereford began to repeat himself, Radnor laughed, but seeing no other way to quiet him he enveloped him in his own arms. Cain grunted with pain as Hereford lashed out and strained to get loose.

"Roger," he said firmly, "if you put those broken ribs of mine through my lungs, I swear I will come back from the grave and haunt you."

The earl relaxed the pressure he was exerting immediately. "I cannot believe there is anything more we have to say to each other," he gasped furiously.

"Only come upstairs again where we may be private," Cain replied in a low voice. "If you so desire, I will go down on my knees and beg your pardon, but not before my men—it would be very bad for them. Let me explain what befell and why you were not told. You can be angry after the explanation as well as before it if you insist on being angry. If I let you go, will you come?"

"Very well," Hereford said sullenly, "but if you want me up there, get rid of that lying little bitch you married. I have had enough of watching her paw you."

Lord Radnor's expression grew rigid for a moment, but Hereford was too important to his present plans for him to display his jealousy or to take offense at anything he said or did. "You are heated," Cain said slowly, "and I will let that pass, although it is no way to speak of my wife. You may have cause to be angry, but not with her. Nonetheless I would show how much in earnest I am to please you, and if you insist, Leah can wait in the antechamber until our talk is finished."

"No, I do not insist," Hereford snarled. "If you can no longer think what to say unless she hangs on you, let it be as you will. I expect any day to see you take suck."

Leah heard that as they were coming in and blushed hotly. Such a view of her affectionate behavior to Cain had never occurred to her, and she was shocked. She blamed herself for never having looked past her own pleasure in caressing him before his friends. The idea that her husband should have corrected her she dismissed. She knew him well enough now to understand that if he were satisfied he was arrogant enough to care little or nothing about what anyone else thought.

Turning on her the frown that he really wished to bestow upon Hereford, Cain snapped, "Leah, go busy yourself with your maids and your work. I want this room to myself for a time."

She lifted her head, her color fading. Perhaps it was true that she had made a mistake in making her lord look foolish, but it was her right to be reprimanded privately. Besides, this was her chamber. Under the circumstances it was comprehensible that Cain should wish to display his authority, but Leah was still a little sore from the earlier discussion with Giles and she felt that he could have phrased what he had to say differently. She dropped a deep curtsy, a thing she had not done since they were married except as a joke, and deliberately lifted her lids to show the hurt eyes filled with tears.

Cain had no time to give a sign of weakening because the other soft heart melted first. Hereford was much woman-ridden at home, two sisters and a mother frequently making him a victim of their tears. In the beginning he had sworn time and again that he would be firm, but experience had brought him wisdom and by now he accepted defeat gracefully.

"Do not weep, madam," he said hastily, "there is no need for you to go. I do not suppose there is anything which Lady Radnor does not already know that you have to tell me," he added, very neatly placing the blame for the incident on Cain's innocent head.

"It is your choice, Hereford," Radnor replied, trying and failing to put the shoe on the foot it really fit. "Of my affairs it is true that there is nothing she does not know."

Wine in large silver goblets, cool and sweet, did as much to calm Roger of Hereford as Radnor's explanations. Indeed, the only time he showed any interest was in Cain's comment that Maud would now try to seize Leah.

"She tried once before, thinking to wed her to a man of her own choice if I died. Now that I have escaped that trap she will try harder. She knows I love the wench," Cain said, smiling at Leah, "and Maud believes she could make me dance to her piping if she held Leah hostage. Truly, it is the only weapon good enough to use against the tale told by the prisoners you hold for me."

"Maud tried to seize Leah before the tourney?" Cain nodded and a look of enlightenment mixed strangely with both relief and apprehension came into Hereford's face. "I will be strapped and tied—. Listen. I received a note from Elizabeth Chester telling me not to take a lady into my house. You may suppose I did not take that kindly for—for reasons of my own, but Elizabeth must have been trying to give me warning that I should not try to protect Leah because Maud would look in my house first. Good Lord, this is horrible! When I last spoke with her, I—." He closed his eyes with a positively sick expression.

"You did not tell Elizabeth of Chester that your women

291

were your affair and not hers—Roger, you could not have been so stupid." Radnor's voice was hushed with a combination of humor and horror.

Hereford swallowed nervously and nodded. "She will cut out my liver and eat it—heaven help me. I—I had better go at once and make my peace with her."

Radnor shuddered eloquently. "Can you? You are a braver man than I, Hereford. If I were you, I would take a trip, a long trip, even go on crusade. It might be that in ten years time she will no longer be wishing to drink your blood. A long, dangerous voyage would be—. By God's ten toes, you are going to take a long trip."

Leah, listening, wondered what sort of woman it was that could make two grown men turn pale. Apparently Elizabeth Chester had that power, for here were two of the finest knights in England looking at each other with despairing eyes. Lady Elizabeth, no doubt, would never be thought of as a brood mare or ordered out of her own solar. Yet Elizabeth did not seem so different from other women. She was beautiful, gay, and her tongue could be very sharp, but Leah had used sharp words once and they had cost her a beating. What defense was a tongue against a heavy hand?

Leah's nature was yielding and she had a desperate need to be loved. She did not understand the force of hatred that a certain type of woman could send forth, or how that cold force could numb a man even while he struck so that the blows gave no satisfaction. Leah was afraid of pain; it was inconceivable to her that one could fight back against it physically returning blow for blow. Furthermore, although she knew that Cain was different from her father, she still did not realize that her father was in the minority among men, that most men preferred to live in peace if not in affection with their wives, and that long periods of semi-isolation in a keep with a sharp-tongued woman could finally wear down even a strong-armed man. Cain touched her with his goblet and she started, her attention returning to the men's talk.

"I am?" Hereford was replying, coldness returning to his voice. "Because you order it, Radnor? Because you wish to be rid of me? Do you think because you rule Wales you can rule me also?"

"For God's sake, Hereford, you begin to sound like Pembroke. I do not wish to be rid of you nor, in spite of what you think, have I the faintest desire to rule anything but my own lands—I have trouble enough with those. I wish you to go because it is essential to the cause we both wish well. Come, sit down again. We can make use of your trouble with the king, I hope. You, like everyone else, have heard that Henry of Anjou is expected, but you have not heard some very important matters regarding this."

"Of course I have heard. Why do you think Chester and I involved ourselves in that insane effort to dispose of Stephen? Do you think we wanted the throne for ourselves?"

"What you say shows that you do not know what I do."

"I suppose I was not secure enough to tell. You suspected that I would run to Stephen for blood money?" The bitter sarcasm, the incandescent eyes told how deep the hurt had gone.

"Roger, I am sorry, but at that time you were not safe." The earl got to his feet with an outraged gasp. "Sit down! It was your honor I feared, not any tendency to dishonor in you. Think! You were bound by oaths to Pembroke and Chester. Would it not have been your duty to tell your oath-bound comrades what you heard? You would willingly do no harm, I know, but Chester is sometimes not very wise and Pembroke is a plain traitor."

Hereford took the goblet which Leah pressed into his hand and resumed his seat, his hot color returning to normal. "I cannot gainsay you. You are even kind not to say that I too am not very wise."

"You are perhaps a little hasty, but time will amend that. Nay, do not look so crestfallen. I trust you for all of that as far as any man can trust another, as you will hear if you will only listen. The most important thing you do not know is that Henry's coming, although urged by his mad mother, suits no one, not even herself. The court is in terror of whom he will bring and who will join him, but there is no support for him at all. Neither Matilda, nor Gloucester, nor Arundel will give him a man or a mil. Chester is in prison and you alone cannot withstand the might of the king. The time is not ripe. Henry must go home, and quickly, before Maud finds a way to capture him or men like Lincoln and, forgive me, your own brother Walter, use this as an excuse for more rapine, arson, and raid. One way alone we have benefited. Leah, where did Giles set those letters? Ah, thank you, my love. Here, read this."

Radnor tightened his robe which had fallen open and

293

made a gesture of eating to Leah, who went to give orders for a meal to be brought up. Cain closed his eyes, waiting without impatience for Hereford who read very slowly from little practice to finish perusing the rather complicated documents.

"This is something, Radnor, if it is, as you say, true that we cannot bring Stephen to battle and win."

"It is true, and you know it or you would be arguing with me. Therefore, when Henry arrives, someone must go posthaste to him, someone he will be willing to trust. Philip and I were to undertake that journey. Philip—Philip must undertake another, even longer journey all too soon, I fear." Cain paused, refocused his eyes upon Hereford's face, and continued briskly. "I can go, and will if I must, but I think it more essential that I remain here to see if I can free Chester."

"You want me to ride west?"

"I do."

"But I have seen the boy only once. He will not remember me."

Cain smiled encouragingly. "He will remember your father; he will have Robert of Gloucester's word to your good faith and good will; he will have my letters supporting your embassy; and he will have these letters of Stephen's which I will entrust to you."

"Is it not more *my* duty to see to Chester?"

"What can you do for him? Will the king or queen even receive you, much the less listen to anything you have to say about him?"

"I suppose not, but to leave—. Would it not seem as if I were running away and abandoning him?"

"What does it matter what it seems," Radnor snapped. "If you are conscious of your own honor, what does it matter what the brutes and fools think? Two other matters of importance can be seen to at the same time. The prisoners you hold for me must be conveyed to Painscastle. From Wales they may well make a lever long enough and strong enough to lift the weight of prison from Chester as well as ensure my well-doing."

"That I can see. The story would make pretty hearing at council and the queen will be most anxious to keep it from getting there. But should the men not be kept here where they can be produced at need?"

Lord Radnor shifted in his chair and gestured toward the food that had been placed before them by Leah. He was a little unsure of how to introduce his next plan to Hereford. What he was about to suggest would go greatly against that fiery young man's grain. To be truthful it went against his own, but he was more practiced in the arts of expediency. Good food and good wine were, fortunately, very calming to the hottest of tempers. Both were provided here in plenty and Radnor meant to use them. When he spoke again, his utterance was somewhat impeded by a full mouth, but his meaning was clear.

"I do not intend to bring them into council. I intend to threaten Maud with the revelation of their tale so that she will be induced to convince Stephen to release Chester. So far, it is all well, but Chester has committed treason, and after swearing to be faithful to Stephen too. Even Maud could not move her husband without some punishment for Chester and some gain for them. I am going to propose that Chester yield certain keeps in return for his freedom, and I hope that you will undertake to convince the barons who have done homage to Chester that this is necessary."

"No!"

It was a long, long argument. Candles were lighted and another meal served before Hereford had been talked around to agreement, even though he readily admitted that the particular castles Radnor wished yielded were of little or no value to Chester. Most of them were deep in areas sympathetic to Stephen and were strategically useless because they were counterbalanced by other keeps which were in the king's control. Others were only technically Chester's, being so far from his major holdings and his major interest that they virtually ruled themselves. Of these Stephen would have a choice, but it would matter little what he chose.

Neither the keeps themselves nor the additional fine which Radnor proposed to offer was what disturbed Hereford. It was the principle of submission that stuck in his craw. Again and again he returned to the notion that if Radnor could only discover where Chester was being kept, he would summon Chester's vassals and his own to free him by force.

"Roger, for the fiftieth time, I beg you to have some sense. What is the use of the vassals fighting when the leader is already taken? If too much resistance is shown, Chester might have an accident in prison—a fatal accident."

Kindling again, Hereford slammed down his wine

goblet. "I say we go wrong about this. We should fight. A man has certain rights. If Stephen cannot be brought to honor these, then I say that he, not we, should die. Henry, you say, is coming. Let us drive Stephen out then and worry about freeing Chester later."

Lord Radnor was too tired now to meet heat with heat. "Who is to drive Stephen out? You alone? I have told you, again and again, that this is the wrong time for war. Even if we were ready, which we are not," he said with bitter intensity, "what profit would we have from setting a boy of fifteen on the throne?"

"I was little more when I took the lands of Hereford under my hand. Did I so ill?"

"Nay, Roger, you did well, but Hereford is not all of England with its bitter hatreds bred by so many years of war. The vassals wished to test you, perhaps, to see whether you were worthy to lead them, but in love for your father and respect for your own strong ways, they were half disposed from the beginning to accept you. You miss the very point of the argument and that is that it is not Stephen who is at fault. Largely it is those around him who do the evil and they would be no better counselors to the young Henry." Suddenly Radnor let his head drop into his hands. "Hereford, I can talk no more. I am so tired I feel faint. Go home and come back tomorrow."

He yawned and scratched his head. "I suppose the rumor that we have quarreled has been killed by your running over here every day when I was hurt, so now it is safe for you to come openly and inquire about my health." Another yawn, as though the admission that he was tired had broken the resistance he had put up so long against sleep. "Anyway, I think the worst of this hiding and whispering is over." He received Hereford's kiss with still another yawn and patted the younger man's shoulder affectionately. "It seems to me that I did not get so sleepy when I was your age."

"Nor," said Hereford, turning in the doorway with a mischievous smile, "before you had a wife. I go, I go. Do not throw that goblet, you will dent it."

The word "wife" and the suggestion in Hereford's manner recalled the events of the morning. "Leah," Radnor began when the door was closed, holding his eyes open with an effort, "I am sorry I was so rude. This is your chamber, but the boy was so upset and there was no other place—"

"Yes, I know. Come to bed now."

"Are you angry?"

"Come to bed. This is no time to begin another discussion."

"You have not answered me."

Perhaps Elizabeth Chester could use rage as a weapon, but she could not. Leah lowered her eyes and murmured, "No, my lord, I am not angry."

Satisfied and completely unconscious that there was something beneath his wife's submission, Cain removed his robe and untied his chausses. Before he could do more, Leah took his right arm to examine the newly formed scar. His body tensed as she touched it firmly, but he did not jump as he would have if there had been a pocket of pus under the new-formed tissue. Thus far Leah could not ask for better healing. She ran her hand somewhat more gently along his still discolored right side and Radnor tensed again. That was not quite as good. There was still tenderness and some swelling, but if he would take no rest, one could not expect better progress.

As if it were a matter of course, Leah now knelt to take off her husband's shoes. "That is not necessary," he said quickly.

"To me," Leah said raising her eyes to his, "it is necessary."

Their glances met and fought and this time it was the man who bowed his head in submission. "Have your will of me, then," was his resentful reply, but he did not feel truly resentful. Each time she examined him he was newly afraid, but each time the fear was less piercing and was followed by a greater sensation of relaxation.

When she was through with him, Radnor lay down and pulled the red coverlet up over him. He could hear Leah moving about softly, putting the wine and the goblets on a chest near the wall and replacing the chair Hereford had used before her embroidery frame. The sounds of movement stopped, and Cain turned on his side to watch his wife undress, his eyes almost closed.

"Leah," he murmured sleepily, "why are a woman's clothes so much less fine when she takes them off? That tunic shone like silver on your body and now it looks like an old gray rag."

Leah smiled quickly with relief. She had won and he

297

was not angry. "The body, perhaps, is not so fine without them either."

"Some day, perhaps——. Listen."

Leah stiffened with terror. "What is it?"

"Rain! The drought is over.

CHAPTER 20

THE DAYS SLOWED DOWN until they seemed bogged in the same mud that jammed the wheels of the heavy carts which brought produce into the city. Horses and oxen strained and slipped, and cartmen, mouthing uncouth curses, got down and put their shoulders to the wheels in the sliding dirt if they wanted to deliver their wares at all. Still the rain poured and the water rushed down the kennels in increasing torrents, dragging with it the odorous filth accumulated in a three-month drought. Even the great Thames River rose, for it was raining all over England; its current became swifter, and the river gave forth a dull roar that was somehow threatening. Men shook their heads as they watched the banks slowly being swallowed day by day; the fords disappeared, large ships snapped at their anchor ropes, and small ones did not venture forth or were swept away.

The serfs, like sodden, shaggy animals, watched with hopeless eyes as their crops, thin and scraggly with drought, were beaten into the earth before they could be harvested and were completely destroyed by the rain that came too late. The cut hay was rotted by wet; the new seed drowned in the earth.

Stephen rode back to London, sullen, soaked, and dissatisfied, but convinced that Pevensey was impregnable. Most of the court returned with him, but Philip of Gloucester was not one of these. He and his men had turned slowly westward, for the end was very near and Philip wished to die near the rolling hills and deep bays of his own country. When Cain received that last letter, the writing so uneven and the tone so wandering, he had been tempted to ride after his foster brother. He had not gone, first, because it was plain that Philip did not want him. Perhaps Philip did not wish to have anyone he loved so well see the horror of those last lingering days or weeks, perhaps he realized that he needed peace to die in, not strength to keep on living, and Cain could bring only a fruitless struggle for life. Secondly, Cain had remained in London because, although he did not admit it, he no longer needed Philip desperately. Emotionally his wife was an even greater security to him than Philip had been, and politically his way was plainly marked out. One brief night of bitter protest had ended his struggle with the inevitable. He had wept and been comforted in Leah's arms and, as Philip himself had promised, the parting grew easier to bear when he had accepted it.

In contrast with nature, the court had put on a gaiety so febrile that it was near to hysteria. As the tension of waiting for Henry of Anjou to arrive grew greater and information no more abundant, the men around the king drowned their nerves in drink and play; the women danced and flirted and added jewels to jewels until they glittered like the star-strewn heavens. Only the pro-Angevin lords were quiet, and their lack of preparation drove the neutrals and Stephen's adherents wild, for the inaction gave no hint of what was coming. All men, however, had one thing in common. All spoke of the weather, and under the feverish activity or the quiet, above and beyond all politics, all thought of the lean year coming.

Leah lived her public life during this period as if in an unhappy dream. She took part in court functions without becoming a part of them, and when Maud approached her about filling Elizabeth Chester's place as her lady-in-waiting, she answered with pretended regret that she did not think her husband would permit it. Maud tried to explain that Leah might do as she liked with him, for Lord Radnor's infatuation was apparent to all and he made no attempt to hide it, but at court Leah continued to play the shy and timid simpleton. She merely gaped and gasped at the queen.

"Oh yes, I should like it. To stay here always where there is so much happening and you are so kind—but I would not dare ask him. Oh, madam, you ask him for me. Surely he will refuse you nothing," Leah had twittered.

Maud did not bother. If she could not bring the girl to weep and plead to remain, nothing else could move Radnor. She cast around for other ways to take Leah, willingly or by force, for there was no doubt that there lay the only method of controlling Radnor, but every faint hope was quickly destroyed. Yet the need to take Leah was desperate for as long as Radnor held hostage the men she had hired to kill him, she dared make no political move inimical to him. If any harm came to him, or if he felt her actions to be dangerous, his father and friends would raise a scandal that could topple her husband's uneasy throne. If she could only take Leah into her power, he would do nothing—not even use the one weapon he had against her—that could endanger his wife's welfare. Maud probed for weak spots in the relationship between the Radnors and tempted Leah with this and that and spied on her daily movements, but she was constantly frustrated by the stupidity of the girl and the cleverness of the husband.

Her frustration had a good cause, because Leah seemed more dazed and frightened every day by the attentions showered on her by her husband and the queen. Soon, Maud suspected, she would be incapable of understanding any offer made to her instead of just being too timid to take advantage of it. In addition, Leah was not alone for a moment. When she talked with the women, Radnor lounged against the wall, well within earshot and eyesight of his prize. If she left the hall, even to go to the garderobe, he went with her, waiting patiently with his back to the wall, his eyes fixed on nothing, and his hand on his sword hilt. No conversation was too interesting or important to break off if Lady Leah moved; no game so absorbing that his attention could be diverted. The house she lived in was guarded and stocked as for a siege. She did ride out sometimes to market—it rained too hard for women to ride for pleasure—but fifty or sixty hard-eyed fighters as well as her husband rode with her, each one conscious that his life was worth less than nothing, that dying would be a pleasure eagerly sought, if one hair on my lady's head were injured.

Lord Radnor was no happier than the queen, for his plans too hung midair, unfulfilled and unfulfillable. Pembroke and his father had, apparently, disappeared off the face of the earth. No word came from Pevensey after the siege was abandoned, and the letters Cain received from his men in Wales made it plain that Gaunt was not there. Leah was adding considerably to his problems, completely aside from the burden of keeping her safe. She was acting very strangely, pettish with the servants, easily annoyed, and easily moved to tears. She did a great deal of complaining. Her head ached, her back ached, she demanded, or rather asked whiningly, for almost constant attention. For some time Cain bore her petulance with patience, thinking that the aguish weather might be making her unwell, but when his temper failed and he had scolded her, she had become nearly hysterical, crying out that she was afraid, so afraid. She would not say of what she was afraid, however, and he had given up questioning or scolding, his love giving him endurance.

Leah herself was almost as puzzled by her behavior as her husband. She did not know why she was so irritable and depressed. Her fears, however were another matter entirely; they were very clear and very real. Simply, Leah was now sure she was breeding and was afraid of childbirth. She was afraid of the pain and afraid of dying. The process was no mystery to her; she had heard it discussed in detail often enough and the bitches and cats were forever bearing their young all over the castle. Although she had never been present when one of her mother's women had delivered, she had heard the screams of the women in labor. More than one had screamed and screamed and brought forth nothing but her own death and the still blue body of a babe that never breathed. More than one also had brought forth her child successfully but then had bled and bled, the slow red drops seeping through packing and padding, dripping, dripping, into a pool on the floor until the life had dripped away.

She had reconsidered her desire to tell her husband of her pregnancy as soon as she was sure of it herself. Too many women cast out lures for him at court, Joan of Shrewsbury not the least. Perhaps if he knew she was already with child, he would forget that he had promised not to look at other women; she would tell him when they were safely alone at Painscastle. Nonetheless, Leah was fiercely glad of the burden she carried because there was a vision stronger than that of a wandering husband or pain and death. Always in the worst moment of her terror it came to save her, the vision of the pride and pleasure in the faces of the women who held their hardly won children to their breasts and rejoiced.

The secret was scarcely so much of a secret as Leah thought. True she managed to be less irritable in public, but she refused to join in the rougher games, refused to

301

join in a hunt specially organized for the ladies on a day when the downpour changed to a drizzle, and listened with a more bright-eyed interest than ever when the women spoke of child-bearing and child-rearing. The older women who knew her exchanged pleased glances and smiled. Joan of Shrewsbury's tongue grew more venomous than ever about her and to her, for her fury was fanned to white heat by Radnor's behavior and by the look of stupid incomprehension Leah gave her whenever they came into contact. Maud tried more desperately and more deviously too woo Leah before the girl was snatched out of her reach. The queen knew that Lord Radnor had not been informed of Leah's pregnancy because once he knew his wife was with child he would remove her to Painscastle and the safety of his well-guarded lands no matter what the political consequences. Why Leah did not tell her husband, Maud could not guess, but she did everything in her power to increase Lady Radnor's reluctance to declare her condition.

In the third week of the month of September, Cain came home from the royal hunt so plastered with mud that his wife made the menservants sluice him with pails of warm water in the courtyard before she would allow him into the house. He was irritable, his nerves keyed up because Hereford, who was still in disgrace and not invited to hunt, had taken the opportunity to slip out of town. Hereford and Giles were riding west on the route Giles had prepared, bearing with them the prisoners of the tourney and Stephen's letters. It seemed simple; the king and queen were both with the hunt and could not be reached to give orders to stop him. Nevertheless Radnor knew that the young man was closely watched, and he had made elaborate plans for shaking the pursuers who would carry news of Hereford's route and purpose to Maud and Stephen. Radnor hated complicated arrangements of this type which he could not personally oversee, and he hated still more the pretense of ignorance which he was forced to assume. The idle talk and assumed concentration on the chase put a strain on his temper which released itself in snapping replies to Leah's questions on the day's activities. She subsided at once, sullenly helping him to remove his clothes and rub himself dry, and she spoke only to order the maids to bring up hot spiced wine to ward off a chill.

"Has there been any word?" he asked irritably for the third time.

"Only that Hereford passed the gate, which I have told

you twice already," Leah snapped. "It is too soon for anything else. He will send us word when he starts in earnest, after dark."

Cain paced the room. "Hell! How I hate to wait and do nothing." To this Leah made no reply, biting her lips and trying to control herself. After some bad-natured slamming at the furniture, Cain came up behind her and stroked her hair. "You are very quiet. Does the rain make you sad? Have I made you sad?"

Leah struggled against an irrational impulse to cry, to scream. "No," she said faintly, "you never make me sad. I—perhaps it is the constant rain which troubles me. It will be a hard year—a hard and bitter winter."

He lifted the heavy braids, coiling them around his hands. "Ay. My stewards write that things are bad at home too, though not so bad as here, for war has wasted our lands less. There will be less fighting if the people starve, but it will be needful to hunt for meat instead of pleasure, and that work is almost as hard. I must thin the animals or they too will starve, and somehow there must be meat enough to keep the serfs alive."

"Keep the serfs alive?" Leah questioned, astonished. "*You* must hunt meat for the serfs?"

Lord Radnor sighed. Always the same reaction, from men and the so-called tenderhearted women alike. Why could no one understand that serfs too had their uses? That hunger could make even those lower animals dangerous? "Leah, if they may not hunt themselves—a privilege I certainly will not give them because God knows what might follow from such freedom—and they have no fodder to feed their kine and no crops to exchange for fish and meat, they will die."

"What matter if they do?"

"In one way, none, really, except that if they all die, who will sow and reap crops next year?"

"Yes, but they never do *all* die."

"Well, then, think on it another way. Their ancestors swore in some manner, though not in words, to serve us, who are doubtless stronger and wiser, with their labor so that we might be free of that labor to protect them from their enemies."

"God knows you do that, my lord. You are scarred all over, my darling, with the burden of keeping the peace."

"Yes, yes, but is not hunger also an enemy? I feed and care for my horses and dogs so that they will be strong

303

and willing to serve me. So must I regard those other dumb and helpless animals. So too do they regard me. Their little quarrels, so simple yet so impossible for them to solve, they bring to me, and when the children are hungry, they bring those also. It is, perhaps, a weakness in me, but I cannot see children cry for food. Not even the children of serfs."

"It is true," Leah murmured, "often I have turned aside so as not to see the little ones with the bones sticking through their skins and the swollen bellies. You do well in this, my lord, as in all things."

Cain sighed and smiled; she seemed better-humored now. "At least you believe so." He kissed her hair and turned away. "I wish I would hear from my father. I cannot imagine——." Leah glanced upward quickly with lips compressed over an "I told you so," and Cain left the remark unfinished. It was impossible to believe that Pembroke could have played Gaunt any dirty trick for which he was not prepared, yet it also seemed impossible that Gaunt should have sent no news if he was well and free. He is old, Cain thought, his heart contracting with sudden fear.

Since she could not say what was on the tip of her tongue and these days seemed to be incapable of making soothing, meaningless speeches, Leah remained silent. Cain looked at her, his black brows drawn together in an ugly scowl, not certain whether he should ignore her sulks or lesson her on how to behave to a troubled husband. Before he could resolve his indecision there were sounds of imminent entrance from the door. Relieved, Cain called "Come," and Beaufort stepped into the room.

"There is a messenger below who desires that you come with him, my lord. He said to give you this token."

Cain accepted the ring which Sir Harry passed to him, glanced at it and saw that it was his father's signet, and paled. "I will go down."

From the messenger, who was a monk, Cain could learn nothing. A great lord, elderly, had stopped at the hospice and had asked the abbot to lend him a man to run an errand—that was all the monk could tell. Cain fingered his scarred face nervously. It could easily be Gaunt who had ridden far, had something of importance to say, and wished him to come quickly without argument. Certainly if Gaunt was alive no one else could have that ring. If Gaunt was not alive—

"Beaufort!"

"Yes, my lord?"

"Tell half the men to prepare to ride out with me. You remain with the other half to guard her ladyship. Hold the house until dawn if you are attacked. If I come not again by dawn, try to escape and overtake Lord Hereford and Giles. I will tell her ladyship nothing of this because I do not wish to alarm her. You may have to remove her by force—do not hesitate to do so."

He hurried up the stairs to say goodbye to Leah, only to be met by her high-pitched, querulous tones scolding at a maid. Cain gritted his teeth, gestured the maid out, and said gently, "I must go out, Leah."

"Out, in this dark and rain? To where? For how long? May I not come?"

"No, you may not," Radnor replied with an edge to his voice. "Pray give me no more trouble. I have had a message to go to a hospice near by. My father is here and needs a word with me."

"You will not sleep away? Cain, I am afraid in the night."

"I will do my best, Leah, but I know not what will be asked of me. I leave you in Beaufort's care. Do as he tells you to do. As to sleeping, take one of your maids to bed with you if you desire company, and try for some peace of mind. You must use yourself to my being away sometimes. I cannot carry you to battle with me."

"You do not go to war tonight?" Leah cried, starting up.

"No, no. I spoke of the future only. Do calm yourself. I can stay no longer."

Perhaps he could have spared more time, but Cain was thoroughly annoyed with her. He had so much deeper trouble, and she clung so and whined so that he could not think. Even though he could feel his temper fraying, he did not want to fly out at her and leave her to cry herself to sleep or, worse, leave her with that as her last memory of him. Before Leah could say another word, he had kissed her with a flare of passion that was frightening in its controlled brevity, and flung himself out the door. She was surprised at his abruptness, but her major feeling was one of irritation with his inconsistency and, when Beaufort came to the door to ask if she wanted anything, Leah smiled and bid him come in to amuse her.

"You have recovered well, Cain." Gaunt's voice was indifferent but his eyes raked his son from foot to head and down again.

"What do you here?" Cain asked furiously. "Why did you send that messenger without any word except that I was to come? Why did you not write? I have been sick with worry."

"Over me?" came the caustic question.

"Our plans may well have gone awry because of your ill-considered silence. I knew not whether to dare send Hereford out with the prisoners, and now because of this crazy demand that I come to you I know not—"

"Are you telling me my duty?" the old man snarled.

Cain choked, his face flaming, then answered childishly from long habit, "No, sir."

"Hereford is safe away, I met him on the road—so now you know that and it saved the danger of a messenger direct from him. I returned hither instead of going home because I had something to tell you which I did not wish to commit to writing just yet. Pembroke is dead."

Lord Radnor closed his eyes to stop the room from whirling and swallowed to still his heaving stomach. In many ways he and his father disagreed, but he had always believed the duke to be a man of honor. That cursed bond of blood. It had made him the slave of a woman and his father an assassin.

"How did you kill him?"

Gaunt had walked restlessly away, as if he did not wish to meet Cain's eyes. Now he whirled about to face him. "Has your mind and heart gone as rotten as your body? What filth is this you spew? Faugh! You are as foul as you look."

"You mean he simply died!" Cain had the oddest impulse to kiss the old man, at this moment being better pleased with curses than blessings. At least his father had not committed murder. He sighed with relief. "Let your horn-hoofed devil of a son sit down and ease his pain," he said almost gaily, "and give him a chance to get used to the change of company. The months at court have corrupted my mind."

The Duke of Gaunt stared at his son with blank astonishment. "What did you say?" he roared.

"That Pembroke died—you said that. By the by, of what did he die?"

"Not that." Gaunt shook his head angrily.

306

Cain was puzzled. "That my mind has been corrupted by the court? Why should that surprise you? I am grown so sour and suspicious that I listen for nothing but plots and think of nothing but such filth."

"No, not that either. What did you say before that?"

The eyes which could be so softly, liquidly dark were suddenly as opaque and black as coal. "Before? Oh, that I was a horn-hoofed devil? That my foot hurt?" Lord Radnor raised his brows and met his father's eyes squarely. "Why? Is it not true? Are you ashamed of it, you who told me what I was? I have been thirty years your son. It is time you grew used to my imperfections." The expression on his father's face showed Radnor that the old man remembered the scene to which he referred as clearly as he did himself. "Nay," he said, quivering with nerves and striking out bitterly again, "I know what I am. Do you want to look again to be sure? Shall I strip and show you what a devil looks like?"

"Pah! You idiot! You can exhibit your beauties to me some other time if you desire it so earnestly, but there are matters of more note to deal with now. Those pains Pembroke complained of on the ride were doubtless real. By the time we reached Pevensey, he could not sit the saddle. He was too weak to move and I dared not leave him lest he recover. Whether he ran back to Stephen to sell him our heads or ran to his own lands to stir trouble made little difference, so I had decided that Pembroke needed a keeper. When I saw how sick he was—I will not lie to you, I did not kill him—but I did not help him grow better either. Now we must move quickly."

The calm disdainful tone, the harsh voice, were soothing. Cain sank into a seat beside the fire and said wearily, "Ay, but why?"

"Because it has come to me that Maud may be more afraid of us with Pembroke in our hands than with him dead. She will think that we could make him speak for us as she made him speak for her. As soon as may be you must go to the queen."

The Duke of Gaunt's face was perfectly expressionless, his voice perfectly steady and normally harsh, but Radnor who was on edge and bitterly ashamed of what he had said, shifted uneasily in his chair because of the tension he felt. "Very well, but why are you here in secret? From what are you hiding?"

"So that when you go to the queen, you will have more

than your tongue with which to defend yourself. Probably she will be constrained by knowing you have those men to speak against her, but what if she has discovered some way out in these months and she fears them no longer? When you go to her—tomorrow night will be best, I believe—I with my men will lie in wait watching the doors of the tower. If you come not out by dawn, we will go in and ask for you."

Cain stared at the scarred hands in his lap. Why had his father come instead of returning to his estates when the Welsh were still restless? To tell him Pembroke was dead? To watch the gates of the White Tower? Why had he come from Wales at all? He came at the time of the tourney to save me from Pembroke's plot. The revelation was a stunner to Radnor. And now he comes again to protect me from the queen and to see me because on the road with Pembroke I had so much pain and was far from well. Cain recalled the other time he had been so near death. Then his father had hung over him and struggled with him for his own good. To preserve the heir to his lands? Perhaps. Or had he made his own sorrow all these years through blindness? Had he dwelt so long on things past that he had not seen the present?

"What ails you, you dolt?"

The sharp question startled Cain into speech. "Nothing—. Only I am so tired of threats and half-truths and half-oaths."

"And I too am tired, my son." Gaunt put up a hand and let it drop. "If that wife of yours brings forth a manchild—." He stopped suddenly, chilled by the flash of fear in Cain's eyes. "The task must be done," he began again more briskly. "Chester and Fitz Richard must be freed and you must wrest sufficient gold from Maud to pay off the men Henry brought and to pay for ships to carry him home. Bah, you are yawning fit to split your head. If you used your bed to sleep in once in a while, you might be able to attend to business better. Go—get you to the bed you covet so much."

Always the bitter gibe. Radnor's raw nerves jumped and twitched. "To say these few words you have dragged me three miles in the dark and rain?"

"No," Gaunt snarled, "it was to see you wet and discomforted!"

A fool's question justly received a fool's answer, Radnor thought, as the old man walked down the hall toward the cell he would sleep in. His father did value him. Perhaps only as the heir to his lands, but it was still pleasant to know that he was of value. The sensation of pleasure, however, was mixed with resentment. Why could Gaunt not say he had summoned him to see with his own eyes how he had recovered from his wounds? Why for that matter could he not have come to the house to see him? A slow smile curved Cain's lips in spite of his irritation. Gaunt's pride would never stoop so far.

By the time Cain arrived at home, he was not only soaked but bruised and muddy. His horse had stumbled in the total blackness of a moonless and starless night, throwing him into the muddy street. It was a great relief to him that Leah was asleep, curled up in a corner on the side of the bed that was usually his. Radnor shrugged and began to remove his clothes as quietly as possible. He would not disturb her for that. It was an unpleasant shock to him, as he sat in the dark idly rubbing his hair dry, to be grasped in a passionate embrace. First, he wanted nothing but to be left alone to digest his thoughts. Second, the boldness was not womanly, to his mind. He enjoyed Leah's response, but he wanted to be allowed to make the advances.

"Just a moment, Leah. I have news for you. I hope you will not be distressed, but I must tell you anyway—your father is dead. It was of an illness—not any doing of mine."

"God is merciful to the just," Leah replied, but to Cain's intense surprise she did not release him.

It was all very well to dislike so unnatural a parent—Pembroke certainly did not deserve love—but to seek so avidly for a sexual embrace after receiving such news was somehow wrong. There was a note of distaste in his voice when he spoke even though he had already decided that a bout of lovemaking was a small price to pay for peace.

"Let me take off my clothes. I will come to you quickly enough." To strip and lie down was the work of a minute. Radnor slid a hand automatically up Leah's thigh.

"Oh, do not. Please, do not."

"What?"

"Please, please. Do not be angry, but do not do that."

"Has the devil got into you? First you grab me as if you could not get at me quickly enough despite the news I have given you, and then you deny me. Is this a new game you have discovered to torment me with?"

"I only wanted you to hold me. I will deny you nothing, my lord, only give me a little time."

Merciful Christ, Radnor thought, may I not have one night's peace to think? He could feel that Leah was trembling, however, and he made a last effort at control, saying gently, "What is it, Leah? Why do you weep? Is it for your father after all?"

"I am afraid," she sobbed.

"Of what are you afraid, dear heart?"

"I will tell you, my lord, but, please, in my own way."

"Of course, love. Wait, I will make a light. I do not like to talk in the dark." And he thought wryly, if we talk in the dark I am like to fall asleep over it. Why did everyone always want to discuss things in the middle of the night? Did no one need to sleep except himself? "Well?" he asked.

Leah's eyes were red and her lids swollen, and she snuggled into her husband's arms before replying. "When do we return home to Painscastle?"

"I have told you some hundred times," he began sharply, and then as she began to shake again, more softly, "soon, love, soon. Do not be afraid. Very soon now we will go. Tomorrow I will go to the queen. Then we need only wait for her to deliver up the gold and free Chester. A few days or, perhaps, two weeks. Not long. Soon." He stroked her long hair and her smooth skin comfortingly.

"When I am there, may I have someone with me?"

"Who? If it be reasonable, my darling, you may have anything you want, anything I can get for you."

"I care not who, so long as it be a noblewoman of good character, or two perhaps, older than I." Leah began to cry again softly.

"You are lonely, my sweet. You miss your mother." A pang of jealousy passed through him, and he smothered it. "Poor child. You are so wise so often that I forget you are but a child. Do not cry, love. I will take you home, to your own keep, if you desire it, to see your mother." He did not remind her that Pembroke was dead. "Perhaps she will visit Painscastle for a while until you are comfortable there."

"I do not wish to go home. I would like to see my mother, but it is not that I miss her. I am happy with you alone."

"Then what do you weep for, Leah? You know I could not refuse so reasonable a desire as for womenfolk of your own class around you."

"When we return to Painscastle, will Beaufort still live with us? Did you not say you needed a castellan for Radnor Keep? Can he be trusted with such a task?"

There was a moment's stunned silence as Radnor's weary mind tried to take in the jump from one subject to another. "Of course he——. Why should you ask such a question about my man?"

"Let me get up for a moment." Leah bent down by the bed, then walked out of the light of the candle into the darkness. When she returned, she took a deep, shuddering breath and stood looking down at her husband. "Because he cannot be trusted with me." She threw herself down upon Radnor, knocking him flat as he started up, gasping, "No, my lord, you cannot rise up and kill him. I have taken away your shoes. Be still, he did me no harm. There was nothing but words. He did not even kiss my hand."

This last was not true, for Sir Harry had forced her so far as to kiss her lips before she fought free of him. That she would never tell because it would have been the man's death warrant. On one pretext or another, Radnor would destroy anyone who meddled with his property. Leah wanted to protect Beaufort because she felt, guiltily, that she had encouraged him. She thought her husband would be paralyzed without his special boot, but she had underestimated his determination and ability. Enraged as he was, he did not even feel the pain as he flung her off him and started across the room. Leah leapt at him again, clinging like a limpet and trying to trip him. At first he only thrust her away, but her insistence in keeping him from his objective finally pierced his fury.

"What did he want? What did he say?" Radnor snarled at his wife, gripping her arm brutally.

"Cain, he is very young. He is very unhappy. He——"

"You would like an exchange, perhaps?"

"Ohhhh!" Leah shuddered.

"He is years younger than I and not so marked. Thus he is even more—beautiful. Why do you protect him? Why?" He shook her until her teeth rattled, the pressure of his hands leaving red welts on her shoulders. "Nay, I need no answer. Your eyes go there and elsewhere too, I hear. You are only too lily-livered to take what you want like all the other sluts so you come sniveling to me. Damn you! Curse you and rot you and damn you!"

He lifted one hand to strike her, and she wrenched herself out of his grip, ran across the room, and threw his shoes at him out of the dark. "Go, go kill him if you will. I tried to protect him because I know if you slay him you will bear the burden of regret all your life. He did you no wrong. A man cannot help loving, no more than a woman can." Perhaps he did not even hear her. He was dressing, his back coldly turned. "Love is a thing that comes unaware, against the will," she sobbed. "So did I love you from the first time you kissed me in the tower room at Eardisley, though I knew that my love must bring me pain and grief. I did not will it; I could not help it. Cain, do not give credit to the name you bear. Do not destroy a man who saved your life three times. Send him away. Give him a castle. Find him a wife. What could give me greater pain than that if I did desire him," she cried despairingly as her husband straightened up and dragged his mail shirt over his head.

Leah moistened her lips at the sight of his face, but she could not make another sound, not even cry out with terror. Her husband groped behind him and his fingers closed on the broad belt that fastened his surcoat together.

"Beaufort's fate is for me to decide, justly or unjustly, but I will teach you once and for all that your will must not cross mine. I will teach you to protect those who have sought to shame me. I will teach you to look with lust upon another man. I will teach you to make my life a misery to me with your complaints and your clinging. Afraid, were you! I will teach you where to fear truly."

The belt cracked and Leah winced. It cracked again, curling around her shoulders. Her lips parted stickily, but she still could find no voice. A harder blow made her stagger and fall against a chair. A still harder one made her reel toward the bed.

"Stop, oh stop! Have mercy, do not beat me." Leah sank to her knees. Radnor's belt came down again. The pain was dreadful, but it was one with which Leah was very familiar. She might even have endured it to the end without protest, knowing that once his wrath was spent on her Beaufort would be saved, but she was afraid that if he beat her until he was tired she would be sick, sick enough to miscarry.

"Stop, my lord," she shrieked, "in the name of God, stop. I am with child."

The raised belt sank slowly. Leah watched the rage drain out of her husband's face and an expression of overwhelming terror take its place. She knew what was coming

312

and slid flat on the cold floor, panting like an animal. The rain had stopped and the sound of a rushing wind filled the room. That, and Leah's panting breath, were the only sound for several long minutes.

"Whose?"

There was nothing more calculatedly cruel he could have said. Lord Radnor did not doubt that the child was his. She would never have mentioned Beaufort's attack if she had such a guilty secret. Cain would have killed Leah, not beaten her, if he had the slightest real doubt of her physical fidelity. It was that with her confirmation of the rumors and smiling hints of pregnancy which he had so long ignored, his own smoldering fear had been ignited and he was driven by his terror to inflict pain in return.

The blow had fallen—the final rejection of the prize she had offered. At the moment, for all Leah cared, Cain was welcome to kill her as well as Sir Harry. She got slowly to her feet and met his eyes. Even that night in Oxford Castle when she had fainted, Radnor did not remember her being so white. He turned on his heel and left the room. Below in the guardroom, Beaufort came face to face with him, white as Leah, wordless but not defiant, offering himself for the punishment he knew he deserved. His presence hardly impinged on a consciousness filled with a far deeper agony.

Lord Radnor struck him down with a single blow, and flung orders at Cedric to hold him in close confinement. He left the house, rode through the howling wind bareheaded and without his shield, rode back to the hospice where his father was, and lay down on the floor beside his father's bed.

CHAPTER 21

WHEN THE DUKE OF GAUNT woke in the morning, he almost stepped on his sleeping son. Without a flicker of expression, he lifted his feet and gazed for a long time at Cain's ravaged face. When he was satisfied, he kicked

313

Cain awake and, without comment or question, began a long and involved discussion about future political plans and arrangements for circumventing the effects of the coming famine. His only response to his son's abstraction and deep expression of trouble was a spate of irritable insults and several sharp blows.

The hours dragged by. From time to time a particularly cruel remark or painful bruise would rouse Radnor and he would apply himself to the topic in hand, but his mind soon slipped away, and when he rose from the dinner table to escape, Gaunt made no attempt to stop him. Cain did not know what he wanted. The pain he had run to, which in the past had eased or erased all other troubles, had failed him. Perhaps somewhere dark and quiet he could find the shaft which was tearing at his gut and wrench it out. There was a chapel, empty and silent, but Radnor found that this fear was not like the arrow he had once torn from his own flesh, fearing to die but knowing he could not live with it in him. This fear could not be torn out, nor conquered, nor destroyed; he must live with it in him. He burst from his solitude into his father's presence crying aloud for work.

The old man looked impassively at his son and shook his head. "There is nothing more to do. You must see the queen and find if you can bend her to our will before we can even plan our next move. Sit down and stop behaving like an idiot. I will give you a game of chess."

They played equally badly. The Duke of Gaunt should have been more satisfied with the situation than he was, for politically matters were going in his favor, but some disaster had overtaken his son, and for the first time in his life he did not know what it was that troubled Cain or how to help him. He thought again of the bitter recriminations thrown at him the night before. Had he been wrong to have forced the boy, beating him and frightening him, into an absolute pretense that his deformity did not exist? Honestly Gaunt admitted that he had begun the process because he could not help himself, because he hated the child for the death of the mother and less for the death of the perfect twin. As the years passed, however, and the boy showed the promise of the fine man Cain had become, Gaunt had continued his harshness to protect the child from the cruelty of others. And when his son was finally a man, it was he who would not let the matter rest, he who returned again and again to the bitterness between them. He had done right; Gaunt was sure of it. Why then was his heart so heavy? Why did he long to speak and be spoken to—to receive the kiss of peace from his child? He was getting old, he thought, nearly three-score years, old and soft. He shook himself, as if to free himself from a physical encumbrance, and knocked the chessmen out of place.

"Go," Gaunt snarled, "you are useless to me and the dinner hour is passed. Go to the court and hear what people say. From one hour after the sun sets until dawn I will wait for you at the main gate."

The court was very gay and everyone was glad to see Lord Radnor. A dozen men fell upon him with questions—jesting questions, idle questions, and desperately perceptive questions. He dared not let his tongue slip, and the fear in the foreground of his mind sank into a steady twisting misery in the background. It was very late before Radnor was able to seek his audience with Maud, because he wished to be sure she would be free of Stephen. When he sent a page up to her quarters with his request for admission, however, he was not refused. Lady Shrewsbury came out into the antechamber to tell him that Maud would soon be with him. She had offered to go out to Radnor, this being the first opportunity she had of private communication with him since the tourney, and Maud had agreed very willingly. To watch Joan being refused in the way Radnor was likely to refuse her was one tiny bit of salve which Maud could safely apply to her lacerations.

"Tell him," Maud said dulcetly, "that I will receive him in a few moments." Joan nodded and moved toward the door quickly with the eagerness of triumph. Maud bowed her head to conceal her bitter smile, reopened the door which Joan had closed, and stood listening.

"Did you receive my letter?" Joan of Shrewsbury came up close enough so that her scent reached Radnor. His nostrils spread as he breathed it, and his body stiffened as he resisted the impulse to step back.

"Ay."

Joan misread the stiffening and the restraint of the voice. "You need not fear to speak. Our voices will not carry." She glanced upward at the frozen face archly. "Well, first you must say your thank you for the risk I ran—then—"

"What risk? You told me little enough."

So he was angry still. "Will you never forget a mistake?

315

What more can I do to redeem myself? You have never given me an opportunity for even a word with you."

"Mistake?" The face was blank, the voice indifferent. "Oh, I have forgotten everything. My mind is washed clean of all such matters now."

Color flew into the smooth white cheeks and the blue eyes glittered. "You think that mawkish idiot you married—"

Radnor's eyes narrowed and his lips twisted with pain. He would gladly have let matters rest, for if the woman had hurt him once the fact was insignificant to him now, but if she dared even name Leah—. Radnor cleared the huskiness from his voice and raised it so that it traveled quite clearly.

"Do not do it, Joan. Say nothing to me of my wife. So long as you talk about yourself or me or on indifferent subjects I can force myself to bear you. I will not have you soil my Leah's name by speaking it with your mouth. My temper is not to be trusted, Joan, and it would make for peculiar explanations if you make me lay you out with a blow. I assure you," he added, cruelly and crudely, convinced that there was no other way to deal with this woman, "that I have no desire to lay you out any other way. Hold your venomous tongue—and keep it and yourself away from my wife."

Behind the door Maud smiled. Joan of Shrewsbury had met her match and it had been a privilege to hear it. The smile faded quickly and she prepared herself to go out. It was entirely possible that she too had met her match. When, without even replying to her courteous greeting, Lord Radnor plainly and bluntly asked for Chester's release and told her that his prisoners and Hereford were beyond her reach, she knew the worst. She stood silent for a moment, her eyes on the floor, whipping up her courage and her rage. When she spoke at last, her words were uncontrolled and vivid. She used every expression a long life and exposure to all kinds of people had taught her, but her fury beat unavailingly against the big man's stolidity. Finally she talked herself silent, gasping for air and searching for a single sign that she had pricked a raw spot. Radnor's expression, however, held nothing but a mild distaste for her gutter language, a mild regret that a great lady should so demean herself.

"Have you done, madam? Are you through with my

manners, morals, and ancestry? Can we speak of the Earl of Chester now?"

"Chester, Chester. I will hold him till he rots. Do not tell me you will bring those men into council to lie for you. You have outmaneuvered yourself by sending them away to be safe. Even if you have lied again and they are indeed within recall, you cannot use them, for they will name Pembroke also. Moreover, to raise such a noise would be a great act agasint the king."

"I never said I intended to bring your killers into council, although they will not name Pembroke. They know only of Oxford, madam, and of you. The act is one of self-defense, which no oath binds a man against and, moreover, if those men speak in council they will not speak against the king who is, indeed, blameless. If your unwise actions should topple him from his throne, what fault is that of mine? Ay, madam, you look strangely now. In future it might be well to remember that it is not so easy to remove 'that devil of Gaunt' from your road."

Maud gasped at his effrontery and insolence. They were standing some distance from her ladies and gentlemen, and Radnor had kept his husky voice too low to carry. Still, Maud could not remember being so spoken to by any man except her husband since she had become queen.

"What I will do," Radnor continued calmly, "if I do not have my way, is to go to your husband with my tale."

"You would not dare!"

"You know me well. Can you say there is anything I would not dare? Moreover, what do I dare? I report a treachery against myself—all saw it happen—and against the king also. Your husband, madam, is too good a knight to appreciate efforts on his behalf made in such a disgusting way. Especially when those efforts have recoiled and are about to intensify his troubles. Nay, nay, I am but a good subject doing my duty. I could have brought the men into council to make trouble for my king, and so I will tell him. It is out of consideration for him that I withheld this knowledge for his private ear. Do you think he will disbelieve? Do you think he will credit that I set those men upon myself, or that Pembroke, my father-in-law, did? Does he know you so little?"

Radnor's face was a hard mask of revulsion and bitter determination. It was not against Maud alone that his feeling was directed, but the entire system and situation. His own behavior disgusted him as much as hers, for he

317

recognized that she was driven by necessity as he was. Hereford's way was clean, at least, even if disastrous. This keeping of the word of an oath and disregarding the spirit would never cease to distress him.

"Give me Chester," he cried finally, "and it will be quits between us. I am sick with this planning and plotting."

Maud had met her match, and her terror of Stephen's anger far more than the fear of political repercussion had defeated her. "Lord Radnor," she replied quietly, a barely perceptible note of pleading in her voice, "I cannot. To allow him who has so openly plotted against the king—who has not even denied the plot—to go scot free—. Even you must acknowledge that to be impossible."

This, then, was the beginning of the end. Radnor sighed. "If you please, madam, let us sit down." He covered his eyes with his hand. "I did not mean that you should allow Chester pardon without punishment. Indeed, that is as evil for my cause as for yours. Such easy pardon will make a rebel of every petty warrior in the realm. Hear what I propose."

In rapid outline he detailed the castles Chester would offer as forfeit and the truage he would be expected to pay. In return, however, Fitz Richard's lands were to be returned to the young man and both Chester and Fitz Richard were to be allowed to depart in peace.

Maud balked at that. "Fitz Richard was a warranty for Chester. It is our right—and no man will say us nay—to keep his lands in our hand."

"That is the price which must be paid, or I will have no peace in Wales. Madam, it cannot matter to you. What you planned in Wales is finished. Pembroke will not fall into your hands again. Hereford guards the north between Chester's lands and Gloucester's. There is no way now for you to put a knife to Gloucester's back."

"You say you desire peace and you tell me to release a man who, no sooner gone from here, will raise up an army and make war."

Lord Radnor shrugged and shook his head. "What can I do? What influence I have will be brought to bear for peace, and I can promise the same for my father. I will be warrant for Fitz Richard's behavior, but who can manage Chester? You should not have spited the Lady Elizabeth; she can do more with him than any other. He is my godfather. I may not leave him to languish, even in the loose confinement of mandatory attendance at court."

"How can I know what you promise will be given? We have not Chester's word—for whatever value that has—that he agrees."

The pot calling the kettle black, thought Radnor. "I will also be warranty for the delivery of the castles. Those you may have before Chester leaves London. The truage I cannot hold myself responsible for. I will urge him to pay. Part may, no doubt, be had from Lady Elizabeth, but you know yourself that he must go to his lands to collect the remainder. What he does then is beyond my ordering, and I will not raise my hand against my godfather."

"It will take a little time," Maud finally replied sullenly. "I must talk Stephen round."

"If that is all we need to wait for, it will be done quick enough. We are agreed on the price of Chester's freedom then?"

Maud looked up at him, startled. "There is more?"

"Ay, more. I have had news—needless to say I will not name my source for it—that Henry of Anjou is here." The brief anxiety faded from her eyes and was replaced by caution and curiosity. "I thought you knew and I see that I was right. Did your husband tell you what letters I wrung from him concerning the Angevin?"

After the faint flush of relief, Maud's sudden pallor made her sallow skin look greenish. "Letters?"

"Ay. Assuring him the succession as agreed. In Stephen's own hand, madam, and dated."

"They are not sealed with the Great Seal." Maud had recovered swiftly and she answered with narrowed eyes.

"No." Lord Radnor's lips twitched. There was, after all, a certain amount of humor in the situation. He and Maud knew each other so well that the moves of the game might almost be called in advance. Briefly Cain regretted that he had never played chess with her. "That I could not quite manage. But something else I can and will. I will promise you that both the letters and Henry himself will go back to France without any major engagement of arms—for a price."

"Dirty usurer," she jeered. "You are rich enough, I hear, to buy the kingdom and you are content to grow filthy begging and stealing more. I would not put a copper mil into your hands that sweat with greed. Who do you think you are to ask for gold—Philip of Gloucester? You promise for a price what even he could not perform."

That touched him. Radnor's complexion darkened and

319

his hands knotted together as he fought the impulse to strike her. How Maud would have loved that. Such a simple way to end all her troubles. No excuse could have saved him if he struck the queen, and she had a dozen witnesses present. Up until now she had despaired of making him angry, for she had already insulted him in every way she knew how. Possibly, she thought, with her own flash of humor, this hurt more because it was perfectly sincere and uncalculated; she had only said the first thing that came into her head.

Maud was a good judge of men, but she had miscalculated this time. Radnor's rage was in response to the slur cast upon Philip, his poor dying Philip. What she said about him was not true and was of no account. "I never promise what I cannot perform," he said when he had his voice under control. "The price is for Henry to pay off his French adherents in lieu of English land. I care nothing one way or another. If you do not pay, they will loot, and it will not be *my* vassals' keeps they will raid."

"Why not take it and let others believe that is its use. Philip of Gloucester did no less and we have continued to content him. It is an easier life than one of war, and leaves a man more time to lie abed."

Radnor's face went as white as it could go, and the scars stood out like two newly burnt brands. Maud sought desperately for something else to say. The last gibe about his uxuriousness, she thought, not realizing that he believed her to be sneering at Philip's recent behavior as if she did not credit the excuse of sickness, had hit him hard. One more remark about his wife and he would be completely out of control.

"I do not deny, Lord Radnor, that I have a score to even with you, and it gives me pleasure to tell you this. You doting husbands are all alike. She drips honey on your neck, and you can taste nothing but the sweetness. Well, it is venom she drips into my ears. You should hear what she says of you. You should see how she looks at William of Gloucester—and what she says of him."

Instantly, Cain saw what the queen had meant all along. He shut his eyes completely and took a breath so deep that the seams of his surcoat strained to open. Leah had been trying to make Maud believe her indifferent to Cain and Cain's watchfulness to be mere distrust. She understood that if Maud thought her valueless to her husband, it would be useless to abduct her. For a flushed triumphant second, Maud believed she had won, but what Radnor was fighting now was a laughter close to tears, not wrath. He had to drop his head into his hands to conceal his face, and a strangled sound worked its way out of his tortured gullet in spite of himself. He must not laugh; it would give all away—but why William? Could Leah not have fixed on a more likely object? One more convulsive shudder and Lord Radnor lifted a face drained of all emotion.

"You finished my character earlier. If you are now done insulting my wife, we can discuss the price further."

"I am not helpless and undefended. You are a fool, also, to come here unsupported." The challenge was bravely flung, but Maud's eyes were hopeless.

Radnor smiled and shook his head, almost with sympathy. "You know I am no fool, madam. My father is returned and waits for me beyond the gate; my men wait in the hall below. They will rouse every Marcher lord in the whole city if I come not forth."

"What do you want?" Maud asked dully. There was nothing more she could do.

When the gates of the White Tower opened to release Lord Radnor, his father had but one word for him, "Done?"

"It is done."

"You sound ill content. Is it as we would have it?"

"Yes." The voice was drained, empty.

"Then I will ride home at once. We have left the lands too long to underlings. There is no need for more than one of us to be here to see that she fulfills her promises."

Gaunt should have left to get what sleep he could before starting his long ride. Instead he sat, staring at his son who had not replied. At last Radnor nodded and touched his horse gently with a spurred heel, turning its head automatically toward the house where Leah was. Surprisingly Gaunt's mount moved with his. Each was immersed in his own thoughts, and, although those thoughts were on similar subjects, the ride was silent, as their rides together usually were. They were nearly at the door when Radnor pulled his horse to a stop and spoke.

"Father—"

"Yes?"

"I hope when this is finished you have no more plans for me."

"Why?"

"I wish to take my wife to Painscastle and settle her there. I have some news that will please you. Leah is with child. There may soon be an heir to the lands of Gaunt."

So that was Cain's trouble. He had suspected it, but had hoped that his son would not so soon be wrenched with fear. The old man still hoped he was wrong, and strained his eyes to see Cain's face in the silver moonlight that made all so soft and deceptive.

"You do not sound as if the news gave you much pleasure." In a long pause there was no reply, and under the shadowing hood Radnor's face was a mystery of black hollows. "My son—" Gaunt stopped. He was so sure he was right and wished so much to be wrong about what Cain was thinking. In any case, he would not add to the trouble by talking about it, not even to start the bitterness now so that it might be less bitter later. If he was old and soft, so it was. He could not be otherwise, not even to be wise, just now.

The younger man dismounted painfully, and Gaunt followed with more agility in spite of his years. "I have no plans for you, Cain. You well deserve a rest. Take your wife home by easy stages. I hope to settle all in Wales before you come. You need do nothing then but watch."

"Will you be there when I come?"

Was there fear in the question or desire? It did not matter; they would be better apart. "No, what need for us both to be at Painscastle? I will go to Chester and do what I may with him. I may even go as far north as Scotland to see King David. I have been thinking that it would be well to have young Henry knighted on this soil. To cajole Stephen so far will be impossible, so David is the only man with rank enough to do it." I am babbling like an idiot child, Gaunt thought, and as he saw Cain draw breath to speak, babbled on. "When a man grows old he grows restless again, as in youth. I have been too long at war in Wales alone. I would look on the rest of the world. Perhaps I will give all into your hands and join the crusade. To go on pilgrimage has been long in my mind."

Through all this Radnor stood like a stump, awkwardly, his right hip jutted out to relieve the pressure on his left foot. It was a position his father hated and had reproved him for often in the past, but now Gaunt said nothing.

"Women die in childbearing."

The words dropped into the silence that had fallen when Gaunt had run out of breath and senseless talk. Why he had said it, Cain did not know. To expose a raw hurt to his father seemed madness in the light of his past experience, but to whom else in the world could he speak?

"I know. On that rack your mother died." Gaunt only meant to say that he understood his son's fear, but he saw Cain wince and realized that his words had again been taken amiss. "My son—good God, do you look to me for comfort? What can I say to you?" So great was his desire to express his sympathy and so unknown to him, who had never expressed it before, was how to do it that his voice was unusually harsh. He grasped Cain's shoulder before his son could turn away. "She is young and strong. Many women bear successfully. In Jesus' name, do not dwell upon it. That way lies madness—I know—and worse than madness. My son, my son—"

They stood quietly in the silver light, the two men of the same blood. There was nothing to be said and Gaunt had offered his son all the comfort he had for him—the knowledge of his own agony. Radnor cleared his throat.

"Will you return before the spring?" No definite meaning could be attached to the words but the voice cried out not to be left alone at that time. Gaunt's hand trembled on his son's shoulder and was withdrawn.

"Before her time, if you desire it, yes, I will return to you." There was a pause and then the old man rushed into brisk speech as if to conceal what he had said. "I will leave in the dawn, Cain, and will not see you again. I will let you know where to reach me and how things progress as always." Another pause while each pair of eyes strained to read the message in the other pair. Gaunt's voice, uncertainly now, began again. "Write me word if you need me—I mean, if there is trouble at home—that is, in case of more rebellion—I will come back."

"God speed you."

That was all he said, but with a gesture as natural as though it were not completely new, Cain kissed his father on one cheek and then on the other. Instinctively Gaunt's hands came up and pressed his son close, but only for a half-second. Then he grunted, pushed his child roughly away, mounted his horse, and rode off without a farewell.

The serene stars, tiny blue gems set on black velvet, sailed slowly across the heavens. Lord Radnor leaned against the quiet warmth of his horse and watched them. Whatever happened now, there was another human soul to which he was linked, for the wall between his father and

323

himself had been breached. They would still fight bitter battles and say bitter words, still hurt each other and hate each other, the habit was too long ingrained to be broken, but it did not matter for at the bottom the blood bond was firm. This too, Radnor realized, in some way he did not understand, Leah had given him. Quite suddenly he thought of the word with which he had left her. The memory brought him from a perfectly mirthless laugh. He was his father all over again. Because he loved Leah and was afraid for her and afraid of the pain she might bring him, he had said the cruelest thing he could think of to her.

The men who stood guard passed Radnor silently. Guided only by the last flickering of the fire, he picked his way through the sleeping men-at-arms and found the stairway to Leah's chamber. He felt along the walls by memory and opened the door.

"Leah?"

"Yes, my lord." There was neither surprise nor fear in her voice, only indifference.

"May I come? I want to talk to you."

"You are master here. Do as you like."

He stood irresolute—maybe it would be better to leave his explanations until morning. Leah lay still, not caring what he did. She had passed through every stage of bitter resentment, trembling fear, and warm forgiving so many times that the emotions had destroyed each other. Now she felt nothing.

"Do you have a light?" Radnor asked finally.

"Flint and tinder are by the bed."

"May I sit down?"

"As it pleases you."

"What you told me, Leah, is it true?"

"Yes. I am with child and the child is yours. Whether you believe that or not, I no longer care."

Radnor lifted his hand as if to ward off a blow and then let it drop. "Nay, I know it is mine. I always knew it. I—how—how long?"

"I have missed two fluxes."

"Why did you not tell me sooner?"

That was not easy to answer. The memory of her jealousy of other women, a newly awakened fear of what he had been doing away from her, made her breath come a little faster and wakened her emotions. It was useless to say she did not care about him. She did, and she always would.

"I wished to be sure, not to disappoint you with false hopes," she replied.

"I see. When is your time?"

"The end of March, perhaps, or mayhap sometime in April."

"So soon?"

The anguish of his tone made her turn to look at him for the first time since he came in. She sat up, distressed for him although she knew not why. "What is wrong? It is the same for all." Then recalling his unjust treatment of her, she added coldly, "If the time is not convenient to you, my lord, I cannot help it. You need not be there. I will cling and complain no more, but bear my troubles as best I may."

"Did I say that too?" he asked in a stricken voice, but she made no reply. "I have just parted from my father," he added, seeking something to say.

"Did he fret you, my lord?" Leah asked dully. She did not care or want to know, but to be on bad terms with her husband was stupid and could only hurt her.

"Not at all. He was very kind, softer to me than ever in my life. He offered me what consolation he could."

"Have you suffered some disappointment?" Against her will there was concern in her voice. Political disappointment meant fighting to her.

"No, I——." What was he about to say? Could he ask this timid girl to console him because he was afraid she would die? He was truly mad.

"It was nothing," he began again in what he hoped were more cheerful tones. "He gave me good news in return for mine. When the queen has fulfilled her promises, we can go to Painscastle, traveling at whatever speed will be comfortable and safe to you. For the present, at least, I have naught to do but see to my estates and rest. You need have no fear for me——." He turned his face from her suddenly and his voice dropped. "If you have left enough affection after what has passed between us to fear for me."

Leah's resentment had been melting steadily. Something very dreadful indeed must be preying on her lord's mind to make him sound so hopeless, to make him assume so dreadful and forced a manner of good cheer. He had done wrong to hurt her when she was struggling to help him, but he was a man of hot temper and his temper had been sorely tried. Leah had thought over her behavior in the past few weeks and realized what a burden she had been to an already overburdened man. Her voice was soft and her hand went out to touch him tenderly.

"My love, why are you unhappy? You have told me that there will be peace in the land, at least for a time, and also that you are at peace with those nearest you in heart and blood. Indeed, I thought I had given you news to make you rejoice. Whence comes this sorrow? Unless you truly do not trust me——"

"Oh, Christ's Blood, Leah, no! I did but wish to give you pain and said the worst thing that came to my tongue." He lifted the hand that lay gently on his and kissed it. Leah could feel his lips tremble against her palm.

"Dear heart," she whispered, "let me help you if I can. At least speak out your trouble. Whatever it is, if two share it, the burden is not so heavy."

"Are you not afraid?" he burst out, clutching her hand so that she winced. "You said you were, over and over, and I did not understand—would not understand—why. I should have known. It was hinted to me with smiles often enough but—but I would not believe it."

"Did you not desire it?" Leah was incredulous, her world suddenly upside down.

"Yes, yes, of course. You know how much I want—wanted—a son. But when I thought—when I came to consider the price—. A son might cost too high. Oh God, God, I am sick with fear."

There was one stunned moment of silence. Then Leah's laugh trilled out until it filled the room and filled the ears of her astonished husband. This was the end of her jealousy, the end of any fears she had ever had. The bud of love had burst into a perfect blossom. The flower of Leah's marriage could never die. More than the continuance of his name, more than his hope for posterity, not as a breeder but for herself alone, her husband loved her. With a cry of joy she came from the bed to his arms.

"No," Leah answered, her eyes alight, "no, I am not afraid. I was, but now I am not. My dear lord, there is nothing to fear. All will be well."